Thinking About Forever

Chrissie McCauley

Quarterpath Publishing

Cover design by Jennifer Stimson.

ISBN: 979-8-218-60542-1

❋ Created with Vellum

For my mom – who worked tirelessly to instill a deep (if not slightly delusional) belief that I can do anything.

For my husband – who encouraged me to write for years before I ever typed a single sentence, and who supported me without hesitation once I did.

Part One

Chapter 1

Monday

I'm sitting at my desk, working through emails, when my favorite charge nurse and longtime friend pops her head into my office.

"Hey, Jules, we just got a call from downstairs. They're sending up an eighty-two-year-old male with suspected congestive heart failure. He had a minor fall in his apartment, waiting for the CT and X-ray reports. He has an aide who got him here right away. COVID negative, BP is low, sats are not great, but he's holding steady. The guy has got some spunk. Admitting doc wants at least forty-eight hours observation before we discharge. Everyone is slammed. If you could do his intake, that'd be great. His power of attorney is on the way."

"Got it. Thanks, Christine—I'll be there shortly," I reply.

The door is almost closed when her head reappears.

"Hey...how are you doing today?"

"I'm good."

"Really?" She scrutinizes me.

I wait to see if any old familiar feelings make their way to the surface before I answer. Nothing.

"Yes, really. I'm fine. Thanks for asking."

"You sure?"

"Yes."

"Want to talk about it?"

"Nope."

She looks relieved. "I was hoping you'd say that. See you on the floor."

Once she's gone, I glance around my office, watching the early afternoon light stream in through the windows. If I look hard enough, I can catch a glimpse of the Hudson River in between the skyscrapers.

I've only recently redecorated after spending the better part of five years with a hodgepodge of hand-me-down furniture, decorations I swiped from vacant offices, and a few personal items. Last year, after telling a patient struggling with depression that "your space matters, what you see every day matters," I decided to take my own advice and give my office a much-needed makeover.

Now, every morning when I walk in, I'm greeted by gray-blue walls, a sleek acrylic and glass desk, a well-loved and very comfortable navy love seat, and my chair—a mid-century modern antique I'd found and had reupholstered in a soft blue linen. A large woven area rug sits in the center of the room, and a few low-maintenance plants are scattered around, an attempt to liven up the place. My heavy textbooks from grad school are stacked neatly on two large bookshelves on the far wall along with a wide variety of fiction, nonfiction, poetry, and other works I reference often in my clinical work and enjoy in my personal life: Michael Singer, Morgan Harper Nichols, Viktor E. Frankl, Lao Tzu, Mary Oliver, Anne Lamott, and dozens more.

The one framed photo on my desk is of my dog, Murphy.

I grab the frame and smile at his happy, goofy face. I turn it over and unclasp the prongs. I pull off the backing, then peel away the layers.. Behind the photograph of Murphy is another—one I've kept in the frame but safely tucked out of sight for over two years. I pick it up cautiously and decide I'll allow this single, solitary moment to feel sorry for myself.

I flip it over and see myself, Murphy, and my ex-husband, Nick.

We're kneeling next to Murphy in the backyard of our old house. The sun is setting, and we are caught midlaugh. Murphy's pink tongue hangs out the side of his mouth. It is one of the last happy photos I have of us.

I sigh, and a wave of disappointment washes over me.

My eyes wander to the painting displayed behind my chair, my first *fancy* art piece, meaning it wasn't purchased at HomeGoods. It's a mixed media abstract full of bright pinks, oranges, blues, and greens, a contrast to my neutral office walls. It's one of those paintings that presents itself differently every time you look at it—my own personal Rorschach test. I love when my patients offer up their interpretations during therapy sessions. Today, it reminds me of another piece of art that hangs in my living room—a similar piece by the same artist but in much more muted tones, pensive and solemn. I applied the same motto of "my space matters" to decorating my apartment in Midtown. I've lived there for eight months and have finally adjusted to life with just me and Murphy.

I glance down at the calendar on my desk. Today marks exactly one year since my divorce from Nick was finalized, though our separation began the year before. And things had been steadily going downhill for months and maybe even years before that. Only recently have I felt like I've worked through most of the all-consuming existential dread I experienced when I realized my marriage was a complete and utter failure.

My marriage to Nick fizzled out with little fanfare and even less fight. The fact that it was so amicable in the end made me question if any of the early years of our love were even real. How did we go from being so confident that we'd spend the rest of our lives together to apathetically dividing household items on a shared Excel spreadsheet? I can't decide what would have been worse—the way we did it or perhaps passionately duking it out in court and ruining each other until the bitter end. Both are depressing, but the indifference I felt was crushing.

The only friction in our otherwise amicable mediation came over custody of Murphy, our three-year-old, sweet but slightly manic black Lab-hound mutt. *I probably still have those emails.* I impulsively type a few keywords into my inbox search bar.

I find them easily.

My fingers hover over the mouse. *Is this going to be helpful or hurtful?* One of my own therapeutic phrases echoes in my head. *Fuck it.* This is the only moment today I'll allow myself a pity party, so why not go all in?

I click them open.

50/50 custody seems like a logistical nightmare. Maybe I can stop by occasionally and see him if I'm not traveling for work, or maybe he can stay with me a night or two, Nick wrote from his work email.

This is absurd. He's a dog, Might I also remind you how anxious he gets when I'm not around. Unless you want him whining, pacing, and staring out the window every time he's with you, it's probably best for all involved if he stays with me. You can visit if you want.

His response came three days later. *Fine. You can keep him. Let's just be done with this.*

Our entire relationship summed up as *this.* It stung.

In my lower moments, I take the majority of blame. If I'd noticed him drifting sooner, paid closer attention, if I had done more—whatever *more* was. If I'd somehow dulled parts of my personality that annoyed him or changed parts of myself entirely to suit his needs, if I could've just "kept him close," as my aunt unhelpfully suggested, maybe I wouldn't be thirty-eight and divorced.

It isn't a fair summary, as Nick certainly contributed to the demise of our union, if not overtly, then by his abysmal, nonexistent participation. I've spent the better part of these past two years combing through my memory, looking for anything that might give me a hint as to where it all went wrong, as if it was one specific moment.

The idea of a debrief felt essential to me. If I couldn't learn a single thing about myself or glean a tiny life lesson, it all felt even more hopeless. Like our relationship was truly just a colossal waste of time. A waste of over a decade of my life. A waste of my precious and fleeting youth.

Eventually, with the help of my therapist and lots of self-reflection, I landed on the fact that the pandemic was ultimately our undoing. Saying that out loud still seems like a cop-out to me, but the series of events that contributed to our downfall may have never amounted to anything had they remained separate events at any other point in history. But collectively, and amid a global pandemic, it all proved to be insurmountable, starting with a hasty exodus from the city to the New Jersey suburb of Morristown in the early weeks of lockdown. It was there we found ourselves trapped in Nick's childhood home with his parents, his sister, her husband, and their four-month-old baby. It wasn't ideal, but we weren't alone in our plight.

In the first weeks of government-mandated isolation, I noticed how much our relationship had been built on a foundation of socialization, of being with other people. When that was yanked away overnight, the silence and forced stillness we were thrust into was jarring. Without all the usual trappings and distractions of life, elements of our relationship I'd never noticed before were laid bare and impossible to ignore.

I saw how much we depended on others to make us feel whole. Nick and I both loved spending time with our friends, individually and as a couple. Dinners, brunches, concerts, a coed softball league, trivia nights, sporting events—these were an integral part of our lives and our relationship. When I think back, I can hardly remember any moments that consisted of just the two of us for any substantial amount of time. Even vacations were group events. There were always other people to bounce off of, to change up and influence our dynamic. Even in the absence of our friends, we always had New

York City with its pulsing energy and its colorful people to be another ever-present, living and breathing part of our relationship.

In Morristown, I saw traits of his that I'd always known were there amplified like one of those toys you submerge in water that grow to ten times their original size overnight. He seemed selfish, stubborn, and not particularly self-aware in any meaningful way. He seemed more than content to let me fill in the gaps in *his* life and follow along with *his* plans, without any thought of me or mine, without any consideration of what I might want or need. I guess it was then that the first fissures of resentment appeared.

Plus, early on in our exile to the Jersey suburbs, my role as one of six directors of clinical social work at New York Grace Hospital was deemed nonessential, and I was moved to full-time remote work. So, I joined the work-from-home warriors and sat at the kitchen table with Nick and my brother-in-law from the hours of nine to five. Our workday was promptly followed by several happy hours, and even more hours scrolling on our phones, bingeing TV shows, and overall feeling like our brains were slowly but surely melting out of our skulls. Which was not beneficial to either of us, individually or as a couple.

But, the scrolling paid off when Nick found a fixer-upper on Zillow with great bones on a half acre lot a few miles from his parents' house. Before we knew what we were doing, an offer had been made and accepted. The closing date was set for two weeks later, and we officially moved out of the city to the Jersey suburbs.

Despite our team effort in doing a home reno, I still felt the growing unease that something was wrong with our marriage. *These are crazy times, everyone is struggling.* I'd repeat these phrases to myself frequently to quell the rising unease. Rumors of vaccines being rolled out were everywhere, and it felt like normalcy was just within reach. It was easy to believe that all the problems in our relationship were merely symptoms of the problems in the world, and once the world was good, we would be, too. An ambiguous finish line emerged, and I felt positive once we got there, Nick and I would return to the same people we were before the pandemic, happy and in love.

I was wrong.

One random night a few weeks before the separation, Nick once again opted to watch TV in our bedroom rather than on the couch with me, and I thought I'd never been so lonely. I couldn't think of anything worse than feeling lonely in a relationship, lonely while sitting a few feet away from someone I vowed to love and cherish all the days of my life.

It felt like a wake-up call, and I jumped into crisis mode, unearthing all my old textbooks from grad school and getting to work. I spent weeks consuming every article and podcast I could find about relationship slumps and asked many hypothetical questions of my colleagues who worked with couples.

I told no one about the dire state of our marriage. Not only was I embarrassed it had gotten to this point, but I did not feel equipped to handle the myriad opinions that would come my way if I confided in anyone. I worried they would judge Nick or me or us. But the isolation I felt quickly gave way to full-blown resentment, and I realized I was turning bitter—something I never thought I'd be. And yet I still had glimmers of hope that my pragmatism and sheer determination would be enough to pull us out of the hole we were in. It had never failed me before. I was committed to fixing us, though I wasn't sure what exactly needed to be fixed.

Finally, after many covert attempts to reconnect with Nick, including one humiliating dalliance into role play that I didn't think I'd ever recover from, I asked him point blank if he was happy in our marriage.

To which he replied, "I love you, but I don't think I'm in love with you anymore."

This was a particularly low blow for me, as Nick and I had spent years laughing at the clichéd ways in which relationships ended.

A year before the pandemic, I came home from work and said,

"One of the guys who works in my HR department is getting divorced. Guess why?"

Nick ticked off a list of our usual guesses. "He was sleeping with his secretary? Wait, wait, that's too obvious. What about, he was staying with her 'for the kids' but then realized the kids knew exactly how miserable they both were? Or is it our favorite, he loves her but he's not *in* love with her anymore?"

"The first one!" I said. "But he doesn't have a secretary. It was a woman he met at Equinox."

"Ha!" Nick exclaimed. "I knew something was up when he showed up to that work dinner with the botched Just For Men hair color correcting look. Another one bites the dust."

How jaded we were to think these lowly relationship issues would never affect us. And then there I was, standing in our newly purchased, renovated, and decorated home at our beautiful soapstone kitchen countertop that took me three trips to a quarry to pick. Nick sat at the barstool I picked out, dressed in the same pair of ratty sweatpants that he'd been wearing for months, his COVID beard patchy and light blond, all suddenly so repulsive to me, and listened to him tell me our marriage was done.

I couldn't help but laugh at the absurdity of it all. Soon I was crying, but I did notice something that felt like relief the moment he said it was over. I took that as a sign we maybe weren't meant to be, and instead of taking a minute to let the weight of reality sink in, I was hell-bent on making this uncoupling as healthy and mature as possible for both of us.

We got lucky when the pandemic ended, and the real estate market soared. We sold our little fixer-upper for three times what we bought it for and split the earnings equally. It felt like hitting the lottery, and the money gave both of us a nest egg to restart our lives. I took that as another sign that maybe we weren't meant to be after all.

That was it for us. Nick moved to Hoboken, and I found my place in Midtown. We started our lives apart, waiting for the final divorce paperwork to process. The Hudson River between us seemed an appropriate divider, symbolic, even poetic. Him over there, me over here, close enough to touch but not quite, like those crushingly lonely nights I had on the couch with him in the next room.

He eventually stopped asking to see Murphy, which felt like another blow. I was never more grateful that we had not had children together. When I was honest with myself, I could never quite picture him as a dad, not for lack of trying. The times I attempted to conjure up the image of him rocking a baby in a nursery or walking through the park with a baby strapped to his chest, his face would strangely disappear, and it'd be like looking into a void.

I grab my coffee mug and feel the warmth in my hands. I take a long sip and think about that uncomfortable memory. Kids are another topic that will not help my current melancholy mood. I know my clock is ticking. I'm thirty-eight, and most of my friends have at least two kids by now. I do, however, have twenty-one eggs on ice at the office of Dr. Melinda Goldburg, a reproductive endocrinologist on the Upper East Side, after my mom badgered me incessantly about it for months.

As soon as I broke the news to her about Nick and me splitting, she said, "You'll have plenty of time to be sad about that, but for now you better go get some of your eggs frozen while they're still good!"

I wasn't surprised by her directness, but at the time I was not in a place to even think about potential children. I was mourning my marriage, and even more so my friendship with Nick that had been such a constant in my life . Eventually, in my weakened state, my mom broke me down, and I scheduled the appointment.

I have to give her credit. Despite the inconvenience of the shots, ultrasounds, and the retrieval itself, I felt a calm settle over me knowing my eggs, "geriatric" but still viable, are waiting for me some-day. It feels like an insurance plan for my future. A future I can finally imagine.

* * *

A new email pops up, yanking me off memory lane and back to reality. It's from my best friend, Meredith. Just a question as the subject line: *Margs tonight? To celebrate?*

I laugh. She is the only other person besides Christine and maybe Nick who would be tracking this day. She is the best friend a girl could have. I type back a quick response. *Maybe next week. I'm fine. Love you.*

I take one last look at the picture of me, Murphy, and Nick. I toss it in the trash and put the frame back together. Pity party is officially over.

I stand up and switch out my shoes, trading the comfortable sherpa-lined clogs for heels, and smooth out my linen pants and sleeveless blouse. I grab my badge off the keyboard, clip it to my belt loop, and head into the hallway. I swipe onto the unit and stop by the nurse's station, which is always buzzing with the best people in health care.

"How's it going this afternoon, everyone?"

"Oh, good. The usual. Room 413 ripped out his NG tube again. The nursing student got sprayed with bile and almost lost her lunch." Dave laughs.

I look at the nursing student in her clearly borrowed oversized scrubs. "I wasn't expecting it, that's all," she says sheepishly.

"It happens to the best of us." I offer a sympathetic smile.

"The new admit is in room 416," Christine hands me his chart.

The critical care unit in our hospital is a step down from the ICU and a step up from regular patient rooms. A lot of the time, the job of this unit is stabilizing and observing before moving a patient to a different level of care. My role, though mostly administrative nowadays, is to assess the patient's needs, both medical and mental health, and offer support in any way possible: care coordination, discharge planning, grief counseling, and individual therapy.

Sometimes that looks like making sure they have walkers or wheelchairs to take home, sometimes it's providing support and psychoeducation for the patient and their loved ones, and sometimes it's as simple as holding a hand.

I knock twice before I walk into the room and see my new patient, a short and stout white man with wiry white hair that forms a horseshoe around his head. He's wearing big horn-rimmed glasses and has a chin that sticks out a little like Jay Leno's. He is cursing under his breath at the remote that controls his hospital bed. I smile. I love the geriatric population.

"Good afternoon, Mr. Johnson. I'm Julia, one of the social workers here at the hospital. How are you settling in?"

"I'd be better if you could tell me how to raise this damn bed so I can get out of here. I'm fine. I told the fellas in the ambulance I was fine, I told the people downstairs I'm fine, and I'm telling you again up here, I'm fine! I just had a little flutter. I think I overdid it on the decaf."

"Hmm ... I'm not sure you can overdo decaf, but I'll take your word for it. Let me help you sit up. How are you feeling?" I ask, adjusting the bed.

"Like I said, I'm fine. I've been fine. Rita, my aide, is a worrywart, and I don't like being in these places. The food is terrible, everyone is in my business, and I can't get any sleep!"

"All valid points, Mr. Johnson. How about I hang here with you for a little and ask you a few questions that might speed up the process of getting you out of here? I'll be honest, though. All the doctors have agreed you need at least two nights of observation to make sure that heart of yours is doing everything it should. So, we should at least prepare ourselves for forty-eight hours together. Hopefully I can help make it as painless as possible for you."

He replies with a grunt. "Well, all right."

I sit on the swivel stool next to his bed. "So, Mr. Johnson, tell me a little about yourself."

"First of all, stop calling me Mr. Johnson. I'm old but not that old. Call me Sid. What do you want to know?"

"Whatever you want to tell me."

"Well, all right. I grew up in Allentown, Pennsylvania. Do you know where that is? I'll tell ya, it's the heart of the Amish country. I got stuck behind horses and buggies on my way to school, and I'd visit the farm stands every week of the summer to get produce with my mother. If I was good, she'd let me get a whoopee pie, do you know what that is? Those Amish are some of the best damned bakers in the world. They use the real stuff, real butter, real sugar, real cream—none of this low-carb, low-fat bullshit Rita keeps telling me to eat. Now, let me tell you, if you could get me one of those whoopee pies, I might stop complaining."

"Believe it or not, I have had a whoopee pie, and I agree with you. They are delicious," I say. "Who helps take care of you? Though it seems like you do a pretty good job taking care of yourself, you mentioned an aide. Anyone else?"

"Rita? Yes, she's my aide, or what I like to call my paid friend. My son is a worse worrywart than she is and has insisted Rita come check on me every damn day. He spends his money like he's got a forest of trees full of it in his backyard. I keep telling him he better save it for a worthwhile investment, like a nice piece of property, or better yet, spend some on a good steak dinner for a nice young woman. I swear I'll die before that boy settles down."

"Okay, so it sounds like you have a son who cares a lot about you. Does he ever help with your day-to-day needs?" I try to assess what type of aftercare Sid might need.

"Sons. Plural. I have two sons, Matt and Eric. Eric died of lymphoma when he was sixteen. But he is still my son."

"I'm so sorry to hear that, Sid."

"Thank you. I promised myself I would still tell people about him even though losing him was the worst thing that ever happened to me. It nearly broke me. Some would say it did. It broke my marriage, that's for sure. We couldn't survive a loss like that. My wife could never get over it; she wanted to stay in bed and pretend the world didn't exist. That's a story for another day, but I knew that feeling. Feeling like there was no point in living in a world without Eric, but we had Matt. Matt was eighteen and just trying to figure out how to be an adult. Yes, he was old enough to vote, to enlist himself in the military if he wanted, but he was still a boy to me, and he needed a parent. He lost his brother and his mom for all intents and purposes. I had to step up. And I am damn proud of him. Even if he is hardheaded."

I smile at his love, pride, and the weight of his loss. "Is Matt your power of attorney? Does he help you make major medical decisions?"

"Yes, he insisted on that, too, but I can make my own damn decisions."

"Okay, well, when he gets here maybe we can talk about what we can do to help support you when you get out of here."

I see Sid's eyes dart over my shoulder, and his face breaks into a wide smile.

"There you are, my boy. Took you long enough!"

He turns back toward me with a twinkle in his eyes. "This is my son, my power of attorney, Matthew."

I spin on my stool and see a man in the doorway: tall, at least six three, a bit lanky but with broad shoulders and a full head of incredibly thick, wavy dark brown hair. He takes two steps into the room, and I get a better look. He is dressed in well-worn dark brown pants, scuffed boots, and a plain black T-shirt. He has a sleeve of intricate and colorful tattoos cascading down his muscular right arm and a black backpack slung over his shoulder. He looks vaguely familiar, but I can't quite place him.

One thing is for sure, he is gorgeous.

"Jesus, Dad, if you want to see me, all you gotta do is ask. We don't need the theatrics." He walks to the other side of the bed and bends down to give his dad a kiss on the cheek.

"Matt, this is Julia, my nurse." Sid gestures toward me.

I lock eyes with Matt and see his are brown and soulful, topped by a furrowed brow that makes him appear contemplative. His mouth is full, with lips almost too perfect to be on a man. My eyes go right to them. I worry I am staring and snap out of it.

"Close, Sid, but sadly, I am not a nurse. In fact, I am terrified of blood, so don't expect to see me here during any procedures. I'm Julia Anderson, one of the social workers here. I was just coming to check in on your dad and make sure he was settling in okay. Nice to meet you." I reach out to shake his hand.

"Matt Johnson." He leans over Sid's bedside, his hand reaching toward me. We shake and I glance down, noticing how elegant his hands are. Baby soft skin, warm. They are easily twice the size of mine.

"I'll let you two catch up, and I'll be back to check in on you later, all right, Sid? Matt, he is on Dr. Patel's service. She is fantastic, very thorough. Christine is the nurse in charge on this shift, so if you need anything at all, grab her or tell her to get me. I'm here until six and happy to help in any way I can." I stand to leave.

"Thank you," says Matt, his gaze still on mine. I stare back, caught off guard by him, the intensity I feel radiating off him.

"You're welcome."

* * *

I walk out of the room in a daze, past the nurse's station. I am almost out of the unit when I hear *"Psssssst"* coming from behind me. Dave waves me over to where the entire unit of nurses and nursing students are all huddled around a computer screen.

"Ummm, Julia, did you know that room 416's emergency contact is *Matt Johnson?*" he practically squeals. He turns the monitor, and I see Google images of the man I just met plastered all over the screen. Him walking down the street, him on a red carpet, him on stage playing a guitar, him smiling for a fragrance campaign. If possible, he is even more beautiful in person than in these photos.

"Holy shiiiiiiiiiiit," Beth, an OG nurse, sighs. "What I wouldn't do to get my hands on him. How long is his dad here?" She clicks into Sid's chart. "I need this eye candy. I *need it*. We deserve this." She leans back in her chair.

"Who is Matt Johnson?" chimes the nursing student.

"Are you serious? How old are you?" questions Dave.

"Dibs on that room!" shouts someone else.

I can't shake the zap I felt in the room with Matt, and I now wonder if it's simply the effect he has on people, like everyone twitterpated at the nurse's station right now.

"Okay, okay, people, yes, he is gorgeous, but he is here with a patient, and as such, we will treat them both with the utmost professionalism," scolds Christine from the other side of the station.

"This is not our first famous person, and it will not be our last. No sneaking around to gawk, no trying to get assigned to that room. In fact, that patient room is mine and mine alone for the next three shifts. Absolutely no taking pictures, and no pervy comments—yes, I am talking to you, Dave. Let us all remember the dire consequences of violating a patient's HIPAA rights."

I give her a nod of gratitude. I can always count on her to keep this ship righted.

I sneak away to my office as they all continue to whisper and ogle at the computer. I stare out my window, trying to conjure up anything I might know about Matt Johnson. I know he is a wildly successful musician, a singer, songwriter, and guitar player who performs in sold-out arenas all over the world, but I'm blanking on any of his songs. I vaguely remember some controversy with him many years ago, but in this day and age, who in the public eye hasn't been touched by that? I still feel rattled by the intensity in his brown eyes. I sit a few more minutes before moving back over to my desk. I slip off my heels and put my clogs on to start working on a project due at the end of the week.

* * *

Before I know it, it's almost six o'clock. I change shoes and walk out to do one last round on the floor before heading home for the day. I save

Sid's room for last, and when I arrive, I find myself a little bummed to see that he is alone.

Sid, sharp as a tack, sees it on my face. "Aw, darling, don't look so sad, he'll be back. He just went to get me some dinner. I told you, the food here is garbage."

"What makes you think I'm sad, Sid? I'm not. In fact, the very opposite, since I see here your numbers are staying nice and stable, which is exactly what we want to see. Maybe you'll get your wish and be out of here before we know it." I glance at his chart.

"You can't pull one over on me." He narrows his bespectacled eyes at me. "I've been around long enough to know when a woman looks disappointed to see me. I've also been around long enough to know that my son is a very handsome young man. Can't say I blame you for making those eyes at him when he walked in."

My face flushes. "I can assure you, I didn't make any kind of eyes, but he does seem like a nice guy who really cares about his dad."

"You've got that right. And I'm the first to make a joke at his expense, but he is the greatest blessing of my life. He is considerate and kind. And even though it's unnecessary, he takes care of me. He takes care of all the people he loves, without ever expecting anything in return. Now, I don't know if you know this, but he's a real whiz on the guitar. He dug one out of my father's basement when he was six years old, and it was practically glued to his hands for the next two years. I could only get him to give it up when I promised to get him a brand new one all his own, so long as he tried his best in school. I regret discouraging him from pursuing his dreams, but you gotta understand how ridiculous it sounded when he told me his plan was to play the guitar wherever, whenever, and as often as he could. I told him, 'That's well and great, son, but it's a hobby. How the hell are you going to make a living like that?' I was worried he'd wind up like the guy down there on the corner, singing for the change in his coffee cup. But I couldn't have been more wrong. He did it. My boy did it. He made all his dreams come true," he recounts wistfully.

My heart warms at the well-worn story of a proud parent.

"Now if only I could get him settled down before I die. That would be a big relief for me, to not worry about him and what he'll do when I'm gone." Sid looks at me pointedly. "Speaking of which, Julia, I notice you don't have a wedding ring on. Does that mean you're on the market?"

I feel my face flush again. "You don't miss a thing, do you, Sid? I'm not sure my relationship status is the important thing here." I try to deflect.

"It sure is, especially if you want my health to improve. Don't you want to help a dying man fulfill his last wishes?"

I laugh awkwardly. "You're not dying, last I checked. All these tests say you're doing just fine."

"We're all dying, sweetheart." He's so earnest it breaks my heart a little. "I just want to see my boy happy and settled. Throw an old man a bone. Are you on the market?"

I stare at him, weighing my options. This curmudgeonly octogenarian is disarming.

"Yes. I am," I admit eventually.

"Well, that's all I need to know. I'll take it from here. You have a good night, now, Miss Julia. See you tomorrow."

And with that, I leave room 416 and head home in the hot, sticky summer air.

Chapter 2

Tuesday

The next morning, I arrive at work early, eager to busy myself with something to help me stop thinking about the soulful eyes of Matt Johnson. I'm startled to find those exact eyes looking at me as I reach my office door.

"Good morning, Ms. Anderson."

"Good morning. Please call me Julia."

"Okay, Julia. Sorry to be hovering around your door like this. I just had a few questions and figured I'd see if you were in yet."

"Yeah, sure. Come on in."

I unlock my door. I let him in and take a few moments to put my things down, open the blinds, and plug in my laptop. He stands by the window, taking in the view of the city with the morning light breaking through the clouds. I glance at him discreetly as he moves toward my bookshelves. He is tall—taller than I thought yesterday. Probably six four, but it's tough to tell because he does the thing tall guys do where they stand with their legs wide, shoulders slightly hunched.

His hands are in his pockets, and his hair is so thick and wavy, I have the distinct urge to touch it. He's wearing a different version of the outfit from yesterday—dark blue jeans, the same brown boots, a blue T-shirt, and a long silver necklace full of charms. I watch as he stands in front of the bookshelves, his fingers drifting slowly along the spines of my books, his head cocked to the side as he reads the titles.

"Want to sit?" I ask.

He does.

"Great office." He looks around.

"Thank you."

"I can see how people would find this space to be very soothing. That must be helpful in your line of work."

I raise an eyebrow.

"I looked you up on the hospital website." He leans forward. "So I could explain to my dad for the fifth time that you are not a nurse but a therapist—a licensed clinical social worker, actually."

I smile. "Well, thanks for that. Makes me feel better since I know a little bit about you, too."

"Oh, like what?"

"Just that you're this unknown, up and coming musician hoping to get your big break soon."

He laughs. It's warm and deep. "Yes, that's me."

"How can I help you this morning, Matt?"

"A few things, but mostly just some stuff that's been weighing on my mind. I don't think they are unfounded worries, though my life has been saturated with anxiety, so please tell me if I'm off base here."

I nod, encouraging him to go on.

"I know my dad says he's fine pretty much all the time, but I have noticed some decline in his cognitive functioning in the past few months. It seems like it takes him longer to retrieve words. He isn't as quick-witted as he once was, and that has been one of the most defining parts of his personality. It's like there's a break in the circuit, like when you start driving somewhere and forget where you're going halfway through and find yourself on the other side of town. Sometimes he looks like he isn't quite sure where he is or what we were just talking about, though he plays it off well, usually by making a joke. When I push him on it, he tells me to get a hobby and that I'm nothing but a busybody. And he's right, but I'm also worried. He's pretty much all I've got in the world, and while I know I can't have him forever, I want to try to make it as long as possible. Does that make sense?"

I like the way he talks, like a steady stream of consciousness—a therapist's dream, really.

"Yes, it makes sense. I can see how important he is to you, and you are to him. He did mention a few times how much you worry. Some of what you're saying could be nothing, or at least just very normal parts of the aging process. Why don't we mention it to Dr. Patel and follow her lead? Like I said before, she is the absolute best and will leave no stone unturned. By my calculations, we have at least another twenty-four hours of observation time, so we might as well do a full workup."

"That would be very helpful, for him and me. A little peace of mind."

"Have you ever talked to someone about the anxiety?" I ask.

"You mean do I have a therapist? The answer is no, but I have seen one before. Shortly after a few ... personal crises." He trails off. "It was helpful in the moment, almost like a problem-solving mode, but we never dug in to examine the depth of things. Not to say I wouldn't be open to it." He pauses. "Are you taking new patients?" The smile he flashes at me is so charming it seems to hit me right in the gut.

Before I can respond, he goes on. "Apart from that, I'm probably hyperanalytical myself—I replay things I've done in my head for weeks and months and years, trying to figure out what I could've done differently, or why I did what I did. Now, granted, it's a bit of an echo chamber 'cause it's just me in there—no objective, nonjudgmental third party. Even despite all of that, I've always felt like I am relatively well adjusted.... Do well-adjusted people say that?"

"Sure."

He smiles. "I do have the occasional bout of fear paralysis and never-ending overthinking. But that's normal, right? Not to mention, all the angst has given me some of the greatest insights of my life and created some great records in the process."

I nod. "Yes, to some extent. Anxiety is an unavoidable part of the human condition. That you've been able to harness it for art and creativity most of the time is fantastic. And no, I'm not taking new patients, though I'd be happy to add you to my waitlist."

His eyes light up, like he's surprised, and he smiles at me again. I can't help but smile back, and he starts talking again.

"The other thing, and I know there's probably no good answer for this, but I feel like Dad should be living with me full-time. Or at least have full-time care. Don't you think? How do I make that call? He says over his dead body, and I know he has Rita. But I just worry about the times he's by himself. I worry he's lonely. I'd feel better if he was with me and I could always check on him. The only problem is my life and schedule can occasionally be chaotic. I basically live in two separate places, but I have a lot more autonomy over my schedule now and could plan for the times I'm gone." His brow furrows with worry.

"Taking care of aging parents is complicated, and you're right, there is no one-size-fits-all answer. Some are thrilled when their kids want to take care of them, and they thrive. Others feel like they have become a burden, like they've lost the last little independence they had, and that's a huge challenge. There's no way to know until you try. Not to mention there are a lot of options to fill in the gaps between those two sides of the spectrum. It's probably worth a conversation. Do you think he'd be receptive?"

He rests his head in his hands, and they grab my attention. Again. His hands are so big and beautiful—they look soft and warm. I force myself to look away as he contemplates my suggestion.

"Hmmm, receptive? Probably not, but he is currently a captive audience, so maybe now is the time." He grins conspiratorially.

"I'm happy to join you for moral support, if you think it might help."

23

"Ah, yes, safety in numbers. That's a good call. I'd appreciate that."

"Sure, I'll meet you up there later today. I'll bring some resources. Maybe around four?"

"Sounds great. Thank you for your time this morning," he politely says and stands to leave. He pauses as he rises, looking at my painting. I stand with him.

"That piece of art makes me feel hopeful."

"In what way?"

"I'm not sure. I'll have to come back and look at it again sometime, but the way the colors are put together—like it's meant to look chaotic, but I find it oddly calming and exciting. Hopeful."

"Interesting." I feel myself smile.

He opens the door and starts to walk out before stopping and turning back toward me. "Have you read *An Inquiry into the Good* by Kitaro Nishida?" His voice is so deep it feels soothing, like dark brown honey.

"No, I haven't."

He nods and wanders into the hallway, gently closing the door behind him.

* * *

By the time I make it to room 416, I peek in the window and see Matt has spruced up Sid's bed with some very high thread count sheets, blankets, and extra pillows. I knock twice and walk in. Sid is eating a deli sandwich, the fresh rye bread permeating the air. Music—soft blues—plays from a speaker on the windowsill.

"Ah, yes, another one of my wardens. Can I get out of here yet?" Sid grumbles.

"I wish! But unfortunately, I'm not a doctor, and you're under doctor's orders." I glance at Matt, who is watching me from across the room, chewing on the straw in his to-go cup.

"Well, can we get that damn doctor back in here? Where did she go? I can never find anyone in this place. Is that part of the plan? If I can't find anyone, I can't get out of here?"

"I'm sure she'll be back sometime before she heads out for the day. What can I do to help?" I sit down on the swivel stool at the foot of the bed. "I have a Fire TV Stick in my office you can use to stream any show you want. We've got a pretty good book collection on this floor; you can come take a look. Or I can get my hands on some top shelf beverages from the nurses' station—apple juice, orange juice— all from concentrate, unclear if there is any trace of either of the actual fruits in it. Or snacks. We've got pretzels, cookies, chips— anything that is highly processed and has almost no nutritional value or taste. I know, the irony of feeding people trash when they're here trying to heal. Either way, it's all yours ... your wish is my command."

He looks at me and brings his hand to his chin, narrowing his eyes. "If you're a genie fulfilling wishes, then you'll go to dinner with my son. Tonight."

I'm so caught off guard I involuntarily scoot myself backward in the stool. Matt chokes on his drink, and as he sputters and coughs, I suspect he feels the same.

"Now, Sid, that wasn't within the scope of my offer...." I stammer, trying to recover.

"Nope. You can't backpedal now, young lady. That's what I want, and it turns out Matthew does, too, because he was just telling me right before you came in how much he enjoyed talking with you this morning. And how much he'd like to take you to dinner tonight. His treat."

"Dad, come on! I told you to play it cool! You're making me look desperate, like I can't ask her out on my own...." He trails off with good-natured exasperation.

"Well, considering you haven't been on a date in at least two years, I would say it's pretty clear you *can't* get a date. Sometimes a father has to take matters into his own hands."

I laugh at their sweet interaction but feel my cheeks flush with embarrassment. The last thing I want is a pity date. I tell them both as much.

"Pity date?" exclaims Sid. "The only thing that's a pity is you two young, beautiful people withering away in this hospital tonight alongside me. For Pete's sake, get out of here! You've gotta eat, don't you? Go out into the world! Enjoy your damn selves! At least do it for me, while I'm trapped in this beeping purgatory." His glare is fierce.

Matt looks at me, and in his most chivalrous voice says, "I'd really like to take you to dinner, if you're free."

I stare at him and then at Sid and back again, hoping to convey to them both how uncomfortable this situation is.

"Don't say no, sweetheart," Sid interjects. "Look at that handsome face of his. And remember, you're fulfilling a dying man's wishes."

"You aren't dying!" Matt and I say at the same time. I look at Matt, his eyes twinkling with good-natured fun. God, he is gorgeous.

"Fine," I concede as I turn to leave the room.

"I'll meet you in the lobby in twenty?" Matt calls out after me.

Once in the safety of my office, I am equal parts grateful and pissed that I have agreed to this last-minute, very coerced dinner with Matt. I don't have enough time to go home and change, let alone freak out about it. I rush over to my desk, rummaging for the emergency supplies I keep in the bottom drawer.

I reapply deodorant and brush my teeth. I dressed this morning in anticipation of seeing Matt again, so I have a relatively sexy yet still professional outfit on—a sleeveless navy knit dress by Reformation that is tighter and shorter than I'd normally wear to work. I flip my head upside down, running my fingers through my long dark hair, hoping to add some volume, then finger comb it around my face. I walk over to the mirror behind my fridge and blot my face with a napkin before patting on some powder and bronzer. I recurl my eyelashes and put on another coat of mascara, making my espresso brown eyes look brighter, add lip gloss, grab my purse, and head for the elevator before I can overthink the absurdity and borderline ethical issues of this situation. As I ride the elevator down, I shoot a quick text to Dave.

> I am informing you for safety purposes that I am going to dinner with room 416's son.

He immediately texts back:

> !!??!!? WHAT !!???!!!

I toss my phone into my purse and take a deep breath.

* * *

Matt is waiting in the lobby with his back to me. He is hard to miss despite all the people milling around. He looks even taller down here with the high ceilings, but I notice the slight hunch of shoulders, almost as if he is being pushed down by gravity. My heart swells, and I wonder if the worry about his dad is taking a toll. When he turns and sees me, a wide smile flashes across his face. I try my hardest not to blush.

"You look lovely. Ready to go?" He leads me toward a waiting SUV. I nod and watch with curiosity as he glances side to side before leaving the safety of the hospital lobby. He holds the door open as I slide across the bench seat and then hops in behind me.

"There's a place in the West Village that is one of my favorites. I got us a table." Just as I start to wonder how he got a table so quickly, he tells the driver, "The Waverly Inn, please."

"You got it, Matt."

And I realize this is not a random Uber but his personal driver, and he can get a last-minute table no problem because I am going to dinner with the world-famous Matt Johnson.

* * *

We walk down the steps to the restaurant and are quickly led to a table in the corner of the covered back patio. I sit against a wall dripping with greenery and Matt sits with his back to the restaurant. As I glance around the room, I am hit with a memory—Nick and me here together once, years ago at Christmastime. We sat by the fireplace and ordered hot toddies and burgers. We were buzzed from the drinks, the charming ambiance, and the festive mood swirling around the city. By the end of the night, we were making out at the bar. I cringe and shake the memory away as a server appears with a carafe of water and two glasses.

"Hi, Matt, welcome back. Do you want the usual?"

"Yes, that'd be great, Amy, thank you kindly."

She turns to me. "What would you like to drink?"

"I'm fine with water for now, thanks."

We sit in silence as Matt opens the carafe and pours water into my glass before filling his own. I start reading through the menu, not absorbing any of the information. I feel like all my senses are heightened, sitting across from Matt, outside the safety of the hospital. I can't concentrate on anything besides not making a complete ass of myself in what is most definitely a pity date. *Do I have no dignity?* I wonder. The server comes back with a glass of scotch with one giant ice cube and what looks like sake in a smaller cup.

"Did you see anything you'd like to drink yet?" She waits patiently.

I glance back to my menu. I don't even see sake on it, but all the words blur together as I use all my energy to try to remember what I like to drink.

"Hmm ..." I murmur, stalling, searching. My palms dampen with sweat. I feel them staring at me.

"I think I'm good with the water, thanks," I blurt before staring blankly back at the menu.

I look up to find Matt watching me intently. He seems amused.

"What's going on in that mind of yours?"

I blink, embarrassed he's somehow read the panic on my face and surprised that he noticed.

"Do you really want to know?"

"Yes, I do."

"I'm trying to think what it might say about me—to you—that I didn't order a drink."

"What do you think I might be thinking?"

"Maybe I have a drinking problem? Or maybe I'm a purist who puts no toxins in my body? Neither is true, for the record. I like alcohol. In a normal, socially acceptable, nondiagnosable way. I was just drawing a blank. I'm nervous, and I'm not usually," I answer honestly. Too honestly.

He laughs. "There is nothing I can relate more to than overthinking. And just so you know, I wasn't thinking that at all. I'm a little nervous, too."

I don't know if I believe him, but I feel some of my jitters dissipate. His voice is comforting, his presence calming.

"Tell me more." He leans back in his chair, casually crossing his arms across his chest, his tattoos on full display.

"Okay." I take a breath. "I was running through what I could order and what it might convey—maybe a vodka martini, straight up with three olives, because that might make me seem sophisticated or mysterious. Or like a real WASPy upper crust kind of gal. But I'm none of those things, and if I'm honest, I'm not convinced I even know what *straight up* means. Plus, I never know how strong martinis are going to be, and I'm a bit of a lightweight and do not want you to have to carry me out of here. So that's out."

He laughs, and I feel it in my stomach. "So, then what?"

I settle in. "So, then I'm thinking, maybe a vodka soda or tequila soda with lime. Simple, right? But no. That might scream sorority girl, counting calories, ordering two at a time at a bar with a sticky floor where there's no cover for ladies on Tuesday nights. So, then what? I could order a beer, which I do enjoy from time to time, especially in the summer or at a sporting event, but I think that might make you think I'm trying too hard to be cool. Like I'm just one of the guys. And I am not that. I love men but have no intention of ever trying to fit in with them. After that, I guess there is the white wine option, a safe bet, but that feels like I'm instantly transported to the life of a fifty-something stay-at-home wife whose kids are all at insanely expensive private liberal arts colleges and who buys buttery chardonnay in the big bottles from Sam's Club. That's depressing all by itself, notwithstanding the inevitable headache white wine always gives me. That leaves me with a glass of red wine, which would be my go-to, except the price range is so vast I don't know what is reasonable for a ... coerced dinner. Plus I can't even tell the difference between a twenty dollar bottle and a two hundred dollar bottle, but my real concern is the fact certain reds are more likely to stain my teeth. So that's a huge gamble. I'm not sure if you have a George Washington kink, but that's not quite the look I'm going for."

He is fully laughing at this point as I ramble on.

"Wait, what? A George Washington kink?"

"His teeth," I say. He shakes his head, not getting it.

"George Washington had wooden teeth. A little red wine stain on teeth can make them look exactly like that."

He bursts out laughing, leaning forward onto the table. "That is the most ridiculous thing I've heard in a long time."

"See my struggle?" I smile, finally feeling calm and warm and delighted.

"So where does this leave you, drink-wise?"

"I could go around and around all night, but that sake you're drinking looks good, so maybe I'll try it."

He passes his glass to me. I raise it to him as he lifts his scotch.

"To your dad."

"To my dad."

After we order our food, a mercifully easier decision for me, Matt asks me thoughtful questions. Not the typical interview-style first date questions—*not that this is even a date*, I remind myself. He asks with the intent to listen rather than formulating his own response as I speak. Listening is a skill I've spent years of training and supervision to master. That he can do it so well is impressive to me ... and very sexy.

He doesn't seem interested in where I went to college or what neighborhood I live in. Rather, he asks me, "What is something you see in your job that most surprises you?"

I take another sip of my drink, thinking hard about the question.

"A lot of it is the obvious things. Like the resilience of the human spirit. Like in my first job out of grad school in Baltimore. I was working with kids and families who were having a very hard time. These families would welcome me into their homes, willingly reveal all their skeletons, to let me walk with them toward change. It always seemed like such a great act of love to me. These families lived in some of the most dangerous neighborhoods, with the bleakest conditions, and yet love and hope grew like wildflowers. I noticed it was the women, mostly, who watered their communities. I still think about those kids, the ones with the all the odds stacked against them, and hope and wish that they are okay."

He leans forward, listening even more intently.

"Conversely, sometimes a health or mental health crisis brings out the worst in people. Fear looks different on everyone. Sometimes it looks like anger, sometimes hopelessness, sometimes an endless pursuit for answers. Once I started to understand that, it was easier to navigate. That's another thing that surprises me. That I have been fortunate to witness hope as something tangible—something I can see with my own two eyes. It's a jolt of recognition that comes across a person's face when they feel understood for the first time in their life. Sometimes that simple connection is all it takes to keep them tethered to earth. I'm always surprised and amazed when people begin to feel the power they gain when they realize they don't have to be held hostage by their emotions and thoughts or their demons and traumas."

Before I know it, we've finished our dinners and order another round of sake. I have not asked him a single question.

"I promise I do get out from time to time and interact with other humans," I joke, embarrassed I've somehow spoken so freely to him.

"No, no, it's fascinating. I can't tell you how much I enjoy listening to you. It's not every day I talk to someone who is so clearly passionate about their work. Plus, it's so different from the world I'm in. Things I don't often think about. It's very cool."

"Well, now it's your turn."

"I'd much rather hear more about you and what is going on inside that mind of yours. But sure, what do you want to know?"

I pause, taking him in over the low lighting. He is so handsome it almost doesn't seem fair. "What's something, let's just say in your professional life, that you're *not* good at?"

"Hmmmmm." He rests his head in his hand. "Probably a lot of things I haven't yet realized. But I know I struggle, at least in my music, to collaborate. To let other people in. To release that control I have and the control I feel like I need in everything I create. I'm pretty sure of myself most of the time, at least when it comes to sounds, melodies, lyrics. What works and what doesn't. But I am very much in my head about the entire process until the last possible second. Once I've got it all figured out, I'll call my guys up—they're the best around—and we will lay it all out based on the blueprints of that original architecture I've already created in my mind. Sure, they have some creative liberties to do their own thing, but if I'm honest, it's probably a little constricted, given the parameters I set out. The flip side is that it's worked for me so far, which is why I haven't tried too hard to change anything."

"Is changing things something you want to do?"

"Good question."

"I know."

He smiles. "I'm not sure. I sometimes wonder if I'm coasting. I'm at a point in my career where I'm not sure what's next for me or where to go from here. Over the years, I've been equal parts lucky and dedicated to somehow mitigate a lot of the risks most newer artists face. I've kind of shown the world, and myself, I'm a known quantity. I'm consistent. I may not be chart topping every time, but I make music I love and that some people still want to hear. I've got the most loyal and supportive fans in the world. They'll listen to anything I put out, so from that standpoint, I don't know why I would change. But at the same time, I wonder if I'm stagnant. If there is more somewhere. If I just pushed myself a little bit, maybe I could get to the next level. Next level for me is not something that might be measurable by anything out here in the world, but something only I can truly know."

"That's a tough balance—pushing and stretching versus sticking with what works and enjoying the ride."

"Exactly."

"Where do you get ideas for songs?"

"Ha." He laughs good-naturedly. "Standard interview question. And the standard answer is everything, everywhere, everyone, life in general. And to answer the next interview question, no, my songs are not about specific people, they are just about the ideas of people. Themes. Patterns. Feelings."

"What's the non-standard answer?"

"It's generally the same, 'cause the standard one isn't dishonest. It's just more nuanced than I usually care to go into most of the time. Sometimes an idea for a song will hit me as I'm showering or stuck in traffic. Sometimes it feels like it's been living inside me, and I haven't quite been able to figure out what it was until a very specific moment. Sometimes it feels like when you have to sneeze, and you stop and brace yourself—that anticipation, and then nothing happens, so I have to dig a little. Sometimes it's born out of pure chemical reactions, super high highs, and the lowest of lows. Sometimes it's a story I've made up in my head. It's anything and everything. The only thing I've learned is that I just have to pay attention."

I cock my head at him, surprised by his insight. "That is something I say to myself and my patients, often. Pay attention."

33

"What do you mean by that?" he asks.

"I mean that we spend most of our waking hours, and our lives, on autopilot. Going from task to task, checking things off our to-do lists, and any time in between is spent scanning the never-ending tasks and thoughts and worries. That makes it hard to pay attention, so we spend a lot of time going through the motions. Making a million little decisions every day without even thinking about it. Mindfulness —a big buzzword right now—to me is simply practicing the art of paying attention. To know what is happening, when it's happening, because you are purposely ignoring everything else to be in the present moment."

He gives me a look I can't interpret and says, "So, kind of like, 'sit, be still, and listen.'"

"Yes. Exactly. That's Rumi."

He squints his eyes and looks at me, like he's seeing something new.

"You are incredibly beautiful," he says suddenly, confidently.

It catches me by surprise, and I feel adrenaline surge through my veins. Through the candlelight, he smiles a half smile at me that is so smoldering, several unholy thoughts cross my mind.

"Thank you," I fight the urge to look down at my lap.

Our conversation carries on naturally and gracefully, like a river flowing downstream. We both seem happy to ride along through the different bends it takes. We pass on dessert, our plates are cleared, and more sake is brought out. I feel buzzed from the rice wine, the conversation, the unexpectedness of sitting across from this very attractive and interesting man on a random Tuesday night. It feels like no time has passed, and yet like I somehow have been sitting with him at this table forever. When I take a second to look around, I see the servers sweeping the floors and tallying up their tips.

I start to gather up my purse. "This was great. Thank you for dinner—even if you were coerced."

"You're very welcome. I can't tell you how much I enjoyed this."

"Me too."

"It was a pleasant surprise to meet you. And I haven't worried about my dad for a single moment since we sat down." He checks his watch and does a low whistle. "Shit, I should probably get back to check on him."

"I can check in with Christine quickly, she's on tonight."

"That'd be great."

I grab my phone from my purse and furiously swipe away the seventeen text messages from Dave, ones with thousands of angry question marks followed by one that says, *YOU MUST TELL ME EVERYTHING.*

I click Christine's contact info, and she picks up on the first ring. "Hey, I'm with Matt, how's Sid?"

"Interesting ..." she murmurs, and I hear her get up and walk down the hall. "He's sound asleep. For someone as pernickety as him, he looks angelic when he's asleep."

"Anything new?" I ask.

"All continues to be on the up and up. Dr. P thinks she might discharge tomorrow evening if all looks good in the morning. I'd tell his son there is no reason for him to come back and sleep in this god-awful recliner. His dad is out for the night, and he's got me at the click of a button."

"Thanks, Chris. I'll tell him. See you in the morning."

"Have fun," she grumbles and hangs up.

"Your dad is asleep, and everything looks good. No reason to wake up with your back in a pretzel from that recliner. She will take good care of him, so you can get a good night's rest."

He looks relieved. "That is great news. Thank you for doing that."

"No problem."

"I really enjoyed this," Matt says.

"You already said that."

"Well, I'm saying it again, for emphasis." He reaches for my hand across the table. I give it to him and feel the warmth coming from his palm.

"Thank you," he repeats.

I look at him and feel the same electrical current I felt the moment I first laid eyes on him yesterday. It almost makes me flinch, and I pull my hand back. "You're welcome."

We both stand to leave. "Take my car home," he offers.

"No, no, it's beautiful out tonight, I'm happy to walk."

"Please, I insist."

"Okay," I concede. "But how will you get home?"

"I think I'll float," he says with a cheeky smile.

I lean in to give him a quick hug. I catch a scent in the spot between his neck and his shoulder. It smells like crisp, clean woodsy, mixed with something citrusy. It overwhelms me, and I stay there a moment longer, breathing him in, feeling his arms wrapped lightly around my lower back. I back up, suddenly feeling the urgent need to get out of there.

"Good night," he calls after me.

"Good night," I echo.

Chapter 3

Wednesday

I show up to work the next day feeling hungover from the sake, the unexpected and riveting dinner, and staying up way too late playing every Matt Johnson album ever produced. Listening to his music felt almost voyeuristic in the context of my personal connection to him, albeit about thirty-six hours old.

It felt like reading his diary—wrong, and yet I couldn't stop. Some of the songs were familiar to me—the big radio hits—but the ones I love are new to me, the deep record tracks that seem soulful and inspired. I'm blown away by the depth he weaves into a three-minute song. I am amazed at his ability to layer so much meaning and cleverness while offering up big, profound ideas in a way that feels accessible and relatable to everyone who might be listening. His singing voice sounds different than his speaking voice, deeper and yet raspier all at once. It's provocative.

I didn't stop at looking up his music. I Googled him and saw hundreds of photos, many of which showed him on stages and red carpets with beautiful women—actresses, fellow musicians, and models. All gorgeous and talented in their own right. *Is this his type?* I felt a pit form in my stomach. While I've certainly never been short on confidence, I do not consider myself to be anywhere near the level of these other women.

Why do I even care? This is a patient's emergency contact who was coerced into sharing a meal with me, nothing more, nothing less. Strangely, I did not see any interviews with Matt about the women he was linked to. No outright confirmation about any one relationship. It was all speculation, though the proof in the photos is undeniable. I ended up drifting off into a deep, dreamless sleep, but as soon as I woke up, I thought about him.

I swipe onto the unit and make my way toward the nurse's station. Dave greets me with a furious look on his face.

"I texted you fifty times last night! Not a single response? Did you know I could hardly sleep? How could you do this to me?"

"Dave, it is not my responsibility to fill you in on every single detail of my boring pity dinner."

"Boring, my ass! You got to sit across from that perfect specimen for at least two hours, so you better spill."

"Want to have lunch with me today?"

"Fine," Dave says begrudgingly.

* * *

After an uneventful morning full of paperwork and a vibrant lunch with Dave at which I shared some, but not all, of the details, I make it to Sid's room. He is sleeping soundly, and Matt sits by the window, headphones on, working on his laptop. I gesture for him to come out into the hallway.

"How's it going? How are both of you doing?"

"I think we're doing just fine. My dad is as ornery as ever because Dr. Patel told him he has to stay through tonight. I have to say, everyone here is fantastic, but especially the nurses. They somehow placate him, and I know it isn't easy."

"Good. I want to talk to you both about some of the discharge resources we have, so maybe I can come back when he's awake."

Matt watches my mouth while I speak in a way that makes me very aware of how close together we are standing.

"Do you have plans tonight? My dad wants to order in Thai, and I was just going to camp out in his room. Want to join us?" He is now looking into my eyes.

"I'm sorry, I can't. I'm busy," I say quickly.

"Yeah, of course, no worries. Maybe another time." Suddenly diffident. It's cute.

"I feel like I'm going a little nuts being in here for so many hours of the day. I can understand why he is so adamant about going home. Hopefully, it happens tomorrow." As he runs a hand through his thick hair, his brows furrow.

"My thing tonight isn't until seven, but I'm going home to walk my dog beforehand. You can join me if you'd like. Get some fresh air," I say impulsively.

"I'd like that." He smiles that half smile.

"I'll text you when I'm at the entrance of the park. It's only a few blocks from here." We exchange numbers, and I once again head back to my office wondering what the hell I am doing.

* * *

I stand at the entrance of the park, anxiously awaiting Matt's arrival. I shift my weight from foot to foot and twirl the leash around my wrists. Murphy, completely unaware of my mounting nerves, sits wagging his tail, restless to begin his walk.

What am I doing?

I know Matt has approached me from behind; it's like I can somehow sense his presence. Murphy jumps up, ripping the leash from my hands and taking off in a full sprint toward Matt.

"I think your dog likes me," he says with smile, walking back toward me holding Murphy's leash.

"A lot of people think that. He is the most excitable forty pound mutt in all Central Park."

Murphy jumps all over Matt with absolutely no manners and begins frantically sniffing at his right jacket pocket. With Murphy serving as a buffer, my eyes rake over him. He's wearing a tight gray T-shirt with an old-school, eighties-style white windbreaker over it, black shorts, and Nike sneakers. He looks the part of a musician, effortlessly cool, all six foot four of him confidently on display. I smile as he pulls out a piece of bacon wrapped in a napkin from his coat pocket.

"I hope you don't mind. I came prepared. It's from the cafeteria breakfast my Dad refused to eat."

"Not at all. You'll have a fast friend."

We fall in stride together, heading for the usual loop Murphy and I do most nights after work. The first few moments are filled with comfortable silence. We see the regular crowd of dogs, and I notice their owners slow down, doing double takes. Matt notices, too, and ducks his head. I glance at him, wondering if he notices the ways he shrinks himself.

He breaks the silence. "I'd like to say you get used to it, but that's not completely true. At least there aren't any paparazzi."

"How can you tell the difference?"

"If I can see them, the paparazzi will usually ask me questions. Some I've gotten to know a little, not here, but in LA. They're okay guys, for the most part, just doing their job. Plus, it's not exactly rocket science to figure out where they will be and avoid it. It's taken me a long time to figure out how to navigate the press in general, but that's a story for another day. The problem now is iPhones."

I laugh. "You sound like a real Boomer when you say that."

"I know, I know, but it's true. Because of iPhones, anyone can be paparazzi. I've started getting this spidey sense when someone is on their phone trying to take a picture of me. Sometimes they end up on blogs or gossip social media accounts. It's mostly fine but still a little unnerving. It doesn't get to me so much anymore. New Yorkers are generally much better about it. They don't give a shit, and most of the time I can go about my business unbothered."

"What a strange way to live," I murmur, mostly to myself.

He shoots me a look, and I worry I've offended him. "Yeah, it's not for everyone." He recovers quickly, "So, tell me more about what's going on in that interesting mind of yours today."

"Just trying to think of what I'm going to have my team do at practice tonight. That's the thing I have. I volunteer as a field hockey coach at the high school in my neighborhood. We do preseason workouts every Wednesday night."

"Coach Anderson." He says it slowly, trying it out. "I like it. What's that like? I've never played an organized sport in my life."

I look at him in all his rock star glory and try to conjure up what a young Matt Johnson might've looked like in high school.

"It's a lot of fun. There's a lot of overlap between coaching and therapy. I love the girls, they're energetic and hilarious, and it's a nice balance for me. Plus, it makes me feel rooted in this community. I know you know this, but New York is full of transplants, like me. I didn't want to feel like I was just passing through. Coaching has been an antidote to that for me. It makes New York feel real."

"That makes sense."

"Apart from that, my only other pressing issue is to book a trip to see my brother, Ryan, as soon as possible. He lives in Denver, and it's been way too long. The pandemic halted our quarterly visits, and we never got back into the swing of things."

"What's Ryan like?" Matt asks.

"He's awesome, a typical older brother. We're only eighteen months apart, so we got mistaken for twins often as kids. He works as an environmental scientist, mostly focused on conservation efforts. He moved to Denver in 2018 to work on a giant project focused on restoring the Native trout populations out there. We are close, we always were, but even more so after my parents split up and my mom had to go back to work full time. She worked a ton of hours, so it was just the two of us a lot of the time."

I leave out the fact that Ryan was essential in nursing me through the early weeks of my divorce. He flew to New York unprompted and helped me move all my stuff out of Jersey and into my new apartment. Then, he camped out on my couch for an extra two weeks, working from my kitchen counter during the day and dragging me out for margaritas and long walks at night. He even went as far as to schedule a hair appointment for me after informing me I looked like the girl who crawled out of the well in *The Ring*.

It wasn't lost on me that Ryan had to process the loss of Nick, separate from my own grief. They had been incredibly close, especially in the early years of our relationship. But there was never any doubt where Ryan's loyalty would lie. He had even reached out to Nick behind my back before the divorce and talked to him about trying a little harder, putting in some more effort, after I'd broken down and cried to him about our dwindling marriage. When his suggestion was rebuffed, Ryan drew a line in the sand and stood firmly on my side. As far as I know, Nick is dead to him.

On the topic of brothers, I say, "Your dad told me a little about Eric. I'm so sorry. What was he like?"

Matt blows out a breath.

"Eric was the coolest little brother you could imagine. He was only two years younger than me, but I swear I have a memory of the day my parents brought him home. Does that make sense?"

I nod.

"We shared a room, even when he was a baby, so I was always the first one to hear him cry. I made it my mission to take care of him, giving him his pacifier, patting his back, singing to him. Probably the first person I ever sang to, now that I think about it. I felt so important that I got to help with this little baby.

"And then suddenly, he was big enough to play with me. And from that moment on, we were inseparable. Every single memory I have from my childhood includes Eric. He somehow managed not to be the annoying little brother. He had the best imagination and made everything fun. He could read a room faster than anyone I knew and defuse a tense situation with a perfectly timed joke. The kid was *funny*. I have no doubt he would've had a long and successful career in comedy if he were still alive. He could somehow neutralize my parents' anger, especially when I was the one in trouble. I get stuck in my head a lot, wondering what my life would be like if he were still here. He would've been the perfect wingman to be on this ride with me. I think he could've kept me grounded, helped me navigate some of the more turbulent times."

"You seem pretty grounded to me."

"Thanks, but I wasn't always this way. I went a little off the rails, in my own way. But I know Eric would've kept me in check. He had that way about him—talking me down, keeping me balanced."

Midway through the walk, we hit a stretch with no other people. Murphy trots ahead of us, his proud little walk. I feel Matt's hand brush against mine. Electric. I focus on the path ahead.

"What is life like for you, with your job? You've seen my life, my work, my day-to-day at the hospital. I can't help but think it couldn't be more different from yours," I ask.

"It's not so different, believe it or not. I know my life might sometimes seem glamorous, but it's a lot of the same. I try to treat my music like a nine to five. I go to the studio every day during the week, working on new stuff, fine-tuning old stuff—the consistency of a schedule is very important to me. When I'm on tour, it's a ton of travel, obviously. But I try to keep my same routine. It's the only thing that keeps me sane and well. I did the whole party every night after a show thing when I was younger, and it burned me the hell out. I couldn't keep performing like that, so I'm a little rigid when I'm on the road, just to make sure I don't get back there again. Apart from that, I feel like I have a lot of free time. I'll do dinners with friends, dabble with some hobbies, come back and forth to see my dad. Not quite the rock star life some people imagine."

"Yeah, you're just an average Joe." I angle my head at the man walking toward us, wide-eyed and openly staring at Matt.

Matt laughs at that and gives the guy a quick nod. We circle around and head back toward the entrance of the park, where we started.

"Was your dad serious that you haven't gone a date in two years? Or was he just busting your chops?" I ask.

"A little of both, I guess. I have gone on a few dates here and there but nothing that ever panned out, nothing worth mentioning to him—which is exactly why he mentions it all the time. What about you?"

"Same, a few dates here and there, nothing worth mentioning," I say.

"It's not that I don't want to date, despite what some people may think. It's just that I took a very intentional break for a very long time —actually, at the advice of my therapist a few years ago. It got me out of the loop of making the same mistakes. Since then, it's been a little easier to see what works and what doesn't work for me. I'm a little cautious, probably too in my head about a lot of things. I just want to be sure. To feel sure. Plus, I'm not at all interested in the entire modern day dating process, as we know it. Mostly the online part, but also the interview process of it, the performative part. Maybe that's a mistake, but I just have this hope that when it's right I'll know, and the overthinking part of my brain that has plagued me most of my life will magically disappear. Wishful thinking, I know. I just kind of have a picture in my head of how it all should be, should feel, and I'm not willing to settle for anything less. If that makes sense. But anyway, because of all that, I kind of ended up in this perpetual state of singledom," Matt says.

"I know what you mean. I've found myself in a similar position. Part of me wonders if it's just inertia or being cynical, or both. But it seems like a hell of a lot of effort to date at this point in history, especially at my age ... which is only thirty-eight." I watch his face for a reaction, not that I expect one, but I've had enough experience seeing the way in which certain men find women over thirty-five to be invisible. Matt doesn't bat an eye. I go on.

"It's daunting to stare down the barrel of online dating. Like what you said—the performative part of it. The curated part of it. A dog and pony show, showing only the desirable parts of you. Plus, all the

44

unwritten rules and waiting around. How exhausting. Why can't we just be honest? And the never-ending apps and swiping is so depressing to me. Nothing ever goes anywhere, and it perpetuates the idea that there is always someone better on the horizon. The unicorns. It's not real, and it just sets everyone up for disappointment." I've obviously spent a lot of time thinking about this.

Matt nods emphatically. "I couldn't agree more. And I'm only forty-two. A young, robust, forty-two."

I smile, "I had no doubts about your sturdiness."

"That makes me either an elder millennial or a very young Gen Xer. Not a Boomer. For the record."

"Elder millennial has a better ring to it."

He laughs.

"Are you ever lonely?" he asks. The way he cuts to the chase is refreshing.

"Sometimes. Not really. I have a full life. I've been able to invest a lot into my friendships, my relationships with my family, my coworkers, my field hockey team, my career. It hasn't yet felt like I'm missing something." *Plus, I had that something, and it turned out to be not that great.* "Maybe the occasional Sunday night, I'll feel a wave of sadness or loneliness. Same goes for the holidays, or rainy and snowy days. Maybe some special occasions, like weddings, or other places when people are paired off, too. But they're just waves. Moments, really. Not a permanent state of being. Murphy fills the gaps pretty well." I sound more confident than I feel.

While I believe everything I am saying, I often feel like it is sitting on the surface of my skin, not wholly sinking in. The truth is, I second guess myself often and spend a lot of time reconciling the life I thought I would have as I near my forties and the life I do have.

"Is a long-term relationship and marriage something you want?" he asks.

"Yes," I answer honestly. "For you, too?"

"Yes. I want it all. I want the marriage, the kids, the white picket fence. I always have. And always will. That can feel a little heavy sometimes, like, why don't I have this thing I want so badly? What am I doing wrong?"

"What makes you think you're doing something wrong?"

"Well, what else could it be? I guess I can only understand my part in it."

"I'm impressed you can take accountability for your part in it. A lot of people can't do that. But the other person matters a ton, obviously—their history, their wounds, their goals, dreams, etc. Also, you can't discount the environment."

"What do you mean?"

"I mean, sort of like, the collective unconscious. The world in which we live and all the different elements of culture, society, politics, religion, etc. Everything. It plays a part, maybe not a huge part, but still a part. It can impact our beliefs. Which impacts the way we think. We have a lot of beliefs about dating, love, marriage, that may be outside of our awareness. Like *everyone has one perfect match*, or *your partner should be able to meet your every need*. Or *relationships should not require effort, and if you do have to work on it, something is wrong*."

He nods, brow furrowed, staring ahead. "That makes a lot of sense."

"What do you think some of those unhelpful beliefs might be for you?" I ask.

His face breaks into a wide smile. "Are you going to bill me for this?"

I laugh. "Touché. I didn't mean to pry. I just like hearing your take on things."

"I really like hearing your take on just about everything."

My cheeks burn.

"So, why mental health? What got you into the field?" he asks as we approach the final stretch of our walk.

"Me and my brother were very anxious kids."

"How so?"

"We both worried all the time. For no identifiable reasons, besides maybe just genetics. But from as early as I can remember, I always had this feeling that something terrible was going to happen. It was relentless. I could never figure out how to get ahead of it. So, I was always on the lookout for potential threats and was constantly on edge."

"My brothers worries were similar to mine in a lot of ways but also different, and his got worse when my parents divorced while mine got better. It got so bad my mom dragged us to a therapist when I was nine and he was ten. This was way before therapy was mainstream. It was a horrible experience—we only went once. The therapist was cold and judgmental. She didn't seem interested in connecting with us or helping us. I walked out of that session thinking, if I had a chance to sit with a kid as anxious as me or as Ryan, I would do better. At the very least, I would make sure they didn't feel alone."

He looks at me inquisitively, like he is trying to figure me out. "You don't seem anxious to me. You seem very calm and even keeled."

"I am. Well, I am both, I should say. Anxious and even keeled. It's all part of me, but it's not an all or nothing thing—more like in the continuum of me, all these different parts exist. And don't get me wrong, I still have the *something terrible is going to happen, the other shoe is going to drop, don't get your hopes up* panic stuff. But I've had a lot of practice at catching it before it sidetracks me."

He nods slowly, seeming to take in everything I am saying.

"Hmm. I like that. *I contain multitudes*," he replies thoughtfully, rubbing his hand against the stubble on his jaw.

I smile. This guy continues to impress me. "Yes. That's Walt Whitman."

He nods. "This has been fascinating. And eye-opening for me. You're giving me a lot to think about. You might actually need to bill me."

"I'll consider it pro bono," I say.

We make it back to the entrance of the park and stand to the side.

"Thanks for letting me join you and Murph man." He kneels to give him some ear scratches. "You know, every time I talk to you, I find myself not wanting it to end."

Butterflies fill my stomach. "I feel the same way." It's easy to be honest with him, knowing how honest he is with me.

"Can we do it again?" He seems wide open.

"Considering you're camped out at my place of business, I feel confident we'll run into each other again very soon," I say.

"Okay." He dips his head in a little bow.

"Thanks for joining us. Murphy was thrilled."

"Were you?"

"Yes, I was equally thrilled."

"Have a good practice, Coach Anderson." He leans in and gives me a quick hug and a kiss on the cheek. I feel the contact all the way in my toes and notice the slightest hesitation as he pulls away.

His scent lingers for a moment longer than his lips. Thank God I have practice tonight. I need something to take my mind off him.

Chapter 4

Thursday

At work the next morning, I am giddy and energized both from my walk with Matt and from seeing my team last night. Practice was a blast—the girls were in fantastic moods, blaring music the entire time and working their asses off. One of the senior captains, Addie, called me out on the goofy smile I had on my face all night.

"Hey, Coach, what's with the smile? You got a new man you're trying to hide from us?"

That's all it took for the other eighteen girls to join in heckling me.

"OOOOOOhhhkayyyy, Coach!"

"Who is he?"

"Or she? We're cool with either!"

"You know we can find anyone on the Internet."

"Just give us his initials."

I managed to evade their questions ... for now.

At my desk, a new email pops up with today's discharges. Sid is on the list. I smile, knowing how happy he will be to get out of jail, but my heart sinks at the thought of not seeing him or Matt anymore.

Later that day I head down to the hospital cafeteria for a coffee to get me through the mid-afternoon slump. I'm standing in line to check out when I feel the air in the room shift, almost like the atoms are rearranging themselves.

I turn to see Matt strolling in, his hands in his pockets, dressed in dark jeans and a white T-shirt, with a lighter-wash denim shirt unbuttoned and billowing in his wake. He scans the room, and when he sees me, his eyes light up. He beelines toward me.

"I was sent to fetch some food," he tells me with that sexy half smirk. "'Something that doesn't look like it's been scraped off the side of the road and fried,' and that's a direct quote."

I laugh. "And I am here to prevent myself from face-planting on my keyboard." I lift my large coffee cup toward him. "At least it'll be your last time doing this. Big day. Sid is getting out of here."

He nods. "Yeah, he's ecstatic. Already listing off all the meals he wants to cook. In his own kitchen. Complaining about how long it's taking. I guess everyone has to come do one last check before signing off on it. So, we're just waiting."

We're still in line to pay, once again enjoying a comfortable silence.

Matt interrupts it. "I know I keep saying this, but I'm going to say it again anyway—I very much enjoy spending time with you."

"Me too," I admit. "We should do it again." I'm suddenly emboldened by the fact that his dad is being discharged and I may never see him again after today.

"How about now?" he asks with a boyish smile.

My heart kicks up a notch. I find us a table in the corner, and Matt sits with his back to the cafeteria in an attempt to hide from ogling eyes. By this point in Sid's hospital stay, word has traveled that the famous Matt Johnson is a regular visitor of New York Grace. We both take a sip of our coffees and Matt starts coughing.

"Did they siphon this from a tanker? God, this is bad."

I take another pull from mine without so much as a flinch.

"This coffee is the lifeblood of the hospital. It runs through our veins. It will put hair on your chest and toughen you up a bit."

He looks at me pointedly. "Does it put hair on *your* chest?"

I laugh out loud. "Is that a line?"

He grimaces. "Okay, yeah, that was bad. Please pretend I didn't say that." He covers his eyes with his hand.

"Okay, but rest assured, my chest is hair-free."

We choke down our coffee and chat about what we love about the city, the people, the energy, and what we don't—the rising crime, the small businesses that didn't survive the pandemic. Matt talks about how he is trying to pave over some of his bad memories of New York during the lockdown. He describes how he felt trapped in California and was desperate to get to his dad and mom but didn't want to put them at risk. When he was finally able to safely make it to the city, he describes how empty, haunted, and terrifying it seemed. The once bustling metropolis, a ghost town. Now that the city is fully reopened, he wants to visit his old favorite places—and new places—now alive and bustling with people, to forget the scary scenes that still play in his mind.

"Anything you haven't crossed off your list yet?" I ask.

"I'd love to go see a movie. Like a real classic film, playing at an old-school New York City theater. I want to get in there, give my ticket to a real guy, not some machine, get popcorn, a soda, maybe some Junior Mints, and sit down next to other people, no masks, nothing scary, and just shut my brain off and watch it. Just sit there and listen to someone else's story for two hours and enjoy the entire experience. Does that make sense?"

"It does." I smile at him, liking the way he often asks me if something makes sense. A little verbal tic that is perhaps rooted in a lifetime of feeling misunderstood. It's endearing.

Matt tells me that Sid wants to go back to Allentown as soon as he is discharged—that despite having a beautiful apartment in the city, Sid goes back to his house in Pennsylvania as often as possible. He tells me about the mixed feelings he has visiting his childhood home, the place where all his dreams were born but also a place that holds so many memories, including reminders of his losses.

I tell him about my mom, the admiration I feel for her knowing her plight as a single mother raising two mischievous kids. We're laughing at something when I hear the overhead PA system beep on.

I see all hospital staff in the cafeteria pause midbite or mid-conversation and perk up their ears—something we all do any time there is a code called hospital-wide. *Not my patient rooms,* we silently chant. Before I fully realize what is happening, and a split second after I hear "Code Blue, CCU room 416," I grab Matt by the hand and bolt for the doors, leaving our coffees and Sid's food on the table.

"What?" He is wide-eyed and confused. Clearly, he didn't hear the code or recognize the room number.

"Sid," I say, pulling him toward the stairwell.

We bound up the stairs together, taking them two at a time. When I swipe us onto the unit, we're both breathing hard, and Sid's room is a swarm of activity. We freeze at the threshold, and I rapidly try to assess the situation.

"Code blue means your dad is in distress. It means the nurses need help immediately and anyone available shows up. That is why all these people are here. It doesn't mean he's dying—that's just in movies," I say quickly, softly, trying to exude calm despite my hammering heart. We walk toward the jam-packed hospital room, fingers still interlocked. I navigate us to the back corner by the window and begin to talk Matt through exactly what's happening.

Sid does not look good. His skin is gray and clammy. His eyes are closed. He looks so old and so frail in the hospital bed.

"It looks like he is having some respiratory distress—that might've caused him to lose consciousness," I say softly. "No one is doing chest compressions. That's a good sign because it means his heart never stopped. If his heart never stopped, it means his brain and all his other organs were not deprived of oxygen. Those tubes Dr. Patel is putting on him now are connected to high flow oxygen—that will help keep everything functioning as it should while they figure out what happened." I gesture toward Christine, who is working quickly and efficiently. "It looks like Christine is giving him an IV to push fluids and probably a medicine to help him breathe."

I turn my head away from the bed and hover it two inches from Matt's chest to avoid seeing a needle go into Sid's vein. Even though I'm not looking, I still feel woozy. I lean my forehead against his shoulder and take three calming breaths. Even amid the chaos I can't miss his smell. He holds my hand even tighter.

After what feels like hours, the team has stabilized Sid, who is now resting peacefully as the room clears out. Dr. Patel comes over to us. She looks exhausted, but her eyes are warm.

"Hi, Matt. Your dad's sats dropped suddenly and without any obvious reason. I am confident this is something we can figure out and treat. This happens in older people—sometimes for no reason and sometimes there is one, and that is what I'm looking for. There is no need to panic despite how intense that seemed. I want to reassure you he is in the best care, and we will do everything we can to get him through this. At a minimum, I am adding another twenty-four hours of observation to his stay and want to run a few additional tests." She goes on about the specific tests and procedures while Matt stands silently, nodding in agreement.

When he finishes signing the consent forms and Dr. Patel leaves the room, I finally turn to look at him. He is standing in the dark corner; the sun started setting sometime during the chaos. His face is deathly pale.

"Are you okay?"

A dumb question, especially coming from me. He doesn't respond. I tug his hand, gently guiding him to sit in the recliner next to his dad's bed. His eyes are wide, staring at a spot on the floor, unseeing.

"Matt?" I kneel in front of him. "Your dad is okay. I know how bad that seemed, it's overwhelming and scary every time, even for me, and I see it almost every day. Can you try to take some deep breaths for me?"

I worry he is in shock. I take both his hands in mine and squeeze gently.

"Matt. Can you hear me?"

His eyes focus on our intertwined hands and then slowly move up to my face, like he is just realizing where he is. He finally looks at me, and his eyes fill with tears. He drops his chin to his chest and takes a shaky breath.

"That was ... terrifying," he mumbles into his shirt.

I look at him—at the top of his head and his thick, wavy hair. This man I've just come to know, so shaken. I impulsively move forward and run my fingers through his hair, to touch him, to comfort him. He leans into my hand, and I skim the backs of my fingers across his cheek.

"He's okay," I repeat. Matt nods slowly, trying to digest what I'm saying. "He is okay," I say again, my fingers now openly caressing the side of his cheek. Matt catches my wrist and slowly brings it to his lips. He gives me a single, soft kiss on the back of my hand.

"Thank you. For being here," he whispers, eyes still full of tears. We stay like that for what feels like a very long time.

Eventually I stand up, not sure what to do next, and head for the door. He seems startled by my movement.

"Where are you going?"

"I just have to go check on a few other patients. I can come back...."

"Please don't leave," he pleads, eyes panicked. My heart flip-flops in my chest.

"I'll come back in just a few minutes. I promise," I respond.

"Okay. Okay, good." He turns toward Sid as I slowly exit the room.

I walk back onto the unit, Matt's words echoing in my head, my heart rate finally slowing after the adrenaline. I stop by the nurse's station to say job well done to everyone who responded to the code. I do a quick round on my other patients, rushing through my usual questions, before I head for my office. Christine hops up from her chair and heads toward me.

"I'll join you. I need a minute away from the desk," she says. We walk in silence, and I know my longtime friend and colleague is chewing on something.

"You seemed pretty cozy with Mr. Johnson's son during that code."

"He was rattled. I was doing what I would've done for any other loved one of a patient."

"Hmmmm." She eyes me suspiciously. "Jules, I've been working with you for how many years? We've seen the good, bad, and ugly parts of humanity together, and yes, you're right, I've seen you hold people's hands in their time of need, but this ... seemed different, and not just because you had dinner with him."

"What are you trying to say, Chris?"

"I know it's been a while since things ended with you and Nick and that eventually you have to get yourself back out there. I'm just a little cautious of it potentially being with 416's son. I have heard about that man nonstop from Dave for the past few days. I don't know what is true and what is not. But as a friend, I might suggest dipping your toe back in the dating pool with someone a little less ... scandalous."

I laugh at that. It feels ridiculous in the context of what I know about Matt, which admittedly is not a lot. Also ridiculous in the sense that there is absolutely nothing happening here that would extend past Sid's stay.

"Noted. Thanks for your input."

* * *

I push the rest of my tasks for the day onto tomorrow's to-do list, unplug my laptop, and throw it into my purse. I grab two Cokes out of my fridge and head back to the unit to check on Matt and Sid.

Matt is in the same place where I left him over an hour ago, but this time he is turned toward his dad's bed, chin resting in his hands, watching Sid sleep. He looks deep in thought.

I hand him a Coke. "Sugar helps with the shock." He takes it but doesn't open it.

I sit down on the window seat by his chair. "How are you doing?"

"I'm having déjà vu," he says eventually. "I used to have this reoccurring dream when I was a kid that something terrible happened to my parents and they were gone. Remember how you said you always thought something bad was going to happen when you were a kid? I had a similar fear, but it was only ever about my parents. It was always something different: they went to work and never came home; they moved to the next town over and forgot me; they got scooped out of the driveway by a giant bird. It didn't matter what happened, exactly, but that feeling of them being gone and me being alone was a constant. I would wake up in a panic and sneak down the hall to peek into their room and make sure they were all right. I've always had this fear of losing them. I know that is normal for everyone, but sometimes I worry I'm thinking about it so much it's all I can see. Like I'm on this train and I can't get off, but I know exactly where it's headed." He takes a deep breath.

"I thought losing my mom was going to be the worst of it. Don't get me wrong, Eric dying was a tragedy of epic proportions, and though it didn't make it easier, the fact that we knew he was sick, and fighting, and then fighting but losing, gave us some semblance of preparation. But losing my mom ... I mean, watching someone who is still very much alive fade into dust right in front of you is just a sadness I can't even scratch the surface of.

"And it's human nature to think it's about you. To think, If I was important enough to her, or if she really loved me, she'd snap out of it and be my mom. It's something I couldn't wrap my head around for a long, long time. It created this hole somewhere inside me that I was desperate to fill, usually with the wrong things or the wrong people. But the older I get, the more I realize that my mom is my mom, and she is also a human just like me. A complicated, messy, flawed human

56

who suffered a devastating loss—one that I can't quite comprehend because I'm not a parent. Once I could sort of understand all of that and lean into it, I felt less angry about her abandonment."

He stops, still looking at Sid, then continues. "But what happened just now, with my dad, feeling like I could've just lost him." He pauses, voice thick, eyes full. "That hit me like a sucker punch to the gut. I know he is going to die someday, but thinking something in my head and watching it happen in front of my eyes is very different. It has been just the two of us for so long. He has been the only constant for me. He's been with me every moment of this wild ride, in this life I've made. I have been sitting here since you left trying to figure out where he ends and I begin. And I couldn't tell you." He swallows hard.

"So, what does that mean for me when he's not here anymore?" he chokes out.

I walk over to him as his tears overflow, spilling down his cheeks, his chin working hard to contain the emotion flooding out of him. I sit on the armrest of the recliner and wipe the tears away instinctively as I feel my own eyes well. We sit in silence, his words hanging heavily in the air. I know there is nothing to say right now, no platitudes or assurances will make him feel better. I bend down to hug him, to comfort him as he reaches for me, leaning in, lips parted. I panic and move away, which results in an incredibly awkward half hug, his beautiful lips grazing my cheek.

I pull back to face him and wonder how someone can look so gorgeous and devastated at once. His glassy eyes roam my face, moving back and forth between my eyes and my mouth, like he can't decide where to look or what to do. I bite my lip, not sure what is happening. He leans in again, and I do not back away. I am at once hyperaware of what is happening and feeling disembodied, like I'm watching from the ceiling. His lips press against mine so softly I may have missed it if I weren't frozen in place. My face must register shock, because he pulls away quickly.

"Shit. I'm sorry." He blows out a big breath and runs his hands through his hair and down his face. He stands up and starts pacing the tiny hospital room. "I'm all over the place right now. I'm not usually this ... unguarded. Or impulsive. And that, the kiss. I, uh, don't get me wrong, I wanted to do that, but it seems like it was probably terrible timing," he rambles on. I stay still, speechless, trying to let my brain catch up.

"What are you two yapping about over there?" grumbles Sid hoarsely from the bed. "Can't you let a man rest in peace?" His eyes are still closed, and Matt bolts next to him, wiping his eyes with the backs of his hands.

"Jesus, Dad, are you okay? You scared the shit out of me."

Sid opens his eyes to find Matt and me hovering next to his bed.

A slow smile creeps onto his tired, lined face. "Now, there is a sight for sore eyes. Look at you two. You look good together, if I do say so myself." His voice is weak.

"How are you feeling?" Matt asks, desperate.

Sid, exasperated, says, "Don't be so dramatic, son. I'm fine."

I see Matt's shoulders relax slightly. At least his dad's cantankerous disposition remains intact.

I take that as my cue and glance quickly at Sid's monitors before excusing myself for the night.

"I'm so glad you're okay, Sid. I'll check on you in the morning." I feel Matt's eyes on me, laserlike, as I leave the room.

* * *

By the time I get home, I am exhausted. I barely have the energy to take Murphy for his nightly walk. The emotional rollercoaster of the day is more than I'm used to. Images keep flashing in my head: Matt sitting across from me in the cafeteria, eyes bright and smiling, hand in mine; his pale face in the corner of his dad's room, the fear rippling off him, the vulnerability in his eyes, the feeling of his lips on mine. It's overwhelming. I don't know what to make of any of it.

I draw myself a piping hot bath and soak my body, trying and failing to clear my mind of everything, but especially of Matt.

I cannot deny the instant connection I feel with him. I rack my brain for similar experiences, the most obvious being Nick, but there is no comparison. Nick and I were always in agreement that our story wasn't a love at first sight situation. I was in my second year of grad school and Nick was working his first finance job out of college. We kept running into each other at the same bars in Fells Point, so much so that I eventually turned to him and asked if he was following me.

"I could ask you the same thing," he shot back with a warm smile.

Nick was very attractive, a solid six feet of athletic grace with sandy blond hair and warm hazel eyes. He had a confident if not cocky way about him, like he'd never had to try too hard at anything. After that first interaction, it was several weeks before we saw each other again and he asked me out. When I go back to that moment, I remember feeling excited by the idea of Nick, amused by the situation. It was markedly different from what I am feeling now with Matt, like a physical force that cut to my core the moment I saw him. It only intensifies with every new interaction as I learn more about him.

After today, I feel untethered, like I'm swimming through unchartered waters—a place I do not like to be. I can't be sure what parts of this are real and what parts are symptoms of different issues, like me being single and lonely, or Matt's innate magnetic pull that isn't special just to me. It is too much to sort through, especially after a day like today.

I manage to fall asleep eventually, but my dreams are full of Matt —the same images from earlier, but a few more: his lips on my neck, his hands on my hips, his fingers dancing down my body, his head in between my legs.

Chapter 5

Friday

I wake up early the next morning to take Murphy for a run before work. I feel the same restless energy from last night and want to burn some of it off. I hit the street as the sun starts rising in the summer sky. As I run, I can't stop imagining the feeling of Matt's lips on mine. I pick up the pace.

Two miles in, my mind is clear, and I have not a single thought besides the welcome ache in my muscles from exertion. By the time I get back to my apartment, my favorite doorman, Neil, is on duty. He kneels to rub behind Murphy's ears, offering him one of the treats he keeps in a jar behind the desk. Neil has been working here for as long as I've lived in the building.

"How was your run, Ms. Julia?"

"Good, good. We are both a little out of shape," I say, wiping sweat from my brow.

Once I'm back upstairs, I head into my tiny white galley kitchen and toss my keys, headphones, phone, and Murphy's leash onto the counter. I fire up my Nespresso and wipe down Murphy's paws, then rummage through the fridge for his breakfast and fill his water bowl. I walk into my bathroom and strip down before stepping into the shower.

My bathroom, and specifically my shower, is the only home improvement project I did before I moved into my apartment. Now my shower is massive—at least by Manhattan standards. I cut into the precious square footage of my tiny walk-in closet to accommodate both the shower and a soaking tub. It's probably my favorite room in the entire apartment. I let the water hit my shoulders, breathing in the steam.

I roll my neck and think more about the interactions I've had with Matt. Do I legitimately have feelings for him after only a few days? Of course it's possible, it's just never been something I've believed to be real. I am a little too pragmatic when it comes to love and can count on one hand the times I've felt infatuated with someone.

Could this be the result of watching my parents' failed marriage, or maybe a consequence of my profession and hearing all the dirty ins and outs of relationships? Lust at first sight seems reasonable enough, but real love? I'm not convinced. And yet all that feels like it's been turned on its head the past few days, since the moment Matt walked into room 416.

After I lather and rinse, I dry off and stand in front my closet. I've spent more time thinking about what I will wear to work this week than I have maybe ever in my life. The anticipation of seeing Matt makes me feel like I'm back in high school, waiting to see my crush in the hallways. I pick a cream Ralph Lauren knit skirt and matching short sleeve sweater. I put on a pair of black pumps and my diamond stud earrings—a gift from Nick for our two-year wedding anniversary after he received his first bonus. I go back into the bathroom to dry my hair, noticing a rogue gray hair amid the thick dark brown strands. I recently added some caramel pieces for summer, but somehow this gray survived. I pluck it out and toss it in the trash, making a note to schedule a color touch-up today. I lightly apply makeup, skipping the concealer on my nose, deciding to let my few freckles shine through today. I swipe on my favorite mauvy pink lip balm and give Murphy a quick kiss before heading out the door.

* * *

The first thing I do when I get to work is swing by room 416 and check on Sid. He appears to be sleeping as I peek in the door. Matt is nowhere to be seen. I check in at the nurse's station, and Beth tells me everything with Sid has been smooth sailing since the code yesterday. We both knock on the wood under the desk.

My morning moves quickly, full of meetings and emails. I eat an early lunch at my desk with Christine so we can go over scheduling for the next few weeks.

"We need more staff," she tells me for the hundredth time.

"I know, I know, we have ads posted everywhere. The career fair is in a few weeks, maybe we'll get some leads. And it's not just us, Chris, it's everyone."

"I know it's everyone, but it doesn't change the fact my staff is burnt the hell out."

I know it's true. They have worked around the clock for years at this point. The trauma of the pandemic on our staff has had a ripple effect that seems to have no end in sight. No one has had any substantial time off, and salaries remain stagnant as the hospital hemorrhages money. So many nurses took early retirement or straight-up quit amid the chaos of early in 2020, and we are seriously struggling. Not to mention, despite the pandemic being over, we are busier than ever with a backlog of very sick patients who neglected all medical care during that time. It is a clusterfuck of epic proportions.

"What if we do a stress management group or something for staff?"

"I think they'd rather just be paid more. Or have more time off," Christine says. As always, I appreciate her candor.

"What about a masseuse coming in once a week or something? Or we get lunch catered in?" I spitball ideas.

"I think that would be nice to boost morale, but I think we'll stay stressed until we have more bodies in here. Competent bodies, I should add."

"Speaking of competent bodies, did you apply for the director of nursing position yet?" I've been on her for weeks to throw her hat in the ring for a serious promotion.

"I'm thinking about it still."

"If you think about it any longer, it's going to get filled. You're perfect for the job, Chris. No one would do it better. It'd be a huge raise, too."

"I don't know if I want to deal with any more administrative bull-shit," she says bluntly.

"Fair enough."

* * *

I don't see Matt or Sid until late that afternoon after my two outpatient groups. When I peek through the window into room 416, Sid is up and out of the bed, looking much like his normal self, and Matt is on the bed, his long legs crossed lazily at the ankle. They're playing along with *Jeopardy!* on the TV, Matt keeping score in the notebook on his lap. I knock twice before letting myself in.

"How is everyone doing in here?"

"Hi there, Julia. We're doing much better than yesterday's little kerfuffle, and I'm kicking Matt's ass in *Jeopardy!* Care to join us?"

"Sure." I pull over the swivel stool to sit at the end of the bed between them.

I steal a glance at Matt, who gives me a tired smile. Upon closer examination, he looks exhausted. His face is pale, with dark circles under his eyes, and his hair is sticking up in twelve different directions. I doubt he got any sleep last night, and I feel more than a little guilty about not checking on him until now.

Even depleted, he is stunning. He again seems to be studying me in a way that makes me hyperaware of my every movement. I turn toward the TV.

We listen to the clues.

This number, one of the first twenty, uses only one vowel—four times.

"What is seventeen?" says Sid. Matt puts a tally on the paper.

Who succeeded James Madison?

"Who is James Monroe?" says Matt.

In 1690 this English philosopher wrote, "Wherever law ends, tyranny begins."

"Who is John Locke?" says Sid.

There's no oxygen below 510 feet in the center of this sea the Russians call Chernoye More.

They both pause, and Matt taps his chin with the pen.

"What is the Black Sea?" Matt says.

I watch them go back and forth for several more questions—like a tennis match.

"You two are like human Google processors. How do you know all of this?"

Matt smiles. "We've been playing together for a long time."

I hear the next question.

According to C.S. Lewis, it was bordered on the east by the Eastern Ocean and on the north by the River Shribble.

"What is Narnia?" I say quickly. It's the only answer I've known so far. They both look at me and smile. Matt logs my one point in his notebook.

We play several more minutes, me getting zero more questions and Matt and Sid answering every one correctly.

"What do you want to do for dinner?" Matt asks Sid.

"I'm in the mood for a chicken salad sandwich. On a croissant, with lettuce, tomato, salt and pepper. A side of salt and vinegar chips."

"Very specific," I say.

"He doesn't mess around when it comes to food." Matt pulls out his phone.

"You expect me to eat the food here? The breakfast they brought this morning was like slop!"

"You're not a fan of powdered eggs?" I tease.

Sid gags.

"There's a deli around the corner that has chicken salad sandwiches," I tell Matt.

"Great. I'll run out and grab it." Matt looks up from his phone. "Want to join me?"

"I should probably get home."

"Oh, would ya just join him? He's been moping around this room all day, watching me like a hawk. It's getting on my damn nerves," grumbles Sid.

"Murphy needs his walk," I protest. Sid looks at me pointedly. Matt is quiet.

"What if I buy you a sandwich?" Sid asks.

"A real big spender, this guy." Matt laughs.

"Okay," I acquiesce, realizing how much I want to spend more time with him.

Matt's face lights up. "Great, let's go."

"Get me an Arnold Palmer if they have it!" yells Sid as we walk out of the room.

We head toward the elevators, and I find myself standing dangerously close to Matt as people pile in on each stop on the way down. The tops of our arms touch, and I feel a tingling sensation go all the way down to my toes.

As we start walking down the block to the deli, Matt finally speaks.

"I'm glad I got a chance to talk to you alone after yesterday. I'm grateful you were there. To help me, mostly, and tell me what was happening. I know it's your job, but it felt like you went above and beyond, and I can't tell you how much I appreciate that. I think I'm okay now, especially because Dad seems back to his usual self, but that was probably one of the scariest moments of my life. So, thank you."

"You're welcome."

"I also wanted to clear the air. I'm sorry about the kiss. Not the intent behind it, because it was genuine, but the timing ... I don't know what I was thinking, and I've been stewing about it all day. I think it was probably inappropriate of me, and I hope I didn't make you feel uncomfortable...."

I grab his forearm, stopping us in the middle of the sidewalk. His eyes lock on where my hand is connected to his skin. "Matt. You did not make me uncomfortable. I want to be very clear about that. I was flattered. It was nice. My only concern was that emotions were running high, and I wasn't sure if the kiss was maybe a byproduct of that. I've seen stranger things happen in a crisis."

"It wasn't a byproduct," he says quickly. "I wanted to kiss you after dinner at The Waverly Inn, but it felt insane. Too soon. I think yesterday, after all the chaos, my guard was down. And so, I just did something I wanted to do without overthinking it."

"Okay. Well, consider the air cleared."

We resume our walk.

A few moments later he asks softly, "Was it really just 'nice'?"

I laugh.

"Yes, it was nice."

"Not like mind-blowing? Like the greatest kiss you've ever had in your life?"

"It was sweet."

"Sweet?" He cringes. "Not sure that's much better."

"Are you self-conscious about your kissing abilities?"

"Apparently. I never was before, but now? Yes, maybe."

I laugh. "How about this—it was surprising. Pleasantly surprising. Given the circumstances surrounding it, it ranks as one of the most memorable first kisses I've ever had. How's that?"

"I'll take it."

* * *

After we pick up dinner, the sandwich for Sid, two Chinese chicken salads for Matt and me, and three Arnold Palmers, and walk back to the hospital, Matt's color has returned, and he seems less tense.

He asks me to stay and eat dinner with the two of them in Sid's room, and I can find no good reason not to. I can't help but notice how comfortable it is to be doing this seemingly mundane task with Matt.

We walk back to room 416 to find Sid holding court with three of the nurses. He has them all hysterically laughing—about God knows what. Eventually everyone gets back to work, and Matt, Sid, and I spend the next hour together laughing, talking, and eating our dinners on our laps.

Sid tells me stories about Matt as a kid, how he'd disappear for hours at a time, creating imaginary worlds that were so elaborate and detailed that Sid feared "something might be wrong with him."

He talked about how Matt somehow convinced Eric to do all the dirty work for him, coming up with ideas he knew would get them in trouble and having Eric execute them. And how Eric never once sold his brother out.

"It was always part of the plan," Matt explains. "He was the baby and you guys never laid into him like you did with me. Ever. He was willing to take the risk. We were a good team that way."

Eventually, I get up and excuse myself. "I should be heading home. It was a pleasure dining with you two gentlemen tonight."

"The pleasure was ours, sweetheart," Sid says.

"I'll see you tomorrow, Sid. Get some sleep."

Matt stands. "I'll walk you to your office."

I nod.

We head down the hall, the familiar path to my office. Once inside the door, I kick my heels off with a sigh. "It's about two hours past my daily time allotment in these." I slip on my comfortable clogs.

I pad around and sit down at my desk while Matt walks toward the windows, his hands in his pockets. He does not seem to be in a rush to leave.

"I think my dad has a crush on you."

"Ah, well, I think I have a crush on him, too."

"Man, so now I have to compete with him? This is new territory for me."

I look at him and my stomach flip flops.

"Can I sit?" He points to the loveseat.

I nod.

He stares at my painting, and I stare at him as I shut down my laptop.

"Any more thoughts about the art?" I ask.

"I'm not sure yet."

"I've heard the entire spectrum of interpretations of that painting. Ranging from paint splatters a three-year-old could do, to oysters at the bottom of the sea, to one of my most long-standing patients who insists it looks like several pairs of women's breasts."

He laughs. "Very Freudian."

"Exactly."

"I wouldn't consider myself an art aficionado, but the more I look at this, the more I see. It's like the artist wanted to make it look complicated. Confusing. Maybe even chaotic. But if you keep look-ing, it's simple. The brush strokes—the colors are all cohesive. Bright, exciting even. I think that's why I felt hopeful. It's like a metaphor for life. We make everything so complicated. But underneath it all, if you can just take a minute to look at something, to find the heart of it, it's pretty simple."

"I like that," I say from across my office.

I am fascinated by his depth, by his observations, his mind. I wouldn't have expected it, which isn't fair. It's easy to get absorbed in his physical appearance—he is undeniably and objectively very attractive. But I am beginning to think that might be the least inter-esting thing about him.

I go and sit down across from him in my chair, leaning back, uncrossing my arms and gently folding my hands on my lap—"the therapist stance," my friends have joked.

"Tell me about your childhood, Mr. Johnson," I say in my most clinical voice.

Matt laughs. "I think I already have. Come sit next to me." He pats the couch beside him.

I do, and I instantly realize it is a mistake. We are touching, the left side of my body to his right side. His face is so close to mine. The chemistry is undeniable. It feels like a force, like gravity or something else I have no control over.

"What are you thinking about?" he asks me, his hand brushing against mine.

"Strangely, absolutely nothing. What about you?"

"I was just thinking about how badly I want to redo that first kiss. You know, the one you described as 'nice.'"

My breathing goes shallow, my heartbeat quickens. The air around us grows charged.

"Okay," I manage to say, barely a whisper.

He turns to me and takes my chin ever so gently in his substantial, soft hands and tips my face up toward him. He takes a moment to look at me before he leans forward and plants the sweetest, softest kiss on my lips. It is agonizingly chaste.

Not enough. I react on impulse.

I surge forward, capturing his mouth again. I can't help myself. I feel a deep want—no, a need. *More.*

I kiss him harder than he kissed me, and passionately, possessively even, his tongue slides between my parted lips. My proximity to him enhances that delicious woody smell I've come to associate with him. The combination of it and the kiss is dizzying. I bite down on his pouty bottom lip. I let go, heart racing, and open my eyes to find him staring at me, a hunger in his.

He rushes forward this time to close the gap between us, his hands in my hair, lips on mine, tongue in my mouth—he explores me. I wrap my arms around his shoulders, leaning into him, heat prickling my skin, heart hammering in my chest, an ache between my legs.

We keep kissing so deeply, I lose myself, and all I can focus on is his mouth and his hands that start to wander my body, drifting down my hips, along the hem of my skirt, back up my bare arms. Every place where our bodies connect feels like fire sparking.

I could easily slip off my skirt and slide him inside of me, right here, right now. It has been so long for me. So long since I've been touched like this, since I've felt so wanted, desired. The intensity is enthralling.

But then I think about this couch we're on, where all my patients sit. A place of respite. Of healing.

I'm at *work*.

The thought brings me back to reality. I pull away from him, both of us breathless, his pupils dilated—almost black.

"We should probably stop." I try to catch my breath.

"Okay. But ... I don't want to stop."

"It's just that this is my office ... where I work ... where my patients sit. This would be ... This is inappropriate..." I stammer.

"No, totally, you're right. I'm sorry. I just—wow. Yeah. Okay." I'm relieved to see him just as flustered as I am.

"I'm going home. I have to get back to Murphy. Thank you for dinner. And the kiss. It was ... lovely. I'll see you tomorrow." I stand and straighten my skirt, trying to get hold of myself.

"Lovely?" he shoots me his half smirk as he regains his composure.

"There's probably a better word for it, but I'm at a bit of a loss right now."

"Sure. Get back to me on that." Matt stands up and heads for the door. I walk over to him, and he wraps his arms around my waist, pulling me close and giving me one last kiss—brief yet so unmistakably affectionate, I have a horrifying feeling that I might cry.

"Good night," I say quickly.

"Good night, Jules."

* * *

Once the door closes and I am alone, I stumble to my chair and plop down.

The only thing I can think is *holy shit*.

I walk home in a daze. *"Good night, Jules"* echoes in my head.

Jules. Jules. Jules. Hearing my nickname come out of his mouth felt intimate. Too intimate? Too soon? *Not really, given the context of that earth-tilting kiss.*

As I am trying to process everything that transpired in my office, I realize I will not see Matt tomorrow, as I suggested. Because tomorrow is a Saturday, and I do not work on Saturdays.

What is happening?

Chapter 6

Saturday

I wake up to Murphy is licking my face and the sun is streaming through the bedroom windows. I look at the clock. Eight thirty a.m. I get up, brush my teeth, throw on some workout clothes, and head downstairs to take Murphy out. We walk our usual morning loop—a few blocks to a green space near Greenwich Village and back. On the way back, I grab an iced coffee and a bagel from my favorite place on the corner.

I have absolutely no plans today and am looking forward to doing nothing but catching up on chores I've put off all week. I start a load of laundry before sitting down at my counter to write out a grocery list. I pick up my phone to look for some dinner ideas and see a text from Matt.

> Good morning, hope you slept well. Dr. P says she'll discharge Dad on Monday, so we'll be here through the weekend.

> That's great news! I'm sure she's just being cautious. I slept very well, thanks. You?

He replies immediately.

> I need a chiropractor.

> The pull-out recliner—never good for backs, especially robust forty-two-year-old backs.

> Very funny. What are you up to today?

I send him a picture of my coffee, bagel, and Murphy in the background.

> Lazy Saturday.

> Looks amazing. It's not the same here in room 416 without you.

He sends a picture of his legs propped up on the rolling stool, Sid in the background looking grumpy. Another text comes through.

> I haven't been able to stop thinking about last night.

Butterflies fly into my stomach. My thumbs hover over the keyboard.

> Same.

> Are you still thinking it was lovely?

> Hmmm ... yes, lovely. But something else, too.

> Yes. Something else, too.

I see three dots appear, then disappear.

Chrissie McCauley

I fly back to LA on Monday night after Dad goes home. Can I see you before I go?

I'd like that.

How about tomorrow? I have something in mind. I'll let you know the details as soon as I figure them out.

Sounds mysterious. Looking forward to it.

Have a great day, Jules.

You too.

Jules.

Chapter 7

Sunday

At eleven a.m., I walk to the address Matt texted me. It's in Chelsea, a short walk from my apartment. I smile as I approach—it's a movie theater. Exactly the classic old-school NYC movie theater Matt told me he'd been looking for. Art deco features throughout, slightly crumbling, and a tiny vestibule box office that sits unmanned. There are no movie titles shown, and the place looks closed.

I move toward the entrance, adjusting my cutoff denim shorts, plain white tank, and oversized cashmere cardigan draped over my shoulders. I've only been here a minute before I see Matt's head pop out from behind the closed doors.

"You're here!" He smiles brightly and pulls me into a tight hug.

"This is very cool. Just what you were looking for, right?" I point at the building.

"Exactly." He reaches for my hand and leads me inside.

"They usually do Sunday matinees, but I convinced the owner to let me borrow the whole place for a few hours."

Which explains why it looks so empty. In the lobby, I take in the vintage movie posters, the worn carpet, the concessions stand. A teenage boy at the counter is boxing up buckets of popcorn, sodas, and half a dozen candy boxes.

"We're doing this right, Jules." He grabs the box of stuff and slides the kid a wad of cash. His enthusiasm is contagious.

I carry the drinks, and we walk back toward the theater.

"Okay, my disclaimer is that there wasn't a ton of variety in movie choices. This place is rad, but it's limited in selection. I wanted something, like, super classic, black and white, *Casablanca* or *A Streetcar Named Desire*. Something like that. But that was out, so then I was like, okay, well, we have to do something romantic, because I am trying to impress you here. But the only choice they had in that genre was *Romeo + Juliet*, and nothing against Leo, great actor, but that wasn't quite what I was going for. They also didn't have *Sleepless in Seattle* or *Notting Hill*."

I laugh. "You picking a movie sounds like me picking a drink."

"Yes, very similar."

"So, where does that leave us?"

"*Sliding Doors*. You know, the movie about how a single decision —or chance, if you will—can lead to parallel lives. And lots of possibilities."

I smile in disbelief.

"Yes, of course. I love *Sliding Doors*." My best friend growing up, Meg, and I watched this movie at least a dozen times over Christmas break in the early 2000s. We were so obsessed with Gwyneth Paltrow that Meg convinced her mom to let her cut her hair into a pixie. She pulled it off, but it was a hellacious process to grow back out, which she wanted to do almost immediately.

Matt and I settle into our seats, smack dab in the middle of the empty theater. The same pimply kid from the concessions stand comes in and asks if we need anything else before showing us the exits with his light-up baton. The movie starts, and Matt grabs hold of my hand, interlacing our fingers. Gwyneth's face fills the screen, and

I find myself absorbed by the movie the same way I was over twenty years ago. Toward the end of the movie, I feel the anticipation of my favorite part coming—Helen and James kissing wildly, passionately, in the rain.

I feel Matt's eyes on me, and my skin prickles. I turn to face him, and I'm still smiling from the movie scene as Matt tilts his head down to kiss me. As soon as our lips touch, I know this is different than the do-over kiss in my office on Friday.

It is not shy or sweet. It is a continuation of the passionate, bruising kiss at the end that almost had me ripping my clothes off in my place of employment. Matt seems focused, almost possessive. I lift the arm rest between us, and he grabs me by my hips and hoists me onto his lap, my legs straddling him, my chest pressed against him. I hesitate momentarily, glancing around the theater, ensuring we are alone.

"That kid isn't coming back anytime soon," he murmurs against my neck.

He brushes my hair out of my face, his hands caressing my cheeks, my chin, his fingers on my lips, salty from the popcorn. He kisses me more, deeply, hungrily. Me on his lap, my hands in his hair, so thick, easy to hold on to, his hands on my hips, drifting up my back, then back down to my ass—where he grabs me tightly. I gasp and peel away to look at him. He bites his lip and pulls me close. I can feel him underneath me, rock hard. My panties dampen.

Oh my God.

"You are so beautiful. And sexy—and I don't think you have any idea." His voice is low and raspy.

I answer by tilting his chin up to me. I kiss him hard, instinctively moving my hips against him.

It isn't until the theater lights slowly begin to brighten that we pull away from each other. Matt's face is flushed, his lips chapped, eyes blazing, his hair a mess. In that moment, he is the sexiest man I have ever laid eyes on.

I start laughing and bend forward to kiss his forehead, his nose, both of his cheeks, and his mouth.

"I don't think I've ever made out with a boy in a movie theater before." I am still straddling him, attempting to brush some of his hair back into its usual coif.

"Isn't that a rite of passage for hot girls?" His hands are warm on my hips.

"I guess I missed that one. And I wasn't always hot. But I bet you've done it."

He laughs. "No, you're forgetting I was a total nerd in high school. I don't even think I took a girl to the movies till I was in my twenties."

"Hmm ... I don't know if I believe that. Even if you were a nerd, you still looked like this. With these lips," I say, tracing them with my finger. "Isn't the thrill of making out at the movies the fact that other people are around? A little exhibitionism."

"Ah, good point." He pats my ass. "Though that was thrilling enough for me." He plants one last kiss on my collarbone. "Next time."

It sends chills down my arms.

I peel myself off his lap and flop back into my seat. I can't help but sneak a peek at his lap, where I see him hard, straining against his jeans. I feel desperate to touch him. So much so it makes my cheeks flush. I look away while he adjusts himself. We stand, and he grabs hold of my hand as we walk out to the lobby, my heart still pounding.

"What did you think of the movie?" he asks.

"I think Gwyneth is lucky her eyebrows recovered from the over-plucking nineties era. I'm lucky mine recovered too, honestly. It's just as good as I remember. I've always liked the idea that nothing is too inconsequential."

"That part kind of stresses me out. Seems like a lot of pressure."

"Really? I think it's empowering. So many times, we think we have to make these grand gestures or these giant changes in our lives for it to feel significant—it can be overwhelming or feel impossible to even start. But the *Sliding Doors* moments are much easier things to do to facilitate change. Like holding the door open for someone. Picking up an earring. Letting someone go ahead of you in line. Everything matters. Every little kindness has the potential to change the world. Great acts are made up of small deeds."

Matt smiles. "Who is Lao Tzu?"

"Small deeds done are better than great deeds planned."

He squints his eyes, thinking.

"Who is Peter Marshall?" I answer for him.

"Ahh, I like that one."

"What did you think?" I ask.

"I love the part where he says, 'If we're *not* going to be together, let's make sure it's for the right reason.' I think I have a tendency to overthink why something won't work instead of realizing all the ways it does work. Just a good way to think about it. I also like the serendipity of it all. It had me thinking a lot about you."

"What about me?" I ask.

"What are the chances you were the person assigned to my dad's room on that exact day, at that exact time? What if you got stuck on the subway, or Murphy got off his leash somehow and you were ten minutes later than you normally were, or my dad was on a different floor, or the ambulance took him to a different hospital, or I was in LA instead of New York? Or a million other things happened, and an entirely different reality could've unfolded. Where I never would've met you."

I stop in my tracks, feeling the weight of his words, the butterflies are back.

"I've thought about that, too. And the fact that I don't often pick up patients on that floor. We just happen to be chronically under-staffed. I could've been in a meeting. I so easily could've missed you."

"But you didn't. And I didn't miss you. Which is good, because that just wouldn't work for me. Meeting you this week has been one of the best surprises. I'm so glad you came to the movies with me today, Jules."

I feel rooted to the ground. Frozen. "Thanks for inviting me," I say eventually.

"Will I see you tomorrow? Before Dad goes home?"

"Yes, I'll be there."

"Okay." He leans down to give me one last gentle but full kiss.

Chapter 8

Monday

Sid officially gets the all clear from Dr. Patel and the rest of his team, and they start processing his discharge paperwork. She determined his respiratory distress was likely the result of a bacterial infection and started him on an antibiotic regimen that should clear it right up. His cardiology reports show worsening symptoms of congestive heart failure, but the team feels confident he can manage at home. He is thrilled. I finally get to meet his aide, Rita, who is as lovely and warm as Sid and Matt have described. She has a maternal disposition and frets over Sid like a mother hen. Despite his complaints, I can see he enjoys it.

Sid tells me Matt has a few last-minute errands to run before his flight back to LA this evening, and he'll be stopping by this afternoon to help take Sid back home. I find myself looking for him every time I walk the hallway of the CCU, hoping for a glance of his familiar tall, gangly but strong frame, that thick dark hair.

Frankly, it makes me feel a little pathetic, and I internally yell at myself to get a grip. I get pulled into several meetings throughout the day, and it is after three p.m. by the time I get back to the critical care unit. I have a brief moment of panic, thinking I may have missed him.

But then I see him wheeling his father out of the room while Rita follows with a bag of Sid's belongings.

I approach them. "Sid, I'm so happy to see you go, but I'm sad you're leaving. It won't be nearly as fun around here without you. But please never come back." I lean down to give him a hug.

"Well, young lady, I plan on never coming back here, but I sure hope I get to see your face again. I thank you for your help, especially with my boy here. Lord knows he needs a hobby or maybe a lady friend instead of worrying about me all the time."

I look at Matt, who gives me that sexy half smile. "Yeah, yeah, Dad, she's heard all of your lines by now."

I ride down to the lobby with them, offering a last round of good-byes and well wishes. Rita takes over driving Sid's wheelchair and busies herself helping him into Matt's waiting car. Matt hangs back, looking at me closely in that way of his that makes me feel naked.

"Thank you for all your help, with Dad and with me. I'm not sure what we would've done without you."

"You're welcome." I take him in for what might be the last time. "I'll keep tabs on Sid for the next thirty days just to make sure all the discharge services are happening as they should. If anything comes up, or if you have any concerns, feel free to call me."

He nods slowly before turning to leave. My heart sinks, and I feel mortified at the lump in my throat. I swallow it down. *Get hold of yourself.*

Matt turns on his heel and quickly spins around, getting to me in two long strides. "Can I see you when I come back to town in a few weeks?"

"Yes," I say without an ounce of hesitation.

He smiles and leans in to give me the briefest of kisses.

"Okay, perfect. See you then."

And then he is gone.

Part Two

Chapter Nine

Once Matt is back in LA, I try my best to get back to normal life and enjoy the end of summer in New York City. It's not easy. I'm captivated by him—I feel a pull toward him with an intensity I've never experienced before, especially in the context of only spending time with him for seven days. I can't shake the feeling that this chance encounter with him means something—a *Sliding Doors* moment. I have to acknowledge that I misinterpret signs at about a fifty-fifty rate, but this feels different. Even if I want to forget about him and our week together, I can't. We have been talking almost nonstop since his departure.

I ask one of my best friends, Meredith, to meet me for drinks. She is one of my oldest friends in the city—I met her years ago through Nick and Meredith's husband, JP. Nick and JP played club soccer together in college and are joined at the hip. I was instantly drawn to Meredith the first night I met her at a party in someone's tiny apartment on the Upper East Side. She was holding court, telling every single guy at the party exactly what she disliked about them in between shots of tequila.

She is hilarious, smart, and unapologetic. We talk frequently about how we are each other's "bury a body in the middle of the night, no questions asked" phone call. She seriously considered ways to fuck with Nick in the wake of the "I'm not in love with you" line, including getting dog poop delivered to his doorstep. "There is an app for that, you know," she told me.

I get to the restaurant first and grab a table outside. I order two top shelf margaritas and tableside guacamole. As I wait for Meredith, I pull out my phone and smile when I see a new text from Matt.

> What are you doing?

He's been spending long days in the studio, plugging away at new music. It seems like our conversations were a way to power through some writer's block, and I am more than happy to keep him company.

Our conversations range from intriguing and deep to light and fun—all with heavy doses of flirtation. The chemistry—even over text—is undeniable.

A server drops off a basket of chips and salsa.

> Dinner with a friend.

I send him a picture of the margaritas.

> You haven't told me what that drink means yet.

I laugh.

> Margaritas—one of the few neutral drinks. They can be consumed almost anywhere, anytime, with anyone. No preconceived notions or limitations. Except maybe that in Mexican restaurants they are a requirement.

> Haha. Very true. And brilliant.

> What are you up to?

He sends back a selfie of him in the studio, all furrowed brow, smoldering eyes, pouty lips. A fire erupts in my stomach. He is exquisite.

Meredith bustles in, a flurry of high heels, blond hair, and an overflowing Celine tote. I put my phone away.

"Sorry, sorry." She gives me air kisses. "You are an angel," she says as she takes a long sip of her drink and flops into the chair. "I got stuck at work. My boss and his small dick energy continue to reign supreme, and apparently, I am the only one in the entire fucking company who dares to call him on it."

Meredith works in corporate communications, and while I don't understand what that means, it seems like she faces high-pressure situations often. She is my only remaining married friend who doesn't make being married a defining part of her personality. With so many of my other married friends, I sit quietly at dinners and brunches while they complain about their husbands: their golf trips, their inability to load a dishwasher, their socks on the floor. Which quickly morphs into talk about ovulation, breast pumping schedules, or the cost of childcare. Most of the time, I don't mind that I can't relate to them at this point in my life, but it wears thin on occasion. Meredith, on the other hand, doesn't talk to me much about JP, and they are one of the only couples who've managed to stay completely neutral throughout the divorce and continue to maintain close friendships with both of us. Meredith never mentions Nick, and I never ask.

"What is new in your life, Jules?" She signals the server for another round.

"Nothing, same old, same old," I lie.

I'm not convinced anything will pan out with Matt when he gets back to town, so I don't mention it. Our week together was a whirlwind, physically and emotionally supercharged. Despite the continued texting, I'm trying to be realistic about what it might be ... nothing. And I decided a few days ago that I'll be okay with that. Just to have the experience of him—the knowledge that men like him exist, that the week we spent together was possible—could be enough for me. The thought is slightly depressing, however.

"Okay, don't say anything until I'm done. *But*, I think I have a guy for you." She gives me a conspiratorial smile.

I roll my eyes.

"*Don't*. You haven't even heard me out!"

"Fine." I sip my drink.

"Okay, so the stats are, he is forty-one, also divorced. Very amicably, like you. No kids, no baggage. He is a client—the head of one of our big accounts. I met him at a conference a few months ago, and we've been working closely with them for the past few weeks. He's tall, at least six feet, muscular, like he lifts heavy weights regularly, dark hair with some salt and pepper, very distinguished, piercing blue eyes, absolutely dreamy, Jules. He's smart and successful—he makes more money than you and I combined, judging from his custom suits and Nolita address. And he is funny—sharp, quick-witted, observant funny. He's a Princeton grad, but he doesn't reek of it like the other Ivy Leaguers we know. I think he's a winner. And before you dismiss me, please let me remind you, I have never once—until now—suggested you go out with someone of my choosing. But this guy is it."

Meredith is a fantastic pitch woman. I try to imagine the person she is describing, but all I can do is conjure up Matt. His dark brown eyes, soft smile, his messy hair and worn jeans. The guy she is describing sounds like the exact opposite.

"Hmm ... no."

"Come *on*." Meredith groans. "You are so completely boring. What is the point of saying no? At the very least you get a nice dinner and some good fodder for our next girls' night. I also know you need to get laid. There is only so much a Magic Wand can do."

She is right. Meeting Matt has made me very cognizant of how long it has been since I've had an orgasm with someone else in the room.

"Can I think about it?"

"Fine, but I'm going to put an expiration on this offer. He's not going to be on the market very long, and I can just see the two of you and your future dark-haired, blue-eyed babies, or maybe brown-eyed? I can never remember what color is recessive or dominant...doesn't matter either way —so gorgeous. You have one week."

"All right, deal."

* * *

By the time I get home, it's after ten p.m. I have just settled onto the couch in my pajamas when I hear the buzz. Neil's familiar voice fills my apartment. "Miss Julia, I know it's late. There is a courier here for you. Should I send him up or away?"

"Up is fine. Thanks, Neil."

A few moments later, I open my door to find a twenty-something guy with a bag and something wrapped in brown paper and twine. He hands me a note and a clipboard to sign for the delivery. I thank him and start opening the envelope as I head back to the couch.

Jules—To help with your drink decision angst, I figured I'd save you the struggle and send one of my choosing. And a book to keep you company until I see you next week—M.

I open the bag to find a bottle of Yamazaki twelve-year-old single malt whiskey, two lemons, a jar of sugar cubes, and handwritten instructions for how to make a whiskey sour.

I open the package to find a hardback copy of *An Inquiry into the Good* by Kitaro Nishida. I smile as I walk over to my counter and set about mixing the cocktail as instructed. When I'm done, I call Matt. He answers on the first ring.

"You are very thoughtful. Thank you for the gifts."

I can hear voices in the background, instruments clanking.

"You are very welcome. If you give me two minutes, I'll make myself a drink and FaceTime you back so we can have it together."

"How 2020. Sounds good."

Five minutes later, I pick up the FaceTime and watch his handsome face fill my screen. I hold up my drink to him. "Cheers."

"I can't stop thinking about you. Is that crazy?" he asks.

Butterflies. "Yes. But the feeling is mutual."

"Good. When I'm back in New York, can I make you dinner at my place?"

"Yes, I'd like that."

We chat a while longer and say goodnight. He clicks off, and I curl up on the couch with Murphy, sipping my cocktail, reading my new book, and can't help but notice the lovestruck smile plastered on my face.

I text Meredith.

> Thanks, but no thanks on the corporate sexpot.

> Ugh, suit yourself.

Chapter Ten

"Does anyone want to offer any last-minute thoughts? Any takeaways? Or topics to talk about next week?" I ask my group as we wrap up our session.

"Can we say the Serenity Prayer?" Larry asks from my right.

"This isn't AA. And you aren't even an addict," says Curtis from my left.

"My takeaway is that I still don't believe in God. You want to get into it again, Larry?" says Herman from the back.

"I'll say it," Geoff chimes in.

"Substitute the word *God* for something else, Herman. You can pray to a doorknob for all I care," says Larry.

"We can say the Serenity Prayer. Herman, maybe you can pay attention to what makes you uncomfortable. It's got some good messages even without the God part," I suggest.

"Next week I have some problems with my lady I need to discuss," says Curtis.

We say the prayer, and I tell everyone to have a wonderful and safe weekend. I clean up the small room and turn the lights off. I start walking down the hallway to the elevator back to my office. I check my phone—it's only eleven a.m. I have a text from Matt.

Eight more hours.

I write back.

Can't wait.

By seven tonight, Matt will land in New York City and I will go to his apartment to have dinner with him. I cannot believe it, nor wipe the grin off my face.

I'm waiting for the elevator, staring at my reflection, when I see a man behind me, a familiar faded blue hat with a colorful patch of stripes sewn on and the words Vietnam Veteran perched atop his head.

"Daryl! It's so good to see you. How have you been?" I exclaim at one of my oldest and most favorite patients of all time. I met him years ago when I was brand new to the city and working in the ED. I worked with the VA to get him connected to services and he made it a point to show up to my outpatient therapy groups. But I hadn't seen him in months, maybe even a year.

"Hi, Miss Julia. It's good to see you, too. I'm just fine and dandy. I'm here for some follow-ups, and I'm going to swing by that new group for my era of vets."

"Good, you look good. Are you feeling good, too?"

"As good as I can. I'm almost eleven months sober. Never thought I'd see the day."

"Fantastic. That is huge. I'm happy for you," I say.

"Thank you, thank you. What's going on with you? You look like you're glowing from within. Is it money or a man?"

I smile at him and deflect. "Just happy to be here. Even happier it's Friday,"

He gives me a knowing glance. "What is that shit you always told the group? Secrets can keep us sick."

I chuckle at my own line coming back to bite me in the ass. "You're very perceptive, you know that?"

"Yes. What's that other shit you taught me? Being sensitive isn't a weakness, it can be a superpower, but only if I learn how to manage it. Not numb it with booze and drugs and women. I pick up on all types of shit. Especially after seeing everything I saw. And I'm picking up on you being positively giddy about something."

He's got me. "Do you believe in love at first sight, Daryl?"

He pauses, smiling, bringing his hand to his chin. "Yes. Yes, I certainly do."

"Tell me more."

Daryl was notorious for dodging personal questions when he was in my group. I dubbed him the class clown because of his ability to evade disclosing anything by cracking a well-timed joke. But that is one of the huge upsides of group therapy. Even if you don't fully participate, you can still get something out of it.

"I saw her sitting across the room in my eleventh grade English class. I felt firecrackers going off in my body. She was perfect. Everything I had ever imagined. I fell in love with her on the spot."

"What happened?"

"We fell in love quickly. We were never apart. She became my entire world; she was the sun, and I just circled around her. But then Vietnam happened. And my number came up. We didn't have enough time to do the things I wanted. I wanted to give her a ring, ask her daddy for permission, the old-fashioned way. She deserved it and more. But I couldn't afford the ring, and I ran out of time. So promised her I'd marry her the minute I got home. But then those fourteen months in the muck happened."

I knew parts of this story from our individual sessions. That he was willing to share now, without my probing, seemed huge.

The elevator had come and gone twice, but we stayed standing there in the empty hallway.

"What was the takeaway for you?" I ask him, one of our typical group therapy closings.

"My takeaway is that I'd do it all over again. Love her all over again. Even though I thought I might not survive it. Even though the pain of that loss carried me straight back into the pits of hell. The only change is that I would have been more honest with myself after the war. Maybe that would've saved me. Saved us. I fight that feeling of regret by reminding myself that I got to love her—and she got to love me, the good me. Even though it wasn't for long. Knowing that love was possible—that gave me hope. Isn't that what life's all about? The highs and the lows. You can't avoid pain without accidentally avoiding the good stuff, too."

I nod, blown away by Daryl's profound insights. I mull it over, wondering if there is something in it for me to take away, too. He looks at me with his big, toothy grin.

"You know all this shit, Miss Julia, why are you kicking it around with me? If you're in love, enjoy every moment of it, 'cause you don't know how long you'll have it."

The elevator dings.

* * *

I'm in my apartment after work, taking my sweet time getting ready, waiting to hear that Matt has landed back in New York City. I do a hair mask, a face mask, and shave almost my entire body in a steamy shower. I dry my dark hair with a round brush to give it some volume and straighten out the waves. It hangs loose around my shoulders, past my collarbones. I apply my makeup slowly and deliberately, adding a little more eyeliner and lipstick than I would for my day-to-day look.

Finally, a text comes through.

Just landed. I'm sending a car to get you so
I can get started on dinner. It should be
there in twenty min. See you soon.

My heart soars, and I am giddy. I dress carefully in my favorite jeans and a sleeveless black satin top cut low enough to show a hint of cleavage. I spritz myself in perfume, put on my favorite gold hoops and strappy sandals, and head down to the lobby.

I show up at his apartment with a bottle of the best cabernet sauvignon in stock at the bodega on the corner by my apartment. I stand at his door and adjust my top, my nerves reaching a fever pitch. I can hear a smooth jazz saxophone playing inside his apartment, and my heart is in my throat.

I knock.

He opens the door an instant later, like he was standing on the other side waiting for me. He's wearing a vintage Phish concert T-shirt, his signature jeans, and that sultry smile. His hair is perfectly mussed, and there's a dish towel slung over his shoulder. Joy and nerves fizzled in my chest like freshly poured champagne,

"Hi." His smile is wide.

"Hi."

"It's really, really good to see you." He leans forward and kisses me on the cheek before wrapping me up in a hug. The moment his lips touch my skin, dopamine floods my veins and my previous notion that I'd be okay just knowing men like him existed flies out the window. I will not be okay. I want—*need*—more of him.

Fuck.

"Come in! Dinner is almost ready."

I walk in, looking around his apartment. It's huge—easily five times the size of mine—an industrial space that has been renovated beautifully. The ceilings are at least twelve feet high, with exposed pipes and brick. The living space is one big room, a living room flowing into a kitchen and dining area. Matt has thick Persian rugs in dark reds and blues atop the polished concrete floors, dark woods and modern leather couches, low light that makes the cavernous space feel cozy.

"Wow. I love your place," I say as I put my purse down.

"Thank you. It was my first big purchase after I signed with my label. I finally feel like I'm old enough to live here. For a long time, I felt like Richie Rich, like this kid who was just pretending. I wish I could spend more time here in the city, but a lot of the people I work with are based in LA. Most of the time it's just easier for me to be there. And after almost twenty years, LA has finally grown on me. Not enough to call it home without feeling like a fraud, but pretty close."

I sit down on a barstool at the black marble counter and watch Matt flit about the kitchen, moving from the cutting board to the stove. He tosses me a wine opener, and I open the bottle and pour us each a glass. My heart is beating so fast, I feel sure he can hear it. Being in his presence heightens all my senses.

"How was LA? How is your dad?" I keep my voice light and calm.

"Dad is good. He's still in Pennsylvania but coming back to the city tomorrow, so I'll see him while I'm here. LA was good. I made some headway on my newest album. I'm really excited about it. I think it's going to be something special."

"What's the inspiration behind this album?"

"It's *fun*. I know that sounds lame, but that's the best way for me to describe it. Every song is fun for me to play. All the rhythms are familiar but new—nostalgic but fresh. I think every song is a bop. That's what kids say these days, anyway. In the early pandemic days, I found so much solace in just playing my guitar, not for the purpose of creating an album, just for the fun of it. I felt like a kid again back in my room in Allentown, plucking those strings for absolutely no other purpose but sheer joy. That's the same energy I took into this album."

"I can't wait to hear it."

"Maybe I can give you an early private listening experience," he says with that half smile.

Innuendo hangs in the air.

"What's your house in LA like?" I change the subject.

"It's comfortable—a bright, Spanish-style bungalow. It has a lot of original features: the exposed beams, classic barrel roof tiles, and stucco design. It feels too big most of the time, since it's just me out there. I turned one of the extra three bedrooms into an in-home studio and redid the backyard. It looks out over the canyon. I had a condo downtown for years, but it started to get a little overstimulating for me. I got sucked into the vortex of the social scene, and I was slipping into some habits that weren't good for me—going out every night, sleeping till the early afternoon, waking up feeling like absolute dog shit and not being able to do what I needed to. Three years ago, I moved up into the hills, and I haven't looked back."

I watch him meticulously plate the food, his brow furrowed in concentration, his hands working quickly.

"Done!" He tosses the dish towel off his shoulder and walks around the counter carrying two big, steaming bowls of what looks like ramen. He sits on the stool next to me, and I tip my wineglass to his.

"To you being back in New York."

"To getting to see your face again," he replies.

We each take a giant gulp of the red wine, and then he turns toward me and his face breaks into a huge smile, showing me all his teeth: big, straight, slightly crowded on the bottom but decidedly perfect.

"George Washington?" he asks.

A laugh bubbles out of me. "No, no, you're all clear. How about me?" I grin widely.

"Nope, definitely post-Revolutionary War teeth."

I study the bowl in front of me. The ramen looks divine, and the colors are vibrant—the deep green bok choy, a perfectly poached jammy egg with its bright yellow yolk. The crunchy nori sits in a broth that smells spicy and salty. I take a bite, and my tastebuds explode. Pure umami.

"Do you like it?"

"This is the best ramen I've had, and I think I've tried every single place in this city," I answer honestly.

"Thank you. Ever been to Japan?"

"No, but I'd love to go."

"When I was there in 2016, there was this place about an hour outside of Tokyo, a place I'd been hearing about from some of my Japanese friends for years. As soon as I got a chance, I finally made the trek out to this little hole-in-the-wall spot—it didn't even look like a restaurant, more like someone's house with a tiny kitchen. There were two tables inside, one of which was covered in paper, plastic bags, and other junk, so I sat down, and the guy in the kitchen just started cooking. I watched him prepare the bowl of ramen, so fastidious, yet he moved so quickly—it was like watching art. I wrote down exactly what he was doing. The way he made the pork broth—letting it simmer with the ginger, the garlic, the spices, the seared pork. He said something which I roughly translated to, *let it simmer for a day.* The way he carefully seasoned the vegetables with a special salt that he got shipped in from the Rikuchu Coast, layering flavor throughout. When he finished, he handed me the piping hot bowl and a plate of cold noodles on the side. You're meant to dip the noodles into the broth. *Dipping ramen* is what they call it. That was my inspiration for tonight's meal for you, a little bit of Tokyo right here in Manhattan."

"I like that."

"Like what?"

"I like how you manage to find beauty and art in unlikely places. I like how excited you get about seemingly mundane things. Your passion for things ... is palpable," *And a huge turn-on,* I think.

"That man making ramen is as much an artist as I am. His medium is just different." After a pause he adds, "No one has said that to me before, by the way. It means something that you noticed."

I shrug. "Noticing things is sort of an occupational hazard for me."

He reaches for my hand, intertwining our fingers. I am quickly reminded how his touch is like a spark plug. My pulse hums.

"I missed you." His eyes are fervid. "While I was in LA, I thought about you all the time. How is that possible?"

I hold his gaze. "I don't know. But I missed you, too."

We work our way through the ramen, and I catch him up on the latest news at the hospital, Murphy's unfortunate new obsession with a cat who lives somewhere on my hall, and some of the antics of my field hockey players. He tells me about the mudslides that are threatening a lot of houses in LA, a new technique his sound engineer is trying on the album, and all the newest updates on Sid's health. The entire dinner is so enjoyable, so comfortable, I start to feel like I've known him forever.

We finish dinner, and I grab my glass of wine and wander over to the media console on the far side of the room while Matt deals with the dishes. The console houses a vintage record player and a record collection that rivals any store I've ever passed by. I look through, noting all the familiar names: Eric Clapton, John Coltrane, Joni Mitchell, Tom Petty, Jimi Hendrix, Etta James, and B.B. King, plus dozens I've never heard of before. I thumb through them, imagining a young Matt listening to records in his bedroom somewhere in Allentown, Pennsylvania, dreaming of what his life would be like one day.

I'm lost in my thoughts when I feel him behind me, solid and firm. He reaches beyond me to change the record. My every nerve stands at attention where his body lightly touches mine. His hips are against my back, his chest pressed against my shoulder blades. I take a few shallow breaths.

He grabs an album I don't recognize and puts it on the turntable. A low, slinky beat comes thumping out over the Bluetooth speakers. A woman's sultry voice sings and time stands still. I try to concentrate on the music and the feel of him.

Breathe.

He gently takes the wineglass from my hand and sets it down on the console. I lean back into him, and he wraps his arms around my shoulders. I hold on to his forearms with my hands and look at the veins that wrap around his muscles and at the tattoos full of intricate designs, bright colors, and dark lines—signs and symbols I don't yet know the meaning of. The anticipation of this moment has been building from the first time I saw him. I want to pay attention. To feel everything.

We move together slowly, almost imperceptibly, with the beat of the music. I lean my head back against his shoulder, and I hear him suck in a breath. Every point of contact between us is on fire. Smoldering. A slow throb starts between my legs.

He holds me like this for a minute and then brushes my hair behind my shoulder as he bends down and plants the tiniest of kisses on my exposed neck. Goosebumps explode on my skin, and I have the distinct urge to sink my teeth into his forearms.

"I have been thinking about doing that since the moment we met," he murmurs into my neck before biting my earlobe. The sensation flies down my spine.

I turn and face him, the top of my forehead barely reaching his chin. I look at his gorgeous brown eyes, framed by full, dark lashes, and glance at his mouth—those lips are beckoning me. I lean in, kissing him, pressing my body against his with a force that makes him rock back on his heels. Suddenly one of his hands is in my hair, at the base of my skull, a gentle tugging on the strands, his other hand on my cheek, holding me in place.

I feel it all—his lips and his tongue and his teeth—as we explore each other. The apartment is spinning around us, and I can't get enough. I put my hands on his chest, so firm, so steady. I feel his heart pounding against my palms. He reaches around and grabs my ass, hard, yanking me closer to him so he can keep kissing my neck, my ears, my collarbone. My hands roam his body. I reach down and feel him—hard and straining against his pants.

"I want you. I want this," I say softly as I grip him, feeling completely uninhibited, like I simply cannot help myself.

It dawns on me that I am no longer in control.

His eyes go almost black with desire.

"I want you too, Jules. So badly." He grabs my hand and pulls me toward his bedroom.

He dims the lights, and with a few clicks, a new song floods through the bedroom speakers. Something more modern. Familiar. Sexy. I stand next to the bed as he closes the door, and I try desperately to focus on the music, anything to stay grounded. The anticipation reaches a fever pitch. My mind shuts off as Matt walks toward me.

"You are so beautiful," he whispers as he kisses me slowly, passionately. My hands drift to the hem of his shirt.

"Take this off," I beg.

He smiles the sexy half smile and pulls the shirt over his head. I see the tattoos on his chest, more symbols and shapes and colors. I trace them with my finger. He shivers.

We stand, kissing, and I feel like I could be here, doing this, forever. He gently pushes my shoulders so I sit down on the bed. He kneels in front of me and starts undressing me, pulling my top over my head, undoing the buttons of my jeans and tugging them down over my hips, my thighs, then tossing them into the corner. He kneels in front of me for a while, almost too long, and I can feel every single ounce of his attention focused on me like a laser.

"You are so unbelievably sexy," he growls into my collarbone as he begins to slowly and systematically devour me. "I want to taste every. Single. Inch. Of. You." His eyes flare.

He is not kidding. He lays me down and works his way over my body with his mouth, his tongue, his hands, and those mind-numbing, perfectly nimble fingers. He is thorough and so, so good—like an archaeologist unearthing the next wonder of the world. Every freckle, every scar, every painstaking detail of my body he takes in with his brown eyes, his pupils fully dilated and hungry.

I expect to feel self-conscious, but that is dwarfed by the sensation that I have been lit on fire. The desire between my legs is so powerful I can barely hear the music over the roar of the blood in my ears.

He finally makes his way south of my belly button, kissing and teasing me. I arch my neck and grab two handfuls of his thick hair, forcing his face to the place where I need him desperately.

"Someone is impatient." He smiles into my thighs.

He starts slowly licking the slit over my panties. The silk and his tongue are overwhelming.

Finally, and all at once, he slides my panties to the side, closes his mouth around me, and plunges one and then a second of those skillful fingers inside me. I gasp and arch my hips against him instinctively. He pushes them back down. This man knows exactly what he is doing, and we both know it.

It does not take long.

I explode around him with such force I see stars. Wave after wave of pleasure courses through my body as Matt stays exactly where he is.

My body finally stills, and my heart rate begins to slow. I look down and watch Matt emerge from between my legs, a victorious smile on his face, which is now slick with me. I take the opportunity to sit up, unfasten his belt, and free him from the confines of his jeans. He springs out, long, thick, heavy, and wrapped in veins. My mouth waters at the pure masculinity. I stop for a minute to take him in—this beautiful man, with his perfect dick, standing completely naked in front of me.

"This is very, very nice," I say, grabbing him in my hands, so warm and smooth. I lean forward to gently lick around the head—it feels like velvet in my mouth. He goes completely still, sucking air in between his teeth, eyes closed.

"Jesus Christ."

I spend some time licking him, his hands in my hair, and I find my own pleasure ramping back up simply from knowing how turned on he is.

He guides me to lie down on the bed, his arms outstretched as he hovers over me.

As confident as I felt a few moments ago, I am suddenly nervous. "I haven't done this in a long time," I say to him.

"How long?" he asks.

"Too long to keep track of."

"I'll be gentle." He kisses me sweetly.

He reaches toward his nightstand and pulls out a condom. He places it between his perfect lips, rips it out of the wrapper, and rolls it on in one easy motion. Just watching the grace and the ease with which he does this sends a new flood of moisture between my legs. He nudges my knees apart and settles himself above me.

I feel him waiting at my entrance, all the blood in my body rushing to the exact spot where I anticipate him.

Slowly, inch by inch, he slides inside of me.

He is gentle, as promised. I feel so full, so stretched by him—it's almost painful but not. A mind-numbing pulse flows throughout me.

He finally gets his entire length inside of me and he stills, letting out a groan into the sheets.

"Fuck."

I rock my hips against him to coax him along. He begins to move inside of me with slow, rhythmic movements.

The tension builds in me again, faster than I expected. Before I know it, I am at the edge, and I think he is, too.

"Matt," I pant. "I'm close."

This is his undoing.

"*Fuck*, Julia," he moans as I feel him bury himself deep inside of me. I feel him pulsating over and over as I uncoil again.

He collapses next to me, breathing hard, hand draped lazily across my chest. I stare at the ceiling, completely speechless.

"Wow," Matt breathes.

Wow is right. We both doze off in a naked heap, a sheet haphazardly covering us.

* * *

I wake up in the middle of the night to the sound of soft music coming from the living room. I wrap myself in a blanket and pad out into the hallway.

I see Matt sitting on the couch in sweatpants and no shirt, strumming his guitar. I stand in the door frame and watch as he adjusts the strings and plays a few notes before readjusting. I know next to nothing about music and musicians, but even I can sense the connection he has to his guitar.

It looks like it is a part of him, like a limb or a vital organ. I watch his fingers traipse up and down the guitar strings, so quick, so sure of themselves. They may as well be in between my legs with the effect they have on me. Matt seems immersed in his thoughts, and I don't want to interrupt, so I tiptoe back to bed.

A few moments later, I feel him slide in beside me and tuck himself against me. I curl into him and rest my head on his chest, listening to his heartbeat as he traces circles on my back. Before I know it, I fall into a deep, dreamless sleep.

Chapter Eleven

My next memory is waking up to the bright sun, the warm sheets, and the feeling of Matt's body pressed against my back. I turn my neck and find his chocolate brown eyes staring at me lazily.

"Hi," I say. "Trouble sleeping?"

"Best sleep I've had in years." He smirks. "But I've been lying here for the past twenty minutes staring at you, naked like this, and it is torture." He traces a finger from my neck down my spine, all the way to the top of my ass. "I've been waiting and waiting for you to wake up."

"Hmmm... Someone is impatient." I repeat his line from last night. "What do you want to do, Matt?"

He says nothing but gives me a predatory smile and pushes his hips against my back. I gasp when I feel that he is already rock hard. I turn to kiss his face, his jaw—now peppered with morning stubble—and his cheeks, his lips. His hands explore, caressing every inch of me. I think of how meticulously he devoured me last night.

My body reacts instantly, moisture pooling between my legs. I stay on my side, hypnotized by his hands and the way he touches me.

It feels like he's leaving behind a mark with every caress—like he's branding me.

When his hand finally finds its way between my legs, he moans into my ear. "How. Are. You. So. Fucking. Wet. Already."

He rolls over to his nightstand to grab a condom and is pushing against me in no time. We stay spooning, and I use my hand to guide him inside of me ever so slowly. We rock together, against each other, the sex just as intense as the night before.

Afterward, we lay there for a while, not speaking, limbs intertwined, him inside me, still hard. I grab his forearm and absentmindedly start tracing his tattoos.

"I like these."

Matt's eyes are closed; I wonder if he fell asleep.

"They're a mixed bag," he says eventually. "I started getting a few here and there. Some mean something—like these." He points to a few symbols. "These mean prosperity, luck, good fortune. And these"—he points to a series of three numbers: thirty, eighty, eighty-two. "These are the birth years of my dad, me, and Eric. But some of the others mean nothing—like this." He points to what looks like a tiny hot dog. "Someone dared me to do that one. At some point, I realized it looked ridiculous, so I found a guy to help me create the full sleeve to try to make it all look cohesive."

"Do you want more?"

"Have you ever met a tattooed person before? Of course I want more." He smiles. "I didn't notice any on you during my inspection last night."

"No, none for me. Not that I wouldn't. I'm a little indecisive with big choices."

"I like it. A blank canvas. Perfect as is."

I grab his hands and bring them to my mouth. "I think I like your hands best."

"Really? Not my lips?" He laughs.

"I like those, too. But these," I say as I hold mine up next to his, marveling at the difference in size. "These are magnificent."

* * *

We emerge from the bedroom by midmorning to find sustenance in the form of bagels and iced coffees he had delivered. He also insists on making banana pancakes with the browning bananas that sit on the counter.

"One of my few specialties," he tells me with a shy smile as he mixes together the batter.

"Were you planning on me sleeping over, Mr. Johnson?"

"Planning? No. Hoping? Absolutely."

The pancakes are delicious and we eat sitting side-by-side at the counter in nothing but our underwear.

"This is good," he chews through a bite.

"The pancakes?"

"No, me and you. This." He gestures between us. "I know we haven't known each other very long at all, but it feels good. Feels ... right."

I nod in agreement, but I'm not sure what to say or what more it might mean. I slowly get up and start gathering my belongings.

"Do you have to go?"

"Yes, I do. I have standing plans with a friend most Saturdays."

He pushes my hair back behind my shoulders.

"When can I see you again?"

"Soon," I offer. It's impossible to think clearly with him this close to me—his smell, his eyes, his lips.

"Okay." I see a flash of disappointment cross his face, but he recovers quickly.

I accept Matt's offer to have his driver take me home—walking the streets of New York in my outfit from the night before stopped being cute about fifteen years ago. As I sit in the back of the black SUV, watching the city streets zoom by, I can't help but smile. My lips are chapped, my hair is wrecked, and I have a dull but very pleasant ache between my legs.

Chapter Twelve

I had the foresight to have my dog walker keep Murphy for the night. Turns out I wasn't the only one hoping to stay the night together. Lisa lives in my building, and Murphy loves her desperately, which does wonders to alleviate the guilt I feel from leaving him overnight. By the time I get back to my apartment, Lisa has returned Murphy, and he is spinning and twirling, begging to go on a walk.

I check my watch; I have some time to kill before I meet Meredith for lunch at the farmer's market. We have a standing date most Saturdays so long as we are both in town and the weather cooperates. We walk, buy fresh produce, sample the new food trucks, and catch up. My plans with her are the only reason I was able to drag myself out of Matt's bed. I've been away from him for only an hour, and yet I still feel like I'm under his gaze. I can't stop smiling.

* * *

I stroll up to the market with Murphy, and it takes me a few minutes to spot Meredith's freshly highlighted blond hair as she sorts through a bin of peaches. The market is bustling today, filled with peak summer produce.

"Did you find a new facialist? Why do you look so glowy and dewy? Hi, Murphman," she says in greeting.

"No, just mind-blowing sex," I say casually, with the hope of catching her off guard. It works.

"*What?* Tell me. Now." We find our way to one of the small bistro tables set along the sides of the market.

"I may or may not have had the best sex of my entire life last night. And this morning." I can't help but gush. I cannot stop thinking about Matt. My brain is on an endless loop of his lips, his fingers ... his dick.

Meredith sits slack-jawed as I fill her in on the overview of my night. I am purposely vague about the identity of my mystery man, but Meredith does not let it slide.

"Tell me who he is. Now."

"The son of one of my patients," I settle on. "It's not unethical—at all. I actually looked it up because you know I'm paranoid. I am in no way, shape, or form treating him."

She arches a perfectly shaped eyebrow.

"First of all, you know I don't give a shit about ethics. Second, is this a one-time thing or will you see him again?"

"I hope I'll see him again."

"Color me shocked." She fans herself. "Here I thought you were wasting away, building up walls, never going to put yourself out there again, and you're actually *seeing* a person long enough to having mind-blowing sex, without so much as a hint of any of it to me."

At that moment, Murphy starts whining and pulling on his leash. A hush falls over the tables surrounding us, and I notice people elbowing each other and pointing. I look up, delighted to see none other than Matt Johnson walking toward me.

I push my sunglasses up off my face and let go of Murphy's leash. He takes off, dodging people and chairs as he beelines toward Matt. Matt sees him coming and turns around, looking for me. When our eyes meet, we're both smiling the same wide, disbelieving smile. Matt kneels to give Murphy a full rubdown and talks to him in a ridiculous voice. Murphy spins and whines and makes a scene as Meredith watches the whole thing unfold with her jaw dropped. She looks at me, then Matt, then back at me, realization slowly registering on her face.

"You've gotta be kidding me," she says under her breath.

Matt walks over to our table, ducking his head, trying to be inconspicuous, clearly aware people are watching.

"What kind of person lets an unruly beast terrorize a neighborhood farmer's market?" He gives me an easy smile.

He is wearing classic black Wayfarer sunglasses, shorts, a familiar well-worn black T-shirt, and a colorful silk scarf tied around his head, holding back his hair. Even if he wasn't famous, he'd be impossible to miss. His height and his hair, his unmistakable sleeve of tattoos—he is stunning.

"What kind of person wears a silk scarf in their hair outside of a Guns N' Roses concert? Who do you think you are? Bret Michaels?"

His eyes twinkle with delight. He lifts his sunglasses and takes me in, his eyes raking over my tank top and jean shorts, like he knows exactly what is under them. He does.

"Meredith, this is my friend Matt. Matt, this is my friend Meredith."

Meredith, for once in her life, is speechless. Good manners prevail, and she stands to shake his hand. "Not sure we're the same type of *friends*, Jules. But nice to meet you, Matt."

"Nice to meet you too, Meredith."

"What brings you to the Union Square farmer's market?" she asks, looking at me suspiciously.

"I'm on a reconnaissance mission, looking for Amish baked goods, or something as close to them as possible, to take over to Dad's." He continues petting Murphy.

"Grab a coffee and join us," Meredith decrees.

"No, no, no, I wouldn't want to impose...."

"Are you kidding? This is the most interesting afternoon I've had in a while. Please do. No, wait, I'll go get you something. I need another. Coffee? Latte? Cappuccino?"

"Iced coffee. Just black is great, thank you." She jumps up and walks over to the coffee truck.

Matt and I sit at the table silently, waiting for Meredith, both of us smiling at each other like idiots.

"Did I tell you I was coming here today?" I ask.

"No, not that I remember."

"There are eight million people in this city."

"Yes." He reaches for my hand under the table. "Though it is a pretty popular spot," he adds, glancing around.

"*Sliding Doors,*" I whisper.

He shifts in his seat to move closer to me.

"I have not been able to stop thinking about last night," he says, eyes on my mouth.

"Me, too."

"You felt so good. You tasted even better. I need more...." He trails off as Meredith rejoins us with an iced coffee. My body flushes from the tips of my ears down to my toes.

This fucking guy.

"So, Matt, Julia was just filling me in on the details of how she met you. How serendipitous."

"Very," he answers. "What's life in New York like for you?" he asks her. I love how he never asks the run-of-the-mill questions, the *what do you do* types.

"Life in New York is fantastic. There's nowhere better."

"Meredith was born and raised here," I add.

"Where do you live?" she asks.

"Mostly LA, but I have an apartment here. Probably a seventy-thirty split. Though, depending on what I'm doing for work, I'm here, there, and everywhere."

"LA? Sorry to hear that." She cringes. Meredith is staunchly anti-

LA and immediately judges anyone who chooses to live there. "And what is it you do for work?"

I glare at her. She is generally unimpressed with celebrity and status, but this, acting like she doesn't know who he is and what he does, is too much.

Either way, Matt humors her. "I'm a musician. Guitar mostly. Piano. Harmonica. I sing and write songs, too."

She stares at him, cocking her head to the right. "What's the career trajectory for someone in your field?" she asks bluntly.

Matt laughs, unfazed. "You mean like how long till I burn out and am just strumming a guitar and singing at family barbeques?"

"Yes. Isn't there a shelf life for musicians?"

"Mere," I say harshly.

Matt is unruffled. "Yes. Most of the time, yes. And depending on who you ask, I might be expired. I kind of hit it big early on and there was a ton of pressure to keep up the pace. To produce hit after hit. But it doesn't quite work like that, for me, at least. I floundered there for a while. I still might be—the jury's out. But I've managed to figure out what works for me and make a pretty good go of it. It pays the mortgage, at least. I've got a tour coming up in the fall."

This is news to me.

"That's gotta be cutthroat," Meredith says. "I've always admired that about artists. The skill and courage it requires to take something from inside of your brain and bring it to life. It's impressive. Even more so because your work is created to be consumed—and critiqued. I imagine you've got a strong stomach."

Matt gives her a genuine smile, and his eyes soften as he realizes she isn't here to interrogate him—this is just Meredith's way of getting to know someone.

"My stomach isn't as strong as I'd like it to be. But I've found some ways to make most of the noise more digestible."

"You know my best friend here"—she gestures to me—"has one of the strongest stomachs around. Nothing rattles her, and if it does, she has me at her disposal. And I assure you, absolutely nothing rattles me," she says sweetly, issuing a warning.

"Except for that blood-needle phobia thing, right Jules?" Matt asks.

Meredith looks impressed that he knows something like that about me. Already. She lightens up even more.

"So, how's your dad doing?" she asks.

We sit there for another half hour, me watching Matt and Meredith go back and forth, getting to know each other. He fields her questions with grace, ease, and his signature honesty. He asks her more of his pointed questions, and I can see her getting a bit dazzled by him. It's hard not to be. He eventually excuses himself, giving Meredith, Murphy, and me a quick hug and promising to text me later. As we watch him walk away, Meredith turns to me with a wary smile.

"Damn, Jules. You're fucked."

Chapter Thirteen

att is only in town for two more days. I feel a sadness creeping in, thinking about him heading back to LA, almost three thousand miles away. I have no idea what is transpiring between us, only that it is thrilling, and I do not want it to end. It's a Tuesday morning, and he texts asking if he can see me.

I am not used to dating, if that's even what this is, and I certainly am not used to the directness, the honesty, of Matt. Asking for something you want—what a concept.

> How about I cook for you tonight?

I offer, thinking it is probably easier for him if we are in the safety of one of our apartments rather then out in the open. I've started to pick up on some of the tricks of how he manages to stay under the radar of the press—a huge one being opting to stay in. Or only going places he knows will prioritize privacy.

> Sounds great, what can I bring?

> Wine? And your hands.

> Just the hands? Might have a hard time separating myself from them ...

> An arm is okay, too. Preferably the right one. I like the art on it.

> Roger that. See you soon.

I skip out of work early to head to Whole Foods. I'm making roasted pork tenderloin in a garlic butter sage sauce with steamed broccoli, fresh sourdough dinner rolls, and a simple salad. I drop my bags off and take Murphy for a quick walk. When I get back, I freshen up and change into a short black cotton dress and pull my hair back into a loose bun before setting off to the kitchen to throw on an apron and prep dinner.

As I melt the butter and add garlic and sage in a cast-iron skillet, my mind wanders. I think about the last time I cooked for someone besides myself.

It was Nick. My memory flashes back to us dicing peppers and onions for fajita nights in our tiny apartment in the West Village. Our hood vent worked only thirty percent of the time, so we had to open all our windows and turn on fans to keep the smoke alarm from sounding.

I wonder how I became a woman who settled for breadcrumbs of affection.

You didn't settle—you made a very difficult choice not to resign yourself to a life like that, I remind myself.

I shake my head, trying to rid myself of the memories. I do not want to be thinking of Nick right now, or ever, for that matter. I know I should just ride the waves of grief, let them surge and recede, but I am still annoyed when they show up.

My sauce is simmering, and I prep the tenderloin to go in the oven. I've just finished washing my hands when I hear the buzzer.

"Miss Julia," Neil's voice sounds through the intercom, "there is a Matt Johnson here for you. Should I tell him to scram?"

I laugh. "No, he's okay. Please send him up. Thanks for always having my back, Neil."

I turn on a Tom Petty playlist, toss off my apron, and wait at the door. The anticipation of seeing him is staggering. I am a live wire. And when his tall frame appears in my doorway, clad in vintage olive dress pants, a striped short-sleeved button-up shirt, hands holding a bottle of wine and a stunning bouquet of pastel ranunculus, the joy I feel is extraordinary.

"Hi." He kisses my cheek before setting down his stuff on the counter. "It smells incredible in here."

"Thanks. And thank you for these." I search around for a vase for the flowers. Murphy leaps off the couch, impatiently waiting for Matt's attention.

"Hey, buddy." Murphy grabs his ball and drops it at Matt's feet. His efforts at playing fetch are futile, given he can only ever chase the ball about five feet before running into the other wall of my small apartment.

"So, this is home?" Matt asks, tossing the ball to Murph.

"This is home," I answer.

"I like it. It feels ... homey."

I laugh.

He looks around. "This looks familiar." He points to the painting over my couch.

"Yes, good eye. It's the moody sister to the piece in my office."

"I'm definitely picking up on the moodiness." He looks at it, hands in his pockets, as he wanders toward the kitchen. "Can I help?"

"Pour us some wine?"

He does. I suddenly feel nervous and don't know what to say. I'm caught off guard by how strange it feels to have him in my house, in this space I've created to be my safe haven. I can count on one hand the people who have been in my apartment.

"Are you okay?" he asks.

116

"Yes, fine," I lie, busying myself making the salad. He isn't buying it. He comes to sit on a barstool, watching me closely. He passes me a glass of wine, and I take a long sip.

"What's going on in that beautiful mind of yours?"

I give him a nervous smile.

"I don't know if there's ever a good time to mention this, and I hope it doesn't ruin our night, but I feel compelled to tell you that I was married once."

"Really?" He seems genuinely surprised. I don't know how to take that.

"Yes."

"Do you want to tell me more?"

"No, not really. Do you want to know more?"

"I'm not sure." He pauses. "When?"

"The wedding was six years ago—I was thirty-two. Which sounds young now that I say it, but didn't feel young at the time. He was my longtime boyfriend. We were married for almost four years before we separated. The divorce has been official for over a year. This place was my fresh start. My reentry to the world post-divorce. Post-pandemic, too."

"That must've been hard."

"It was. It was brutal. But I think I've gleaned all the silver linings I could from it and I'm happy to be where I am."

He nods. I get the sense he wants to ask more but is holding himself back. I look at him over my tiny countertop.

"What's his name?"

"Nick."

Murphy nudges Matt's leg with his ball, and Matt rubs behind his ears. "Is this guy his, too?"

"Initially, yes. We adopted him together. But not anymore. He's mine and only mine. No other pets. No kids. No real baggage, apart from the emotional kind." I give a half-hearted laugh.

He nods. "Got it. Well, thanks for sharing."

"What do you think about that?"

"About what? The fact that you have an ex-husband?"

"Yes."

"I think the older I get, the easier it gets to have empathy and compassion for other people—just in general but especially with relationships. We both have pasts—mine is not something I usually ever offer up willingly. It's... unpleasant to rehash decisions I made, things I'm not proud of. I appreciate your honesty."

I do a full body exhale and walk behind him to wrap my arms around his shoulders.

"Well, that's a relief."

"Since you're being honest, I feel like I should be, too."

I tense again.

"I know I've been vague about things from my past. Some of the stuff you can find on the Internet, but the bulk if it happened before the Internet was what it is now—a small mercy. The CliffsNotes version is I fell in love with someone, very hard, very fast. She was wrong for me in so many ways that should've seemed obvious at the time." He stares at the counter and sighs.

"Mostly because she was married. Married to someone who had a lot of sway in the entertainment industry. And I was an idiot. I want to say it was because I was young, but I can't make those kinds of excuses, though I can use them to get some insight—that's something my therapist told me. I was right in the middle of accepting that my mom was not coming back, I was new in the business, and the relationship was volatile, which I mistook for passion. I did a lot of things that were not characteristic of me back then, or at least what I thought was me."

He takes a long pull of his wine.

"I got out of that relationship by the skin of my teeth. I could hardly recognize myself at the end of it. And it set me on a path where I continued to make bad choices. For a while. I compounded the problem, if you will. I'm unfortunately very good at that. I was drinking too much, having sex with the wrong people, and saying things I shouldn't to people who I shouldn't have trusted. The combination of everything almost decimated me.

"But it didn't, mostly thanks to the people who truly know and love me and who refused to let me go under. So, very slowly, I clawed my way out and back to myself. I had to figure out who I was before, during, and after that. Why I did what I did. How to not do it again. Who I wanted to be. And how to be that. It was about a five-year slog, but I made it to the other side—I think. It might be my single greatest accomplishment."

I nod slowly, trying to digest all he said.

"Do you want to tell me more?" I recycle his line.

"Not really. But ask me anything," he gives his half smile.

"What's her name?"

"Jackie Myers."

I stop. I know who Jacqueline Myers is. I think the entire world does. An exquisitely beautiful model who quickly became one of the original reality TV stars. She'd had a very public and fraught battle with substance abuse, ditto a string of toxic relationships, most notably one with an A-list actor. ...And Matt Johnson. I don't know how I missed this in the reconnaissance mission I did of Matt after that first week in the hospital. *Maybe it was too long ago?* Jacqueline was basically was patient zero for gossip websites and publications like Page Six in the early 2000s. I want to know more, every detail, actually, but I don't push it.

"Okay. I won't ask. But thank you for sharing."

We stay with my arms wrapped around his shoulders, and I kiss him on the cheek. He passes my wineglass to me, and I take a sip.

"Well, now that the hard stuff is out of the way ..." He spins the stool around so I am in between his legs, and his hands drift toward my hips. He looks at me in that way of his, like he is studying me.

It makes me feel naked—borderline uncomfortable—especially after our mutual disclosures. But then he presses his lips to mine and I am captivated. The kiss is slow and sizzling. I melt into him. His hands find their way underneath my black dress. When he feels that I'm not wearing any underwear, a growl rumbles deep in his chest.

"What is this?"

I shrug.

"You've been standing here this entire time with nothing on underneath this dress?"

"Yes."

His hands slide up the backs of my thighs. He traces the curve of my ass where it meets my legs. "How am I supposed to eat this dinner you're making. And act like a gentleman. And try to impress you, knowing this?"

"Nobody asked you to act like a gentleman."

He bites my bottom lip, tugging on it with his teeth, and grabs me—my ass fitting almost perfectly in his huge hands—and yanks me toward him.

The fervor begins.

I fumble to unbutton his shirt, and his lips are on my neck, my collarbone. His hand is between my legs.

"Fuck, Jules. I want you in the worst way." He yanks my black dress over my head and tosses it onto the couch. His hands are cupping my breasts, he focuses all his attention on them, kissing and nipping, my head thrown back at the sensation overload.

Beep, beep, beep blares the timer. I snap my head toward the sound. "Alexa, off," I shout and start toward the oven.

Matt holds me in place by my hips, eyes ablaze.

"Our dinner ..." I start.

"Let it burn," he says between kisses. "I'll order us something in," he adds, kissing me again.

I surrender.

We are a flurry of hands and hair and lips. Matt fumbles in his pockets, producing a condom. I kneel to tug his pants off, leaving them around his ankles, his boots still on. Every part of me is aching for him. I hoist myself onto his lap, taking the condom from the counter and rolling it onto him slowly, over every perfect inch of his giant, throbbing cock. I hear him suck air in through his teeth, and I begin the measured process of working myself onto him.

Millimeter by millimeter, he slides inside me. I bite my lip to keep from crying out. This position—me on top—feels so much more intense. Eventually, I settle, my arms around his shoulders, his around my waist. I hold still for a moment and take him in—he's slack-jawed and completely silent. He is staring at me in a way that makes me feel like the sexiest person on the face of the earth.

I start moving ever so slowly, still adjusting to his size. A low moan comes from his chest. Soon enough, I hit a pace that is tantalizing, both of us breathing hard. I feel the edge nearing for me, and I move my hips forward to keep him all the way inside.

"What are you doing to do me?" he breathes into my ear in disbelief.

It is the beginning of the end for me. I hold onto his shoulders, gasping into his neck. The smells of him and me and the burning sage sauce all tangle in the air. As he feels me clench around him, he grabs hold of my ass with both hands and cries out as he comes deep inside me.

Chapter Fourteen

I manage to salvage most of dinner by scraping off the burned parts of the pork tenderloin and dumping barbeque sauce on it. The butter-sage sauce was a complete loss, but neither of us care. We sit down at the counter, loose-limbed and smiling. The post-sex haze.

"I know I mentioned it in passing earlier, but my record label is throwing together a tour for me this fall. I'll leave in a few weeks."

I chew slowly. "That's awesome. What's a tour like?"

"It varies, but this time I'm just in the US. It's eight weeks, and every two to three days I'm in a new city."

"That sounds like a lot. Are you excited about it?"

"Yes and no. I'm excited because there's nothing I love more than playing live for my fans. It's hands down the best part of the job. But also no, because I've been feeling this growing tension between me and the label over the past few years. The tour was their idea. They picked the dates, locations, called all the shots. They want me to release a new album early next year. Which is great. Fine. I've already been working on it. But the idea of going through another album with them and the marketing machine that comes along with it just feels ... daunting. Which is not the way I want to feel about putting out new music. And I've never felt that way about it before. I am normally champing at the bit to put new music out. I just feel this friction, or maybe it's just exhaustion from being beholden to them for so long."

"What would you do differently?"

"I don't know. That's part of the problem. I feel like I'm at a crossroads in my life. In my career. I don't really know where to go from here. I've kicked around the idea of switching labels. Or venturing out on my own. Or just retiring altogether, kind of just fading into the background and focusing on other things I'm interested in, like putting together some type of foundation. Nothing has stuck or felt all the way right, so I'm not sure."

"A foundation sounds cool. What kind?"

"A few ideas, but mostly surrounding music. The obvious choice. Whether it's funding research or helping keep music in schools, or putting music in schools that don't have it, or offering opportunities to kids to be exposed to music when they otherwise wouldn't. I don't know, something like that."

"I love that idea."

He swirls his wine in his glass, his dark eyes dazzling in the candlelight. "I want to keep seeing you. Even when I leave for the tour."

I put my fork down and take a big sip of wine. "How would that work?"

"We make it up as we go. I'm pretty good at figuring out how to still have a life, even when I'm on tour. I can plan to be back in New York City whenever I am nearby. But maybe you could come meet me on the road somewhere?"

"Hmm... Yeah, maybe," I try to process what he's said.

He raises an eyebrow. "Are you feeling what I'm feeling, like this might be something?"

I hesitate. My answer is obvious, but I have an instinct to guard it. "Yes," I murmur.

He looks like he's fighting a smile, like he doesn't want to give too much away either.

"Me too."

"We usually take a midtour break. It'll be in November. I've already booked a villa in Mexico for five days for me and some of my friends, the band, and some production guys. We'll spend some time unwinding and working on new things. It'll be the most free time I have for a while, and I'd love for you to come."

"Hmm..." I stall.

He watches me closely.

I can't deny the hesitation I feel to make plans that seem so far away with this beautiful man who I am just getting to know, but who I don't yet actually know at all.

"No? Too soon?" He asks.

"It feels like a lot?" I say, a question more than a statement.

"I get it, but we just agreed that we feel like this might be something."

"Yes, and I do. I guess I don't know what that something is just yet—besides sex so good it almost burns down the building." I nod toward my charred skillet.

He laughs. "I think it's two people who are really, really enjoying getting to know each other. Who want to make plans to continue doing so in the future."

"Okay, that sounds accurate to me," I agree.

"Look, there's no guidebook for this. My life is a little different than the average Joe, as you so cleverly have pointed out. I learned a long time ago that it doesn't work for me to *not* be direct. What I do know is that I like you. A lot. I want to see where this goes. I don't tend to put myself out there like this unless I think it's going to go the distance. That's all I know. I'm excited about this. About you."

The butterflies are back.

"I'm excited about this too, and I want to keep seeing you. That's for sure. But I think I'm going to need to get back to you about Mexico."

He nods and drops it, but I sense his disappointment—sense that he wanted more of an answer, more of me.

I wonder how much I'm willing to give.

Chapter Fifteen

I'm in my office with Christine having a cup of coffee and debriefing her on the board meeting I sat in on this morning. Though I'm not a board member, I am from time to time invited to the meetings to listen in on plans for the hospital, budget concerns, and all the other details that keep our hospital system running. I mainly enjoy hearing all the hospital gossip from the C suite, minus the occasional pervy look or comment—bordering on sexual harassment—from the COO, Chip Barrington.

"Chip had mustard on his tie. And he asked Dr. Flynn's assistant to 'be a doll and grab me another coffee,'" I tell her.

"God, he is such a misogynistic prick."

"They're thinking of creating a pediatric psych emergency department here. We looked at the specs from one that just opened at UCLA. And another in Texas. The board would have to secure the funding, but we have the space now that the intensive outpatient program closed." There have been murmurs about this for months, but this is the first time I've heard any actionable steps.

"That would be fantastic. Mostly for the kids, but for staff, too," Christine says. She is reclined on my love seat, her feet propped up on my coffee table, sipping her iced caramel oat milk latte. The one thing my friend springs for is coffee. "It's one of life's few simple pleasures," she told me once many years ago.

"I'm going to help with some of the preliminary research," I say. "It would be cool to get back to where I started this career, with kids."

"For sure. ...So, how are things going with Matt?" she asks cautiously.

"I don't know what 'things' are quite yet, but I am very much enjoying his company."

"Are you the only one who is enjoying his company?"

I almost choke on my coffee. "What do you mean?"

"I mean, according to Dave, he's had many girlfriends."

"I think the operative word there is *had*. He hasn't mentioned anyone to me."

She snorts. "Why would he mention to you if he was seeing anyone else? He's not a moron."

"I just think it probably would've come up if he was."

She stares at me, deadpan. "Julia."

"Don't look at me like that. We're having a great time. It feels good. It feels right. We want to keep seeing each other. There's been no discussion of dating other people—I assume he isn't. Because I'm not." As soon as the words are out of my mouth, I feel embarrassed that I clearly haven't thought this through.

"Assuming. Really? We know better than that. How would you feel if you opened your news app right now and saw a photo of him out to dinner with another woman, a very young and gorgeous model-actress type?"

It hits me like a blow to the ribs. The prospect of experiencing pain like that again makes my stomach clench. "Point taken."

"So, what gives? Either you're having fun and that's it, or, you're having fun but it's more than that for both of you, and that's great. But if it's more for you and maybe not for him—then you're in a bad spot."

I let it sink in. "It just seems ... unnecessary for me to ask him that at this point."

"Aren't you the therapist? Aren't you the one always harping that everyone should have open and effective communication skills all the time? Why not just have an honest conversation with him? It's better than being blindsided."

I push away from my desk and spin to face the silhouette of the city outside my window. One of my office's best features is this view —calming and invigorating at the same time. I love watching the shadows change throughout the day—a skyline altered simply by the position of the sun. A minute or two can change things, reveal more. Am I missing something? I don't think so.

But I've also been out of the dating world for so long I wonder if maybe this is how it works now. Certainly, dating multiple people at once isn't a new phenomenon. But that is disingenuous, and Matt seems so earnest. I sigh and slump back in my chair.

"I don't mean to scare you," Christine says a little more gently. "I just want you to be smart. There's a chance he's not seeing anybody else. But there's zero chance that other women aren't trying to see him. You deserve to have an honest conversation about expectations."

"Maybe you should've been a therapist," I say, mind racing.

Christine laughs. "What do you think nurses are half the time? The only differences between you and me are that blood doesn't make me queasy, and somehow you get paid more."

* * *

Matt has started touring, and we haven't seen each other in over two weeks. I stop by Sid's apartment on my way home from work one evening. He's in the city for a few days for several follow-up medical appointments, and Rita reached out asking if I'd join them for dinner. I can't stay long but decide to drop in for an hour before field hockey practice.

I walk into his apartment, a beautiful two bedroom, two bathroom on the Upper East Side. Inside is a comfortable living room with a cozy leather sofa and matching recliner, thick rugs, antique floor lamps, and two pine shelves full of books, framed photos, and tchotchkes. A small kitchen is off to the right, and the bedrooms and bathrooms are on either side of the living space. I smile and wonder how much Matt helped to create this beautiful, warm place. My heart swells thinking about how well he loves and cares for his dad.

"My girl!" says Sid from the dining room table, where he is eating Chinese food and drinking a Coke.

I give him a big hug and a kiss on the cheek. "It's so good to see you. You look fantastic. You know you're supposed to take it easy on the sodium, right?"

"Salt is one of my favorite food groups."

"I hear you. I'm not saying cut it out, I'm saying just maybe ... less? Remember the heart failure thing?"

He waves my comment away. "I'm just fine. How are you? How's work?"

"Work is good. The same old. How have you been doing?"

"I'm fine, I'm fine. How's my boy?"

"He seems great. Traveling a ton."

"I don't know how he does it, it looks exhausting. I hate thinking of him by himself all the time. Surrounded by thousands of people cheering for him every night and yet he goes home all alone."

As soon as he says it, sadness washes over me. I hate that, too. "I'll see him soon," I offer, deciding right then that I'll make it happen as soon as possible.

"I know he seems like he's got it all figured out, but don't let him fool you. He was always a sensitive kid—never too sure of himself. I know you won't believe it because he never stops talking, but he used to get a little tongue-tied. It made him quiet. Observant. Stuck in his own damn head. When all this music stuff started to gain momentum, he was the same, but he had to fake it. Put on a face for everyone and then figure the rest out once the curtain closed. I think that sensitive kid is still in there."

129

Another layer in the onion that is Matt.

"Anyway, I'll stop blabbering, but what I'm trying to say is that I think you're a good match for him. I see the way you two shine when you're talking about each other. I just hope he doesn't get in his own way."

"I hope so, too."

I sit with him while he eats his dinner, catching up on all the Allentown gossip. Before I leave, I probe Sid to see how he might feel about relocating to LA to live with Matt full-time—which he immediately dismisses, grumbling something about "over my dead body."

* * *

At home, I shower and get into bed to scroll on my phone. It dings with a text from Matt.

> Dad said you stopped by. That was very kind. Thank you.

> I'm always glad to see him. I did have to harangue him a bit about the salt intake.

> He is stubborn.

> I also tried to put some feelers out for you about him potentially moving to LA. Initial assessment is it'll probably be a hard no, but sometimes he surprises me, so who knows?

> Thank you for doing that. I forgot that was our original plan, to talk to him about that together. How did I get so sidetracked ...

> Could it have been the coerced first date at the Waverly Inn?

> Yes. But it was in no way coerced. You are quite distracting.

I smile. A few minutes pass. I see another text bubble appear and disappear.

> I miss you. Can I say that?

> You can say anything to me.

> Come meet me in Minneapolis. I can have a plane ready for you in two hours.

My adrenaline surges at the idea of it. *Can I?* But as quickly as the idea comes, it passes. I am not a fly-by-the-seat-of-my-pants type of girl.

> I wish. But I'm already in bed.

I send him a selfie, Murphy in the background.

> You're beautiful. I wish I was next to you.

He sends back a picture. He's in a hotel bed somewhere with a sleepy smile, his arm over his head. So unbelievably sexy, I reconsider dropping everything for him.

> Me too. Soon.

> Promise?

> Yes.

* * *

Matt has a show in DC Friday night. After too many days of talking and FaceTiming, often into the wee hours of the morning, I feel a longing to see him, to touch him, that I can no longer ignore.

"What if I come down to DC and meet you after your show this weekend?" I say one night on FaceTime. He's once again in a hotel bed in a white T-shirt and messy hair; he is so alluring I can hardly stand it. He sits straight up.

"That would be fucking awesome. Let's do it! I'll book you a flight."

"No, no, it's an easy train ride. I'll get on the Amtrak right after work Friday and meet you after the show. I like the train."

"Well, I can't wait to see your face."

* * *

By the time Friday rolls around, I am giddy at the idea of seeing him. I seriously consider blowing off my entire day and going down early to see his show. I'm forced to nix that idea after I get bogged down with meetings about the new peds psych ED. The board has greenlit the preliminary proposal and we are moving full steam ahead, which means I have a long list of things I need to do before we can even consider breaking ground.

I catch the six p.m. train from Moynihan station and head south to Union Station. I love riding the train. The city lights blur together as we zoom by. No traffic, and with the overpriced cocktails from the beverage car, it couldn't be better. I listen to music and imagine what this weekend might hold for us. My eagerness is juxtaposed with a tiny pang of doubt that has been lingering since my conversation with Christine. Regardless, my anticipation continues to build as we pass through each stop: Philadelphia, Baltimore, BWI, and finally Washington, D.C.

By the time I get to the Jefferson Hotel, it's almost nine p.m. and I am humming with excitement.

Matt left a key for me at the front desk, and I make my way

toward his suite. It is huge and gorgeously decorated with stately grandeur, all well-designed, polished wood furniture and ornate drapery. The sitting room has two narrow French doors that look directly at the Washington Monument. I step onto the Juliet balcony and take in the views of the White House, the Mall, the monument, and downtown DC. The warm end-of-September air curls my hair at the ends.

I make my way back inside to survey the rest of the room. There's a kitchen, where a bottle of Japanese whiskey sits in an ice bucket, and a private study that houses all of Matt's guitars—the castoffs and ones he opted not to use for tonight's show. The bedroom has a large four-poster bed, and in the closet Matt's clothes are hung neatly: several pairs of jeans, vintage T-shirts and funky robes, along with three pairs of his chunky brown boots and sneakers in various states of wear. The bathroom has toiletries all lined up on the shelf. Very tidy. I've learned Matt is a a neat freak, with a touch of hypochondria.

"My voice is my money maker. If I get sick, I'm screwed," he told me once.

Matt texted me before the show and asked if I wanted to meet him for a late dinner at a restaurant downtown.

> As much as I want to have you all to myself in the hotel room, I'm going to be famished, and this place has the best burger in DC.

> Are you sure? Seems a little out in the open.

> Yes, totally sure. I know the manager, they'll take good care of us.

I freshen up in the bathroom and change into a beaded Veronica Beard miniskirt, a crisp white button-down and nude slingback pumps. I bought this outfit specifically with Matt in mind, also with Christine's words ringing in my head that he may be seeing other people. I want to stack the odds in my favor, to somehow try to ensure there is no one else he'd even consider dating after seeing me tonight.

I arrive at Le Diplomate, and the restaurant is bustling. The maître d' leads me to a secluded table in the back. I see Matt sitting at the banquette, his back against the wall. His hair is wet, like he's freshly showered. He's in a black T-shirt, jeans, and his familiar brown scuffed boots, with a chunky black watch on his wrist. There's a glass of scotch next to him and a glass of red wine at the place setting to his right. For me. I smile. He's staring down at his phone, his head propped up on his hand.

He must sense me, because he looks up as I approach, and the look he gives me is pure sex. I feel desire coil low in my stomach. He stands to greet me, a quick kiss on the cheek before pulling me into a tight hug. He has at least four inches on me, even though I'm wearing heels. I bury my face in his neck, planting a kiss beside his Adam's apple before I join him to sit next to him on the banquette. I need to be able to touch him.

"I can't believe you're here. God, you look incredible," he murmurs into my neck.

I feel myself tense, shocked by the way I am somehow ignited just being in his presence. I notice him briefly glance around at the other patrons before he leans in to give me a longer kiss on the lips. Everyone in the restaurant looks harmless to me, no obvious phones pointed in our direction, but Matt is the expert here.

"How was your show?" I turn to face him.

"It was magnificent, the crowd had the best energy. I switched up my set list at the last minute, and I think it worked out well. How was your train ride? Do you like the hotel?"

"It was good, easy. The hotel is gorgeous. What a view."

"I know. It makes me feel very patriotic every time I'm here. Also makes me feel kind of on edge, like there's this dark undercurrent, the politics and the scheming, and the secrets. All the government agencies, all the things that they know and we don't. Do you ever wonder how many foreign dignitaries have perhaps sat at this restaurant, in these exact seats, and all the shit they might've been up to?" He laughs. "I watched a lot of *House of Cards* during the pandemic."

Matt—expansive as always.

"Yes, this place undoubtedly gives off a Francis Underwood vibe." I lean into him.

"I can't believe you came."

"Why are you so surprised?"

"I've asked you a few times to come meet me, and you say no."

"Yes, but it's not because I don't want to see you." I grab his hand under the table. "I'd love to drop everything and come hang out with you while you're on tour. But I have a job and a dog, and friends, and a life in New York."

We've discussed all this before in one of our marathon phone calls.

"I know, I know," he says. "That's one of the things I like most about you. That you have your own thing, and that it's so different from mine. I've only dated people in the same industry as me. For a while, I thought that was just what was in the cards for me. It made sense. We could understand each other and all the parts of this world, this business, that don't make sense to a lot of people. But obviously all those relationships ended, and while I don't think it was solely because we were all in the public eye, it was a contributing factor. I think I was desperate to feel understood. I thought certainly the one person who could do that best was someone who did the same thing as me for a living. But it always ended up more complicated somehow. This seems different. Simple. In all the best ways," his voice is raspier than usual because of his show.

This is my opening to ask if he is dating anyone else. To clarify what we're doing here.

But I don't want to ruin this moment. Sitting next to him, drinking a glass of wine, listening to the chatter and clash of dishes in the restaurant. It seems reckless to sour any of our time together. It happens so seldom and always feels magical.

But I need to know that we're on the same page. If we aren't, I need to figure out how to manage that, because damn—just imagining it stings. I'd love to bury my head in the sand and enjoy that magic for what it is but decide to take the leap.

"Matt, I want you to know that I'm not seeing anyone else. Or sleeping with anyone else. Just you." I force myself to hold his gaze.

I see the smile in his eyes before it hits his mouth.

"That's ... exceptionally nice to hear."

I stare at him, waiting for a similar response.

"Do you think I'm dating other people?" he cocks his head.

"I don't know. I try not to make assumptions. It seems like we've both been on the same page up until this point, so I wanted you to know where I stand. I'm only seeing you; I only want to see you." I stare at him. Honesty in a new relationship feels very uncomfortable.

"I haven't been with anyone but you since that first night we spent together in my apartment."

I frown and bite my lip.

"And I plan to keep it that way. I don't want to see anyone else—just you, Jules." He nuzzles into me, his hand resting on my thigh under the table. "I told you this once before and I meant it. Meeting you has been the greatest surprise, and I don't intend to squander it away. I'm sorry if I made you wonder."

I exhale. The relief is palpable. This surprises me.

"Okay. Let me know if that changes." I kiss him and then lean into his shoulder to take a deep inhale. "I love the way you smell."

"Oh, yeah?" he asks.

"Yeah."

"I love the way this skirt you're wearing is just short enough to make me wonder what would happen if you bent over just a little bit," he whispers softly into my ear. The warmth of his breath has me suppressing a shiver. His hand on my thigh starts moving in lazy circles.

"What would happen is that you'd see I'm wearing a teeny, tiny scrap of fabric. It hardly counts as underwear." I scoot closer to him and brush my hand against the outside of his jeans, where I feel him harden.

I watch his pupils dilate slowly.

"What, exactly, do you think you're doing?"

"Nothing. I just missed you. And this," I say innocently as I grab him under the table.

"I think I'll ask our server to just box up the food. We can go back to the hotel." He stiffens and starts glancing around, looking for someone.

"No, no, let's stay and enjoy." I take a sip of my wine.

His eyes scan the restaurant, everything seemingly in order, before he turns his attention back to me. His hand creeps farther up my thigh, playing with the hem of my skirt.

"Did you wear this just for me?"

"Yes." I try to keep my breathing steady.

He leans into my ear as his hand still plays around my thighs, those long, languid fingers dancing in between my legs, up and down, teasing me.

"I don't know what turns me on more. You in this skirt or knowing that you're thinking about me when we aren't together."

I instinctively move my hips forward, toward his touch.

"I do a lot more than think about you when we aren't together."

He eyes darken.

Our server appears and assures us our food will be out shortly. He asks Matt if we need refills on drinks.

"Yes, another round, please." He says it stoically, as if his hand hasn't continued its mind-numbing ascent up my thighs.

He's back to whispering in my ear. "You know, I cannot stop thinking about you. You are driving me crazy." His raspy voice, his hand—the combination sends chills down my spine. "And I'm very glad you mentioned the dating thing tonight, because I really, *really* like the idea of having you all to myself."

My head lolls to the side, and I grip him even harder over his jeans. I watch him bite his lip and try to keep a neutral face the crowded restaurant. It gives me such a thrill, I think this might be a game I want to play with him for a very long time.

"Why is it that I can't stop thinking about you?" he asks rhetorically. "It's not just this." He moves his hand fully in between my thighs. He feels the wetness there, and his eyes go dark.

"Could it be that?" I ask, breathless. His eyes are fixed on me.

"That has something to do with it. And I will take care of that in just a minute." He moves his hand over my panties. "But it's more than that, more than the sex, more than the off-the-charts chemistry. It's more than your big, beautiful brown eyes—the cleverness in them, the depth, the wit, the passion, the kindness. I think ... I think it's the way I feel when you look at me. Like you *see* me."

He moves his other hand to my cheek, brushing his thumb lightly over my mouth then down my neck, where it lands on my chest. He flattens his palm—wide and smooth, right over my heart.

"But I think it might be this that I like most of all." He presses down for emphasis. "There is a goodness here that I just want to be around all the time. It makes everything feel better. It makes *me* better."

I feel myself liquefy.

"Are you feeling what I'm feeling?" he asks again, seriously, suddenly vulnerable. His eyes search my face.

"Yes. All of it."

He nods, satisfied. He then moves his hand inside the seam of my panties, where he discreetly and expertly uses his glorious fingers to touch me. I do my best to keep my face calm—bored, even, while my newly anointed boyfriend gets me off beneath the table at Le Diplomate, unbeknownst to the Friday night crowd.

Chapter Sixteen

"Scott invited us to his house out East for the weekend. Can you come?" Matt asks over FaceTime. He is back in LA for the week, and I am in a Hilton hotel room in Houston, Texas, sweating my ass off. The heat down here is no joke.

I smile at the *us*. I am still getting used to the idea that Matt is my boyfriend. Still flying high from our time in DC and still getting used to the idea that I am approaching thirty-nine, have been married and divorced, and now once again have a boyfriend. I feel like there should be another word, more mature, more meaningful, but here we are.

"That sounds fun."

"So, I'll tell him we're in?"

"Definitely. What have you told him about me?"

"Oh, just the usual. That you're brilliant. And beautiful. And funny. And that you have the greatest vagina on the entire planet."

"Excellent. Just as I'd hoped."

I laugh. I'm nervous to meet Scott, one of Matt's oldest and best friends. He talks about him often, and I know their friendship dates back over twenty years, right before Matt's music career took off.

Matt passed my friend test with Meredith with flying colors. I hope I'll do the same.

"How's Texas?"

"Hot. As hell. Still. If only the board could've waited until winter to send me here."

"What's the plan while you're there?"

"Tex-Mex first, then visiting Texas Children's Hospital." I filled him in earlier on the details of my trip. Texas Children's Hospital is spearheading a new initiative to meet the demand of a recent surge in children's mental health concerns. I've got back-to-back meetings scheduled for the entire two days, including with their director of clinical services. This is an ongoing part of my research mission to see if this is something that can be achieved at New York Presbyterian.

"According to their numbers, they've seen an eight hundred percent increase in emergency room visits for kids under eighteen experiencing a serious mental health crisis, and that is just since the pandemic," I tell him.

"Man, what do you think is causing all of that?"

"I'm not sure exactly, but that is what everyone is trying to figure out. Certainly, the isolation, lack of social connectedness, upheaval in routine—kids just don't have the brain development to understand that, and consistency is incredibly important in childhood development."

"Yeah, and how did anyone even get help when we couldn't leave our houses?"

"Exactly. Kids are completely dependent on their caregivers. And parents were and still are stressed the hell out, completely maxed out, and maybe their own mental health issues worsened. Loss of jobs, food insecurity, housing insecurity, it's all part of it. There are so many contributing factors, and we probably won't understand the magnitude of all of it for years to come. But the reality is we are in a postpandemic mental health crisis, kids especially. I hope we can figure something out. And soon."

"I admire you, Jules."

I like how interested he is in my work, my job, my thoughts on things. He's curious. Concerned. He pays attention, forms his own opinions, asks me questions that illustrate all of that. During the week he sends me links to articles he read that he thinks would be of interest to me—in addition to the memes, videos, etc., usually followed by a text asking, *What do you think about this?*

It isn't something I'm used to.

At the beginning of my relationship with Nick, he loved to hear stories about the kids I worked with. The ridiculous things they'd say, the unbelievable circumstances they overcame. He made me feel like what I was doing really mattered, which was a vital part of my restoration process at the end of challenging days. I couldn't remember when or why Nick's interest seemed to wane, whether it was as I moved into more administrative roles, or if he just became preoccupied with his own work. But in the last few years we spent together, there was usually nothing more than a cursory *how was your day* from him.

"Thank you. I admire you, too."

"I feel like you're making a difference. A big one. It's inspiring. And very sexy." The compliment makes me uncomfortable.

"And you are, too! Think of all the people who have found solace in your music. Who have used it to get through something, or to maybe realize they aren't alone in the world. That matters."

"I accept that. Thank you." I see him walk from his kitchen over to the couch.

"So, tell me ... what exactly is under that top you have on?" he asks with a naughty smile.

I am happy to show him.

* * *

By the time I get back to New York, I am exhausted. Spending two days at Texas Children's Hospital was a roller coaster. On one hand, I was inspired by the ideas and initiatives the hospital has put into action—and so quickly—to address the mounting crisis. The hospital system has teamed up with community-based providers and local elected officials to start three intensive outpatient programs in the greater Houston area. They offer free training to school systems and educators on mental health and have enhanced community outreach by parking and staffing mobile crisis units in each of the major school districts. They work with local medical and nursing schools to incentivize students to consider pursuing a psychiatric specialty. It is even more impressive that they were able to scale it so quickly and get the buy-in. Texas Children's is three times the size of my hospital, and I feel like any new idea or change is riddled with red tape.

On the other hand, it was devastating to see the enormity of need. I spent time in the emergency department, and they were flooded—standing room only. It seemed like half of them were kids in a serious mental health crisis. There were no beds, and safety precautions, standard of care, and hospital liability fears were constantly at odds with each other. Kids were rotting in the ED for days, sometimes weeks, waiting for psych beds. No school, no real treatment, and seemingly no hope for them or their parents. Things seemed bleak, and it felt heavy.

Getting home and seeing Murphy alleviated some of the disquietude I was feeling. Even with him by my side, I am dragging by the time Friday rolls around. Determined not to let my blah mood ruin my weekend out East, I take the day off to go shopping. I stop by my favorite lunch spot on my way to a blowout followed by a mani-pedi. I get back to my apartment and change into jeans, a plain white T-shirt, and a vintage leather jacket Meredith gifted me for my thirty-fifth birthday. I drop Murphy at Lisa's down the hall, with his weekend bag packed full of food and his favorite toys, and walk back to my apartment. By the time I hear Matt knock on my door around three p.m., I'm feeling mostly restored.

I open my door and am, yet again, blown away by how gorgeous he is. Seeing him for the first time after we've been separated never seems to get old. His hair is windblown, and he's in pair of his signature jeans and an incredibly soft pink T-shirt. He's wearing glasses, round frames in a warm brown tortoiseshell, the first I've seen of them. He looks adorable and sexy all at once. I stand on my toes to kiss him in the doorway. He wraps his arms around my waist, and I feel my body do a familiar activation—butterflies in my stomach, a smile so wide it hurts my cheeks, and goosebumps on my skin. The physical attraction is off the charts, and that's only the half of it.

"Hello, handsome."

"Hello, gorgeous." He slides his hands from my waist to my ass.

I touch his glasses. "These are very cute."

"You're dating an older man ... comes with the territory."

I laugh and kiss him on his cheek, on his nose, and one last time on his perfectly pink lips. He pulls me close against him and pushes his hips against mine. I gasp when I feel how hard he is.

"I've missed you. So fucking much," he murmurs into my ear. I grab his waistband and shove my hand downward. Apparently, I have no self-control around him, either. He indulges me for a moment and groans before he pulls my hand out and gives me one last kiss. "As much as I'd like to do this right now, I parked the car in in a fire lane."

Matt grabs my weekender bag in one hand, my hand in the other, and we walk to the elevator. Once inside, I can't help but touch him again. His dick, which I can see pushing against his jeans, is taunting me. He leans his head against the wall. "Jules. Please don't do this to me."

"I'm sorry." I kiss his neck. "Do you know that you are extra irresistible today?"

"Very soon, we will do this. And make up for all the times I've wanted to do this since I last saw you," he whispers into my ear.

A promise.

Chapter Seventeen

We arrive in Amagansett in record time thanks to it being October and past the peak summer season. We pull up to Scott's gorgeous beachfront manse, a beautiful two-story home with weathered cedar siding outlined in bright white trim, set back on a spacious front yard with a perfectly manicured lawn—classic Hamptons. As we grab our stuff from the car, Scott comes bounding down the front porch. He's short and stocky with a full head of white hair, a linen shirt, jeans, and a warm smile.

"Matty! My man!" Scott gives Matt a giant bear hug. "And this must be Julia. We've heard a lot about you. Only good things, of course." He wraps me up in the same giant hug.

"Likewise. Thanks so much for having us this weekend."

"Are you kidding? It's going to be a blast! Forty-eight hours with Matt? This hasn't happened in what, like three years?" he says as we walk up onto the porch.

"Has it been that long?" Matt asks.

"Hi!" Another voice comes from inside the house. Natasha is Scott's longtime girlfriend and another very close friend of Matt's, with brilliant red hair that cascades halfway down her back, porcelain skin, and giant green eyes.

"Welcome to our home!" She hugs us both. "I'm so glad you're here, Julia. Normally it's just these two and me, and they are insufferable."

The house is stunning—open and bright, the design clean and modern with tasteful coastal elements. They have the back doors open, and I can smell the briny air from the Atlantic Ocean a few hundred yards away over the dunes. Scott gives me a quick tour and then lets us have a minute to get settled in our room—a spacious guest suite facing the back lawn, pool, pool house, and beach. The walls are grayish green, and the king-sized rattan bed is covered in fluffy white bedding. A matching rattan chair sits in the corner. The en suite bathroom is done in the same coastal greens.

"This is incredible." I flop down on the bed.

"I know, I love it here. It's so peaceful." Matt lies next to me.

He rolls over to face me, and I take his glasses off and place them on the bedside table. In this early evening light, I can see tiny flecks of caramel in his brown eyes.

"Have you been here a lot in your life?"

"Back when I was lived in the city more full-time, I would come out here as much as possible. It slowly dwindled as I got busy and moved to LA." He looks pensive.

"What are you thinking about?" I ask, pushing a wayward lock of hair off his forehead.

"It just occurred to me that in all the years I've been coming to visit Scott and Natasha, I've never brought a woman with me. What's even more interesting is that I didn't even think twice about it. It's very nice. To not overthink everything."

"Glad to hear it." I look at him and wonder how I got so lucky. I climb on top of him, and he grabs my hips, settling me perfectly. He unbuttons and tugs my jeans down, running his finger along the seam of my lace panties. He maneuvers his fingers expertly inside so he can touch me, pushing the fabric to the side, exploring me. When he feels the wetness, his eyes go dark and he bites his lip. I stare at him, breathing hard, as he pulls his hand out and starts licking his fingers. His eyes roll back in his head.

"How are you so fucking sexy?"

I lean down to kiss him. "I don't know. But I'm flattered to be here with you, with your friends this weekend. This is exactly what I needed after the week I had." I rock my hips against him.

"Don't do this to me, we have to go downstairs and have drinks and dinner!" He flings his head back, exasperated—hand again in my pants. I kiss his neck and run my hands under his soft pink shirt, feeling the hard planes of his chest, his stomach.

"I can't help it. I missed you," I murmur into his neck.

"I missed you, too, more than you know. What I want is to lock that door and stay holed up in this room for the next two days. Even that wouldn't be sufficient. I cannot get enough of you," he whispers.

I sit and pull my pants up, not wanting to tease him, or me, anymore.

"Okay, okay. Let's go enjoy dinner with your friends, and we will pick up where we left off as soon as we get back."

"Fine. I just need to sit here for a second and think about baseball stats, or guitar chords, or the square root of six hundred till this goes down." He winces as he tries to adjust himself.

* * *

We get downstairs and find Scott mixing margaritas in a pitcher at the kitchen island.

"You know, I thought we might not see you two for a while." He winks at us and hands each of us a glass.

We walk out to the back patio, which surrounds a large saltwater pool. White twinkle lights are strung across the top of a massive pergola. A ten-person teak table sits underneath with place settings for the four of us. Natasha is at the built-in grill, firing up skirt steak and veggie kebobs; it smells divine.

We eventually make our way to the table, our drinks seeming to magically replenish themselves thanks to Scott. He and Matt go back and forth bantering, talking about old times, the years when they would wander the West Village going bar to bar, the absurd situations they found themselves in and how they got out of them.

"And then you met me," Natasha says from the head of the table.

"And then he met you, and you were the stabilizing force. For both of us," Matt says warmly.

"Yeah, Nat, you brought us back from the brink. And made it even more fun."

"Jules, there was a time when watching Matt try to pick up a girl at a bar was like watching a newborn giraffe trying to walk," Natasha says.

"She's not wrong," Matt admits.

"It's not that you didn't have game—you did, but only because of your face. And you're tall. And incredibly talented. But the shit that came out of your mouth. Man. So bad." Scott laughs.

I laugh, loving seeing this side of Matt. Getting to know his friends. Watching them bust his balls. After dinner we move to a firepit on the patio with more drinks, and Natasha brings out s'mores supplies. I lose track of time as we sit laughing, telling stories and drinking.

"All right, you two lovebirds, we're turning in for the night. Help yourself to anything you need," Natasha says, reaching for Scott's hand.

We hug them good night and the two of us sit out at the firepit a bit longer, finishing our drinks. I find myself watching Matt in the crackling light, once again wondering how I landed here, with him. He catches my eye and smiles. "What's going on in that beautiful mind?"

"Just thinking about you."

"Want to go for a walk with me?"

I nod.

He wraps a blanket around my shoulders, and we trudge toward the dunes. The moon is full, illuminating the beach like a spotlight. We walk in silence, the wet sand cold on my feet, the waves crashing, Matt's hand warm in mine. He's looking ahead of us with that furrowed brow of his.

"What are you thinking about?" I ask.

He pulls on his lip.

"I'm worried that I've spent too much of my time and energy creating this imaginary world in my head about what my life should look like and what my future partner should be like and all these arbitrary rules and ideas about what is good, what is bad, what would work, what wouldn't work. I always felt like the second I met my person, it'd just be an instant knowing in my bones that I couldn't deny. It'd be forever, and everything else would be cake.

There wouldn't be any problems or disagreements or things to figure out, it'd all just fit into place. I've had the feeling once or twice, a *this is it* feeling, and then something happens, it ends, and I'm rocked. I know how that sounds. Idealistic. Unrealistic. Because of course, all relationships have conflict. It's normal. But it doesn't *feel* normal to me. It makes me want to cut and run. To hide. To do something. I don't know. Does that make sense?" he rambles.

"I don't know what I'm saying, exactly. I think I'm realizing how much time I've wasted thinking like that, because it clearly wasn't working. Maybe if I'd been a little less rigid, a little more open, a little less tied to these ideas I created in my head, maybe that could've cleared a path. Maybe I could've met you sooner."

I look at him, focusing hard to follow his train of thought. He runs a hand through his hair, frustrated.

"I've just been feeling the weight of time a lot more lately. I'm almost forty-three. And I know that is young. But some days it feels like I'm on the downslope. I'm on the back nine. And there's so much good stuff on this side, I love it here for a lot of reasons. But time, man. There isn't enough of it. The older I get, the more aware I am of it, and there's so much more I want to do. I try not to live with regret, but it still creeps in."

148

I'm not sure what territory we've just entered, if he's talking about me and him and us, or if his thoughts are just general, existential, philosophical.

"I think everyone has regrets to some extent," I offer. "I also think it's normal to have a picture in your head about what life should look like. We all do it. When—fill in the blank—when I lose twenty pounds, when I get that new job, when I get married, when I get a bigger apartment, when I finally get out of this town. Whatever it is, we think that once we get there, we will instantly be transformed into the person we're supposed to be. The person we want to be. It's hard to balance the life right in front of you, the one you are living in this very second, and the one you imagine in your head."

He stops and turns toward me, nodding emphatically. "Yes. Exactly. And right now...right now I don't want to ever think about anything besides what is right in front of me this very second. And that is you."

He puts his hands in my hair and kisses me, long and slow. We stay locked together in the moonlight until the ice-cold surf rushes up and soaks our feet, shocking us back to reality. I scream, and Matt turns and pulls me back toward the house.

Once in Scott and Natasha's backyard, I bend down to brush the sand off my feet.

"You can rinse them off in the outdoor shower." Matt points toward the side of the pool house. I look at it, then look at Matt and give him my best come-and-get-me smile before I take off running the few hundred yards toward the shower, peeling off my clothes as I go, dropping them behind me like breadcrumbs.

I hear his deep laugh and turn to see him bare-chested, chasing me. By the time we reach the door, he's caught up to me, and we're both down to our underwear. I shiver in the cold night air, but my entire body feels warm—heart pumping, lungs burning as Matt reaches beyond me to turn on the shower. We strip our remaining clothes off and stand facing each other with matching smiles. He pushes my hair back behind my shoulders and runs his finger ever so gently across my collarbone.

"You are so beautiful, Jules. It almost hurts."

I pull him toward me and kiss him as I back into the shower. We stand under the spray of hot water, skin to skin, and the contrast with the cold night air is heavenly. He kisses me deeper, and I feel his dick, hard against my hipbone. Warmth floods my stomach—the instant turn-on for me, knowing the power I have to get him so hard, so fast.

He turns me around, my back pressed to his front, and slides his hands up my waist, all the way to my chest. He grabs a bar of soap and takes his time lathering his hands with suds, then gently massages me all over my body.

He moves in between my legs and begins circling my clit slowly. Heat floods my core and I feel my arms go limp at my sides, my head lolling back against his shoulder. He works me into a mind-numbing frenzy, my hips jerking toward his hand, desperate for release. He nips at my ear, his free hand now kneading and massaging my tits, doubling the sensation.

He kneels, his hands working their way down my spine to my ass. He is kissing and rubbing and soaping and licking it, like it's his favorite thing in the entire world.

"This. Ass. Is. Unbelievable," he says in between kisses. "I want you to smother me with it." I back into his face, and he groans. I look down to see him stroking his dick, which looks like it's throbbing. The sight of it, of *him*, makes my mouth water.

I want it.

I pull him up to stand and surge forward to kiss him before lowering to my knees. With the shower beating down on my back, I take him into my mouth. He lets out a series of expletives and braces his hands on either side of the shower wall while I work him with my tongue, my lips, my hands. He comes so hard it hits the back of my throat. I swallow and stand, wrapping my arms around his neck, my nose pressed against the crook there—my favorite spot.

"That was ... otherworldly," he sighs, his limbs loose, his eyes closed.

I try to kiss him, making sure to give him a lot of tongue.

He laughs into my mouth. "Hey, hey, hey, I only want to taste you, not me." With that, he turns me against the wall, gets down on his knees, and goes to work returning the favor.

We stay in the shower until the water runs cold and then wrap ourselves in towels, grabbing our clothes strewn about the lawn, and race upstairs to our warm, cozy bed.

* * *

The next morning, we sleep in. Matt and Scott run out to grab coffee and croissants from a place in town while Natasha and I roll out yoga mats on the back patio. In addition to being a private chef and a welcoming and gracious host, Natasha is also a certified yoga instructor. The guys walk out as we flow, Scott letting out a low whistle. I glance back to see Matt sitting on the step of the patio, watching me with an unmistakable look of lust on his face.

Saturday afternoon, I have plans to steal away for a few hours to meet one of my best friends from college, Jenny. She's here with her family for the weekend, and I haven't seen her in months. When I remind Matt of my plans, hurt flashes across his face.

"What? Is that not okay?"

"No, it's fine. Of course it's fine. I just want you all to myself this weekend."

My immediate instinct is to cancel with Jenny. Matt and I already spend so much time apart, surely it's reasonable to blow off my old friend to be with him. I know she'd understand. Plus, I want to spend every second together, too. But another part of me is blinking yellow—caution; reminding me that my friendships are important and shouldn't be taken for granted—they've been lifelines to me many times. I walk over and sit on his lap in the rattan chair in our room.

"Do you want me to stay?" I ask, running my hands through his hair, kissing his temple.

"Yes, kind of. But I know you want to go. And you should go," he replies, his face glum.

"I won't be gone long. Two hours max. I figured you could hang out with Scott and Natasha and catch up without the old ball and chain." I try for levity.

He's suddenly serious. "You aren't a ball and chain. The exact opposite, in fact. I want to be with you all the time. It's a new phenomenon for me. I'm fine, really. You go see your friend. I'll work through it."

"Okay." I decide to drop it and start getting ready to meet Jenny for drinks in Sag Harbor.

He stays sitting in the chair in our room while I walk into the bathroom. I see him looking at me in the mirror as I put on my makeup, tousle my hair, and slip on a Staud pink floral mini dress and nude sandals. I grab an oversized jean jacket to carry along. I can't interpret the look on his face, but he seems preoccupied, and the energy rippling off of him is one I can't quite place. Before I finish getting ready, he walks behind me, holding me tightly around the waist, his head resting on my shoulder.

"You look too sexy to go out tonight without me." He kisses my shoulder.

"Lucky for you, I'm only going for a few hours and then I come right back. To you." I kiss his hand.

"You promise?"

"Yes. Of course," I reassure him.

Then wonder why I have to.

* * *

The moment I see Jenny, I know I made the right choice. She's one of my closest friends, and she was my roommate for three years in college. Despite our separate paths and not living near one another, when I see her, it always feels like no time has passed. Jenny, her husband, and their two kids live in Boston. She was born and raised in the Hamptons, and her parents are still here, so she comes back as often as possible to see them.

"What brings you to the Hamptons? A little post-summer getaway?" she asks over wine.

"Something like that," I answer diplomatically before changing the subject.

I'm keeping my relationship with Matt close to the vest. I've spent too much time overthinking all the ways in which my dating someone new might be interpreted by people in my life. I figure the majority will be happy for me, but I can't ignore the subset of our friends who encouraged me to stick it out with Nick, and who would have loads of things to say—most of them hypercritical. That's all minus the small part about Matt being a very famous artist. I don't want to open that can of worms.

I feel protective of our relationship, like I need to guard it—its newness, its intensity, its potential. I know this isn't possible in the long run, but it feels right for now. I manage to keep Jenny off my scent, and we have a blast catching up and reminiscing about old times over two bottles of rosé and a charcuterie board.

When I get back to the beach house a little after seven p.m., I follow the music and find everyone out on the back patio. The October air indecisive—desperately holding on to the warmth of summer and reluctantly letting in the first wafts of the brisk fall ahead. I see Matt lounging lazily on a chaise, Scott in a matching one next to him. Natasha is going between the patio and the house, a giant glass of rosé in hand, working on dinner—steamed Maine lobster with a gallon of melted butter, roasted garlic rosemary potatoes, and the last of the season's sweet corn. She shoos me away when I offer to help, so I head over to where Matt and Scott are laughing—more like howling, telling old stories. The bottle of scotch between the two of them has a solid dent in it.

"Hello, gentlemen."

"Julia. Juli-uhhhhhh. Juul. Jewel-baby. Jules. Can I call you Jules?" Scott asks, slurring a bit.

"You? You can call me whatever you want, Scott." I kiss his cheek and go to sit between Matt's long legs.

"I like that. I like her," he tells Matt. "Matt and I were just talking about the time he and I were in Mallorca. He insisted he could speak Spanish—which he can't. He just kept saying something about having a hairy tongue? Or not a hairy tongue? But you butchered it. Totally fucked it up. Everyone looked at us like we were insane."

"Someone told me an expression—and now I can't remember it— where the literal translation is something about a hairy tongue. But the idiom is basically, you have no filter or are overly honest."

"You are most certainly that." Scott laughs.

I grab Matt's drink, taking a long pull. I lean against him in the chair, letting my head fall back against his chest. His body keeps me warm from the coolness in the air.

"How was your friend?" he asks, playing with a piece of my hair.

"She was great, I'm so glad I got the chance to see her."

"Well, so am I," Scott chimes in, "But Matty was pouting like a lovesick puppy the entire time you were gone. What have you done to him?"

I turn to look at Matt, and he gives me a casual shrug.

"I'm back. I told you I'd be," I say quietly, planting a kiss on his jawline. He wraps his arms tightly around me.

Chapter Eighteen

After dinner and several more rounds of drinks around the firepit, we stumble up to bed. Matt is officially drunk, and I am delighted to see he is a very, very, happy one. He's laughing as he face-plants on our mattress, fully clothed. I kneel at the bottom of the bed, working to get his boots off.

"Why are you wearing these boots? We. Are. At. The. Beach," I say with each tug.

"Because they're my *thing*," he slurs back.

"Well, maybe your *thing* can be taking them off before you down a bottle of scotch with Scott, okay, buddy?" I laugh, finally ripping them off and tossing them onto the floor. I climb up onto his back, kissing his cheek, trying to rouse him from his drunkenness. He rolls over quickly, somehow managing to keep me on top of him and straddling him. He's surprisingly nimble given his current blood alcohol level.

"Are you mad at me?" he asks, his eyes straining to focus.

"About your boots? Yes, furious." I bend down to kiss him. He tastes earthy. Like the scotch and the smoke from the firepit.

"No ... about me not wanting you to see your friend. Not wanting you to leave."

"I didn't realize you didn't want me to see her. No, I'm not mad. But why did that upset you?"

"Because!" He is exasperated. "I really like you. And I think you really like me, too. But how? It seems too quick. But who cares? Maybe I do? I don't know. But I think I'm falling in love with you. And I'm not just saying this because of the scotch. But I'm falling in a way completely new to me. It's like free-falling.

"And this brain of mine goes haywire," he goes on. "Sometimes I feel like I was born missing a layer of skin—or cells, or fascia—or something everyone else seems to have. And because of that I can pick up on things and feel things way more intensely than everyone else. It's too damn hard to go through life like that. So, a while ago, I managed to build up some protective armor. Made my own skin. Impenetrable. I could keep everything and everyone out unless I decided they were allowed in... or so I thought. Something like that. But *you*, Julia Anderson, have penetrated it all. And I am glad about it, for sure. But now I feel totally fucking exposed. Defenseless, really. And I don't like it. And I don't know what to do. Except tell you about it. So *that* is why I want to know if you're mad at me." His eyes start to close.

I feel myself sober at his drunken confession. "Matt. Open your eyes." I grab his face gently between my hands. "Listen to me. I am not mad at you. I will tell you when I am, you won't have to guess or read my mind. That is not the type of relationship we have or ever will have."

"Okay, whew. That's a relief," he says with a sleepy smile.

"I'm not done." He opens his eyes again, barely. "I do really like you. You are not wrong about that. And I think your vulnerability and honesty—tonight and always—might be my favorite thing about you." He blinks up at me, fighting to keep his eyes open.

"Kiss me." Hr mumbles.

I do, briefly but adoringly, before his eyes close one last time and his breathing slows and then deepens. I tuck the duvet over him, before I curl up beside him, still fully clothed, and fall into a drunken slumber.

* * *

"Wake up, beautiful people! The sun is up, the birds are chirping, there's not a cloud in the sky. It is time to seize the day!" I hear Scott singsong from the hallway.

Sunlight blares into the room; apparently, we forgot to close the blinds. A dull ache throbs behind my eyes, and my mouth is so dry I can hardly swallow. I glance at the clock—it's only seven a.m. What the hell?

Matt pulls a pillow over his head before moaning, "Whyyy? Why the scotch? Why? Why? Why? That was not necessary. *Fuck you, Scotty!*"

I drag my body, which feels like it weighs six hundred pounds, to the bathroom to thoroughly brush my teeth. I splash cold water on my face and swipe on some deodorant, feeling about ten percent better. I close all the blinds and curtains, fill a glass with tap water, and chug it before refilling it and walking it to Matt's side of the bed. I take the pillow off his head and hand the glass to him.

"I'm in bad shape, babe." His eyes are still closed.

"Babe?" I arch an eyebrow at him.

He cracks one eye open to look at me. "Just trying it on for size."

"I like it. Babe."

He smiles. "That makes me feel a modicum better. But seriously, Jules. I don't think I can get out of this bed right now."

"You sleep. I'll find provisions." I give him a quick kiss before putting the pillow back on top of his head.

I mosey downstairs, where I find Scott whistling—actually whistling—in the kitchen as he makes a green smoothie.

"How are you so chipper?"

"Luck—and liver—of the Irish." He smiles. "Want some?"

"No thanks, but I will take some coffee. And Excedrin, if you have it."

"You know, Jules," Scott says as he rummages through the cabinets, "Matty has never brought a lady here. It feels ... momentous."

"Yeah, he mentioned that."

"Don't go breaking his heart," he sings, handing me the medicine and a coffee mug.

"I couldn't if I tried," I say back. Scott laughs.

I sit down at the counter and wince when Scott turns on the blender. My head. "I really don't plan on it, Scott. This thing between us is still fairly new."

"Oh, I know, I know. He filled me in on the whole how-we-met story. But new or not, it seems substantial, no?"

"I think so?"

"I'm going for a beach walk in thirty minutes. Based on my two-plus decades of experience with Matt Johnson scotch hangovers, I say we have until noonish till he's moving. Care to join me?"

"Sure, I'd like that."

* * *

I make two coffees, leaving mine on the counter, and head upstairs with a mug for Matt along with a giant ice-cold water, Excedrin, and a piece of peanut butter toast. I quietly place the items on his nightstand and change into leggings and a T-shirt before grabbing Matt's sweatshirt off the chair in the corner. He doesn't budge.

Scott is somehow even more energetic than before as we head out the back door toward the dunes. The air is fresh and clean, tinged with salt, and I can feel the harsh edges of my hangover begin to soften.

"Where's Natasha?"

"Oh, she goes to Pilates every Sunday morning."

"After the gallon of rosé she and I drank last night? You two are machines."

"Lots of practice." He smiles.

We start walking, and I ask Scott the usual questions. He tells me how he found his way into the entertainment industry, working as an intern in the summer between college semesters, then talks about his love story with Natasha and, of course, how he met Matt.

"He is probably the most genuine person I know. Those are hard to come by in the industry we're in."

I nod.

"He seems very calm around you."

"I feel calm around him, too."

"It's been a long time since he's dated someone. I'm not going to do the whole overprotective-friend spiel, but know that I am. Same with Nat. We were there for the absolute dumpster fire of Jackie Myers and vowed never to let something like that happen again on our watch." He cringes.

"Yeah, he mentioned the mark that left on him."

Scott lets out a woosh of air. "I will never get over it. I've made it my life's mission to avoid her. Which isn't easy in the world in which I work. I have nothing nice to say."

"What happened?" My curiosity gets the best of me.

"The better question is probably what *didn't* happen. Everything that could've gone wrong, went wrong. But Matty was in so deep. God, it was brutal to watch." He shakes his head.

"We'd only been friends for a few years at that point, but I'd been in the business a little bit longer, and I'm a little older, too, though I know it's tough to tell," he says with a wink.

"I thought I had more experience dealing with people like her. But nothing could've prepared either of us for Jackie Myers. She was like the Mount Vesuvius of people. My personal opinion is that she gets off on psychological torture and ruining men. Just Google her track record. But at the time, Matt was so young. Man, he was young. He was still reeling from all the stuff happening back home, Eric and his mom, and figuring that out. But he'd also just broken out of Allentown and was a *hot* commodity in the music world. His first album was so strong, so good, it had Grammy nominations written all over it. Record labels were foaming at the mouth—they all wanted him. And Jackie caught the scent and decided she did, too. Poor Matty didn't stand a chance. She was—and is—incredibly charming. Breathtakingly beautiful, in an evil kind of way. She got her claws in him, and it was a miserable few years."

We pass a pair of joggers. Scott nods hello, and we keep walking.

"The breakups and make-ups were so constant, I stopped asking and he stopped telling. He went inside himself, which made it all that much worse. Jackie's husband, ex-husband, whatever, was hell-bent on destroying Matt for making him look dumb. Like the guy didn't know what he was getting himself into—he was her third husband. The whole thing was insanity. Once Matt freed himself from her clutches, it was another slow trudge to repair the damage. He wasn't in a great place. Which was the saddest part to me, because he was absolutely killing it in the music world. His first three albums all went multiplatinum—almost unheard of. But his personal life was a mess. Anyway, he figured it out. And though he's always been a little leery, a little guarded about love since then, he is still somehow eternally optimistic. It's quite a dichotomy."

I'm shocked. I try to picture a young Matt, even more sensitive and so talented, getting swept up by someone with the charisma and celebrity and beauty of Jackie. It's hard for me to relate that person to the person I know, who seems so self-assured.

"Anyway, that's ancient history now. And not that I'm comparing, but you couldn't be more different from her. Not just her, but some of the other girls he's dated. You guys seem great together. It warms my cold, dead heart."

I laugh at that. "Thank you."

"You're exactly the type of person I told him he'd end up with. Like, years ago. I called it. I told him he needed someone *not* in the industry. Someone normal. Someone who was smarter than him, someone who was funny, someone who could keep him grounded and get him out of his head. He spends too much time in his head."

"You think?"

"You haven't noticed?" He seems surprised.

"No, I mean I know he's very thoughtful and contemplative, but he doesn't usually seem that way when I'm with him."

Scott looks at me with a knowing smile. "Well then, that says it all, doesn't it?"

By the time we walk back to the house, Matt has emerged from bed. He looks worse for wear but rallies for a late lunch before we head back to the city. I'm sad to see the weekend come to an end. It's been so fun, so relaxing, and I've gained so many insights. I love that I had the chance to see him with his closest friends. It brought out a different side of him that I like just as much as all the others I've seen. It feels significant that not only has he brought me into his close circle, but that it feels so natural for me to be there.

I insist on driving back into the city so Matt can nurse the remaining dregs of his hangover. He's reclined in the passenger seat looking at his phone when I hear him softly say, "Shit."

"What?"

"Nothing."

"Okay..." I say. "Tell me."

"It's nothing. Someone sent something in to one of those social media gossip sites."

"Sent what?"

He takes a long pause and reaches for my hand.

"A photo. Of you."

My pulse quickens. "What do you mean?"

"I don't want you to worry. It's vague and dumb. It doesn't identify you by name, and you can hardly make out any of your features besides your clothes. And it means nothing in the grand scheme of things. Nothing but a blip that will wash out of the news cycle by tomorrow morning when the collective ADHD of the Internet moves on to something else."

"That's not making me feel better."

"You're walking on the beach with Scott. The picture is from very far away and it's blurry—clearly, someone took it on their phone, but you can see your gray sweatshirt says *Northeast*. And it looks very similar to the sweatshirt I was wearing in the photograph they got of me leaving the coffee shop in town earlier in the weekend ... also with Scott."

"It looks similar because it *is* your sweatshirt, Matt!" I panic.

"It's one picture and an extremely dubious caption saying something about you as a potential 'love interest' because of it. There are a thousand of those sweatshirts."

"Can I see?"

He holds out his phone, and I glance between it and the road, taking in the photo and the caption, all as he described. Despite his reassurance, I still feel unnerved that someone took this photo without me knowing.

"What do we do?"

"Nothing, babe. We ignore it and keep on keeping on. It's fine. I promise." He squeezes my hand.

I believe him.

Chapter Nineteen

Matt's last stop on his tour before the break is at Merriweather Post Pavilion outside of Baltimore. My hometown. I can't think of a better place to see him perform live for the first time than in the same arena where I saw my first concert: The Chicks in the early nineties. The same place where my friends and I sneaked beers from the beverage carts and sprawled out on the lawn, singing with Dave Matthews Band, Jack Johnson, John Mayer, and Counting Crows at the top of our lungs in the hot and muggy summer nights.

Despite our relationship feeling more and more substantial, I still haven't shared with anyone that I'm dating Matt, besides a few trusted coworkers who watched the entire thing unfold and, of course, Meredith.

I still consider our relationship need-to-know information because I don't want this cocoon we've built to be subject to scrutiny, especially after the little scare we had in the Hamptons. That, plus the potential blowback if anything gets out in the press before Matt is ready. He's only recently opened up about his precarious history with the media. It's a complex relationship that is both needed and dreaded. After hearing his stories, I understand why. One night over sushi in my living room, he filled me in on the whole sordid history and the moments that still haunt him.

"Once I started dating Jackie, it was open season," he told me. "They sat outside my house for weeks and months just trying to get a glimpse of anyone who came and went. My housekeeper came to the door in tears several days in a row after some of the paparazzi screamed things at her about her kids and where she lives to rattle information out of her about who I was dating. I had to meet her at her car every day to make sure she got inside safely.

"My buddy's wife rode in the trunk of his car to avoid being photographed and considered a 'love interest' of mine. There were no rules, especially back then. It is not normal behavior. Not even close to normal. It can make you feel insane," he said, shaking his head.

"There was a lot of deception in those early years, and I had no clue." He still gets worked up even all these years later. "These journalists would take me, this young, dumb kid from this little town, whose eyes were as wide as saucers that this was actually my life now —they'd take me to the fanciest restaurants, the hottest spots, SoHo Houses, the Ritz, nightclubs, the Beverly Hills Hotel, front row at the Knicks games, all these places I would've never in my wildest dreams imagined I'd be. I'd sit there, and a parade of beautiful women would walk by, women who never would've looked twice at me two years before. They'd order drinks, top shelf this and that. Only the best food. *Matt, anything you want. You got it.* They'd get me real cozy, like we're friends, and my guard came down, if it was even up to begin with. And I'd do what I do best: I'd talk. And talk. And fucking talk. And try to be funny and witty, to be clever and charming. To say the things they wanted to hear. And ultimately to win them over, like I'd had to do repeatedly with these types of people for years as I tried to get into the industry. And then again as I tried to carve out my place in the industry. I trusted them. They're supposed to be professionals, right?

"These writers are backed by these huge institutions, and I

naïvely thought there would be some collaboration, like *hey, this is the direction we're going for with this article*, some type of heads-up. Not like *hey, let's exploit all the worst parts about you and your most traumatic relationship*. Or at the very least, a little humanistic approach, maybe just acknowledging that I'm a real person with feelings and a life, not just ad revenue. Right? Wrong. I was so wrong. And then an article comes out, and then another, and another. Next thing I know I'm getting calls from my publicist telling me that I'm the biggest fucking idiot on the face of the planet and I need to fix it immediately. So, then I go into the next few interviews intent on course-correcting the previous discrepancies. And it all backfires. Remember how I told you I compounded the problem?"

I nodded.

"Yeah. I did. Quite beautifully. I just started rambling, trying to overexplain myself, which is never a good thing to do with a potential adversary. It was not good. And after that, it was a feeding frenzy. People could smell blood in the water, and I was the chum. So, I got another call from my publicist telling me that my career was—in no uncertain terms—over. Dead. Never to be revived. And that I only had myself to blame.

"It took me weeks before I could stomach opening a computer. I was terrified at what I'd see. Remember, this was the height of tabloids, gossip blogs, sensationalized headlines. They were everywhere. These piecemeal articles, parts of conversations completely out of context. It painted a picture of me as this real piece of shit—an entitled, misogynistic asshole, completely undeserving of all my success. And of course, it was sprinkled with all the darkest parts of my relationship with Jackie— quotes from her, quotes from me, pictures of us, a timeline of our relationship.

"And to be fair, there was certainly truth in all of it, but only in shades. I was arrogant and uncouth and testing the limits of shock value. I'm not proud of how I handled a lot of things back then. But the general outcome was almost irrevocable. They basically said that no one should listen to my music, no one should bother to work with me, ever. And that no one should *ever* let their daughter within one hundred feet of me." He paused and stared at the floor.

"Feeling misunderstood is something I've been dealing with my entire life. I can mostly handle it, though it doesn't feel great. But to feel like the entire world not only misunderstood me but hated me— and there wasn't much I could do about it—was too much. I was gutted."

My eyes welled. I couldn't imagine how anyone who spent more than ten minutes with Matt could ever misunderstand his intentions, his character, the core of him.

"That was around when I started therapy for the first and only time. It was immensely helpful. The tools I learned there got me through that time. But it was touch and go for a while. I moved back to Allentown with my dad for nine months to decide if I even wanted to try again. Which I did, clearly. But it took a while to rebuild the armor enough to get back out there." He'd laid back on the couch, deflated.

This entire saga, the months and years of fallout that it created, was part of the reason, he explained, that he instituted a "say nothing" policy over the past several years.

"I looked at other people who had long careers in music. Granted, most of them were before social media, before smartphones, so it was just less opportunity to say something dumb or fuck up and have people find out about it, so I didn't have much guidance. But those artists, like the greats, they never said anything unless it was about the music. Nothing ever about their personal lives. I also looked at other public figures in general who had long careers in their fields. Like the royal family. Sure, they get bad press, but the Queen had a saying, "never complain, never explain," and that stuck with me. If I don't say anything, my words can't get twisted. And I never have to find myself in that position again. I get to keep doing what I love, which is making music, and I don't have to deal with the other bullshit."

"But it sounds like you've learned a lot of powerful lessons from those experiences. If it happened again, you'd be way better equipped to handle it. You were basically a kid, thrust into the industry without so much as a cautionary tale," I pointed out.

"I *am* the cautionary tale," he said with a sad smile.

Admittedly, after that conversation, I spent an evening Googling old articles and guessing which ones he had been referencing. In some interviews he gave in his early years, he came off as a little obnoxious and cocky. Some didn't even make sense to me in the context of what the interview was supposed to be about—his music.

I shut my laptop before I could go too far down the rabbit hole. I couldn't reconcile the person I knew from the person I was reading about. And I could see how damaging it would be to only have a small facet of your life, a static moment in time, captured in print. I wondered what it would be like for me to have my every misstep documented on the Internet for all time. What a complete nightmare.

In the few months we've been together, I've watched him navigate the press and the publicity firsthand. He is an expert, no doubt, at evading them, and if he's ever gotten caught in the crosshairs unexpectedly, he never looked it. He knows which spots where they'll likely be and avoids them. He makes sure to build relationships with the owners of restaurants, stores, and coffee shops he frequents, who go out of their away to respect and ensure his privacy. He gives interviews sparingly and only with people he has real and long-term friendships with—those he can trust. He stays off the grid of social media almost entirely, with the majority of his posts prescheduled by a publicist, nothing ever in real time. He knows how to keep me safe from lurking eyes. Arriving at and departing from places at different times, rarely together. Using service entrances, even disguises like hats, sunglasses, and COVID masks to obscure our identities. Part of me feels a rush at the game of it, but another part of me feels like he is hiding me.

I joked about it one night.

"Are you kidding me? I am absolutely hiding you. I would never subject you to the mayhem that accompanies me unless absolutely necessary," he said.

I appreciate the protective instincts but wonder what that means about us in the future. What constitutes *necessary*? At some point, if we continued dating, someone will have to know. How will he react? Moreover, how will I react? I dodge pictures in the very average circumstances of my very normal life. HR had to track me down for two months to get an updated headshot for the hospital directory.

When I was a kid, my mom frequently told me, "Stop looking like you're scared!" any time she took a picture of me. I've never felt like I look quite like *me* in photos. Matt, on the other hand, is living and moving art. Candid photos of him walking, getting in and out of cars, and conducting his daily business look straight out of a magazine.

"Do you practice your angles and poses while you're on a tread-mill or something?" I asked him while I brushed my teeth. He was in nothing but a pair of boxer briefs, lounging in my bed. I stood at the doorway. "Seriously, though, how do you never have a wonky eye, or like three chins in any pictures like most people? Like me?"

He laughed. "No, I don't practice, but I've done enough photo shoots with exceptional people to know what works for me and what doesn't. And for the record, you only have three chins when you make that ridiculous face. See, I can do it, too." He shoved his chin back and down, revealing his own triple chin.

I finished brushing and walked over to him, kissing each one of his chins. "Well, somehow they still look sexy on you."

* * *

I invite Meg to be my plus one for Matt's show in Maryland. I tell her I got tickets from some exec at the hospital and want to relive some of our youth. She replies to my text.

YESSSSS. 100% I am in, and I cannot wait followed by, Did we ever see a Matt Johnson concert when we were in high school?? Drawing a blank on him, but he could've been lumped in all those shows we went to half blacked-out the summer before college.

Hmm, sounds familiar. Maybe?

I've known Meg since the third grade, when we were both trying out for the travel field hockey team in Towson. Meg is fiercely competitive, an incredible athlete, and an even better friend. We've seen each other through all phases of life and relied on each other during tough times like my parents' divorce, her dad's battle with colon cancer, puberty, a dozen heartbreaks, and everything in between.

She was the only person in my life to caution me about Nick— after all, she was there from the moment we met. She shared her warning shortly after I moved to New York, when I was back in Baltimore visiting for a weekend. The two of us were sitting outside at Ryleigh's in Federal Hill on our third round of orange crushes when she said out of the blue, "I'm just not sure Nick is the person for you, Jules." When I pressed her on it, she said, "I can't think of anything specific. It's just a feeling. He's just ... not it." I was shocked and a little hurt. We never spoke of it again after that night, and she dutifully stood by my side as maid of honor at my wedding.

To her credit, she did not mention it at all when I finally told her we were getting divorced. Instead, she and Meredith schemed up ways to torture Nick, mostly to make me laugh, and they also alternated making plans to ensure someone laid eyes on me at least every few weeks. "Welfare checks," they joked.

I pick her up and we drive to the venue, parking in the VIP lot. "It came with the tickets," I explain. Once inside, we are ushered to our front section seats by Matt's personal security.

"Also came with the tickets," I say.

Meg looks at me sideways. "Okay, Ms. Big-Hospital-Donor-VIP-Tickets. I'm very happy to ride on your coattails." We sit down as the opening band warms up. "This is a slightly better view than our usual lawn seats." She turns around and cranes her neck toward the slowly filling back lawn.

"I'm pretty sure I lost a bra and most of my dignity somewhere back there in the summer of 2000." She points.

I laugh. "You and me both."

Out of nowhere, someone brings us tequila sodas with extra limes. The guy delivering the drinks says, "This is called the Sorority Girl—compliments of the band." I smile, and my cheeks flush.

"What the hell does that mean?" Meg asks.

I shrug.

"Whatever, I'll take it. Damn, Jules, this is first class all the way. Class, class, class! I am here for it."

We spend the next hour and most of the opening band's set catching up on life. It's been a few months since we've last seen each other, and since then, Meg, her husband, John, and two-year old Piper have moved out of our hometown to a suburb a little north of Baltimore called Lutherville-Timonium.

"Better schools, bigger yard, yadda yadda," Meg says. "But tell me about your life. I'm married with a kid and bored out of my fucking gourd. Any dating? Better yet, any steamy sex?"

My face burns. Here is one of my oldest, best friends, and I'm holding back. I'm not ready yet.

"A few guys here in there. You know, New York. Full of Peter Pans and finance guys who have a lot of money in their bank accounts and are eager to tell you about it." I try to deflect.

"Seriously, Jules? Don't hold out on me, you know I live for this. No sex, nothing?"

Weighing my options, I decide to tell her about the mediocre one night stand I had with a minor league baseball player named Dean after the ink was barely dry on my divorce papers. My coworker, Beth, set me up with him after losing patience with me and my endless moping. She insisted, "The only way to get over someone is to get under someone new." And while I found this to be both crass and untrue, I was too dejected to argue with her.

Dean was perhaps one of the most attractive people I'd ever laid eyes on; he was truly incendiary. But fifteen minutes into our date, I realized he was about as sharp as a spoon, and the conversation I had to pull out of him was so dull and uninteresting, it was downright painful. I decided to cut my losses and suggested we go back to his hotel room, where he couldn't talk and I could enjoy his chiseled six foot six body. It was fun, but the lack connection made it barely memorable. Especially in light of the chemistry I have with Matt that penetrates to a molecular level.

"Ohhhhh my God, Dean sounds dreamy." Meg swoons. "What's his last name?" She pulls out her phone, ready to Google a picture of him, right as the lights dim and Matt steps out onto the stage.

"Shhhh, I'll show you a pic of the minor leaguer later, the show is starting."

Matt saunters around the stage, the lights turn on, and he strums the first chord of the show. As his hand drives down over the guitar, the hair on my arms stands up. I realize that besides the private concert I saw in his apartment without him knowing, I have never seen him do his craft in person. He knows it, too.

Several songs in, Meg looks at me.

"Holy. Shit," she says.

I agree. I could not have prepared myself for what it would be like to watch him perform up close like this. He is completely captivating. Mind-blowing.

"Is he looking at us?" Meg looks to the row behind us. "Why does he keep looking in our direction? Is he looking at the other sections like this? Wait, is he looking at *me*?"

"No, Meg, he is looking at every section the same. He's just really, *really* good at his job."

"Good at his job? I am good at my job. I make Excel spreadsheets.

He is pure, living sex. I am practically sliding out of my seat over here."

I cannot deny the sex oozing out of his every pore as he sings and plays his guitar on the stage. He is so completely consumed by what he's doing, his every fiber seems to be in sync, connected. I've never seen someone so confident, so talented, so dedicated to their obvious God-given gift. His face contorts, his entire body committed, as he strains to hit certain notes or play challenging parts of a song. I am mesmerized. In a trance. I can't tell if it's the heat under the packed pavilion, the tequila, or the idea that every single person in the arena is probably having the same unholy thoughts about Matt as I am—but I'm somehow the lucky one who gets to live them out. Either way, I am completely and utterly intoxicated.

Matt ends his first set and takes a short break. The lights come on, and Meg is fanning herself with her purse.

"Okay, I cannot emphasize this enough. What. The. Fuck. Julia, he is so insanely hot. Who knew? I'd never even thought twice about him, but watching him sing like that? How do his fingers move so fast? He is like sex on a stick. I'm dead serious, I need to go change my panties. How is that even legal for him to be that hot? I feel like I might combust just watching him. Do you think I could get John into a Matt Johnson role play? Honestly, he fucking better because I will be dining out on the memory of that man for a long, long time, my friend." She babbles on, and I can't stand leaving her in the dark anymore, especially hearing her gush.

"Meg, I'm going to tell you something, and you have to swear you will not say a word."

She turns to me, eyes gleaming in anticipation of a juicy secret. "Like the time we crashed your mom's car when she was out of town and blamed it on gale force winds? Or the time I made out with the substitute teacher after finals week?"

"No, Meg, like the time we saw your mom with the neighbor while your dad was on a work trip—like a *could do harm if discovered, no telling a single soul* type of secret."

The seriousness lands, and Meg straightens up. "I swear."

"I have been seeing Matt for the past few months." Her eyes search my face. Nothing registers.

"Matt? Matt who...?"

The recognition hits her like a bolt of lightning. She jabs her finger toward the stage.

"That Matt? The guy who I just told you made me *literally slide out of my seat?* You are dating *him?"*

"*Shhhhhh!* Keep your voice down!"

She covers her mouth with her hands, eyes bugging out of her head. "I know now is not the time, but very soon, I am going to need every. Last. Detail. Don't you dare gatekeep."

I smile. "Okay, I'll tell you, but after the show I'm going to hang back and see him, so are you okay getting an Uber home?"

"Honey, I would be happy walking home if it means I get to hear a little snippet of what might be happening with you and him behind that stage." I laugh hard and hug my friend. Matt walks back out to thunderous applause and starts his second act.

Somewhere in the middle, Meg leans in and whispers, "Is he kind to you?"

"Very," I answer with no hesitation.

A small smile appears on her lips, and she nods. We spend the rest of the show swaying back and forth together, exchanging wide-eyed glances of shock that this is indeed my life.

* * *

The show winds down, and before the last song, I hug Meg goodbye and walk toward the side of the stage. I see one of Matt's familiar security guards, Marcus, as I approach. He is intimidating, for sure, but as I get closer his face breaks into a wide smile, and I see the kindness there. "Well, well, well, little Miss Julia, I was wondering when you were going to make it to one of our boy's shows."

"He was incredible."

"Always is, baby girl."

I hug him, and he leads me backstage to the dressing room. I see all of Matt's things that have become familiar to me in the past few months. His boots are lined up neatly against the far wall, same for his guitars. A giant two-liter bottle of alkaline water and a half-drunk hot tea sit scattered on a coffee table beside a notebook. Several drafts of set lists are scratched out and rewritten. I walk over to the mirror and see his comb, his cologne that I love so much, and his toothbrush in its LED light antibacterial case. I smile at all of it. *This guy.*

I'm sitting in a chair when he comes off stage and bursts through the door. His eyes are energized, his cheeks rosy. Sweat glistens on his skin. He is completely irresistible. "Babe!" he says with a giant smile. I cross the room and grab his face, planting a big kiss on his lips.

"What did you think?" he asks, picking up a water bottle.

"I think you are spectacular. You have a gift. I was blown away." I help him peel his sweaty shirt off. "And it makes me even more attracted to you. Which I didn't think was possible."

"How attracted?"

"Hmm ... apparently the limit does not exist." I step back and strip off my top as I walk over to a dressing chair in front of a mirror, the bright lights, the waist-high countertop.

"What do you think you're doing?" he asks coyly.

"What does it look like I'm doing?"

He tosses his water on the couch and crosses the room in two long strides, grabbing my tits in his hands.

"God, you are so fucking hot," he says through gritted teeth. "But I'm all sweaty."

I smile and kiss his salty lips and neck. "I don't care."

I laugh and unbuckle his belt, yanking his jeans and boxers down. What a cliché this is—but I don't care.

In a minute, we're both naked, pants at our ankles, standing in front of the dressing room mirror. He kisses me, and it's full of want bordering on need.

"Bend over," he demands aggressively before grabbing my ass so hard I yelp. The fact that this sometimes reserved, incredibly sensi-tive, brilliant, thoughtful man is bossing me around is so titillating I almost come.

"Say please," I demand.

"Please." He bites my lip. Hard. I smile into his mouth. I love this.

Next thing I know, I'm hinged at the waist, my cheek pressed against the cool marble of the countertop. I hear the crinkle of a condom wrapper—where it came from, I do not know. Or care. I cry out as he enters me, slamming all the way in with one swift motion. He fills me, stretching me, right to the brink of pain and pleasure. I lie there as he builds up a rhythm, listening to our skin slapping together and to the crowd out beyond the stage somewhere, collecting their things, heading home. Completely unaware the man they just spent two hours watching is fucking his girlfriend a few hundred yards away.

He grabs me by the root of my hair and yanks my head up so I can look at him in the mirror. His eyes are feverish and locked on mine. It is so intimate, so intense, like watching our very own live sex tape. He lets out a sharp exhale. "Fuck, fuck, Jules, I don't want to come yet."

I turn to look at him with a devilish smile. "But I want you to."

And he does, almost instantaneously.

I feel him jerk inside of me, coming hard, and I take his hand in mine and lead him to the place where we are connected, where he fills me, where I am dripping wet. I use his hand as if it were my own, and with only a few touches I am coming, too, rippling around him, gasping into the counter.

We stay like that, him collapsed on top of me, me collapsed on top of the counter, for several minutes. He carefully pulls himself out of me. I feel stunned, frozen in place from the rush of ecstasy and adrenaline. I watch him in the mirror as he duck-walks over to the trash can to dispose of the condom and then pulls up his jeans and fastens them. Then I see his hands on my ankles, gently tugging my panties back up. His touch is so tender, so loving, as he traverses my legs, my ass, my hips. He bends back over and repeats the same process with my jeans.

I stand up and catch a glimpse of my reflection in the mirror. My hair is wild, my eyes bright and more hazel than brown, my face flushed and completed sated.

I look so *alive*.

And behind me stands Matt, the man who makes me feel this way. I turn toward him, and he wraps me in his substantial arms, now so familiar to me, so comforting. He kisses the top of my head as I hold on to his waist. We stay there in silence, until eventually Matt says with a laugh, "So, we are going to need to get you to more shows."

I smile into his chest. I take a moment to notice what I feel. All I can think is ... *happy*.

Chapter Twenty

I'm walking down First Avenue on my lunch break when I see an incoming call from my mom.

"Hey, Mom."

"Hey, hon! Too busy to call your mother? How are you, what's new?"

"Same old same. Just working on a big project. Coaching. Murphy, the usual."

"Any dates? You know I worry about you being alone."

"I know, Mom, and I'm fine. You do realize you spent most of my life drilling into me that I don't need a man and shouldn't depend on one, ever? And now that I'm not, you're worried that I don't have a man? What am I supposed to do with that?"

"Oh, I don't know, you never listen to me about anything else, so who knew you'd listen with that? Is it too much for a mom to want grandbabies?"

"No, but you have another child who can help you make that dream come true. Stop putting all the pressure on me!"

"Who, your brother? I'll be lucky if he settles down before I'm in a home somewhere."

"Okay, okay." I drop it. "What's going on with you? How's the pickleball league going?"

I listen to all the inner workings of her newest hobby, including her opinion on every player in her senior pickleball league at her local YMCA. She's only recently retired after working for thirty years at various state-level civil service jobs. I had my reservations about her stopping work, as it was always a huge source of connection, stimulation, and satisfaction for her. But she proved me wrong and now seems busier than ever between her new sports, interests, and dozens of friends.

"The reason I'm calling is Thanksgiving. What are we doing? Are you working? Or coming here? Am I coming there? I cannot get your brother to text me back. Do me a favor and call him. I have had several invitations from my gal pals for Turkey Day. Betty invited me to join her at Baltimore Country Club, and you know how much I love it there. Their mashed potatoes are to die for. So, talk to your brother and let me know the plan. Gotta run, love you, hon."

She clicks off before I can respond.

Matt's midtour break is coming up, and he's asked me—several times—if I'll join him in Mexico. I've been noncommittal because the trip coincides with both Matt's forty-third birthday and Thanksgiving. I want nothing more than to spend five consecutive days with him in the sun, no work, no other obligations, but I feel guilty at the thought of being away from my mom. We've always done our best to be together for holidays. I scroll through my phone to find Ryan's number and am shocked when he picks up my call.

"Ry, can you move back East yet?" I ask.

"You sound like Mom. What's up, Jules?"

"Nothing, just strolling down First Avenue. The air is crisp, everyone is drinking hot coffees, the beginning of coat weather is here, and you know New York is only going to get even better as Christmas nears...."

"I've been enjoying that same crispness for the past six weeks, but without the smell of hot garbage lining the streets. I'm staring out my office window, and all the trees are changing. I'm going up to the mountains this weekend to try out a new trailhead with some friends, and there's a brewery on the way. So, I think I'm good. Can you see any trees? Or just gridlocked traffic, people in a rush, and a wall of skyscrapers?"

I sigh. We go back and forth about this often. Ryan has made it clear he has no intention of ever leaving the Centennial State.

"Fine. Fine. You win. But I'm calling because I need some rein-forcement—Mom is trying to lock down holiday plans. She has an offer to go to BCC with Betty. What are you thinking?"

"I haven't even thought about it." *Shocker.*

"Well, let's figure it out, because I have plans but don't want to leave her by herself."

"What kind of plans?"

"A trip to Mexico."

"With whom?"

"A friend."

"Meredith?"

"No, not Meredith."

"Meg? Jenny?"

"No, none of them. They all have husbands and families."

"Then who, Jules?"

Silence.

"A *guy?*"

"Maybe."

"If you want an assist from me with Mom, you'd better start talking."

"Fine. I've been seeing someone for a few months. We met at work. He's funny, smart, and sweet. He's invited me to come to Mexico with him for the week of Thanksgiving, which is also his birthday. I want to go." It feels nice to admit it out loud.

"Okay, well, what's his deal? Where does he live? What does he do for a living?"

"He lives in New York, partly. He's a musician."

Silence.

"Does he have a job?"

"Yes, don't be rude. He has a fantastic job."

"Okay, what's his name?"

"Matt."

"Matt who? Come on, Jules."

"Matt Johnson."

Pause.

A longer pause.

"Are you serious?"

"Yes."

"Like the famous musician?"

"Yes."

"Don't you remember when I tried to teach myself guitar? To his songs?"

I did not remember that at all.

"Well, okay ... is this like a thing?" he asks.

"What do you mean?"

"Like, is this legit? Do people know about this?"

"If you mean legit, like are we dating exclusively, then yes. And no one knows about it besides a few coworkers, Meg, Meredith, and some of his close friends. And now you. Mom does not know, and I'd like to keep it that way. For now, at least. I like him. A lot."

"Okay, okay. I'll invite her here for Thanksgiving. She'll probably say no, especially if Baltimore Country Club is on the table. She loves that place. But this way we can both absolve ourselves of any guilt."

"Thank you." I'm relieved.

"But what are you going to do about Christmas?" Ryan asks. Shit, I haven't even thought that far ahead. My favorite holiday. I don't know what Matt's plans are or if we will spend it together. It seems like a big step.

"I don't know yet, I'll get back to you on that."

"Okay, sounds like a plan."

"Thanks, Ry."

"Of course. And Jules, one last thing."

"Yeah?"

"Does he treat you well?"

My eyes prick with tears at this question. I don't forget that Meg had basically just asked me the same thing. It is both validating and immensely sad to be reminded that the people I love know how brutal things have been. Nick was never unkind to me in all our time together until the end. That, perhaps, was the most jarring element of it all. It wasn't just that he revealed a part of himself I didn't even know existed—a cold, disengaged, indifferent version—it's that he weaponized it.

"Yes," I answer.

"Does he prioritize you?"

"Yes. He does," I say, with zero hesitation.

He pauses.

"Then he's okay in my book."

Chapter Twenty-One

Back at the hospital, I have an unexpected visitor waiting for me at my door—Chip Barrington, the hospital COO. My skin crawls at the sight of him.

"Anderson. Taking a long lunch, I see."

"Not quite, Chip. In fact, most of the nurses on this floor and I average about one lunch break a week, thanks to the insane patient volume and not enough staff. How's that new budget looking?"

"Looking the same as it did last month and the month before that."

Sounds about right. "What can I do for you?"

"Aren't you going to invite me in?"

I fight the urge to roll my eyes and unlock my office door. "Sure, come on in."

He sits on the couch and kicks his feet up on the coffee table, looking around the room. "Nice spot you've got here, Anderson."

"Thanks. I've got a pretty busy afternoon, so how can I help you?" I have zero patience for this man.

"The pediatric psych ED. We need it. The projected revenue

could float other parts of the hospital. Maybe dig us out of this hole we're in. We need it to work, and we need it done fast."

"Okay ..."

"The hospital needs a show of good faith before they'll cough up any money. There are several grants available for this type of endeavor. If we can get at least three of the big ones, they'll give us permission—and more importantly, money—to do the bulk of the work. We'll have to figure the rest out later. But it's a start. And I'm tapping you to do it."

"Do what? The grant proposal?"

"Yes."

"I have no experience with grant writing. It's completely out of my wheelhouse. Don't we have someone who does this somewhere in the hospital?"

"Not anyone who is available. Plus, you know the language, the need, the scope of the unit."

"Okay. I'll do it. It'll take me some time to figure it out, but I'll get it done."

"Well, that's the other part."

I stare at him.

"The proposals are due December first."

"That's in less than three weeks. It's also Thanksgiving." And Matt's birthday, and Mexico, I add silently in my head.

"I know. I figured it shouldn't be too hard for you to squeeze in. You spend so much time here anyway, and there's no partner or kids to steal your attention away," he says, smiling, looking at his fingernails. I fight the urge to smack the smug look right off his face.

"Thanks for your consideration. And my personal life remains none of your business, Chip," I say with a saccharine smile. "I'll get the grant done." I get up and open the door. "If there's nothing else, you'll have to excuse me. I have work to do."

"Happy Thanksgiving, Anderson."

Prick.

Chapter Twenty-Two

I work around the clock on the grant proposal—half my time is spent researching how to even write a grant proposal. The more I realize how complex it is, the more my blood boils that Chip dropped this in my lap at the last minute. I refuse to be defeated by that asshat. I refuse even more to let it ruin my trip with Matt, which is officially happening. So, in addition to bikinis, sundresses, and hats, I fill my suitcase with books, notepads, and my laptop.

My plane touches down in Cancun around eleven p.m. By the time Marcus picks me up from the airport and drives me to the villa, it is well past midnight. I can feel the anticipation of seeing Matt build in my chest as I walk up the dimly lit stone stairs. It's been over three weeks since we saw each other at his show in Maryland, but it feels like much longer.

The villa looks like it's been carved into the side of a hill, all natural materials, stone, dark wood, and greenery. Marcus hands me a key, and I let myself in. I thank him and walk into the room, taking in the cavernous ceilings and woven jute carpets. The focal point is a massive four-poster bed of raw wood draped in white mosquito nets in the middle of the room. I see Matt's guitars, amps, and other equipment leaning against the couch in a small seating area to the left. A tiny half kitchen is off to the right.

"Matt?"

The entire back of the room opens to the outside. The doors are thrown open, and the gauzy white curtains billow in the warm breeze coming off the ocean. I walk toward the door, my body filling with a familiar electrical current. I smell the tangy smoke from a joint, mixed with coconut sunscreen and the salty air. I walk out onto the patio overlooking the beach. The moon is full and bright, casting a creamy glow on the ocean, the beach, the infinity pool before me, and a beautiful man lounging on one of the chaises.

Matt.

He's wearing a short-sleeved floral print shirt, unbuttoned, and linen shorts. His hands are clasped gently behind his head, eyes closed. Somewhere on the patio a slow, sultry song in Spanish seeps out of hidden speakers.

I touch his shoulder. "Matt?"

His eyes fly open, taking me in, and the look in them has such an intensity, a mix of joy and lust and wonder all at once. I wish I could bottle it up.

"You're here." He smiles.

He pulls me down to sit with him on the chaise.

"Long time, no see," I say and grab the heavy glass of tequila sitting next to him. I take a sip while he continues to stare at me, his gaze so piercing I almost look away. He abruptly takes the glass from my hand, places it on the ground, and takes me gently by the jaw, bringing my mouth to his.

"I've missed you," he murmurs. His mouth is ready and waiting, those lips soft and parted. I lean into him, feelings surging through me. Our tongues meet and I taste him, the woody and smoky taste of the tequila, the weed, the coconut sunscreen, all together heady. He pauses and reaches under the chaise to pull out a flower, a single pink dahlia. It is vibrant, the dozens of tiny petals each a slightly different shade of pink.

"For you." He hands it to me.

"It's beautiful. Thank you." I tuck it behind my ear and turn to straddle him on the chair. I can feel him, hard and pressing against me through the linen of his shorts. My hands run down his smooth chest, pushing away the fabric of his shirt. I trace the art on his pecs, run my fingers down the now familiar trail of the tattoos that decorate his arm. I land at his unassumingly soft hands and then his fingers—his gorgeous, long, deft fingers. I have dreamed of these fingers in the weeks we've spent apart. I bring them to my mouth, putting them in, one by one.

I take my time, working my mouth thoroughly up and down each finger, watching him watch me in awe. Then I slowly guide his hand and those wet fingers to the top of my pants. He takes my direction and moves south, brushing the outside of my panties and groaning, mostly to himself, "How are you so fucking wet?"

I answer by kissing him deeply, hungrily. "You."

He rushes to yank my tank top over my head as I fumble to slide his shorts off. Soon enough we're both naked, skin to skin, kissing like it's our last moments on earth, nothing but us and the moon and the warm, salty air, the low, thumping beat of the music and the waves crashing in the background. He stops me, getting up to find a condom. The absence of his body against mine is jarring. I want him back. *All* of him.

"No, don't," I gasp, pushing him back down on the chaise. He looks at me, longing in his eyes. I thought about this on the flight here.

"I have an IUD. I know you know this. I want you. All of you. Just you with nothing between us. Is that okay? Are you good?" I ask, looking down at him, my every sense heightened as I await his response.

"Yes," he answers. "Jesus. Yes. I want that, too. I am good—all clear. I didn't want to be the one to bring it up, I felt like it should be your decision. But, *yes.* Just me and you, Jules. Nothing between us. Not now, not ever."

I kiss him deeply, my adrenaline rushing at the idea of it. He buries his face in my chest, moaning softly, as I take my sweet time guiding him toward me. I rub his throbbing cock against me, drenching it in my wetness, almost coming at the idea that there will be no barrier between us for the first time.

He grits his teeth. "Fuck, Jules."

I tease him at my opening, letting him feel me, me feeling him, the anticipation building. When I can't take it anymore, I slide him inside of me as slowly as humanly possible. Savoring every raw, unadorned inch, loving how he seems to fit so perfectly. The way I'm stretched just enough to accommodate him. My body shudders.

His eyes roll back into his head as it falls against the chaise. "Fuu-uuuuuck, please don't move," he pants. I stay still as long as I can manage before I slowly start rocking on him, feeling the friction building between us. Our breath quickens in sync. "Wait, wait, wait, wait, babe. Slow down, please. I've been away from you for too long, and no condom ... it's too much. I want this to last. I want to enjoy it."

I try to still myself, but something primal takes over, and I can't stop. I grab the back of his neck and start moving again. He grabs my hips, holding me in place on top of him. He brings those beautiful fingers up and around and starts rubbing my clit in a way only he can. Those same fingers that were in my mouth a few minutes ago are now moving in deliciously slow circles, the pressure building. I feel myself almost levitating out of my body and lean backward, bracing my hands against his shins. His hypnotic movements outside of me, and inside, the thickness of him spreading me, all at the same time. It's too much. "*Matt!*" I cry out, gasping for air. I last five more strokes of those fingers before I shatter completely.

I feel myself clench and release again and again around him. My breathing is labored, rasping in my throat. I didn't think it was possible for him to get any harder, but after he feels me come, he turns to granite. By the time I open my eyes and lean forward to look at him, he is staring at me, his eyes huge, glossy, animalistic. I know he is close. I take those fingers, the ones that I love so much, now slick with me, and stick them back in my mouth, sucking on them as I grind against him. That's all it takes. I feel him explode as he flings his head back and screams my name, nothing between us, both of us pulsating in unison.

We stay like that for what feels like hours. We stay like that until I can feel him dripping out of me.

When our breathing steadies, I take a second to lock in this moment—the smells, the sound of the waves crashing behind us, the loose-limbed, hazy-eyed calm, the pure serotonin pumping through my bloodstream, and the sight of the moon's milky white filter on this beautiful man completely sated beneath me, still inside of me. I never want to forget this.

When I start to wonder if Matt fell asleep, I slide off him and rest my head against his chest. "You doing okay?" I murmur.

No answer. I plant tiny kisses on his shoulder, his neck.

"Yes, more than okay," he says finally.

"What are you thinking about?"

"I'm thinking if I died right here, right now, with you, that'd be just fine with me."

I smile, knowing that exact feeling.

Chapter Twenty-Three

Today, after more of the same as last night, Matt heads off to a makeshift studio in a separate villa on the property. He's invited his band and sound engineers to work on new music while we're here—no rest for creators. I have a ton of work myself but decide it can wait, so I grab a book and walk down to the beach. I'm glad for the quiet. My time with Matt is always so intense, I don't feel like I have a moment to reflect on what is unfolding between us. Being with him is a phenomenal practice in mindfulness—but maybe too much so. I feel so present, so completely in tune to my surroundings when I'm with him. Sex is like that times infinity. I've never felt so alive in my body.

I can't help but compare him to previous lovers. With Nick there were fireworks in the early years. The nights in his twin bed in his shitty apartment in Baltimore, us trying to be quiet while his room-mate slept. Then later, when we had space and all the time in the world to explore each other, it was fun, and we were bold. Even early in our marriage, I felt so attracted to him in this new role as my husband. He was the same, but different. The connection, the vows, the years of knowing each other were kindling for desire. It was only in the eighteen months before our marriage ended that I started to feel what I'd heard my girlfriends complain about: sex morphing into something that resembled a chore for both of us. Like there were a million other things we'd rather be doing. Like we were each secretly hoping the other one wasn't interested.

My mind works quickly to fast-forward five years with Matt. Will the sex fizzle? Will the day-to-day stresses and irritations of life be a barrier for us to do this? To get inside each other in every way possible? There is no way to know.

Matt admitted he struggles "when the going gets tough," which I still am not clear on. I work hard to quiet my inner therapist, my need to know exactly what that means. Overthinking has never gotten me anything except a fifty milligram Lexapro prescription. I know myself well enough to know overthinking is often a sign that I'm scared. In an attempt to relieve that fear, I busy myself by preparing for all possible outcomes. Doomsday prep. That does nothing but create a false sense of security—the idea that if I just plan and prepare enough, I'll be safe from harm. Safe from hurt.

But like Daryl reminded me all those weeks ago, you can't avoid pain without also avoiding joy. They are two sides of the same coin. So right there, on the beach, without another soul in sight, I dig my feet deep into the white sand and focus on the crystal water. I sit with the discomfort, the uncertainty that I do not know for sure whether Matt and I will be anything beyond this day, this week, this trip. So, I sure as hell better enjoy it.

* * *

Later that afternoon, I lounge by the pool in my bikini, a crocheted black sarong slung around my waist. I have my laptop open and my notepad out, and I'm working my way through all the infinitesimal requirements necessary to finish the third and final behemoth grant proposal that is due next week.

On the other side of the patio, Matt sits with Seth, his longtime friend and sound engineer. They have their laptops open, headphones on, cutting and laying tracks for Matt's newest album. Occasionally, I glance over to find him staring at me.

Eventually Seth collects their equipment, gives Matt a fist bump and me a quick kiss on the cheek, and heads out. I put my laptop down and pad over to Matt, taking his giant headphones off his ears.

"Whatcha thinking about over here?"

"I was just thinking about how much I like looking at you."

"That's all?"

He smiles. Matt is a lot of things, but brief is not one of them.

"I'm thinking how much I like looking at you while you work. You're doing something you love, something you're passionate about, something you're obviously very good at. I really, really like that about you. I like how we can be together but doing our own thing at the same time. You aren't relying on me to entertain to you, to do anything but just be with you."

"I think that's normal," I respond.

"Not for me, it's not. Or at least it hasn't been. I've been with women before who I felt a strongly that I needed to protect or 'save.' Which they didn't, for the record, that was just my own shit. That therapist I told you about told me that. *Everyone is responsible for identifying and communicating their own needs.* I always felt like they needed a lot from me. And it felt really good to be needed like that at first. It also felt like something easily fixable. But I couldn't leave their side at events, parties, shows. I always worried about them, that they felt uncomfortable, that they didn't have anyone to talk to. I didn't realize a lot of times till it was over that I was constantly stressed, bending over backward to keep them on an even keel. To keep them from getting upset with me, to avoid a fight. I'd sometimes get a pit in my stomach whenever we'd be together because I knew something would happen, something would go wrong, and we'd end up in an argument that would take days or weeks to recover from.

He pushes his sunglasses up into his hair.

"But I don't have to do any of that with you. Which makes me feel even more sure of myself, somehow. It's refreshing and calming. Every time I'm with you I feel like I can be me, and I don't have to do all the mental gymnastics. It just makes everything feel so easy. That's what I was thinking. And I was also thinking how insanely sexy you are. I am so attracted to you, it isn't fair."

"Really?"

"What do you mean, 'really'? Have you seen at yourself?"

"Yes and I'm plenty self assured. But, I am also a woman. And I'm approaching my forties. Things don't metabolize the way they once did. And other things don't sit the way they once did. At least not without a lot of effort. Gravity isn't my friend." I lift my boobs up an inch or two higher.

"I like those exactly where they are," he says and pounces.

* * *

The next day is Matt's birthday. I get up before him and tiptoe out of bed to the place in my suitcase where I've hidden a gift. I wake him by planting forty-three kisses all over his body, softly counting them out loud. His sleepy-eyed smile almost does me in.

"Happy birthday, baby," I save one last kiss for his lips. "That one is for good luck."

"Thank you." He pulls me on top of him, beaming. He looks at me in that way of his, and I feel like he wants to say something but is holding back. I pull a small box from behind my back and present it to him. "For you."

"You didn't have to get me anything. You being here is everything I wanted."

"I had a feeling you'd say that, but to me, birthdays should be celebrated. You only get one day out of the entire year that's just for you. Open it."

He sits up and starts unwrapping. He opens the box to find a watch.

"An IWC Pilot Spitfire?"

"Yes."

Since I've known him, he's worn the same Audemars Piguet watch with a brown leather band so worn and scuffed it hardly passes as brown anymore, such a creature of habit is Matt. I made the mistake of Googling the price tag for his exact watch and my eyes almost popped out of my head. Then I began my impossible quest to find a suitable birthday gift for a man who can buy himself anything in the world.

I thought a second watch—sportier, but just as cool as his current one—might be the perfect gift. The fact that I found one while hunting through every vintage watch store in lower Manhattan seemed like incredibly good luck. The fact that I had time to get it fixed up and could even afford it without selling a kidney made the entire thing seem fated.

He takes it out of the box carefully, like it's a delicate baby bird, and starts examining it. He flips it over and runs his fingers over the tiny place where I'd had something engraved. His eyes shoot up to mine. "416?"

I nod. He screws up his forehead. It only takes him a second to figure it out.

"Dad's room. At the hospital."

"Yes."

"The place that led me to you," he says quietly. He sits, staring at the watch. Nodding his head. Speechless. A first for him.

"Thank you. This is special. I don't know what to say. Except maybe I always hoped it'd be like this." I feel a warm rush of love for him.

"Happy birthday, Matt," I say again, climbing onto his lap.

He carefully places the watch back in the box and sets it on the nightstand. He cradles my face in his hands with a similar gentleness, like I am something precious. He kisses me, and it is full of all the words he can't say. After a few minutes, he pulls me down on top of him, where I happily give him the second part of his birthday gift.

193

* * *

We spend the rest of Matt's birthday lounging by the pool and the ocean, where I give him "the world's greatest blow job," and we dine on all the local cuisine.

His phone rings throughout the day with happy birthday calls and texts from everyone who loves him, which turns out to be a lot of people. We answer a FaceTime from Sid and Rita, who are back in Allentown for Thanksgiving and to spend time with Matt's mom.

"I have your birthday check here at the house," Sid says through the screen.

"Dad. I don't want your money. Keep it!" Matt laughs.

"It's tradition, and you know it. One dollar for every year plus five dollars for good luck. So how much is that, son?"

I smile behind my sunglasses, watching the two of them, Matt shaking his head. "Forty-eight dollars, dad," he answers, ever the good sport.

"You see that, Julia? He's more than just a pretty face."

I laugh and wave to them. Once they hang up, I watch Matt type on his phone, responding to texts, a smile on his face for most of the day. For a guy who never wants much of a fuss made about him, I can see how much it means to him.

But at one point, his smile vanishes and his brow furrows, like a dark cloud is passing over his face. He puts the phone down, only to pick it up again a second later, thumbs hovering.

"What's wrong?"

"Nothing." He puts the phone back down.

"Your smile disappeared."

He forces a smile at me.

"That one's a fake."

He leans back in the chair, closing his eyes, the sun beating down on his lovely face.

"It was Jackie," he tells me eventually, "and you just described her perfectly—she is the human form of disappearing smiles. The grim reaper of joy."

My chest tightens. "Oh."

"I don't know how she got my number. She always comes out of the woodwork at the most inconvenient times. She wished me a happy birthday," he says sourly.

Why is he have such a bad reaction to a text? It's ancient history. Am I feeling insecure about this? Why?

I push my thoughts aside and get up to go sit between his legs on the chaise.

"Hey." I coax his attention toward me.

He opens his brown eyes, and they soften when he sees me. I rest my hands on his thighs.

"Do not let her put a damper your birthday. You only turn forty-three once," I say as I untie my bikini top, letting it fall to the pool deck.

His smile comes back, the real one, and his hands reach out to cup my breasts. I lean forward, giving him a slow, sultry kiss, and when he kisses me back, hard, I know I have him back.

* * *

The rest of our time in Mexico is spent lounging by the pool and the ocean, eating, drinking, and making love. We walk on the beach hand in hand and swap books as we lie on the lounge chairs. Matt, a self-proclaimed grammar buff, proofreads my grant proposal, and I listen to the early cuts of his new songs.

The time together in the sun restores me in a way I didn't even know I needed. I did not expect that I could like Matt even more than I already did, but as I've told him before, the limit does not seem to exist. The uninterrupted time is the longest stretch we've ever spent together, and that it has been so easy, so seamless, so enjoyable, rockets me to cloud nine. As I watch the New York City skyline appear in the distance on my flight back home, enjoying the calm contentment that I've been feeling the entire time away, I have the stark realization that I am head over heels in love.

Chapter Twenty-Four

I t's officially Christmastime in New York. The best time of year. Everything is decorated, and the entire city seems high on the Christmas spirit—most of all, me. As I walk down Bleecker Street, I take a picture of the wreaths, white lights, and red bows that adorn the shops and restaurants. I send it to Matt.

> Nothing better.

He sends me back a photo of the palm trees in his backyard laced with Christmas lights.

> Not the same, but it'll do for now.

> Do you have a tree inside?

> No, I used to do a little Charlie Brown Christmas tree but it kind of bummed me out, so I stopped a few years ago.

> That just won't do. We'll decorate my tree together when you get here.

Chrissie McCauley

I haven't seen Matt since Mexico, and he has plans to fly to Allen-town the afternoon of Christmas Eve. Sid, Rita, and Matt will spend the holiday together in Pennsylvania, mostly so they can see Matt's mom on Christmas Day. Then, they'll all come to the city to see me since I volunteered to work the holiday shift this year, which starts on Christmas Eve and ends in the wee hours of the morning of the twenty-sixth. The other social workers have young kids, so it doesn't feel like a huge sacrifice for me to be in the hospital. Ryan will be in Baltimore with my mom, and they'll take the train up to see me and meet Matt a few days later. This is all Matt's idea—the big family meeting. I'm excited for him to meet Ryan, but my mom is another story.

Even though I have to work on Christmas, it doesn't dampen my mood in the least. In fact, I feel a surge of energy as I bop around the city from store to store. I keep getting misty-eyed at how lucky I am to be shopping for so many new people this year, people I didn't even know existed just a few months ago.

I pick out a gorgeous cashmere sweater for Rita and a six-pack of the finest olive oil I can find for Sid. I get Ryan and my mom their usual gifts—airline vouchers on Delta for him, and Le Mer skincare for her. I buy Meredith a gold heart charm for her necklace and buy myself a matching one.

Matt is far and away the hardest to shop for. Not just because he has everything—or has the resources to get himself anything he wants —but because I want my gift to make him feel special and cherished, the way he makes me feel. I start buying a few small things that make me think of him: a special pillow specifically designed to be placed on your head, a UV light antibacterial phone cleaner, two vintage T-shirts, a case of wine called The Washingtonian, and several other small items.

* * *

The week before Christmas, my field hockey team loads onto a bus and heads to Syosset for a one-day indoor tournament—our last competition of the year. I walk into the arena with the head coach, Lindsay, and I'm assaulted by the smell of turf and sweat and Icy Hot. I smile at the familiarity, remembering my own field hockey days fondly. We find our field and I walk on, feeling the tiny black pieces of crumb rubber in the bottoms of my sneakers, listening to the girls chatter among themselves as they suit up.

Our first game is intense—the girls fight for every goal. We end with a win, and in the middle of our postgame huddle, I feel it. Feel *him.* The same feeling I always get when Matt is nearby, like the air is suddenly charged.

No way.

I glance over to the other side of the field and blink a few times to make sure what I am seeing is real.

Matt.

He's dressed in a blue puffer coat and jeans with a black beanie on his head, and he's casually grabbing a seat in the front row of the bleachers. When I meet his eyes, he gives me his megawatt smile and my heart rockets to outer space. The girls, ever observant, follow my gaze.

"Who is *that*, Coach?" they ask, almost in unison.

"My friend," I answer.

"Okay, sure thing, Coach."

"My friends don't make me smile like that."

"Who he is?"

"Is that someone's dad?"

"Is he, like, famous or something?"

"Why are all our moms looking at him?"

"He looks, like, really hot."

"For an old guy."

"Yeah, like, daddy vibes."

"What's his name?"

"Girls! He's not a dad. And I hope when all of you are older you remember this exact moment, you ageists!" I half scold them, half laugh out loud at the stark reality that Matt and I are closer in age to these girls' parents than to them. And that their parents are the ones more likely to be Matt Johnson fans.

I walk over to him, unable to ignore the pull, and give him a giant hug.

"What are you doing here? I didn't think I'd see you till the twenty-sixth!"

"I missed you. I know how much you love Christmas. I want to spend as much time with you as possible."

"You," I say, leaning in to give him a kiss, my heart exploding in my chest. I have the urge to tell him I love him. But I push it down. *No. Not yet.* I need to be sure.

Matt watches the final two games and is incredibly gracious as strangers ask him to take selfies and sign autographs. Somewhere in the back of my mind, I worry these photos might end up online somewhere, but Matt seems unconcerned, so I follow his lead. When the games end, I bring him over to the team and watch as he masterfully fields the girls' unfiltered and inappropriate questions. By the end they're all giggling and smitten with him. How could they not be? As they load up onto the bus, I wish everyone a merry Christmas and hop in the car to ride back to the city with Matt.

I sigh, holding his hand across the console. "You got some rave reviews across generations. I think your fan base just grew by at least forty people."

He laughs. "I could say the same for you. Those parents are big fans of yours."

My cheeks warm.

I lean across the console to give him a kiss on the cheek. "I can't believe you're here. I thought you had some hard deadlines this week."

In addition to wrapping up the last eight cities on his tour, he's been filling me in on his label's increasing pressure to put his new record out and get another tour together for the spring. And how he's been feeling ambivalent about the label for months at this point and has been kicking around an idea with a few longtime friends and colleagues—his own label.

He's got more than twenty years of experience in the industry, and because of his sustained success and talent, he is universally respected. He's quietly started talking to producers, agents, and engineers and to other artists, who are all ecstatic at the idea of working with Matt. Ultimately, the industry is fickle, and any move he makes could be a giant risk, but their enthusiasm seems to energize him and balance out the stress the idea creates. I can tell it's been weighing on him.

He kisses my hand. "It's nothing that couldn't wait. Priorities, Jules. I've got 'em this year."

* * *

We get back to Manhattan and immediately stop at one of the Christmas tree vendors set up on the street. I already have a fake tree with white twinkle lights, waiting to be decorated, but I'm so excited by Matt surprising me, we decide to get a real one too. It's slim pickings this late in the season, so we settle on a tall, thin, and very sparse tree. After it's wrapped up, Matt hoists it over his shoulder and we walk into my building. He helps me drag a box of decorations out of the back of my closet, and we get to work. Michael Bublé plays in the background, the smell of balsam fir is in the air, and a bottle of very expensive red wine is decanted. It all feels like magic.

Before we finish, I grab a small, wrapped box from my bedroom and hand it to him.

"I thought we were doing gifts the twenty-sixth?" he questions.

"We are, but this is just a little something."

I watch his slow smile as he unwraps it and holds it up—a small blue and white electric guitar Christmas ornament. An almost exact replica of one he owns, the one I watched him play at the concert in October. His eyes light up as he looks at it, flipping it over to see where I've written *Matt* and the year.

"It's a family tradition to give each other one Christmas ornament a year starting the year we were born. The idea being that by the time you're an adult, you'd have enough to fill your own tree," I explain.

I show him some of mine: ballet slippers, field hockey sticks, a black dog, and thirty-five others. I watch as he looks for the perfect spot to hang his guitar. And after he carefully places it on the tree, he turns to kiss me, eyes shining.

"Thank you. This is special. It means a lot that you thought to include me in your tradition."

He walks over to his backpack and pulls out a small, gift-wrapped box of his own. "I wanted to give this to you now. And the second part I'll you give later."

I smile and take the box from him. I open it up to find a beautiful IWC watch with a dark blue face and black leather band. Classic, feminine, sturdy. I love it.

"Wow. It's gorgeous." I go to fasten it on my wrist.

"Wait, flip it over."

416. Just like the inscription I gave him.

"It's perfect." I blink back tears.

"Now we match. You can wear it to work. And even though we can't be together on Christmas, just look at it and know I'm with you."

* * *

I get through my Christmas shift easily, ensuring that every patient on the critical care floor can celebrate the holiday in whatever way they prefer. I feel effervescent as I walk over to Matt's apartment in the early hours of the morning, the air freezing. I lug a tiny fake tree from my office with me. His doorman lets me up, and I use a key he gave me to quietly slip into his apartment. I strip off my work clothes and climb into bed with him, kissing the back of his neck as I press my cold body against his back, stealing his warmth.

"The hottest woman in the world and yet you're ice cold." His morning voice is raspy.

"So warm me up."

He rolls over, brushes my hair out of my face, and pulls me tightly into his arms.

"Merry Christmas, baby."

"Merry Christmas, Matt."

* * *

We lounge in bed until midmorning, only getting up for coffee and the pastries Matt procured the day before. We make love on the couch in his living room before showering and getting ready to host dinner for Sid, Rita, Scott, and Natasha. Matt and I work together all afternoon preparing lobster-stuffed beef tenderloin, twice-baked potatoes, roasted brussels sprouts, and a pecan pie—only the best menu for Sid.

As the two of us dance around the kitchen together, alternating between the stove, the oven, and the island, glasses of red wine in hand, I catch his eye, and we exchange a look that seems to say, *This is everything we ever wanted.*

Once our guests arrive, I set out hors d'oeuvres: crab-stuffed mushrooms, sausage and pimento cheese balls, crudités, and a cheese board. We sip pomegranate palomas and open gifts under the tiny tree. The mood is so cheerful and festive, I want to capture it. I know Matt does, too, because he grabs his phone and snaps photos of everyone all night. We serve dinner on Matt's dining room table over candlelight and several bottles of The Washingtonian wine I gifted Matt.

After everyone goes home and we've loaded the last of the dishes into the dishwasher, Matt and I lounge on the couch, my legs in his lap, listening to Bing Crosby on the record player and sipping a

nightcap of Yamazaki whiskey. I am trying to brace myself—and Matt
—for the dinner we'll be having with my mom and Ryan tomorrow
night. I don't know why I'm so nervous about it. Something about him
meeting my only two family members feels upping the ante.

"Babe, I've survived incredibly hostile interviewers with hidden
agendas, I think I can manage your mom."

I laugh. He has a point.

"You know, we'd have enough space at my house in LA to have
both of our families for the holidays," he says casually.

"Christmas in LA sounds like an oxymoron."

"Are you drinking the same Kool-Aid as Meredith?"

"No, no Kool-Aid. I just can't imagine a warm Christmas. You
said it yourself, it's not the same. And there is nothing like New York
City at Christmas."

"Okay, fair, it was just an idea. But since we're talking about LA,
there's something I want to talk to you about."

My stomach tenses.

"I was asked to be one of the performers at the Grammys this
year. I said yes."

"Wow. Congrats, babe, that's fantastic."

He pauses.

"I want you to come with me. Be my date."

"What exactly does that mean?"

"It means you'd be with me. The whole night. Walk the red
carpet with me. Sit with me. Come to the parties with me. Be with
me. For everyone to see."

I take a second to try to understand what that would be like. My
nerves start jumping. He's watching me closely. "That sounds like a
big deal," I say eventually.

"It doesn't have to be."

"It's kind of what we've been avoiding this entire time, though,
right?"

"I know, and I've been thinking a lot about that. I know I've been
rigid about my arbitrary rules, but this feels very different. I want to

go to the show and do the carpet, the whole thing, which is something I haven't done in years. I sat on the offer for a few days, but I found myself actually wanting to go this year. I *want* to, because of you. I feel like it just makes sense, letting the world know about us. I feel like having you next to me is like a superpower, and I'm excited about it, not terrified or dreading it like I used to be. I'm looking forward to it. And I want to run with it."

I glance at the beams above us, collecting my thoughts. He is clearly excited, but I don't know if I am.

"I don't know if I'm cut out for that type of world," I say lamely.

"What world? My world?"

"No, I don't think that's your world. I've been living in your world since we met, and it is nothing like what I anticipate a giant awards show would be."

"I know, but that type of stuff is occasionally part of my world." He frowns, a storm cloud rolling in.

"What?" I ask.

"I guess I'm just a little surprised. I thought it'd be an easy yes for you."

"It's a lot to think about."

He looks hurt.

"Matt, please don't confuse what I'm saying. *You* are an easy yes for me. But all of the other stuff that's not you but just like your occupational hazards, well, that's something I have to wrap my head around."

"I know, but you can't completely separate the two."

He has a point.

I stare at the Christmas tree, the white twinkle lights reflecting on Matt's face. I can see he's drifted away from me, gone inside himself, his eyes fixed on the floor, thinking. Several minutes pass in silence. I don't know why I feel so hesitant about the idea of the Grammys. Is it a sign that something is wrong? No. That doesn't seem right. Up until this point, I've been happy to defer to him about the publicity of our relationship. In fact, I've even felt pangs of worry that he is keeping me hidden from the world, which doesn't feel great, either.

I can't have it both ways. But I also feel ancient insecurities creep in as I think about what it might be like to be in LA, the city of perfect specimens, several of whom Matt knows intimately.

To knowingly walk into that seems like it could jeopardize what we have, this relatively normal relationship. In New York.

But then I think about how it must've taken a lot of consideration for him to even think about going himself, let alone asking me to come with him. And as nervous as I am about the unknown, I feel sure that being with him is the right choice, regardless of the location.

"Matt."

He glances over at me.

"I'll come."

"I don't want you to come if you don't want to."

"I want to come. I just needed a minute to think about it. Can I have that?"

"Of course you can. But I don't want a pity date."

I smile, crawling over to his lap.

"You know, the only thing that is a pity ..."

Matt looks at me, a smile dancing across his lips as he fills in the rest. "... Is you two young, beautiful people, withering away in this hospital room. You're sure?" he asks.

"Completely."

His face breaks into a wide smile.

* * *

The next night, I ask my mom and Ryan to meet me for drinks before Sid and Matt join us for dinner. Ryan knows exactly what is happening, but I only mentioned to my mom we'd be having dinner with friends. Matt has been adamant for a while that I talk to her about us, but now, with the Grammys a few weeks away, my back is against the wall. My reluctance to share this information with my mom lingers.

Our relationship still feels vulnerable, precious, sacred, and something we've been protecting for months. I can't help but feel like the carefully crafted bubble we created together is about to burst. Without it, we'll be left completely exposed to the outside world—the noise, the criticism. And like it or not, my biggest and most beloved critic and champion is my mom.

At least I have Ryan for backup.

I meet them at Via Carota, my mom's favorite restaurant in the city. After we hug, catch up, and exchange gifts, I decide to just get on with it.

"So, Mom, I have something I want to talk to you about."

Ryan gives me a nod in solidarity.

"You're *pregnant*?! I'm going to be a Gigi!?" she shrieks. She has been doing this little bit for years. It is infuriating and humiliating. Ryan puts his head in his hands, his shoulders shaking with laughter.

"Jesus, no. Come on, Mom!"

"Well, then, what?"

"I'm seeing someone."

"Okay ..."

"His name is Matt. We met a few months ago at work. He's the son of one of my former patients."

"Is he handsome?"

"Yes, very."

"Is he handsome, Ry?"

"I don't typically weigh in on how handsome men are, Mom," he answers, deadpan.

"Okay, well, what's he like?"

"He is kind, a little reserved, thoughtful, incredibly talented, and funny."

"Does he like you more than you like him?" she asks. Ryan chokes on his drink.

"What kind of question is that?"

"I told you, I always thought that was the problem with Nick. You need to be with someone who loves you more than you love them. Nick never had to work for it. He needed to chase you a little more, not the other way around."

"Wow, thanks for the insight about ten years too late. Can we please not discuss Nick? Matt and I both like each other. Equally."

"Okay, well then, I'm happy for you, honey. I've been hoping you'd put yourself back out there sooner rather than later, of course."

"There's one other thing."

She stares at me.

"He's a musician."

"Oh, for crying out loud, you mean he's unemployed? Really, Julia? Have I taught you nothing?"

I glare at Ryan, who had the same reaction. He shrugs sheepishly. Apples and trees, I guess.

"*Mom!*" My patience is wearing thin. "He is not unemployed. Quite the opposite. He is very, very successful. And a little famous."

I see her racking her brain trying to place who he might be. "Matt who?"

I say nothing.

"Matt *who?* Julia Elizabeth!"

"Oh, for the love of God, she's dating Matt Johnson," Ryan yells, exasperated. "The world-famous solo artist? Guitar god? Grammy winner? You know who he is, Ma."

Her jaw drops. "The guy who just performed at Merriweather? Fran went to that. She said that young man would send her to an early grave. He sings that song, the one I like."

I have no idea what she is talking about. My mom often refers to things she thinks my brother and I should immediately know, but we don't.

"Yes, he performed at Merriweather. Meg and I were there that night, remember? Well, he's invited me to be his date to the Grammys next month. There's going to be a lot of photos taken at the event. And he's meeting us for dinner, now. Any minute. Please, try to use your filter," I beg.

"Oh, my God, Julia. I've got to post this on Facebook," she says, reaching for her phone.

"No!" Ryan and I say at the same time.

"You may absolutely *not* post anything on Facebook about this. Seriously, Mom, Matt is very leery of the press. We just want to keep everything normal and low key. Please don't mention it to anyone unless you need to."

"Can I text Fran?"

"Yes, of course. But she cannot post anything on Facebook, either."

"Okay, honey. Well, I'm very happy for you. Just make sure you don't look scared in all those photos."

"Sure thing, Mom."

Matt and Sid arrive, and the dinner goes better than I could've imagined. My mom and Sid talk to each other—more like talk at each other—for over two hours, which takes the heat off Matt. And Ryan and Matt hit it off immediately, cracking jokes, quoting movies, and talking about music. It warms my heart to see what I hope will be the beginning of a long friendship between the two of them—a little something to help fill the void of brothers lost.

After dinner, we move down the block to a bar with a lounge area, where Meredith, JP, Christine, her sister, Dave, and his boyfriend come by for drinks. We sit around, drinking, laughing, and dancing for the next four hours. I have to stop a few times and take it all in—all of my favorite people in one room together. It's extraordinary. It will go down as my favorite Christmas to date.

But suddenly and unexpectedly, I feel something else trying to push into the moment. A familiar, primordial, but barely audible voice in my head saying, *Maybe this is all too good to be true.*

It stops me in my tracks, and I feel like someone poured ice water on my head.

What the hell was that?

Matt notices. He always notices.

"You, okay?" he whispers in my ear.

I force a smile, nod, and give him a kiss on the cheek. I can tell he doesn't believe me, but he lets it go. For now.

After the night ends, Matt and I walk back to my apartment with our faces tucked in our coats to fight off the biting December air. With each block we walk, my mind churns. I wonder why that voice —the all too familiar one, telling me something is wrong—has returned. And why now.

Is it a sign?

I feel like Matt and I are on the precipice of something big, something amorphous I can't yet see, but I can feel it looming in the distance. By the time we turn onto my street, I hear Daryl's voice again: *You can't avoid pain without also avoiding the good stuff.* And with great love comes the risk of great loss. Two sides of the same coin. And it might be insane to let yourself love knowing eventually you will lose, but that is what life is all about. The great paradox.

Right?

Part Three

Chapter Twenty-Five

I take off work the last week in January with plans to fly to LA on the Tuesday of Grammy week. I've been buzzing around the city on a current of nervous energy in the hours leading up to my red-eye flight out of JFK. Matt insists on sending a private plane for me, but that seems completely unnecessary, so I book myself a domestic flight. But Matt being Matt, he upgrades me to first class, which I find out when I check in for my flight.

"I want you to be comfortable," he tells me when I call him from the Centurion lounge.

"I'm fine, Matt, truly."

He's been extra attentive in the past few days, which is saying something, since his baseline is very attentive. I wonder if he senses the nerves I am trying to ignore from across the country.

This will be my first time in LA, and I'm staying with Matt at his house. The week is full of events and meeting the remaining important people in his life, all of whom seem to reside in the City of Angels. I can't yet bring myself to imagine the magnitude of what is about to happen: me going to the Grammys with Matt. As his date. On his arm. It is a public coming out of epic proportions. A hard launch. No turning back. After more than five years of complete radio silence on his dating life, we are willingly walking into the lion's den.

Matt seems calm about the entire endeavor, at least on the surface. But I know the fears he has that lurk underneath, that threaten to boil over at the first sign of trouble. The history of anxiety, the thought that somehow this could be a *Return to Start* roll for him in the game of life, that he'll be opening himself up for scrutiny and criticism—things he's worked very hard to avoid for the past decade.

He asks if his management team can search through my online presence to see if there is anything I might not want discovered. I can't imagine what they'll find besides a few outstanding parking tickets and likely some hugely unflattering, but not illegal, photos of me bonging beers or dancing on a bar somewhere in my early twenties. I say okay.

Matt also suggests I give the important people in my life a little notice about us before they find out by way of mainstream media. I spend the week before my departure making phone calls to my closest friends and a handful of people at work. All are very surprised but happy for me. I feel slightly more confident going into the week knowing that my people are all on board.

* * *

Landed

I text him as my plane touches down at LAX.

> I cannot wait to get my hands on you. I will be back as soon as humanly possible. Make yourself at home.

By the time I get my bags loaded into Matt's waiting car and snake along the 405 to his house, my bones are heavy with exhaustion. After passing through several gates, I walk up the front steps and enter a code into the keypad. His wide front door clicks open, and I walk in. The house is exactly as he described it: bright, modern, with some very cool exposed beams and walls of windows, all meticulously organized.

I quickly find my way to his bedroom and en suite bathroom. I peel my disgusting airplane clothes off and step into the steamy shower. I use his shampoo, conditioner, and body wash, all of which make me smile as they smell so distinctly like Matt. Masculine. Earthy. Delicious.

Once I'm done, I dry myself with a giant fluffy towel from the linen closet, throw on a clean T-shirt I swipe from his drawer and a pair of satin panties, and climb into his bed. The sheets feel decadent against my clean skin, and before I know it, I fall fast asleep.

* * *

I sense him in the room before I'm fully awake—a shift in the energy. The particles in the air feel charged. I open my eyes and see him sitting on the bed next to me.

"You are a sight for sore eyes." He leans down to give me a slow, sultry kiss, with that now familiar and beloved brooding smile.

"Come under here with me." I lift the blankets for him.

"As much as I would love to, and I plan to, there are a few time-sensitive things to discuss."

I sit up.

"I want to show you something, but I don't want you to be worried."

"Ah, yes, that sentence always puts me at ease." I laugh. "What is it?" I rub my eyes open.

"The online stuff came back. Nothing bad, at least from my publicist's perspective, but I want to share it all with you to see if you want anything scrubbed before Sunday night."

He hands me a folder with a packet of paper inside. On top are printouts of my private Instagram profile picture: a tiny circle of me and Murphy on a hike in upstate NY. Decidedly harmless. After that are pages of tweets from a Twitter account I didn't even know I still had. There are a total of eleven tweets, almost all of which are reposts of fundraising requests from my alma maters. Slightly embarrassing, but certainly nothing to scrub. I don't have Facebook, TikTok, or Snapchat accounts. So that's easy. My LinkedIn profile picture is the same photo and info that could easily be found on the hospital's website, nothing but basic information about my education and professional experience. Somehow, his team found an old online photo album from my freshman year of college, full of me and my friends in matching jean skirts, tube tops, and orange Sun-In dyed hair.

"How did they even find these? I thought that website shut down," I wonder aloud.

"They're very thorough."

The last few pages in the packet make my stomach drop.

I thumb through them slowly.

My wedding photos. Me and Nick smiling in the church I grew up in. Me in an off-the-shoulder lace A-line gown. My grandmother's sapphire necklace twinkling around my neck. Too much hairspray. Nick in a tux, rented from Jos. A. Bank, looking handsome but nervous. Us kissing outside the hotel lobby where the reception was held. Dancing to our first song, "You Are the Reason" by Calum Scott. Me hugging my mom after her toast. A sparkler exit. All of it, right there.

It's then I remember my wedding photographer shared all her photos on a blog linked to her website. It would likely be one of the first hits on a Google search if someone ever figures out what my married last name was. I guess I can hope they won't, since I switched back to my maiden name after the divorce. I look up to find Matt staring intently at the photos.

"Do you want to keep these out there?"

"I don't know," I say. "This, these pictures, my marriage to Nick, it was a part of my life. A huge part. A beautiful part, until it wasn't.

It doesn't feel right to have that erased. But I don't want to subject myself to judgment. Certainly not Nick. Or you. What do you think?"

"I'm okay with whatever you want," he offers. "But I think, if you feel like it's right, we just leave them and say fuck it. Every person on earth has a past. Lord knows mine is out there for the all the world to see. Leave it. You just might want to give him a heads-up," he cautions.

"Okay," I agree, feeling a little on edge at the sight of my old wedding photos.

"What's he like?" Matt asks softly, nodding toward the picture of Nick.

"Nick? He's a good man. Confident, ambitious, gregarious."

"What happened?"

This is the question I've been waiting for. We've danced around it for a while, basically since the night we almost burned down my apartment, my own insecurities preventing me from disclosing too much. He knows the gist of my divorce, but I've never felt fully comfortable sharing the intimate details of it all, and Matt's never asked outright. Until now.

"That's the million-dollar question. I don't know. The not knowing was the hardest part to navigate," I answer plainly. "Ultimately, I felt like one day we both woke up and realized we were different people. Like we'd been on this same path together for years, and it suddenly became glaring that at some point we'd gone in separate directions. But I wasn't even sure if we had ever been heading in the same direction in the first place. Our relationship felt hollow, a shell of what it was. I was lonely. And sad. I felt like I didn't recognize myself anymore. Or him. I didn't want to resign myself to feeling like that, living like that for the rest of my life. I tried hard to make it all better, and I failed. Pretty miserably. All of that and the fact that Nick told me he wasn't in love with me anymore—that had a lot to do with it." I choke out a sad laugh. "That part definitely stung."

Matt looks at me pensively. I continue.

"I think had we not been married, if our relationship had just petered out and we went our separate ways, it would've been much easier for me. The fact that we'd promised each other our love and made vows in front of everyone we knew made it much harder to stomach. I felt the overwhelming urge to call every guest who came to our wedding and apologize to them personally. I know how absurd that sounds, but it's how I felt. I felt like a fraud. I never realized how important marriage was to me, like the big picture of it, the institution, the sanctity of it, until mine had already imploded. I felt like part of the reason I tried so hard to revive it was out of my own guilt and worry of what other people might think, not necessarily because I genuinely wanted to be with Nick." I sigh and lean back against the headboard.

Matt nods but says nothing.

He grabs the solo wedding portrait of me from the packet. It's in black and white. I'm looking at myself in a mirror, putting my earrings on. My dark hair is long, well past my shoulders, longer than it is now, and thick with soft waves. My brown eyes are big, emphasized by thick lashes. I have fewer laugh lines than I do now. My full lips are painted a light pink and are slightly puckered with concentration. My dress is on—we went through three rounds of fittings to make it fit like a glove. The tops of my breasts peek out from the fabric, full and round. Matt runs his finger along the photo, a contemplative look on his face.

"You are so beautiful. I wish I could've seen you that day." He traces the outline of my face, my neck, my breasts in the picture. I feel a shift in energy.

"A part of me hates that someone else got to love you like this. That someone else got to have you like this. I know that isn't fair, and I have my own history. But I want you, all of you, all to myself. Does that make sense?" he asks seriously.

"Yes. It does." I reach for his hand, not missing his use of the word *love*. I also think about the number of his exes, ghosts from his past, that I could potentially run into over the course of this week. And I wish I could have had all of him, too. I have him right now, in this moment. But I can't have his past or guarantee our future.

It's an unsettling thought.

Before either of us says anything else, Matt tosses the packet aside and dives on top of me. We spend the next hour making up for the time we've spent apart, using our bodies to say all the things we can't quite speak.

Chapter Twenty-Six

There is a frenetic energy in the city all week as people bounce from event to event, anticipating the big awards show on Sunday. Two weeks ago, I set up a meeting at UCLA to check out their pediatric behavioral health emergency department while I am in town. I want to get a feel for how they run it, especially after what I saw in Houston. It will be a key part of my presentation to the board at the end of the month—the last big thing I have to do to convince the hospital to provide a portion of the start-up costs for the unit. I'm feeling confident about it because I recently found out I have secured two out of the three grants.

The chief medical officer of the unit at UCLA is Dr. Ernest Williams, a pioneer in pediatric behavioral health. He also happens to be a former professor of mine and a longtime mentor. No matter how many times I hear him lecture to a group or even one-on-one, I'm blown away by his knowledge, and more so by his warm disposition and empathy. He is easily one of the best in the business, beloved by patients and colleagues alike. He greets me in the lobby with a giant hug.

"Julia! I worried we'd never see each other again in person after the pandemic."

"Me too. I'm so glad to be here. Thanks for taking the time to show me around."

He walks me through the unit and explains that before this existed, any child experiencing a mental health crisis in Los Angeles and the surrounding area was directed to regular emergency departments. They were being screened by nursing staff, followed by emergency department doctors, and then were briefly evaluated by a rotating psychiatrist. They usually wound up with a laundry list of meds and ultimately left in a similar holding pattern as I'd seen in Texas—one that both Dr. Williams and I considered barbaric. There are so few acute psychiatric beds and residential treatment centers for kids in the state—so again, they were being housed in ED hallways and waiting rooms, their parents hoping and praying that a bed might open somewhere—even if it was eight hours away by car.

"We have our fair share of frequent fliers, but during and after COVID it seemed like a tsunami of them. Some would decompensate so badly in the adult ED that their parents would take them out AMA only to return less than twenty-four hours later and wind up in the same exact situation," Dr. Williams explains.

When I walk onto the unit, I'm elated by what I see. The entire space is done in bright, cheerful colors. Individual patient rooms rim the outside of the wall, and in the center is a giant hangout area. I assume it's used for group, based on the colorful beanbags scattered in a circle, feelings charts on the wall, and tissue boxes scattered throughout. Beyond that is a separate space outfitted as a classroom, equipped with all the newest technology and bright desks bolted to the floor, a typical safety precaution. The unit is staffed with three full-time child psychiatrists, four full-time therapists, and fifteen full-time rotating RNs who specialize in psych. I have a brief meeting with one of the psychiatrists and one of the therapists and sit in on a group therapy session. In that time, a therapy dog comes onto the unit and makes his rounds, transforming the kids instantly into more care-free versions of themselves, if only for a few moments.

Dr. Williams takes me to lunch afterward, and I pick his brain, asking about the more logistical concerns and most importantly, how they secured funding.

"Partly state grants and party very generous private donors who contribute at an annual gala the hospital hosts every spring. There are a lot of deep pockets in LA; I imagine they are even deeper in New York. If you do it right, you can cover your costs for the year and beyond."

He catches me up on his life, sharing that he and his wife recently downsized to a condo in Santa Monica and his daughter is halfway through her sophomore year at Stanford. I brief him on life in New York, leaving out any mention of Matt.

As we wait at the valet, Dr. Williams says, "I know I made this offer years ago, but it still stands. If you ever want to try out life on the West Coast, there is always a spot for you at UCLA, Julia."

"Thank you. That is such a generous offer." I am genuinely flattered. It would be a once in a lifetime opportunity to work with Dr. Williams in this inspired new unit. But New York is home.

* * *

I climb into Matt's giant Land Rover and drive to meet him for an early dinner. I'm bursting with energy and inspiration, feeling more confident than ever that I can make this entire thing a reality at New York Grace. Even the jam-packed 405 can't bring down my mood. I breeze into the restaurant and find Matt at a table to the right near the front door. He doesn't notice me walk in, but I very much notice him. Namely, that he is surrounded by three exceptionally beautiful women. The one sitting to his right, a petite brunette with icy blue eyes, is laughing at something he said and has her hand on his forearm. I feel the hairs on the back of my neck stand up.

"Jules!" Matt exclaims when he sees me. He pushes back from the table abruptly, coming over to wrap me up in his long arms. If I had any doubts about what may have been going on at that table, they disappear a second later when Matt kisses me full on the lips in front of the other women.

He turns to them. "Alex, Jessica, Kara—this is my girlfriend, Julia."

The shock on their faces is very satisfying.

I can now see that these women seem to be some obscure age between twenty-five and fifty, but it's hard to tell because of their distorted, overfilled faces. The three of them offer me polite hellos, but I can see right through the veneered smiles—they are sizing me up. Hard. The excitement I felt five minutes ago evaporates, and I am transported back to high school, walking through the lunch-room, trying not to shrivel under their gaze. I do not like the feeling.

"If you ladies will excuse us, Jules and I have a date that I've been looking forward to all day."

"Bye, Matt. See you on Sunday," one of them says.

He grabs me by the hand, and we walk out to a back patio, finding two seats in the corner overlooking the Pacific. Before I say anything, Matt reaches across the table and squeezes my hands in his.

"They are friends of friends—they saw me waiting for you at the table and came over and sat down."

I nod. I can accept this. It makes sense. I trust Matt. I believe him. But feeling this level of insecurity is not something I've dealt with in a very long time, so I'm surprised and confused by how easily it floods in and stings. I wonder if my reaction is a combination of the nerves I feel about Sunday, the pressure of being in LA for the first time, meeting Matt's friends and colleagues, and ultimately just feeling out of my element. Like I can't quite find my footing here. And even though it's only been a few days. I have a sudden pang of home-sickness.

"How was your meeting? I want to hear all about it."

I fill him in, my excitement returning ever so slightly. When I mention Dr. Williams's offer, Matt's face lights up. "So, you could move to LA?"

"No, no. He said it very casually. He said the same thing years ago. I didn't actually consider it."

"But you could." He gives me his megawatt smile.

I laugh. "I don't think LA is for me."

"What's not to love? It's January! And we're outside. In short sleeves. Look at that beautiful Pacific Ocean. I know you're an East Coaster, but there is a whole lot to love here." He points to the right. The sun is starting to set, and it is mesmerizing.

"It's beautiful." I can't disagree.

"Even more so because you're sitting next to me. You know I always imagined it'd be like this. I wasn't sure if it could be real. But it is." He rubs the inside of my wrist with his thumb.

I kiss him across the table and change the subject. I don't know why but I have a very strong feeling that I don't want to be here permanently.

Chapter Twenty-Seven

We move into a suite in a hotel downtown on Saturday morning.

"It'll just be easier, traffic-wise, to be down here," Matt explains.

He hires a stylist to help me after seeing the terror in my eyes at the idea of having to pick out a dress that will be photographed for the entire world to see. I stand in the middle of the room while a woman with a severe bleached blond bob, and an equally blunt attitude, thrusts different dress options at me. I dutifully march into the bedroom, change, and come out to see what everyone thinks. Matt sits quietly on the couch, watching me closely. His first question is always, "How do you feel in it?" I love him for that. I dismiss the first three options—they feel too high-fashion for me, gowns that are on trend but make me feel ridiculous.

In the end, I settle on a black strapless Saint Laurent gown. It has intricate beading around the bodice, and its heavy fabric falls to the floor in a puddle with a high slit that reveals most of my left leg. It is undoubtedly the sexiest dress I've ever worn. I feel classy and confident with my best assets on display. Plus, the dress needs almost no alterations—a practicality given the time constraints.

The stylist hands me a pair of black strappy sandals, and when she starts fussing over my jewelry, Matt says, "I'll take care of that."

After I change back into my jeans and white button-down, everyone has cleared the suite. Matt walks over to me, a boyish grin on his face, and pulls out a Tiffany Blue box from behind his back.

"I saw these and had to get them for you."

I open the box and gasp when I see a pair of platinum and diamond dangling earrings. The afternoon sunlight bounces off the diamonds, throwing sparkles all over the room. They are stunning and intense. Just like Matt.

"What do you think?" he asks, eyes ardent.

"These are beautiful." I lean forward to hug him. "Thank you, I love them."

"And I love you," he says softly.

I back up, surprised yet not surprised at all. Hearing those words from him feels like something I've known forever. His eyes are blazing and vulnerable as he looks at me.

"I don't expect you to say anything back. But I need to say it. I need for you to hear it. To know it. It's been bubbling up inside me for weeks, months. Being with you has been incredible, more than I could've ever imagined possible. I sometimes feel like I'm dreaming. And I love you, Jules. So much. I just needed you to know that."

I nod, silent. Overwhelmed. He kisses me, and we start the familiar dance that I know will end with us tangled in the sheets, making love to each other. It seems only right to consummate this moment.

* * *

The morning of the Grammys is like nothing I've experienced before. People come and go from our hotel suite faster than I can keep track of. I sit like a statue in a makeup chair for what feels like ten hours as every inch of my body is buffed and polished, my hair is styled, and makeup is lacquered on with what I feel sure is some derivative of concrete. I'm feeling much better about my general everyday appearance knowing that an entire team of people are responsible for making celebrities look so good. Matt spends the day greeting the people in our room, fielding phone calls, doing interviews, and eventually taking a fifteen-minute shower and changing into his charcoal gray custom Tom Ford tuxedo.

"Must be nice," I call out from my perch. "I'm going to need an ice scraper to get all of this off," I say, gesturing toward my face.

"You are beautiful." He kisses me deeply.

"No, no, no! No kissing until after photos!" clucks the makeup artist, shooing Matt away from me. She reapplies my lipstick and gloss before spraying my entire face with what I think is hairspray. "Nothing will move until tomorrow," she explains.

The glam team starts packing up as I head to the bedroom to get dressed. Matt stands behind me, watching me in the mirror as I put on the earrings he gave me.

"Hold on, don't move." He darts into the suite. He comes back with his phone, opening the camera app. He stands off to the side, careful not to get his reflection in the mirror, and says, "Okay, go ahead." I continue putting my earrings on, my mouth pursed in concentration. Matt snaps several photos.

"Perfect." He turns the small screen toward me, showing me the photo. I look good. Really good. My confidence soars. I almost don't recognize myself.

But what I do instantly recognize is the similarity between the photos Matt just took and my wedding portraits we were looking at earlier this week.

"I love you," he says, coming up behind me and resting his head on my shoulder, arms around my waist. We look at our reflection together in the bathroom mirror. His hair and his eyes, just a shade darker than mine. There is no denying how fantastic we look together.

"I can't wait to show you off to the world." He nuzzles my neck.

I smile but can't ignore the flash of discomfort that shoots through me as I wonder why he is trying to recreate a sacred memory of mine. I shove it off, and we head down to the waiting limo.

* * *

My chest tightens and my breath quickens as we join the line of limousines inching closer to the theater. Matt is holding my hand, giving me reassuring squeezes.

"It's going to be fine. Just pick one spot and look at it, smile if you feel like it, and hold tight to me. I won't let you go," he soothes.

I try taking deep breaths, but it is not helping. My hands are shaking with nerves. He pours a small glass of tequila and passes it to me. "Drink this, it'll take the edge off." I down it in one gulp and feel the warmth soak through my body, immediately aware of the fact I've had nothing but coffee today.

Finally, it's our turn.

Despite Matt's pep talks, I am not prepared for the noise and lights that assault us as we step out of the limo. Matt goes first, then reaches his hand down to help me out. I immediately start shaking all over. He turns to me with his sexy side grin plastered on his face. "I am right here. Hold my hand, we will walk through quickly. Don't listen to anything anyone says. I love you."

I grip his arm as the stylist hops out to adjust my dress. She looks at me and notices my quivering knees, and I see the first hint of kindness from her.

"Julia, chin up. You are stunning and perfect. Go show them," she says sternly. It's enough to propel me forward on Matt's arm with my head held high.

"*Matt! Long time no see, dude!*"

"*What song are you performing tonight?*"

"*Who is your date?*"

"*I love you, Matt!*"

"*That's the chick in the sweatshirt!*"

"*What's her name? Is she your girlfriend? How long have you been hiding her from us?*"

"*What's your name, sweetheart?*"

Reporters and fans scream at us as bulbs flash, and I start seeing spots. "Keep walking, we're almost to the first stop," Matt says through his smile. We pause at a spot on the carpet where the bulk of the photographers are waiting. I try to remember what the makeup artist told me about posing: *Give them different angles, keep moving, bend your knee, the one with the slit, lean into Matt, soft smile*, but it all abandons me. I just stand next to Matt and try my best not to appear like a deer in the headlights.

Don't look scared! My mom's voice echoes in my head.

Matt is completely at ease in this situation. He smiles, seemingly unruffled by the deafening barrage of questions and the bright lights. At one point, I step to the side so Matt can be photographed by himself. I feel much more comfortable in this role, lingering in the background.

"Thank you all," he says, reaching out for my hand again, and we keep walking. He picks up his pace as we pass through the next several sections of the carpet without stopping.

"I have to say hi and do a quick interview with my friend before we go in. It won't be more than a few questions."

I nod and follow him. He walks up a few steps to an elevated platform—a mini stage of sorts—and I wait down below, taking in the chaos. I can't hear what Matt is being asked, but I do notice a camera panning down toward me. I do my best to appear aloof, but I start waving at the camera like a complete idiot. After only ten minutes, Matt comes to retrieve me, and we head inside the theater.

"You did it!" He leans in to kiss me on the cheek. "Let's get you a glass of champagne."

"Yes, please." I exhale.

He grabs two flutes, and we find our seats.

Once inside with the bulk of the cameras and noise gone, I feel my nerves calm, and I'm able to enjoy the show. Shortly after it begins, Matt leaves to get ready for his performance. When he takes the stage, I am in complete awe once again.

And once again, I am not alone. During earlier performances tonight, the crowd chattered throughout, but when Matt takes the stage, it's dead silent. I glance around to see a room enthralled by him. He is surrounded by the best of the best in his industry: artists, producers, managers, musicians. His talent and his passion transcend a normal listening experience, practically holding us all captive.

In this room full of powerful people, Matt seems completely unfazed. I know this hasn't always been the case for him, as he once described a bout of crippling stage fright in his early years, the insecurity that followed him around to open mic nights, and the self-doubt he harbored. But all of that is clearly long gone, and I watch him tune it all out and lock into whatever mode he goes to when he performs in another stratosphere.

At one point during his song, he finds me in the crowd. When our eyes connect, the air charges, and I feel like I'm floating. I'm instantly reminded of that night in Baltimore after his performance, my body humming with energy. I feel a slow pulse in between my legs. The lights, the crowd, this giant venue, the buzz from the champagne—I realize in this moment and without a shadow of a doubt that I am completely in love with him. And I should tell him as soon as the right moment presents itself.

His performance ends, and the applause is thunderous. Several minutes later, he makes his way back to me, ducking down so he won't obstruct people's view of the stage. I grab his hand as he sits back down in his seat, and I lean in to whisper, "That was incredible. And I am going to fuck your brains out. At the first opportunity."

A giant smile spreads across his face. "Is that a promise?"

"Yes."

"Well, all right, then."

The show continues, and during a commercial break, I excuse myself to use the bathroom. It is packed, and I find myself standing in line behind someone familiar—one of the women I saw sitting at the table with Matt earlier this week. Alexa? Alison? I can't remember her name, but she turns toward me with a faux smile. "Oh, my God, hi, Julia, you look gorgeous." Her voice is a pitch too high. I know she doesn't mean it.

"Thanks. You too."

"So, I guess it's official now, huh?"

I stare at her.

"You and Matt," she prompts.

"It's been official for a while now, but only our closest friends were in the know."

"That's *so* interesting. Because I know for a fact that he was on a date with a dear friend of mine at the end of the summer. And it wasn't the first date. Maybe third or fourth?" Her smile is venomous.

I keep my face calm, ensuring that this woman does not get a rise out of me. I smile at her as sweetly as possible and say, "Enjoy your night," before ducking out of line. I head back toward the theater doors with a smile painted on my face as I rewind time in my head, trying to remember when Matt and I went to DC.

By the time I find my way back to my seat, I'm feeling unnerved. Matt grabs my hand as I sit down. "I missed you." His eyes are so earnest. I've only been gone for a few minutes, but I know he means it.

He kisses me, and I know in my gut that the woman in the bathroom was fucking with me. Plus, I remember we didn't even say we were exclusively dating until the end of September—which helps to ward off the doubt that is threatening to seep in. *But was that technically the end of summer?* I second-guess myself. *What does it even matter? We are here now.* We watch the remainder of the show, hand in hand.

231

Matt does not seem bothered that he isn't nominated for anything this year. "I've done this whole song and dance before," he told me over lunch earlier in the week. "At first it was all I wanted, a Grammy. I thought it would make me feel like this was all worth it, somehow it would validate my spot in this industry. And certainly, that was a special moment for me. But now I feel like it's just something; it doesn't have to mean anything. I didn't even come to the show for years because I stopped caring, didn't buy into the hype. But then I was reminded of how fun it is to be here, with all the people in my profession who I admire and respect in one room. To be able to play in front of them—that is what gets me amped. And I think it's very cool they still consider me enough to invite me. That's an honor, and really a testament to my fans, the people who love my music no matter where I play it. But winning or losing a statue doesn't define me, not anymore."

After the show is over, Matt is still riding on the high of his performance, and it seems nothing can bring down his mood. His energy is contagious and combines with the adrenaline I've been feeling and the three flutes of champagne I've had. We navigate through the sea of people exiting the theater and are stopped at least a dozen times by friends and acquaintances saying *hey, man* and *great job* and enjoying quick catch-ups.

I'm introduced to more people than I can keep track of. Most are cordial but seem indifferent toward me, focusing solely on Matt. Like he is the sun and everyone else is just orbiting around him. It is then I have the thought: *Matt is a rock star.*

My next immediate thought is, *What am I doing here?*

I do my best to ignore it.

Eventually, we make our way back to our limo and collapse against the seats. Matt loosens his bow tie and tosses it into the cupholder. I watch him with his bright eyes, his tamed hair, his tuxedo—the cut, fit, and color of it divine. He is so insanely sexy that I think I might combust.

And he's mine. The thought is electrifying.

"What a night! And it's just getting started." He briefed me this morning about the handful of after parties he has to stop by. "Some just to show my face, some for us to actually have fun," he said then.

Now, he asks, "What did you think of my performance?"

I sidle over to where he's sitting, gathering my dress around my waist to sit in his lap.

"I thought you were absolutely fantastic. Unbelievable. The room was enchanted by you." I kiss him. "Watching you up there was such a turn-on. You made me—and I think a lot of other women—very, very, wet." Desire floods my system.

"Oh, yeah?"

"Yeah."

I bite on his bottom lip. He twists away from me momentarily to look for the button for the partition in our limo.

"Do you want to make good on your promise?" he asks with a seductive smile as the window separating us and the driver slides up and seals shut with a thunk.

"Yes."

It's on.

We crash into each other, mouths colliding, his tongue sliding in and meeting mine. I lean into him, grinding my hips against him with an urgency I can't quell. We kiss as I try to rip his tuxedo buttons off. At the same time, he tries to get to the zipper on the back of my gown. We're fumbling, panting, the intensity and adrenaline making us both frantic.

"Fuck it, just keep my dress on," I say breathlessly, and I move off him long enough to slide my panties down my legs. I hold the silky fabric out to him with one finger and cock my eyebrow. "Want to see just how wet you made me?"

His eyes go dark as he takes my soaked panties and puts them in his mouth, biting the delicate fabric with his teeth.

"You are so fucking dirty," he growls.

I wrestle with the buttons on his pants, finally freeing him. I take a moment to look at him, so full and thick, his velvet head dripping in anticipation of what's about to happen. I'm practically salivating. At this moment, I see a flash from a camera outside the limo, and I drop to the floor like I've been shot.

"What the fuck!" I scream.

Matt starts laughing. Hard.

"No, no, don't worry, babe, these windows are so tinted no one can see through. Trust me, it's been tested many, many times."

"Oh, thank God."

I get up and climb back into his lap. He is still laughing as he flings my panties across the limo and buries his face in my cleavage. He licks a trail in between my breasts and back up my neck, to the lobes of my ears clad in the diamonds he gave me. It is tantalizing. His fingers work in between my legs, stroking me with a rhythm, *the* rhythm, the one only he knows. The one that builds my orgasm quickly. Too quickly. I gasp and reach down and start pumping his cock with my hand, trying to match the pace he's set. We're all gasps and moans, teeth and hair; the air inside the limo fills with the smell of our sex.

When I can't take it for another second, I grab his shoulders with both hands and lift myself up onto his perfect cock. I tease him for just a second with the wet opening before I plunge down onto him. A moan rips from his mouth as I take a precious minute to work myself onto him fully. I stifle a sigh and feel myself clench, precariously close to the edge, then I move up and down in a deliciously fast pace, grabbing hold of his thick, gorgeous dark hair. Sooner than either of us expect, Matt gasps, "Fuck. *Fuck.* I'm coming," and explodes into me with a shudder. The feeling of his orgasm, knowing that I caused it, that I am the source of his undoing, and so quickly, is all it takes to put me over the edge. I cry out as I come with him.

"Incredible," he says.

"Incredible," I repeat.

"Just when I think it can't get any better..." He trails off.

I catch my breath and pull away to see Matt's smug, relaxed smile plastered on his lipstick-smudged face, his eyes at half-mast. A portrait of a satisfied man.

I climb off and land in the seat next to him, resting my head against his shoulder. We both remain silent. Content.

Eventually, the limo driver maneuvers us out of the crawling traffic to a side street. Matt kisses the top of my head and says, "Just so you know. I'd take that over a Grammy any day of the week."

Chapter Twenty-Eight

W e stop at the downtown hotel suite to change clothes—him, a deep blue tuxedo jacket, white shirt, black pants, no bowtie; me, a strapless neon leather Bottega Veneta dress. The stylist pairs it with metallic heels that make my legs look miles long. The waiting glam team works quickly to put my hair into a messy ponytail and smoke out my eyes before we jet down to a car and head off to the first of three parties.

The Universal Music Group after-party is the see-and-be-seen spot of the night, Matt explains. We walk in and have more photos taken, which only reminds me I'm not even close to figuring out the posing thing. Also, I haven't looked at my phone since we left for the red carpet. That was at Matt's urging early this morning over coffee. "Let's just enjoy the night before we have to deal with whatever is happening on the Internet."

Matt is stopped by an old friend. He introduces me, and after we exchange hellos, I whisper that I'm going to get us drinks. I find my way through the crowd and stand in line at the closest bar. I feel someone approach me on the right, and a quick glance over reveals it to be Kerri Taylor, a Grammy-winning country music artist, a flawless specimen with legs as long as her platinum blond hair. I discreetly scan her face and can't find a single blemish or even a pore. She is perfect. And she happens to be one of the many women Matt dated once upon a time.

"So, someone finally tamed the dragon that is Matt Johnson," she drawls in her faux-Southern accent.

"I'm not sure he needed to be tamed." I smile and hold out my hand. "I'm Julia Anderson." I sound much more confident than I am.

"I heard. Me and the rest of the world, as of just a few hours ago," she says, a Cheshire Cat smile on her perfectly enhanced lips.

"Congratulations on your award tonight," I say, feeling increasingly uncomfortable.

"Thank you. Tell me, how do you keep him from running? From what I remember about Matt Johnson—and a few other ladies have told me the same—he packs it up and heads for the hills as soon as the little honeymoon phase is over." She gives me a steely gaze. I stand there speechless while she orders a cocktail. A vodka martini, straight up.

"I guess they weren't the right ones for him, then."

"Keep telling yourself that, honey." She starts to walk away. Before she's swallowed up by the crowd, she turns around.

"When he starts talking in sonnets and soliloquies and promising you the world, get ready for him to split. Just a friendly warning. We women must look out for each other, right?" she says with a noxious smile, as casually as one would report the day's weather. She walks away, leaving me stunned.

I find my way back to Matt, shaken from the interaction, and hand him his tequila on the rocks.

"Babe, I thought I lost you." He hugs me close.

"No, no, just mingling with some of the other people here." I don't mention Kerri; I don't want to spoil the mood. I smile and chat with Matt and these people, chiming in and laughing at the right times. I don't miss the fact that no one asks me a single question, but I let it roll of my back. This is Grammy night, after all, but I'm starting to assess that even outside the glitz and glam of the night, many of these people are deeply self-involved.

We leave the party after an hour and then stop by a second party thrown by Matt's label. It's more of the same as the first party, but at a different location. By the end, my head is spinning as I try to remember the names and faces.

Finally, we leave the label party and drive to meet some of Matt's closest friends at a private event in a mansion somewhere up in the hills. This party is much more low-key, and I find myself fully relaxing for the first time since the day started at seven a.m. The drinks consumed at each stop along the way help, too. I run into a few women in the bathroom who are genuinely friendly, normal, and hilarious. I spend most of the night hanging out with them and sneaking kisses with Matt, who seems just as relaxed and completely unguarded; he is perfectly comfortable here in this multimillion-dollar house in the Hollywood Hills with these very famous people. The thought lingers, and I wonder if I could ever feel truly comfortable here.

Toward the end of the night, I notice a very curvy brunette indie singer, another ex of Matt's. I watch her from across the room—her confidence, her perfectly polished face, her ability to so easily navigate a party full of this caliber of celebrity. And once again, some ancient insecurities try to rear their ugly heads, creating tiny fissures of doubt. About what, I'm not sure, but it produces an overall feeling of unease.

I do my best to stay present and enjoy the moment—the music, the views of downtown LA in the distance. Matt is attentive and affectionate as always, but it feels new doing it so obviously out in public. He seems eager to make up for lost time. He tells me he loves me often, and I believe him. I know I love him, too, but am waiting to tell him till we can be alone. He doesn't seem to notice the many pairs of eyes on him, half a dozen female admirers. But I do. I see them look at him and then look at me, eyes scanning me from the top of my head to my toes, sizing me up. I'm convinced I hear them whisper, *That's his girlfriend? Who is she?* I do my best to meet their gaze, emboldened by the fact that Matt's hand rests possessively on my waist and the fact that I can still feel him dripping out of me.

* * *

We do not get back to the suite until the sun begins to rise. Matt and I are smoked from the day and night, and we fall asleep in our hotel robes in a heap on top of the bed. By the time we wake, it's nearly noon. My throbbing head is a cruel reminder that I am no longer in my twenties. Hell, I'm barely even in my thirties anymore. Matt lies strewn across the bed with a pillow over his head.

"Why did we drink so much tequila?" he moans.

"I'm pretty sure that was all your idea, rock star." I gather up our belongings and start tossing them haphazardly in bags.

"I am too old for this shit." He rolls onto his stomach.

"You and me both." I walk over and climb onto his back, gently massaging his shoulders, raking my fingers through his hair. He groans with pleasure.

"Let's pack up our stuff and get the hell out of here," I say. "Go back to your house, take a very hot bath, order bacon, egg, and cheese bagels, Thai food, and giant ice-cold fountain Cokes, and sit our asses on your couch for the rest of the day."

"That sounds divine." He reaches to grab his phone from the nightstand.

I watch his face as he scrolls through his messages and alerts.

"I haven't looked at the Internet yet," I say. My own phone sits on the coffee table out in the seating area. "I just read through my texts." I had over one hundred texts this morning, most from my inner circle, at least fifty from Dave alone.

Christine: 🤍

Dave: 🔥🔥🔥 NEED BTS DETAILS ASAP

> Meg: I can't believe this is happening to me (via you). Both of you are insanely attractive. 😿

> Meredith: Wow. You are the chicest woman there. PS- I already checked Twitter and reported any account that said anything mean about you.

> Mom: You don't look scared, good job, hon.

> Ryan: Your boyfriend looks like a real goober in that tux. Tell him I said that.

> Natasha, Scott, Matt in the group text: Cat's outta the bag! Looking good, lovebirds!

> Chip Barrington (work): I guess you do have a personal life. This could be great PR.

I cringe at Chip.

> Rita: Sid says tell Julia she is stunning. Tell Matt his jacket looks too big. Tell them both that I love them and want all the credit for making this happen. From me: You look beautiful and happy, sweetie.

The last is a text from a number that isn't saved in my phone but that I know by heart. It came in late—after three a.m. EST.

> Unknown: I know you don't owe me anything, but I wish you'd let me know this was happening.

Nick.

Shit.

I never contacted him. I couldn't muster up the courage.

"I don't have the stomach to read anything else right now," I say to Matt.

"I don't either. Let's go home, and we'll do it once we feel better."

Home.

* * *

It's a disorienting sensation, feeling like Matt and I are completely fine, unchanged in our world and in our relationship with each other, while at the same time, there is an entire world out there that only exists online, where people are having their own experience of us. It is bizarre.

We ride back to Matt's with the windows down, the cool air blowing my hair all around, music blasting, sun on our faces. It feels perfect.

Once we execute the hangover plan, Matt and I find ourselves snuggled up on the couch, and it seems like now or never.

"You look, and just tell me," I say nervously, hiding my eyes behind my hair as he starts scrolling his phone.

He pauses for a moment and looks at me. "Jules. You know none of this matters." He holds up his phone. "This world is not real, but this"—he squeezes my hand—"what we have, this is real. And this is all that matters."

"I feel like you're trying to prepare me for something bad."

"No, not at all. I'm just saying, I want you to always remember that. The press is fickle. They love you, then they hate you. They'll turn on you, cancel you, faster than you can even refresh your news feed. We cannot tether ourselves to their whims. It's so much noise, and it takes practice to tune it out. Just promise me, you'll trust that this—this thing you and I have, the love, right here in this room—is real, and that is all that matters. Anything you read or see online is just noise."

"Okay, I trust you."

"I love you, Jules."

"I love you, too," I blurt out.

A feeling of peace washes over me the instant the words leave my mouth. I didn't realize how they have been almost boiling over, waiting to get out.

He stops and stills, his face serious. "What was that?"

"I love you," I repeat. "I love you so much, Matt. I'm sorry it took me a minute to say it back. I got too in my head about it. I was scared to say it again, because I wanted to be sure that I meant it in every way I could mean it. And I was scared about all the ways in which I could fuck this up, or you could, or we both could. It's always a possibility, but I don't want to be ruled by fear or uncertainty. I love you. I think I have for a very long time."

I see the smile in his eyes before it travels down to his mouth; he lights up from within.

"Can you say that one more time?" he asks, pulling me onto his lap so our faces are only centimeters apart.

"I love you, Matt."

Pure joy floods between us. He presses his lips to mine, and I can almost taste his happiness.

"Glad to hear it. Because I fucking love you, Jules." He kisses me, and I let myself get lost in it. Until the incessant vibrating of his phone on the arm of the couch brings us back to reality. *The phone. The Internet. Ugh.*

"Can we get this over with?" I say, the dread returning to my chest, though it is significantly less potent than before. Almost like the words we just exchanged have covered me in a giant security blanket.

"Okay."

Matt grabs his phone and scrolls. And scrolls. And scrolls. I sit frozen, watching his face. He's smiling softly at first. Then a giant grin. "Babe. It's fine. It's more than fine. It is all good. The overwhelming commentary is that you are drop dead gorgeous, accomplished in your field, and, according to *Us Weekly,* just the kind of woman everyone wanted me to be with, not that I give a shit about what those people think. But it's good. It's all good."

I exhale, and he wraps me in a hug.
"See, nothing to worry about."
I feel relieved.
For now.

Chapter Twenty-Nine

Before I leave LA, we make plans to meet again in two and a half weeks in Pennsylvania for Sid's birthday on February nineteenth. Two and a half weeks feels like a long time, especially in the wake of our big reveal, but it's the only plausible situation given our scheduling constraints. Despite our relationship being mostly well-received, and Matt and his publicists' kind words and coaching, I still feel unmoored by it all.

When I arrive back at JFK after Grammy week, a few photographers call my name in baggage claim, and I walk toward them, certain I must know them from somewhere. I'm horrified when they lift their cameras. In the days and nights apart, Matt fields a dozen panicked texts and phone calls from me after I feel certain someone is following me or watching me.

"Just go about your day, try to ignore it, and eventually they will lose interest, I promise."

Hearing his calm, soothing voice always manages to feel like an exhale to me.

"Remember what I told you that day in the park? New York is much better than LA with the cameras—there are less of them there, they're less feral, and it's a little easier to blend into the background. But if anyone crosses the line anyway and makes you feel scared, let me know, and I will figure out security."

Security? *What in the world?*

"Also, just make it a habit to stay out of comment sections everywhere from here on out. Those places are insidious. Everything will be okay. I love you, Jules."

What I don't say is that I'm already scared. Not just because of the risk of being photographed and talked about against my will, but more because it feels like we've reached a point of no return. I don't want Matt to think I can't handle this, can't handle him and all the additional parts that come with his career and his life. I believe him when he says this will pass, that I will get used to it and we'll find a new normal. And yet I can't put into perspective what life will be like knowing this is his reality. Our reality.

I worry I'm becoming paranoid.

Work feels like one of the only safe spaces, and I feel my muscles unclench the moment I walk into the familiar hospital lobby. I make time each day to hang out at the nurses' station with Christine and Dave and Beth. Listening to them make fun of each other and hearing Dave's exceptionally inappropriate questions about Matt are just what I need.

"I'm imagining very slow, passionate lovemaking, followed by a serenade. Or is the serenading part of the foreplay? Just blink twice if I'm right. About any of it," Dave says.

"There is no world in which I would ever tell you any of that information."

In more private moments, Christine asks, "So, how are you adjusting to all of this?"

"I'm not, I don't think. The little things, like getting fifty thousand new followed requests on Instagram, I am trying to ignore. Matt says it'll die down."

"Okay, but Matt isn't here to see it. Like me. You seem on edge."

"It's just new, Chris. It'll be fine."

"Okay."

I can tell she doesn't believe me.

It helps that my presentation of my research from UCLA and Texas Children's pays off. The board agrees to fund the unit if, and only if, we secure fifty-five percent of the funding. The grants I won back in November are only a drop in the bucket compared to what we need to get the ball rolling. I pitch the idea to have a gala, just like Dr. Williams did at UCLA. It's a ton more work, but I'm happy to do it. However, the CEO of New York Grace, Dr. Barry Kampf, makes a comment at the end of my presentation that gives me pause.

"You know, you and your boyfriend are going to be good for business. Great press. With his name attached to New York Grace and him attending the event, we should see a significant uptick in donations."

I immediately find Chip across the table. He gives me an *aw, shucks* smile, which confirms my suspicions that this sniveling weasel has been in Barry's ear about my personal life.

"I'm not sure I'm comfortable with that, or if he's even available. But I'll take it into consideration," I say to Dr. Kampf diplomatically.

In between working at work and working at home, I see Meredith and my field hockey players. I'm grateful they've been in the know about Matt for months, because it gives me the sense of normalcy I so desperately want. My players go from ribbing me incessantly about Matt to becoming fiercely protective. I joke to Matt that he could hire them as security with payment in the form of an introduction to Jack Harlow or Lil Yachty.

Neil, my doorman, has also been checking on me regularly. "Everything going okay today, Miss Julia?" he asks when I enter the building.

"So far so good!" I say back as cheerfully as possible. He tells me that Matt sent him "some very wonderful, generous gifts" as a thank you for the potential increase in his workload because of our now public relationship. I'm touched by Matt's thoughtfulness, but the fact that my life choices are potentially impacting an innocent party like Neil is disturbing.

I notice loneliness starting to creep in each night I spend in my apartment alone with Murphy. It begins to feel frighteningly similar to the early days of the pandemic. Like I'm trapped inside these four walls, like I can't leave, and if I do, it could be dangerous.

* * *

Friday after work, I pick up a rental car and Murphy and I head out of the city to Amish country. I wait for Matt's private plane to land at the tiny Allentown airport, and my solace is palpable the moment I see him step onto the tarmac.

Taking in the familiar sight of him—Wayfarers, jeans, a gray sweater, and black coat—is like a full-body exhale. I rush to his outstretched arms. He pulls me into a rib-crushing hug, kissing the top of my head. He holds me out at arm's length, pushes his sunglasses up into his hair, and begins examining me, like he's looking for signs of injury.

"Are you okay?" The care in his voice is too much.

I burst into tears.

"I just missed you. A lot," I blubber into his shoulder.

"That was too long." He wipes my tears with his thumbs. "Let's never do that long apart again, okay?"

I nod, not knowing if that is even possible. He tucks me tightly under his arm and we walk toward the car. Matt opens the back door right away to say hi to Murphy.

"How is the best boy?" he croons at my dog. "Did you do a good job taking care of Mom while I was gone? Should we get you fitted for some steel teeth, big boy?" Murphy spins around in circles, tail wagging so hard black hairs fly all around the car. My heart swells.

"I love you, Matt."

"Love you too, babe."

Chrissie McCauley

We pull up to Matt's childhood home. It is exactly like I imagined: a small two-story structure that looks like every other house on the block. It stands out only because it's been well maintained; the yard is immaculate, and the house itself appears to have been recently painted. The front door is a cheerful red with a green *Welcome* wreath tacked onto it. I glance at Matt, knowing he's responsible for the care and upkeep of this home.

Sid is sitting at the kitchen table with Rita and a few of his oldest friends. "My boy! My girl!" he exclaims as we walk into the room. He rises slowly and gives us both giant hugs.

"Happy birthday, Pops!"

"I've missed you, Sid. Happy birthday!" I kiss him on the cheek.

"And who is this mangy mutt you've let into my home?" he asks with a smile, scratching behind Murphy's ears as the dog frantically wags his tail.

"This is Murphy, the toughest pup in all five boroughs," Matt says.

We bring our bags in, and Matt pulls me into the formal living room to show me the gift he bought his dad: it's a custom made voucher for an eight-course chef's tasting menu and wine pairing by James Beard winning chef, Gabriel Kreuther. I squint to read the fine print that says the dinner can be hosted at home or at a restaurant, with as many guests as he'd like.

"You know how much loves food. But he doesn't love eating out or leaving his comfort zones. So he's got options. It's also tough to find a suitable gift for the man who means the world to me. Especially when he tells me he wants nothing."

I look at him, his mussed hair, his casual stance, his brown eyes. "How did I find you?"

He looks at me.

"You are so incredibly thoughtful. And generous and kind. I don't know how I found you, but I'm glad I did." I press my hands against his chest and pull him close to me. When we kiss, I remember how much I've missed him. His taste, his smell, the feel of his body pushed against me.

"I have been thinking about how good it's going to feel to be inside you after every single moment we've been apart," he whispers into my ear.

"It's time for dinner, kids!" yells Sid.

* * *

"I saw mom last week," Sid says in the car on the way to the restaurant.

"How was she?" Matt asks.

"The same."

Matt nods and sets his mouth into a firm line. I reach across the console for his hand.

We walk into Sid's favorite restaurant, Henry's Salt of the Sea. It's a blast from the past—dark green paneled walls, burgundy napkins and tablecloths, and model wooden ships perched throughout. It feels perfectly Sid. Matt rented out the back room, and it's packed with men all over the age of seventy, at least ten of them. Sid lights up and looks at least a decade younger. There's a giant smile plastered on his face all night. It's no wonder he loves coming back here.

The dinner is a joyous affair. I feel so content to watch Sid and his friends banter and laugh while I hold Matt's hand under the table. After plates are cleared, Matt brings out a cake ablaze with eighty-three candles. Sid turns serious and closes his eyes for a few moments, contemplating his wish. He looks around the table, then blows the candles out in three swift exhales. We clap and cheer, and Sid's friends present him with a group gift—keys to a pimped-out golf cart. With his mobility becoming more limited, it will be a great way for him to visit his friends within the neighborhood in style. He is visibly touched, misty-eyed, and doesn't stop talking about it the entire ride home.

Later that night, after Rita has gone home and Matt has helped Sid to bed, he comes into our room, his childhood bedroom. It was redone long ago—gone are the Joni Mitchell and Eagles posters that Matt says once adorned these walls, as are the guitars, amps, picks, and strings that were once strewn about the floor. Now it is devoid of clutter and painted gray, with simple wooden furniture. Two book-shelves against the back wall still hold Matt's awards and stacks and stacks of journals.

"Matt Johnson original songs. Vintage." He skims through them.

"You could probably auction those off on eBay."

"The content in those journals is so deeply embarrassing, I wouldn't let anyone look at them for all the money in the world." He laughs and changes into shorts before climbing into bed next to me. His long arm drapes across my stomach.

"That was so fun, and so good for my dad. I'm glad you could be here."

"I'm glad, too. I can see why he loves Pennsylvania so much. I've never seen so many short, white-haired men in one room at the same time. I could hardly tell them apart."

Matt laughs.

"How are you feeling, being back here, being close to every-thing?" I ask. Matt's mom lives in a long-term care center here in Allentown.

"I'm planning on going to see her tomorrow."

"What's that like?"

"Depressing. As you can imagine. She's technically in the memory care part of the facility, but no one is convinced she has any memory issues. It's just much better than the alternative, which would be some type of long-term psychiatric hospital." He rolls over to face me in bed. "Will you come with me?"

"Of course. I'd love to meet your mom." I kiss him.

"She's not really my mom anymore. She just isn't the person I'd hope to introduce my girlfriend to. The mom I choose to remember is the one who would dance to jazz music in the kitchen with my dad. She had bright eyes and an even brighter smile. She made my lunch and scratched my back and always told me she loved me. She's very much a stranger now. But it doesn't negate the responsibility I feel to see her. Dad too. You know they are still married?"

"No, I didn't know that."

"It's been almost twenty-five years since she disappeared right in front of us. At first, he hoped she'd snap out of it, that she just needed time to grieve about Eric, to adjust to life without him. But then it was a year in, and then two, and before we knew it, it had been five years. I'd already had two albums by then. I was living in New York and coming back to Allentown every weekend to see her. To visit her. I'd sing to her; I'd read to her. I'd show her pictures of my life. Dad brought her all the magazine articles about me, only the good ones, all my records. He'd show her videos of me on TV. And nothing. She just stared at me, looking at me but not seeing me. She never said a single word.

"I got pissed. I was frustrated. And angry. And sad. I missed her. I felt like she was being selfish. I told Dad at that point he should consider divorcing her and moving on with his life, having a chance to meet someone new and have some happiness. But he refused. He told me, 'I made her a promise, I gave her my word, and I meant it.' I was never able to understand that until I got older. To me, it seemed obvious that the answer was to leave. Why anchor yourself to a sinking ship? But I get now there is so much to learn, so much goodness—reverence, really—in honoring those vows. My dad made it work. He filled his life in other ways, with his friends, this town, me—things to help make the void not seem so big.

"If I'm honest, I think the whole thing fucked me up a bit in terms of relationships. I admire the commitment my dad made, but I

251

still don't know where I land on the whole situation. It's probably caused me to be too cautious in relationships. Saying and doing certain things have felt like they have a lot of weight. I only want to do it all once. I've put this pressure on myself that I must be absolutely one hundred percent sure. I don't know." He rakes his hands down his face. "Being back here always makes me stuck too much inside my head."

His words hit me square in the chest. I can't stop myself from thinking about my own failed marriage. My own vows I tossed in the trash so easily. Nick and I had no real hardships, especially in comparison to Sid and Carol's loss of a child. I feel a surge of panic that Matt might be thinking the same thing.

"Did you ever bring any girls from high school into this room, back in the day?" I reach for him, desperate to change the subject.

"No way. I was way too much of a wimp to invite a girl into my room." He kisses my shoulder, my collarbone.

"You aren't such a wimp anymore though, right?"

"Right," he answers, eyes now focused on me.

I lean over and meet his lips, soft and waiting. We kiss, a now familiar dance that's full of passion and longing. I press my body against his like I can somehow meld us together.

I sit up and peel off my pajama top, leaving on just thin cotton pants and panties, then pin his arms above his head. With him rendered helpless, I kiss his neck.

"If you did this to me when I was in high school, I would've come in my pants by now." He laughs, trying to nip at me.

I quickly shuck off my pants. With my panties still on, I start slowly but steadily moving against his shorts, feeling him harden underneath me. I guide his hands to my chest, my stomach, my hips, before letting him feel of the wetness between my legs.

"You are unreal," he moans, now frantically trying to free his hands from my grasp.

In one fell swoop I peel my panties and his shorts off, climb back on top, and quietly slide him inside of me. My breath quickens as he lets out a series of expletives. I shush him and cover his mouth with my hand.

"Shhhh. You can't. Wake. The. Parents." His brown eyes smile up at me, full of the dark intensity that seems to follow him around—the passion, the lust, the possessiveness.

He laughs through my hand. "Dad is half deaf."

He grips my hips, moving me up and down, back and forth. The anticipation builds, the sensation is in overload. I fall forward, flatten my body against his, feel him pressed up somewhere deep inside me. With my face against the bed, I bite down on the sheets to stifle my sighs as I feel the first tremors of my orgasm start to pulse through my core.

"Wait," he gasps, frantic. "Wait, baby. Look at me. I want to watch you come." I rise and hover above him so close our noses touch. I fight the impulse to look away under the potency of his eyes. I focus and keep moving, both of us locked in on each other. A few more breaths and I'm gone. An orgasm rips through me, and I feel him come with me, his release deep inside me. We ride out the waves of pleasure together, the quiet intensity producing a high-octane moment.

Neither of us moves for a very long time. When I finally look at him, he is serene, calm, wearing the post-sex blissed-out Matt Johnson face I've come to adore. We lay in bed, our legs intertwined, him drawing circles on my back, me doing my usual tracing of his tattoos.

It's only then I notice something different: a tattoo on his right wrist, at the very end of his sleeve. I pull his arm closer to get a better look.

"Is this new?"

I must have missed it earlier, with his watchband covering it. He sits up, and his cheeks flush—he seems reluctant to let me see.

"I wanted to wait for the right moment to show you. But I guess now is as good a time as ever." He offers me his arm, letting me examine it up close. It's small, barely the size of a half dollar, but the design is intricate, the colors bright pink and vibrant—an almost perfect replica of the dahlia he gave me in Mexico.

"What are you thinking?" He looks vulnerable.

"I'm thinking it's almost as beautiful as the original one."

"It reminds me of you. Beautiful, bright, breathtaking, made up of so many tiny petals, so many layers. I did some research on it after we left Mexico. Dahlias were first discovered sometime in the sixteenth century. The Aztecs revered the flower, not only for its beauty but its medicinal and healing properties. It is a symbol for love, devotion, beauty, and dignity. The dark pink ones like mine are a symbol of kindness and grace. All parts of you that I love." His eyes search my face. "I knew I was falling in love with you in Mexico. I wasn't sure how it would all play out, but it's been better than I could've ever imagined."

I'm speechless, blown away by the gesture. A deep sense of possessiveness and love fills me. Matt has permanently marked his body with a symbol that will forever remind him of me.

"I love it. And I love you," I say.

Several minutes pass, and I am wide awake staring at the ceiling in the dark, thinking about everything Matt said, what it might mean. I assume he's asleep, so I'm surprised when I hear him say, "This feels like more than anything I've experienced before. Do you feel the same way?"

"Yes. You've completely swept me away."

He nuzzles in next to me, and I go back to staring at the ceiling. I can't seem to find the words as easily as Matt can. He always manages to make everything sound like poetry. I can't disagree that what the two of us have is remarkable, and I meant what I said wholeheartedly. But getting swept away is only romantic if it ends well, if there's a happily ever after. If it ends in disaster, you're a blind fool. A fine line to walk.

I feel that familiar sense of unease again. I know what it's like to fall in love. As does Matt. Maybe not like *this*, but in general. It's addictive, exhilarating, a high that can't be replicated by any substance on earth. Falling in love is a pure dopamine trip—I have no doubt if I got in an MRI machine at this moment, my brain would be lit up like a Fourth of July sky. But what happens when this phase slows down and evolves into something different? Will love be enough? For me, for him, for us? Yes, we have fallen in love. But what happens when we land?

I finally drift off to sleep hoping we'll be able figure it out together.

Chapter Thirty

The next morning, I wake to an empty bed. I find Matt in the basement, picking at an old guitar. I watch from the stairs as he adjusts and readjusts the saddles, strumming out random chords. He's quiet, lost in his thoughts. I sneak back upstairs to get ready to meet his mom, giving him the space to process what it might be like seeing her for the first time in almost two months. We have a few errands to run before we make our way over to the long-term care facility.

First, we stop by a florist and pick up two massive bouquets of blue hydrangeas.

"She used to grow them in our front yard; they were her pride and joy," he explains.

The next stop is a small boutique, where Matt picks out an expensive plush pajama set in navy blue. The last stop is the Amish Village Bakeshop to grab coffees and treats for the staff, a half dozen whoopee pies for Sid, and a loaf of Friendship Bread for his mom. "It's like a sourdough bread that turned into a cake. It's her favorite," he tells me.

As we walk out of the bakeshop, I notice a young woman milling around the door, stealing glances at Matt. She has a baby in a carrier on her chest and is holding the hand of a little boy. Right before we exit, she approaches Matt.

"Hi, Matt, I'm a huge fan. I have been to every one of your Philly shows."

"All of them?"

"Yes. I especially loved the solo tour you did ten years ago ..." she continues, but her son is tugging on her hand. "Mommyyyyy, I want a muffin."

"What's your name, buddy?" Matt crouches down to his level. The boy instinctively moves behind the safety of his mom's leg.

"Hudson," he says into her jeans.

"And how old are you?" Matt asks.

"Free." Hudson holds up up two fingers.

"Ah, three is a fine age to be. What do you like to do?"

"Twucks. Play with twucks." The boy emerges from behind his mom's legs.

"Fire trucks?"

"Yeah, and trash twucks and 'cycle twucks ," the boy says.

"All very important civil services," Matt responds. "Can I get him a muffin?"

"Um, um, sure?" the mom stammers, starstruck.

Matt offers his hand to the little boy, who reluctantly takes it and walks a few feet over to the counter. I'm left with the mom and her sleeping baby.

"I can't believe I just met Matt Johnson," she says to me but mostly to herself. "He was, like, on posters in my room when I was growing up. I knew he was from here, but I never thought I'd run into him! Wow," she gushes.

"Yeah! Small world," I say. My attention drifts over to the counter, where Matt has picked up the little boy to give him a better vantage point of the muffin selection. It looks like the most natural thing in the world for him.

"You're Julia? I saw the photos from the Grammys," the mom says.

"Yes. That's me."

"Wow, you are a lucky woman. He's going to make a great dad."

They walk back a few moments later. Hudson's face is victorious as he proffers up not one but two muffins.

"He's got great taste," Matt says to the mom. "I'm not playing in Philly for my next tour, but I'll be in New York, which is probably the closest to here. A quick train ride. Tell me your name, and I'll leave two tickets for you at the box office."

"*What?*"

"I'd love you to come to my show. If you can find a babysitter."

"That would be unreal! Fantastic! Wow. Thanks so much. Can I hug you?" she asks.

"Of course," Matt says, and I watch him try to navigate a side hug so as not to crush the baby in the carrier. While Matt takes out his phone to get the woman's information, I stare at the baby—her chubby hands rest under her round cheeks. She has miles-long eyelashes and the tiniest little mouth.

"Do you want to take a picture?" Matt asks the woman. I've become familiar with this strategy of his—he knows that most of the time people want a picture with him, and to ease their discomfort in asking, he will suggest it like it's his idea. His thoughtfulness never ceases to amaze me.

The woman, Matt, and Hudson stand in front of the muffin counter while I snap a photo. "You guys have a great day!" Matt says as we head out.

We walk to the car, but my brain is still inside that shop, watching Matt with that little boy, the preciousness of that baby girl. Something stirs in me, a yearning I've never felt before. We start driving, and I steal glances at him. I picture his big brown eyes, his perfect pouty lips, maybe my nose, our combined dark hair on a baby of our own. He notices.

"I know that look by now. What are you thinking about?"

"Just thinking about how much I love you."

"I love you, too."

"Also thinking about how cute those kids were," I add.

He grabs my hand across the console, squeezing it tightly.

He lifts his sunglasses to look at me and says, "Ours will be cuter."

I think my heart might explode.

* * *

We are forced back to reality when we pull up to the long-term care facility where Carol Johnson has resided for the past two decades.

I feel Matt's tension grow with each step we take toward the doors. I am greeted by the familiar smell of bleach and ammonia; it's strangely comforting, reminding me of the halls of my own hospital. Matt stops by the front desk and drops off a giant gift-wrapped box.

"Well, well, if it isn't the famous Mr. Matt Johnson," the woman behind the desk says.

"Hi, Leah, it's great to see you." He gives her a quick kiss on the cheek. "This is for you guys—the new Nespresso machine and a few dozen pods. Should hold you over for a day or two." He plops it down on the desk. I hand over the other treats we picked up at the bakery.

"You are too good to us. We miss seeing you around here." I see Matt's body language shift at that. His shoulders shoot up as she unknowingly taps on the guilt he feels not seeing his mom more often.

"This is my girlfriend, Julia Anderson."

"Well, this is a first." She smiles warmly. "It is a pleasure to meet you. Carol will be thrilled."

"How is she today?" Matt asks, and we start down the long, brightly lit hallway.

"The same. She's been sitting in the sunroom more often lately, but it's much of the same. I'm sorry, sweetheart."

We stop outside her room, and I hear jazz music playing behind the door. Matt takes a deep breath and gently knocks.

"Hi, Mom."

Carol Johnson sits in a recliner in the corner of the room. Her eyes are closed, but she rocks slowly in her chair to the rhythm of the music. She is tall, thin, all lithe limbs, her beautiful hair— cut to her shoulders—thick and dark brown just like Matt's but with streaks of white throughout. She looks remarkably young for being almost eighty. Her porcelain skin is practically wrinkle-free, probably from being indoors for almost twenty years.

She opens her eyes and looks at Matt. I swear I see a flicker of recognition.

"I want you to meet someone." Matt holds my hand and walks us closer to her chair. "This is Julia."

"It's so nice to meet you, Mrs. Johnson," I say.

She looks at me, and again I feel some sense of awareness or, at the very least, a surveying of me.

"We just celebrated Dad's birthday. Same restaurant as every other year, and we missed you. Maybe you can join us next year," Matt says casually, like he's having a normal conversation.

"Want to see?" He kneels beside her and scrolls through photos on his phone.

She doesn't look.

Matt busies himself unloading the things he's brought her. He puts the bread in her mini kitchen, the flowers in vases by her bedside table and next to her recliner. He places the bag with the pajamas on her lap. She doesn't touch it or move to open it, so Matt does it for her, holding up the cozy pajamas. "I thought these might look nice on you."

Nothing.

I pull up a chair next to her and start talking. "I've heard so much about you. I love Allentown. I've never been here before. Matt showed me the rose gardens, they are beautiful. He said they're one of your favorite places."

She continues rocking, eyes fixed on a spot on the floor.

Matt changes the record behind us. She has almost the same sound system as the one in his apartment in New York. I watch her as Stevie Nicks starts singing "Dreams." She sits up, turns and looks at Matt, and smiles at him. A big, bright smile. A smile that is so much like his, it makes me want to cry. His eyes go wide, and he smiles just as big right back.

"You like this one, Mom?"

Still smiling, she leans back in her chair, rocking to the beat, but she doesn't answer his question. We stay for a few more hours and have lunch together before heading back to Sid's house.

There were no more signs of recognition after "Dreams," but I can see reignited hope shining in Matt's eyes.

"She hasn't done anything like that in a long time," he tells me on the way home.

"It seemed like she recognized you and what was going on. And she seemed very connected to the music."

Matt nods. "What did you think?"

"I think she's lovely, Matt."

"No, I mean, what do you think is wrong with her? What's your professional opinion?"

"Oh, babe, I can't make any type of assessment just based off that interaction."

"I know, I know. But if you had to guess, what do you think is going on?"

I hesitate. "I'm not sure. I'd be interested to see her history. To see how she's presented to other people over the years and what they've noticed. But what I know for sure is that her generation didn't know half as much as we know now about health and mental health—especially trauma and grief. Women with any type of mental health concern, especially moms in her era, were often ignored. Or, at the very least, misdiagnosed and mistreated. That's where all these terms like *hysteria*, *exhaustion*, and *mental breakdown* came from. But even so, I think it would be unusual for her to be like this unprompted."

Matt listens intently, pulling on his lower lip.

"My guess—and it's just a guess—is that maybe she had some preexisting mental health condition—major depression or anxiety-panic disorder—that she was able to cope with until the trauma of watching her child get sick, plus the treatments that followed, and eventually the loss of Eric altogether. The stress, trauma, and grief combination are brutal and overwhelming. Maybe it was too much for her to manage. Maybe it felt safer for her to check out, to go inside of herself, into the quiet, or into a different reality that made her able to survive a loss like that. And maybe it's just been so long at this point she doesn't know how to come back, even if she wants to."

"Do you think it's possible that she could come back?"

My heart sinks. "I don't know, Matt."

"I'm not going to hold you to it, Jules. I've accepted this is how she will be. I just want to know what you think."

I sit quietly, weighing my words. "I think anything is possible."

He grabs my hand and brings it to his lips. "I think so, too."

Chapter Thirty-One

It's an ordinary Wednesday at work, the bulk of which I have spent in a four-hour meeting with the hospital's head of PR to work out the details for our upcoming gala. Invitations have been sent, and we are expecting more than three hundred attendees, including a dozen philanthropists with some very deep pockets. If all goes well, I have an ambitious goal of opening the unit by summertime. I'm back in my office, trying to finish up my last remaining tasks for the day and texting with Matt.

He sends me a picture of himself with a beer and a half dozen oysters somewhere, the sun illuminating his handsome face.

Wish you were here.

I stare out my window—March in New York is depressing. Gray, wet, and cold. Made worse by the knowledge that spring is just around the corner but feels so far away. I wonder for a moment why I live here. Especially since the man I love lives primarily in a place where it's sunny most of the year. It's not the first time I've thought this in recent weeks.

> Wish I was too.

> I can't wait to see you this weekend.

This weekend I'm cashing in on the second part of my Christmas gift from him—a surprise weekend away, hopefully somewhere warmer than New York. Just the two of us. I cannot wait.

I hear a tentative knock on my door.

"Come in!"

Dave pops his head in with an unreadable look on his face.

"What's up?" I ask.

He meanders around my office, his hands behind his back, looking nervous. "Oh, nothing, just thought I'd see what you're doing."

"Okay, except you only ever come here if you want to gossip, take a nap, or steal my snacks, so what's up?"

"Well ... since you mentioned gossip, did you happen to look today at that gossip site I told you about?"

"No, Dave, you know I don't want to see anything on there. It's bad for my health. And probably yours, too."

"Well, maybe you should. I saw something. Today. About Matt. It's kind of roundabout, but it's pretty obvious it's him."

My heart rate accelerates. "Matt says those websites are all bull-shit. Half the time it's the people themselves submitting stuff to drum up PR. I don't think we should pay attention to it."

"Okay, well, I can't *not* tell you, so I'm just going to read it quickly and then you can go back to ignoring it." He pulls his phone out of his back pocket. "'Dreamy solo singer who has been notoriously single for the past several years, save for his big debut with an unknown normie, seen canoodling with a love her/hate her country crooner in Santa Monica Tuesday night. Is our favorite lothario up to his old tricks?'"

It clearly describes Matt. My automatic thought is, *Where there's smoke, there's fire.* I have heard this from my mom for years, in the context of trusting your instincts. I feel nauseous.

"That's bullshit, Dave," I say with as much conviction as I can muster.

"You're probably right, but the comments are blowing up. The Internet has already identified it as Matt and Kerri Taylor. No pictures, though. Not yet, at least."

"I don't want to see or hear about it. This is exactly what he warned me about."

"Okay, Jules, I know you're probably right. I just needed you to know. I couldn't have you wandering out in the world without knowing this is circulating. Just talk to him about it. Clear the air. I'm sure it's a simple explanation. You're seeing him this weekend, right?"

"Right. I will. Thanks for the heads-up."

He walks out of my office with what looks like pity in his eyes. I do not like it.

I can't ignore the insidious thoughts percolating in my head, and I resist the urge to let myself go down the rabbit hole, knowing it is a terrible idea.

I tap my phone open and do it anyway.

As I scroll, I'm flooded with horrible thoughts.

Obviously, he is fucking someone else.

Of course it was too good to be true.

I knew there was no way this would work with me and him.

What was I thinking?

How did I get myself caught up in this shit?

He lives on a different planet, one where I don't belong.

There's no way he would do that to me. He's been nothing but honest from the start.

He loves me. I know he does.

But there were all those rumors years ago about stuff exactly like this. History repeats itself.

Kerri Taylor? That bitch. The hideous, horrible bitch.

If that's what he's into, then obviously there's no way he's into me. We could not be more different. I have a soul, for one.

Why did I put myself in this position in the first place?

I am a fucking idiot.

This is so humiliating. Even if it isn't true, most people don't know that.

Did I betray myself again?

Did I ignore my instincts?

What did I miss?

Why can't I ever get this right?

I scan Kerri Taylor's social media and see she indeed appears to be in LA. So? LA is a huge town. I Google *Kerri Taylor and Matt Johnson*. The gossip site link pops up first, but it's already been picked up by TMZ, and they have a photo. The very grainy, barely discernible picture shows someone Matt's height and build, but I immediately recognize the jacket he is wearing. It's him. Leaving a restaurant and getting into a waiting car. Followed by an equally distorted long-range photo of someone resembling Kerri Taylor leaving the same restaurant, getting into a separate car. Her platinum blond hair is impossible to miss. My chest clenches.

It takes all my willpower to shut down my brain and my Google search and focus on something else. I send a quick email to my coworkers that I'm heading home early. I can't possibly sit here for another minute.

The walk home clears my head, but barely. This is the exact scenario Matt has described. He's coached me, prepped me, reassured me that something like this was almost a guarantee. He told me how to handle it, how to turn down the noise, how to ignore it. *Just keep doing what you're doing*, his voice floods through my head. He's done nothing in our entire relationship that would lead me to believe I can't trust him. And yet, I've had years of lived experience watching my mom, my girlfriends, even myself, in a way, be blindsided by men who change their minds. Back and forth, back and forth I go in my brain the entire twenty blocks home.

By the time I unlock my front door, I decide I won't say anything to him about it.

Chapter Thirty-Two

Meredith invites me for drinks and dinner before I leave for my trip. It's been approximately forty-eight hours since Dave showed me the gossip website. I've held strong and haven't mentioned anything to Matt. But the knowledge of it is eating away at me.

We meet at one of our favorite Mexican restaurants halfway between our two apartments. True to form, I arrive first and order us both top shelf margaritas on the rocks with lots of salt. Meredith breezes in, offering unnecessary apologies. I never mind that she's always late; it is as much a part of her personality as her unwavering loyalty.

She sits down and takes a long pull from her drink. Then squints her eyes at me.

"What's up? You have that look."

There's no hiding with a best friend.

I pour out all my worries, everything that has been weighing on my mind, in no particular order. The comments from Matt's exes in LA that I can't shake, the threat of people taking my picture without my knowing, the gossip that Dave showed me, the photos I saw of

Matt and Kerri. I talk about Matt's intensity in general—sexy, mostly, but also at times teetering on too much. I talk about my insecurities, my perception of his insecurities, the way I've been second-guessing the validity of our whirlwind romance, my lack of clarity on where this is going and what it will look like. I ask if it's even realistic to think I could be with someone again long term but especially someone who happens to be famous. Finally, I divulge my ultimate fear—the fear of making the wrong choice, of fucking up, the fear of failure. The fear that something is seriously wrong with me. By the time I've debriefed her, she's drained her margarita and ordered another round.

She blows out a long breath. "Damn, Jules. I had no idea you've been holding this all in for so long. You have a lot to think about, that's for sure."

"I know. I don't know why it has to be complicated. It feels like I'm getting in my own way or something. Like I can't see clearly."

"Well, why don't we try to simplify it for you, then?"

"I'm all ears."

We order dinner, the usual—enchiladas for her, fajitas for me, guacamole to share. And begin simplifying.

"Okay, first things first, he's obviously gorgeous, and you're insanely attracted to him. I am, too, just so you know, but I think a corpse would be, so the physical part isn't an issue, correct?"

"Correct, but the caveat is that the intimacy in general, not just the sex, is so off the charts, it sometimes it feels like too much. Too intense. Is that even possible? I feel like we're always at a ten out of ten, and it distorts my vision, like my logical side is offline most of the time we're together."

Meredith looks at me, deadpan. "I'm trying to understand where you're coming from, but I am also working very hard not to roll my eyes at you right now. Since when is it a bad thing to be that connected? You know the intensity of the sex part will change."

"Will it?" I can't help but remember how often I'd use sex as a measuring stick for how well or poorly my marriage was going.

"Jules, come on. It will. It always does, and you know it. But that isn't a bad thing. Sex is not the only measure of love. It's not the only measure of attraction, or connection, or even desire. And it certainly isn't the only linchpin for having a happy relationship. Even if it fades a little at times, that doesn't mean it's gone. It comes back. Ebbs and flows. It doesn't make it any less valuable or passionate because it's not the exact same as it is right now. Plus, you'll find new ways to excite each other and make it special. I know all our friends love to talk shit about their husbands and the boring sex, them pawing at them all the time, blah blah blah, and sure, I join in sometimes for fun, but that isn't the case for me and JP, and we've been married for twelve years."

I nod in agreement. She makes an excellent point.

"And we are both well aware of all the toxic bullshit tropes we are fed about love and life and marriage—we've talked that to death plenty of times. You can't let those poison your well. Next issue." She polishes off her second margarita and orders another.

"I want to be married again. I want to have kids."

"I know," she says softly. She knows this has always been a sore spot for me.

"I don't know what that would look like with him. I can't picture it. And I don't want to fuck it up again. Matt's life is ... unconventional. There are so many good parts of it, but I don't think it's considered normal by any stretch of the imagination."

Meredith interrupts me. "This is where you are making things more complicated than they need to be. First of all, you didn't fuck up anything with Nick, that was a dumpster fire you both contributed to equally, so stop using that as some sort of metric. And next, do you want to be married to him? Do you want to have kids with him? If the answer is yes, forget everything else."

"How can I forget everything else? That isn't reality. I don't even know where we would live."

She sighs, exasperated. "If you love him and want to marry him and have kids with him, to me that means you are committed to him.

I'd argue you didn't have that strong conviction, at least with the kids thing, when you were with Nick. If you have the relationship I think you have, you guys talk. A lot. You talk too much, quite frankly. It's not always fun to have a therapist as a best friend. But those lines of communication are open. You can figure out all the details. Focus on the big picture stuff. Not the minutiae. That shit will be in every relationship whether you're with Matt or the next banker who walks into this restaurant. Everyone has their own weird shit to navigate, including you. We are simplifying. Remember?"

As soon as she says it, my brain flashes back to Matt in my office, that first week in July. Staring at the painting on my wall. His amber voice, raspy and warm, saying, *If you can just take a minute to really look at something, to find the heart of it, it's pretty simple.*

I smile at the memory. "Yes, I can picture myself marrying him. And having kids with him. And even more, I can picture all the in between with him. The boring nights, the slog of work, the logistics of travel, the issues we'll have to navigate. I can picture us together through those things, the figuring it out part of life."

Meredith smiles at me, and something washes over her face. Joy? Excitement? A knowing? I can't tell.

"What next?" she asks. She is on a roll.

"The pictures. On the gossip website."

"You mean the ones you never even talked to him about? Seriously, Jules? Aren't you a therapist?"

"Yes, Mere, I am a therapist, but I'm a person first."

"Do you trust him?"

"Yes." I answer without hesitation.

"So, what's the problem?"

"He's told me about instances when he has done less than honorable things in other relationships. He's clearly capable of it."

"But he's never done that with you. You're going to punish him for being honest about past bad decisions?"

She's right. Again. I'm reminded that my entire career is built on the fundamental belief that people can grow, change, and evolve. *Wow, am I a hypocrite.*

She grabs my hand. "Okay. Well, what is that shit you say to me all the time? *In the absence of information, we fill in the blanks with our own subconscious bullshit.* Or something like that. You're inserting your own worst-case scenario without even consulting him. There's an easy way to simplify that one. Just fucking ask him! Get the information and then figure it out."

When she puts it like that, it does seem simple. I feel the tension melt out of my shoulders. Talking it out has proved to be a better option than going around in circles in my own head. Thank God for girlfriends.

We finish our dinner and switch from margaritas to Modelos. Meredith's phone buzzes.

"JP is around the block. He's going to stop by for a beer."

While we wait for him, Meredith fills me in on her ongoing struggle to decide whether she wants kids. When I first met her, she was certain that babies were not in the plans for her and JP. "I feel a calling to be the cool, fun, rich aunt. And I can be all those things because I won't have kids," she told me. But in the past year or so something shifted, which she attributes to many things—her waning egg supply, the patriarchy, and feeling more attracted to JP than ever.

"I feel like after all this hemming and hawing over a decision, I'll wind up being infertile so all these endless conversations will have been for nothing."

"If that's where you're at, then why not just give it a good old-fashioned college try?"

"I think I just might."

She looks over my shoulder. "Well, well, well, if it isn't my sperm donor himself."

I turn to greet JP but stop dead in my tracks when I see who is strolling in behind him.

Nick.

Chapter Thirty-Three

"What the fuck, JP?" Meredith says. "You failed to mention my best friend's ex-husband was in tow."

"We had that pickleball thing tonight, babe, I told you. You know Nick is on my team." Nick stands behind JP, sheepish. I can't remember the last time I saw him. Probably not since we met at the attorney's office and signed our final divorce decree.

"A little warning would've been nice." She looks to me to get a read on what I'm thinking. I shrug and give her a look—it's fine.

As they take off their coats and sit, I watch him. Nick looks good. His blond hair is shorter than it was when I last saw him. He finally got rid of his horrible facial hair and looks clean cut and much younger than I remember. He lost the quarantine weight and seems to have put some muscle back on. He looks every bit the young, cocky athlete I met in Baltimore all those years ago, but slightly more refined.

"Hi, Julia, good to see you."

I give him an awkward wave.

Meredith flags down the server and orders a round of beers.

"You two smell terrible." She scrunches her nose. "Do they not have showers at the New York Athletic Club? For the money you two shell out every month there, certainly you could've utilized the amenities."

I can't stop looking at Nick. A flood of memories hits me: carrying a couch up the three flights to our first apartment, laughing, sweating, and cursing. Picking crabs and drinking Natty Bos in my mom's backyard. Opening a bottle of champagne and drinking it straight from the bottle in our New Jersey house. I try and fail to stop myself.

For the next forty-five minutes, I nurse my beer and listen to the three of them banter.

"You're lucky you're one of my best friends, because you are clearly the weakest link on our team," JP says.

"Are you serious?" Nick laughs. "You're the one wearing two knee braces. Your arthritis is going to force us into the geriatric league."

"It's embarrassing for both of you. What are you guys, seventy-five? What is pickleball even? Actually, don't tell me, I'm so sick of hearing about it," Meredith says.

Eventually, she yawns and looks at her watch. "All right babe, let's go." They get up to leave, and Nick looks at me from across the booth.

"How about one last round?" he asks.

Meredith's eyes go wide.

"Okay," I say.

She mouths to me, "Are you okay?"

I nod.

Text me, she mimes before heading out hand in hand with JP.

"So, how have you been?" Nick asks.

"I've been great, how about you?"

"Good. Hoboken is a good scene for me. I come into the city three days a week but can work mostly from home. It's nice."

"That's great. How's your family?"

"They're good. My sister is pregnant again. Baby number three."

"Congrats to her."

"How are your mom and Ryan?"

"They're good. Everyone is good."

Silence.

"I won't pretend I don't know who you're dating," he says eventually.

I stare at him, remembering his text the morning after the Grammys. The one I never responded to.

"If I didn't know I fucked up before, I definitely know now," he murmurs.

"What are you talking about?"

He takes a deep breath, and something in his eyes seems suddenly old and tired. Like the burden of carrying these thoughts around has aged him. "I've had a lot of time to think over the past two years. I didn't see it for a long time—the part I played in the end of our marriage. I was so sure that what I was feeling at the time was permanent, that it would never change. I didn't realize if I had tried a little bit harder, maybe it would've gone away. Or at least maybe I could have prevented the distance from growing to what it was."

I'm shocked.

"I appreciate that, but I don't think it's necessary to hash any of it out at this point. It's all water under the bridge now, Nick."

"I know, I just wanted to say it. Maybe for the first time out loud, certainly the first time to you. I wanted to make sure you knew. I know you blamed yourself a lot. That wasn't fair."

"Why did we even get married, Nick?" I blurt out. I can't get over how sad he looks. It's making me sad.

"What do you mean, why? I loved you."

"I know. I know we thought we loved each other. But there was clearly a disconnect somewhere."

"I think I loved you in the best way I knew how, and it felt like marriage was the next step. It was the path we were on. We dated, lived together, an engagement and marriage were the next things on the list. We were one of the last couples to get married out of all of our friends."

"You asked me to marry you because our friends were doing it?"

"No, Jules. Of course not. I'm just saying that was the progression of a relationship as we knew it. We never had major issues. We never fought. It felt easy, we were a good fit. And it just seemed like marriage was the next step."

I sigh. "You're right," I say quietly.

"And there's a lot I wish I did differently."

"Me too," I admit.

He starts peeling the label off his beer. "Are you happy?" he asks.

"I don't think that's any of your business." I feel my hackles rise. I would've given anything to hear him ask me that question three years ago.

"Okay, I don't mean to pry." He backs off. "It's just, I know when you and Meredith come here for margarita nights, one if you is usually working through something."

I stop at that, forgetting how much Nick knows about my life, my habits, my friends, despite the fact we have not been together in so long.

"Yes, I am happy."

"I hope he doesn't make the same mistakes as I did."

"And what might those be?" I ask. I can't help myself.

For months after we split, I fantasized about the ways in which I might exact revenge on Nick for his stupidity in letting me go. Part of that included all the ways in which he'd grovel and say it was all his fault. It hasn't crossed my mind in a long time, but now that the opportunity is in front of me, I'm dying to know.

"Taking you for granted, for one. Only caring about me and all my own shit. I stopped noticing all the things that made you *you*, that made me fall in love with you all those years ago. The way you hum to yourself whenever you're doing things around the house. The way you'd absentmindedly thumb through your hair on the couch when you were watching TV. The way you make everyone around you better—calmer, more understood. The way you'd look at me when I was talking to you, you'd squint your eyes a little and I'd know you were really listening. You're doing it now. You're so perceptive, you always have been, another thing I took for granted. But that intuition of yours was unnerving to me at the end, because I felt like you could see me pulling away before I even knew what I was doing."

Putting aside the last few months of our failing marriage, Nick has always known how to cut to the core of me, in the best of ways. Being able to read me so clearly, know me so deeply, was a power he'd earned over time. I'm surprised by how introspective he seems to be now. I always thought his ego would make it near impossible for him to look inside himself and admit any wrongdoing. But the man sitting in front of me seems to be a very different version of the Nick I knew. A newer, more vulnerable one. I soften and feel something like pride at his evolution. Then, almost instantly, a sadness. Grief that I'll never get to know this version of Nick.

"You know, in hindsight, I'm glad you told me you didn't love me anymore. Don't get me wrong, it was incredibly painful, but you saying that made everything so final. We couldn't recover from that, so the next steps were clear. If you hadn't been honest with me in that moment, who knows what we would've done? Dragged out the misery a while longer? Added some kids to the mix and hoped that did the trick? Muddling through thirty-plus years together with no love isn't something I'd wish for anyone," I say.

"I'm not going to pretend seeing you with someone else doesn't hurt a little. I know I have no right to say that. But it does," he admits.

I nod. I feel for him. It cannot help that it would be hard for him to miss me and Matt. Especially after the Grammys.

"I'm not going to pry any more than I have already. But answer one question," he says.

"Okay."

"Does he know how lucky he is?"

I'm embarrassed to find my eyes filling with tears. Here sits my ex-husband, the source of my pain for years. But he's also somebody who I loved and who loved me for a long time prior to that.

"Yes. He does."

Nick nods, and the right side of his mouth twitches into a sad smile.

"Good. You deserve that and more, Jules."

Chapter Thirty-Four

Matt charters a private plane for me to take from LaGuardia to our mystery destination, solely so I can bring Murphy with me. He insists where we're going is "an oasis for Murphy." My dog has never been on a plane, and I've never flown private, so we are both very excited.

It is luxurious. No headache of security lines and baggage claims and delays. The pilot refuses to cave to my incessant needling for information about where we are going. He tells me he's been sworn to secrecy. I can figure out that we are headed south.

I doze off and wake when we begin our descent. I gather we have not been in the air very long. As we land, I see Matt waiting for me next to the runway. Leaning against a giant black truck, his arms crossed casually, he looks tired and a little pale, but still devastatingly handsome. As I walk down the stairs to the tarmac, his face breaks into a smile, one I've come to learn he reserves just for me.

Murphy runs from behind me and jumps all over him. Matt pets him before bounding over to me and scooping me up in his arms. "Hi, babe."

"Hi." I kiss him. "Where are we?"

"Virginia. We've got a short drive to our final destination."

I hop into the truck. "Virginia? This wasn't on my guess list."

"I figured. I thought about pivoting to a more exotic location—warmer. The Caribbean, maybe. But I want to show you this place. I wasn't sure when I'd get another chance. Once you see it, I think you'll understand."

"I'm excited."

We drive in silence, holding hands.

"I realized, on my flight here, that I've been living a pretty nomadic life for a long time," he starts.

"Yeah?"

"I've been thinking about it a lot. Home. What is it? Where is it? What am I looking for?"

"What have you come up with?"

"I always thought home was a place. A structure. Something I could see and touch with my hands. But that can't be right, because I have those. My homes in New York and LA. But they feel ... incomplete. LA feels a little more homey, I think, because of the yard and the space. But still, it's lacking. New York feels like I'm playing pretend. I sometimes feel like it's a very nice, very expensive, personalized hotel that I crash in when I'm there. So, then I was trying to think about the last time I felt at home. And I had to go back. Way back."

"Back to Allentown?" I guess.

"Yes. Exactly. But it's not that house. I still get those waves of sadness when I see the actual house. The home I'm thinking of is a moment in time. Me, Eric, my mom, and Dad. It's a memory. I don't even know if it's real or a fantasy or a mash-up of both. But it's a Saturday morning. Dad's making pancakes. Mom puts Fleetwood Mac on the record player and goes back into the kitchen, pours a cup of coffee for Dad and then one for herself. Eric and I are on our stomachs on the family room carpet, playing with G.I. Joes. Eric's setting up an epic battle, but I'm not paying attention 'cause I'm watching

Mom and Dad. And feeling this feeling of just pure love. Or joy. Or safety. I felt home."

"Home is a feeling," I echo.

"Yes. Up until now, my efforts to find *home* have been fruitless, 'cause I've been looking for the wrong thing."

"And now?"

"Now I think I know what I'm looking for," he says with his half smile.

He jerks the steering wheel to the right, and we head up the side of what appears to be a mountain. There is no road, but a path has been cleared, and the earth is packed down. We pull up to a clearing at the top next to giant oak trees, thirty feet high. Beyond that is a hill that slopes down into endless woods, farmland, and a large pond. The land is surrounded by the Blue Ridge Mountains in the distance, slumbering in the mist. It is breathtaking.

"We're here!" He is so cheerful he seems boyish—I love it.

I blink at him.

"You are standing where a future house will be built. I bought this land. Twenty-eight acres of pure American beauty."

"Wow." I walk around, taking in the vastness of this property. "This is incredible. But where are we?" The only sign I saw was for Charlottesville, and that was thirty minutes ago.

"Somewhere in the middle of Albemarle County. We're about a hundred miles southwest of DC, three hours from Virginia Beach, and about thirty minutes from downtown Charlottesville."

Murphy busies himself exploring the woods in front of us, sniffing and peeing every few feet.

"Walk with me." He takes my hand and heads toward a clearing in the wooded part of the property. "My dad has been on me for years about investing my money in something worthwhile. I couldn't think of a better thing to spend it on than my own piece of land."

"Why here?" It seems so random to me, this place in the foothills of the Blue Ridge Mountains.

"My quest to find home has been ongoing for a while now. I was in a bit of a rut last year, felt like I wasn't where I wanted to be in my life, wondering why I was alone when I didn't want to be, just feeling sorry for myself," he coughs into his elbow, "I opened a map and started typing in different towns, checking out the local real estate. I started looking out West in Wyoming, Montana, Idaho, and there were some beautiful options, it just felt like a bit of a cliché, plus I've always been an East Coast guy, so I started looking here, too. North seemed too cold, Florida seemed too hot; I wanted to be near the mountains, anyway, so I looked south, and this land popped up. As soon as I saw it on FaceTime with a Realtor, I could picture the house, the sunsets over the mountains, the space, the fresh air. Plus, all the amenities I could ever need are nearby in Charlottesville, and I'm within driving distance of my dad and New York in case the world ever shuts down again. It was perfect, so I put an offer in, and here we are."

He points to a tiny structure up ahead with an even tinier front porch, two windows, and a stone chimney. "It's taken forever to get the zoning permits, to get water and sewage and electricity up here. But this little house is almost finished. It's not my end goal, but I figure I can eventually turn it into a studio or guest house when I build the main house," he explains.

I walk inside. It is positively charming—a little studio with exposed beams and stone floors. In the center stands an antique wood burning stove. It has a tiny kitchen, bathroom, and living space. I can imagine two rocking chairs on the front porch and Murphy at my feet.

"What's going on in that mind of yours?" he asks me as I look around.

"I'm thinking you're right. This place is an oasis. I love it." I never saw myself in the country. I grew up outside of Baltimore, and besides my quick stint in the upper-class suburbia of New Jersey, I've always lived either in or directly outside of a major city. The idea of being out here with all this space, in nothing but nature, feels completely foreign. But I can see the appeal of going off the grid, especially for Matt.

"I love you. And I want your input when I start to draw out the plans for the house."

I freeze. He wants this to be ... our house?

"I was thinking about New York. And how when I'm there, we spend almost all our time at your apartment, even though there's more space at mine. Why is that? It's the same when I think back to Christmas—having everyone at my place, the same place I've lived in for years—but me and you, in the kitchen together, music playing, the warmth. These same structures, just typical New York apartments, they aren't anything special. So, what's different?"

I turn toward him, the mountains in the background. My head is spinning, my heart is soaring. I know what he is going to say.

"I think it's you, Jules. You're what feels like home."

I blink back tears and a calm comfort settles in my bones that this is right.

But a split second later, Kerri Taylor's venomous words ring in my ears: *When he starts promising you the world, get ready.*

I say nothing and lean in to kiss him. "I love you," I whisper in his ear, noticing how warm he feels against my face.

"We aren't staying here this weekend—the water is not reliable just yet, and there is no furniture, clearly. I thought that might not be the relaxing getaway you imagined. I booked us at a spectacular little hotel down closer to the town. We're going to sleep and eat, hit up the local vineyards, and I am going to ravish you. Because a month apart from you is way too long, Jules. We've gotta figure that out. As soon as possible. Ready to go?"

I nod. "Yes, we definitely need to figure it out."

* * *

On the short drive to the sprawling boutique hotel, Matt gets the chills. By the time we pull up, his muscles are aching. And once we check in and pull up to our own private cottage, he is burning up. The problem with the gorgeous, expensive boutique hotel is that it does not have a little shop in the lobby where you can buy Tylenol or Alka Seltzer, or Gatorade.

I rifle through the cottage, searching for supplies, barely noticing the beautifully appointed sitting area with fireplace bricks climbing to the ceiling, a blue velvet couch, and the lofted bed with floor to ceiling westward facing windows—everything feeling both old and new.

"Would you believe me if I told you this is called the George Washington suite?" Matt gives me a wan smile from the stairs, where he is hunched over the banister.

I laugh and help him up into the loft and into bed. "I think we're in the land of Thomas Jefferson, though."

"We are. His house ... Monticello is around here somewhere. We should go see it."

"Are you okay? This came out of nowhere," I worry.

"I was feeling tired and run down all week, but I thought it was just from traveling and stress." He starts shivering in the bed.

"I'm going to find a CVS."

"No, no, I'll be fine. I'll just take a nap. I have dinner reservations for us at seven."

I give him a look. "Matt. I love you, but you look like shit. We aren't going to dinner. You need medicine."

"No, this is supposed to be your Christmas gift! I've been looking forward to this weekend for an entire month. I'll be fine. Just give me an hour."

He looks miserable, so I make an executive decision and tuck him into bed. Murphy senses something amiss with his beloved Matt, so he hops onto the bed and curls up next to him. I navigate the giant black truck into downtown Charlottesville and see that Matt was right—anything we could need is right here. Stores, restaurants, shopping, plus the University of Virginia, all brick buildings, white columns, and pristine lawns pressed up against the picturesque downtown. The campus gives the town energy, a vibrancy. I am charmed.

I procure supplies, and when I get back to the room, Matt has piled every blanket and towel on top of himself, and is still shivering.

"I think I'm pretty sick," he says sadly as I walk in.

"Oh no, I'm so sorry." I sit next to him on the edge of the bed and give him some Tylenol.

"This is humiliating. And disappointing," he moans. "This is not what I had planned for this weekend. You should go get a different room, so you don't get sick, too. Leave me here to fester in my own germs," he says through chattering teeth.

"Not a chance. I'm not scared of your germs. Just rest."

I change into my pajamas and climb into bed next to him. Murphy snuggles in between us. I stare up at the ceiling, lost in my own thoughts. I accept that I won't be sleeping tonight between Matt's tossing and turning as he burns off his fever and my mind busily reading through my news ticker of worries.

I replay my conversation with Meredith, reminding myself to simplify. I know that I love Matt. But is that enough? Why do I feel a little nervous about the idea of a house together—isn't that where this was all headed anyway? My conversation with Nick is still rattling around in my brain, and I need to take stock of things before diving in headfirst. But it's a little late for that. Why do I feel such a strong need to know all the other unknowns about us? I need to talk to him about the Kerri Taylor photos, but why? Why am I doubting him? Do I not trust him? Should I just forget about mentioning any of my concerns at all? No, I need to mention it so I can stop filling in the gaps with worst case scenarios. But when?

I reach over and feel his forehead with the back of my wrist. *Not now, he's sick. Maybe tomorrow.*

Chapter Thirty-Five

I wake to Murphy's low whimper telling me he is desperate to go out. It's still dark out by the time we get back inside, and Matt is awake—looking worse for wear, but awake. I check his forehead with the back of my hand. It's cool.

"How are you feeling?"

"Better. I think."

"Your fever broke."

"That was brutal."

"It was. You poor thing."

"My whole body hurts."

"I think you should probably take it easy today."

"Thank you for taking care of me."

"You're welcome." I kiss the back of his hand. He looks toward the windows.

"Think we can catch the sunrise?"

"Yes. If you're up for it."

"I am. I've got a lot of making up to do after yesterday."

I help him up, grabbing a water and some blankets, and we head outside with Murphy. We sit in the Adirondack chairs in the front yard of our private suite, the sun barely visible on the horizon, turning the sky pink and orange over the mountains. Matt is wrapped up in multiple blankets, looking so pale and frail that I suppress a smile.

"What?" he asks with a weak smile.

"You look like the sick kid from *The Secret Garden*. Like you live in a convalescent home and I'm the caregiver, just bringing you outside for your ten minutes of fresh air."

He laughs at that, and it quickly turns into a coughing fit.

"Sorry, sorry."

"Not quite the robust forty-three-year-old I touted myself to be, I guess." He pauses. "But I will say, there is no one else I'd rather be sick as a dog with."

Once the sun rises in the sky, I decide it's now or never.

"I saw a picture on TMZ. Of you and of Kerri Taylor."

His eyes lock on mine.

"I was wondering if you saw that."

"Then why wouldn't you mention it to me?"

"There was nothing to mention."

"It didn't look that way."

"I was at dinner with my friends. She was at dinner with her friends. Same restaurant. We said hi, briefly. The manager let us know the paparazzi were outside. I wasn't in the mood to deal with them, so I left. I didn't even say goodbye to her. But then she left after me, and somehow it became a story. I have my suspicions, but that's all it was."

I nod, relieved by his explanation. It was exactly as I expected and what I knew deep down was probably the case.

"Did you think something was happening between her and me?"

"No. Not really. But it bothered me. A lot more than I thought it would. Especially after some of the comments she made to me during Grammys week."

He sits up at that. "What did she say?"

"Something along the lines of you heading for the hills when things get hard or the passion wears off. That you make promises you won't keep."

He leans back in the chair. "Well, she isn't completely wrong about that. That was what happened with her. But she is not you. She and I were together, very briefly, years ago. I was not who I am now. It's not the same, not even close."

I swallow.

"The thing between Kerri and me is ancient history. I'm sorry she said something that upset you. That was a shitty move on her part, although I'm not shocked that she did it. I think she was the one who tipped off the paparazzi that we were both at the same restaurant in the first place. It would've been a good story, and she needs a lot of attention. I told you, babe, these things happen in my world. It's just noise. Annoying and irritating, but it'll blow over. It always does. We just have to ignore it."

"I know, I'm just not used to it, I guess."

"I know. And I feel bad that my life is subjecting you to this. If I could change it, I would. I love you, Jules. I promise, I will never hurt you."

* * *

We lounge in and out of the room all day, letting Matt recover. Despite the proximity to the mountain, the early spring sunshine floods in, warming our faces and giving me a much-needed hit of vitamin D. By Sunday, Matt is feeling almost one hundred percent, but he is still weak. The color returns to his face, and he refuses to let his sickness ruin any more of our trip, so we shower and head down to a local vineyard.

Pippin Hill Farm and Vineyard is nestled in a little valley south-west of Charlottesville, surrounded by the mountains, grapevines, rolling farmland, and a gorgeous barn that serves as an event space. We walk down a road lined with hedges of dormant limelight hydrangeas trying desperately to grow with the help of the late

March sunshine. I can see how beautiful this place will be when everything is in bloom.

We sit on the covered patio, the beams wrapped in white lights, heat lamps at the ready in case the sun fades away. Matt orders for both of us—a wine flight for me and water for him. I watch at him as he stares at the scenery, both impossible to look away from. His hair is messy, and his eyes are bright, full of laugh lines. His nose is strong. His lips are the kind of pouty, full ones that women spend a lot of money to achieve. He looks completely relaxed—his normally furrowed brow is smooth. He's in his favorite jeans, a T-shirt, and a black corduroy long sleeve button-up shirt, and he spins his sunglasses on the table between two fingers, long legs spread wide. I feel like I won the lottery.

It's in this moment that I can see him here, in this place. Virginia. His vision here, the space, the dream house on the hill—it all makes sense. He'll travel the world, spend time in LA and New York. But he'll always come back here. It will be home. *Home.*

He catches me staring and smiles. "What?"

"I like looking at you," I admit.

He grins so wide it makes my chest ache.

"Look." He points at an arbor where a woman is standing on a chair weaving white flowers into it. Rows and rows of white chairs in neat stacks are being unfolded by staff. They are setting up for a wedding. A large one, by the look of it. "What do you think?"

"I think it's a perfect day for a wedding."

"Would you ever want something like that?"

"A wedding?"

"Yeah."

"I already had something like that, remember?"

"Yes, I mean another one."

"I'm not sure, I haven't thought about it."

A lie.

Of course I've thought about it. I've been resolute that I will never have another wedding. For a while I wasn't even sure if I wanted to get married again—the pain of the failure was so brutal, I didn't know why I'd willingly walk into it again. I've gotten over that, but to have another big wedding seems like a bridge too far, a farce. In my imaginary future wedding, I see myself in a simple, non-white dress, holding the hand of the man I love, waiting in line at city hall. Just us. We'll sign the paperwork, kiss, and head off to a tucked-away bar, toasting ourselves, no one the wiser, our own delicious little secret.

"Do you want something like that?" I ask him.

"Yes. I want all of it."

I nod and start wondering how we'd compromise on that ... but I stop myself. *A problem for another day.*

We stay at the vineyard for hours, me drinking wine, Matt eventually switching to sparkling water, walking the grounds, sitting on the porch, ordering cheese boards and truffle fries and sliders—Matt's appetite is finally returning. We watch the wedding guests arrive, one by one, and I wonder if we're both dragging out our afternoon so we can watch this wedding. Either way, I enjoy the pace. Nothing to do, nowhere to be except here with Matt.

Music starts, and a groom and his men appear from the side of the property, followed by bridesmaids walking slowly down the aisle in pale blue gowns. Then it's time for the bride. She walks out, her mom on one side, her dad on the other. Her face is so beautiful, so hopeful, it reminds me of a Roald Dahl quote about how good thoughts will shine out of your face like sunbeams. The bride is sunbeams personified, only trumped by her groom, who looks beside himself.

I look at Matt, who is watching the scene unfold with his trademark intensity. When I see a sheen of tears glistening in his eyes, I melt into a puddle. Matt is such a sap. Such a hopeless romantic. An eternal—if not unrealistic—optimist. I love and respect that about him so much. It's easy to be cynical, to be jaded. It's almost what the world demands. But not Matt. To stand in the face of heartbreak, tragedy, and despair and say, *yeah, I know that's a possibility, but I still choose to hope for the best* is something I admire about him. I wish a little more of it would rub off on me. I grab his hand.

"What?" He wipes his eyes with the back of his hand. "I just love love."

"I know you do. I love that about you."

We watch the ceremony from behind the hedges, feeling like interlopers but unable to move away. We can't hear the vows, but we can see the emotion written across the faces of the bride and groom. Once they seal their union with a kiss and exit the ceremony space, Matt and I finally get up to leave. The guests start milling around, waiting for cocktail hour, and it only takes a few moments before someone recognizes Matt.

"Are you Matt Johnson?" a woman asks.

"Yes, that's me." Matt ducks his head, shrinking himself.

"And you're the girlfriend? This is like ... confirming it?"

I look at Matt. He says nothing, so I answer. "Yes."

The girlfriend.

"Oh my God, I have to go tell Olivia. Can we take a selfie?"

A commotion is now underway. I see Matt's posture change. Tension ripples off him. He is uncomfortable.

"I wouldn't want to upstage the bride," he insists.

"She won't care! She loves your music, too. Can you play a song?"

I watch Matt expertly and diplomatically extricate himself from the conversation, with several selfies as a consolation prize.

When we finally make it to the truck, he sighs with relief. "Shall we?"

We head back to the hotel to spend our last night together before we go to our respective coasts again. As we drive the winding two-lane road, the sun begins to set, and I see it all in a flash—the house on the top of the hill, a porch that wraps around where we'll watch the sunsets, a stone terrace out back leading to a garden, soup simmering on the stove, Murphy roaming the land, and me and Matt, just us. Together.

Home.

Chapter Thirty-Six

Matt flies to New York to join me for the hospital's big gala scheduled for the third Saturday of April. It's another big event that will be photographed excessively, and I am still not entirely comfortable. Our relationship as far as the media is concerned is still neither confirmed nor denied by Matt in any kind of official statement or social media post—though it's obvious we are together. I ask him what would be so bad about just saying something? He balks when I suggest it, reminding me of his darkest moments. I try to not get bogged down by the optics of it and default to whatever makes him comfortable.

I'm nervous going into the gala, in part because of the pressure to make it a success—we need a very specific number in donations to make the dream of the unit a reality. The other part is the strange sensation I'm feeling about bringing Matt into my work world. Like the first time you bring your boyfriend home to meet your parents and he's covered in tattoos and drives a motorcycle. You know they're going to have opinions, and frankly, I don't want to hear any of them.

It doesn't help that every chance he gets, Dr. Kampf mentions how spectacular it'll be to have Matt Johnson photographed in front of a New York Grace backdrop.

He comes straight to my apartment with his luggage and several guitars. He's staying in New York for a few nights, heading over to a studio in the West Village to work. After a quick rendezvous in the shower together, I'm slightly more relaxed and begin the process of getting ready.

Matt lounges in my bed, scrolling on his laptop. As I dry my hair, I see the frown on his face. He seems miffed.

"What's up?"

"Nothing, babe."

"Liar."

"It's nothing. Nothing to talk about—it's your night."

"It's not my night, it's the hospital's night. And I want to know what's got you looking like that."

"These fucking emails. All the travel is getting booked for tour, and it just feels daunting to know I'm pretty much gone until July. Plus, I just got the details about all the PR stuff I have to do for the album. It's bumming me out. So much has to do with social media. And engagement. The label says you either go viral on TikTok or you're doomed. It just doesn't make sense for me and my music. I'm not doing songs people can necessarily do a dance to. I don't even think TikTok is my demographic. The whole thing just makes me feel very old. And tired."

"A TikTok dance? That's the metric for success now? Yikes."

"Tell me about it. And once the press stuff is done, the tour starts. And I'm excited about that. I love touring. But that just means I'm not going to see you as much."

I step out of the bathroom to look at him. "I know, that is bumming me out, too."

"But maybe it doesn't have to?"

I raise an eyebrow.

"You could come with me. Take a leave of absence."

"Ha ha. No way."

"Seriously? You're just going to shoot down the idea that quickly?"

"Were *you* serious? You want me to leave my job and follow you around the country for four months?"

"Yes, I do," he says quietly. "And I think that's a big part of the reason I've been feeling so ambivalent about the idea of going back on tour. There are a lot of long travel days and lonely nights. I always imagined at some point I wouldn't be doing it by myself anymore. I imagined that the person I love the most in the world would be with me. At least for some of it."

I freeze.

"And since we're talking about things I want, I want you to move to LA with me until we figure out the Virginia house. I want to be with you as much as I possibly can, and I think we can get more time together in LA. And I know there's opportunities for you out there. You even said it yourself, that doctor you used to work with at UCLA ..."

I interrupt him. "What? How long have you been sitting on this pitch? Doesn't New York make more sense? For both of us? Your dad is here, your mom is a short drive. My mom is a train ride away. You can do the same things here that you can do in LA. Plus, I don't think I like LA."

He stares at me, confused, like this wasn't what he expected of me.

I take a breath. "Can we table this for now? I need to think, and it deserves more than a rushed conversation. We've got to be at the gala in an hour."

"Okay. That's why I didn't want to say anything tonight, Jules." He rakes his hands through his hair.

I walk into the bathroom and finish getting ready, my mind racing. Living in New York seems like such a no-brainer. It dawns on me I just assumed this is where we'd land. Where I'd stay. That we'd go to the house in Virginia, someday, when we needed to get away. I try to focus on the speech I have to give tonight. I squeeze into my dress, a long-sleeved black velvet gown by Alessandra Rich. It's classy enough for a work event but still sexy.

"Will you zip me?"

Matt fumbles with the cuff links on his black tux. He walks behind me, and I can feel the tension between us. It's uncomfortable. He must feel it too, because he bends down to grab the bottom of my zipper and kisses each inch of skin along my spine as he closes it. It feels like an apology—for what, I'm not sure. At the top, he secures the hook and brushes my hair over my shoulder to kiss my neck. I instinctively lean into him, relaxing.

"You look beautiful," he murmurs softly.

"We'll figure everything out, okay?"

He nods, and we head down to our waiting car.

* * *

We arrive at the gala and meet Meredith and JP on the way in. Meredith looks radiant in a blue satin Galvan gown. Her blond hair is piled in a messy updo. JP looks dapper in a midnight blue tuxedo. The four of us walk into the step-and-repeat area together and spend twenty minutes taking photos. I answer questions for the press, explaining our goal, the mission of the unit, and the need it will serve. I can feel Matt's eyes on me as he stands off to the side, and when I catch his glance, pride shines back at me. As soon as I'm done, the reporters rush to him.

"So, Matt, are you going to be one of the big donors this evening?"

"Will you be performing tonight?"

"Is this confirmation of your relationship?"

He answers the questions quickly and succinctly, dodging the ones he doesn't like. He says he will not be performing and is happy to be here as a guest, in support of the hospital. *The hospital, not me,* I note. Then he says that of course he's donating to the unit, that he can't think of a greater cause. This is news to me—I never expected him to, but the fact that he does it without being asked touches me so deeply I have a fleeting thought that I'll pack my bags for LA tonight.

I am all over the place tonight and it is annoying.

We go inside and hit the ground running with a whirlwind of introductions. The hospital executives and big donors are eager to meet Matt, and I find myself biting back laughs watching these stuffy old guys act like fangirls. He disentangles himself from them and heads off to find Dave and Christine by the bar. I chat up several people while tracking Matt from across the room. I am not alone. Lots of other eyes in the room find their way to him, like he's magnetic.

Eventually we take our seats for dinner. Matt and I sit at a table with Meredith, JP, and several of the hospital executives, including Dr. Kampf, who is eager to talk Matt's ear off. The conversation and wine flows and everyone seems to be enjoying themselves. I sit quietly, mentally preparing myself for the speech I'll give once dessert is served.

As I run through notes on my phone, I hear Meredith, JP, and Matt talking and laughing next to me. Something about margaritas and pickleball, and then JP's voice, clear as a bell, saying, "You should've seen Julia's face when Nick walked in."

My head shoots up.

"When was that?" Matt asks. Casually. But I have become so attuned to him, I feel the microscopic shift.

"You're a moron, JP," Meredith mutters under her breath.

"A few weeks ago. It was no big deal, she didn't know he was coming. We just crashed girls' night," JP says, oblivious.

"Gotcha," Matt says. He turns to me and gives me a smile that doesn't reach his eyes.

Shit.

* * *

I hear Dr. Kampfs voice over the speakers, "And please let me introduce clinical director of New York Grace Hospital and the person who has been championing this project from its very inception. Please give a round of applause for Ms. Julia Anderson."

I walk toward the stage in a daze, a smile plastered on my face. I get through my speech without stumbling. I look at Matt, who is watching me intently. After thunderous applause, I make my way back to my seat. I grab his forearm to counteract the distance I feel. I pull him close and softly whisper into his ear, "I ran into Nick a few weeks ago when I was out with Mere. He was with JP—it wasn't planned. It was nothing. I didn't mention it because it felt like there was nothing to mention."

I hope he will pick up on the similarities between this situation and the one I've been all wound up about with Kerri Taylor. In both cases, it's ultimately nothing. He nods, but his mouth is set in a firm line. My stomach drops.

"I just wish you'd said something. It seems like kind of a big deal to have drinks with your ex-husband," he says evenly.

"I'm sorry."

We get through the rest of the night, and it turns out to be a banner event. We raise more than our initial goal, two hundred and fifty thousand dollars, from Matt alone, which means we'll have even more resources for the kids and their families, plus additional staff. My elation is juxtaposed by a terrible sinking feeling in my stomach. I watch Matt do and say all the right things, but I know he's upset. I try to bring it up in the car on our way back to my apartment, but he is quick to shut it down.

"It's fine, Jules. I'm exhausted. Let's just go home and go to bed."

It feels like suddenly our unshakeable foundation is very fragile.

Chapter Thirty-Seven

The next morning is laced with an uncomfortable tension, which is something altogether new for us. I want to believe it is from Matt's very normal insecurity and possible jealously that I saw Nick. But it feels like more than that. Like a culmination of little things, water rushing toward a dam. We are out of sync, and it does not feel good.

I try again to bring it up, but Matt shuts me down, insisting everything is fine. Eventually, after a walk full of stilted conversation, we are surprised by a photographer as we exit a restaurant and it leaves me shaken—literally. We get back to my apartment, and as my hands finally stop trembling, I decide I can't stand the tension anymore.

"What is going on, Matt? This doesn't feel like us. Please talk to me."

He lets out a huge sigh and scrapes his hands down his face. "I feel like you're pulling away from me. Like you are actively trying to create space between us, and I don't know why. Today I could feel you flinch as we walked down the street."

"I am not pulling away. There is a difference between me pulling away and me adjusting to this reality that our relationship is now open for public consumption. The perceived flinching is just that, Matt. Not you. That photographer scared the shit out of me. You've had twenty years to adjust to this life, can't I have some time?

"Yeah, but you knew who I was when we met. You knew this was my life."

"Again, there is a huge difference between knowing this is your life and actually living it. I didn't plan for us to meet, neither did you. That has been one of the most incredible parts of all this, the unexpectedness of it. But we, really I, have to figure out how to navigate feeling like someone is always watching me, judging me, judging us. It makes me second-guess myself in a way I never thought I would, especially at this point in my life. It can be overwhelming. I know you're going to tell me to tune out the noise, and I am, I am trying, but it takes practice, and I'm still practicing."

He takes a minute to let that settle.

"Is that why you went to dinner with your ex-husband? Because you're overwhelmed?"

"What? No, not at all. Is *that* what this is about?"

"I don't know, Jules, but it didn't feel great to hear. Especially because it came from JP, not even you. Like I wasn't even a thought in your mind. Why wouldn't you have told me?"

"Because there was nothing to tell. I had dinner with Meredith, not Nick. He showed up afterward. And we stayed an extra thirty minutes. That was it. It was a good conversation, one that answered a lot of questions I'd been thinking about for years. Of course I considered telling you about it, but I thought that might make it significant in some way which it was not at all. Also, it's a little rich for you to be commenting about dining with exes. At least my beer with Nick didn't make front page news," I say with more venom than I intended. It catches Matt off guard.

"You're *still* upset about Kerri?"

"No, I'm not still upset about it, I was just proving a point that we both did the same thing. Neither of us did anything wrong, though certainly we could've handled it differently. And the takeaway is that overcommunicating is always the better option. For both of us." I sigh, deflated. I do not want to argue with Matt.

"And I'm sorry about the Kerri thing. But if it's not that, then what is the problem here?"

I take a deep breath.

"It's what you just said—you asked if you were even a thought in my mind. You are *every* thought in my mind. All the time. You are so consuming. Us, our love, it's impacted every single cell in my body, every part of my life, which is incredible, but sometimes I feel like I can't even see straight."

"Consuming? That's the best you can come up with to describe what we have?" he asks, hurt in his eyes.

"No, of course it's not the only word. But that doesn't make it less real for me. I love you, and that is one thing I am one hundred percent sure about. But we don't exist in a vacuum. Adjusting to the realities of your life and career has at times felt stifling. I'm trying to imagine what our life looks like together long term. I know you are, too—you've told me many times about the pictures in your head of your life and your future partner and what it'll all be like for you. My fear is that this imaginary, one-dimensional person who exists only in your mind never has much of an opinion. And I do."

I'm not even sure what I'm talking about or where I'm going, but these thoughts have been swirling around in my head for weeks, and it feels good to say them out loud.

I keep going.

"I don't want to live in LA. Or at least I don't want to feel like that is the only way to make this work. I don't want to leave my job, my friends, my team, my life—unless *I* want to. I don't want to follow you around the world like a groupie, and I don't want to feel like we always have to be looking over our shoulders, waiting for some next big public crucifixion. I don't want to hear strangers' opinions about me or you or us. I don't want you to feel like you have to move to New York full time and give up your life in LA. I love the idea of Virginia but I can't ever see it being a permanent full-time base for either of us. I don't want you to feel like you have to change anything about yourself, or your life, or your career, for me. I don't want you to resent me. And I don't want to resent you. I don't want either of us to feel like we're settling. Ever."

He blows out a big breath. "I get all of that. I hear you. And I agree, neither of us should ever feel like we're settling, but I think there is a middle ground between compromise and settling. Right?"

"Yes, probably."

"I love you so much, Jules. And I know you love me, too. Isn't that enough?"

"Yes. The love is more than enough. But it doesn't magically erase the fact that we have to figure these things out. Falling in love with each other isn't the finish line. It's more like the starting line. I've seen both. I don't want to make the same mistakes as I have in the past. I'm doing my best to think ahead this time."

He sits quietly. I've never seen him so taciturn.

"I just want you to know what's going on in my head," I add.

"I didn't know you were thinking all of this. When you go inside your head and don't let me in, it makes me feel like I'm losing you," he admits.

"You can't possibly know what is always going on in my head, nor should you want to. I will always be honest with you. And if you feel like I'm pulling away, maybe you pulling away in response is not the most helpful solution."

"I wish things could be like they were at the beginning."

"You mean when no one knew about us? That was not real life. It was an artificial environment. There was no way for us to sustain it."

"Yeah, but it was so much simpler. Why can't we get back there?" he asks with an edge to his voice.

"We can. But it may look a little different than before. That's all I'm saying. We will figure it out." I can feel his frustration and mine, although I think we've made some headway.

"It is okay for us to talk about these things, Matt. We *have* to be able to talk to each other with honesty and trust that we will be heard by the other person, right? After all, how do you think people make relationships and marriages work for thirty-plus years?"

"Well, apparently I have no idea ... and clearly, you don't either."

My jaw drops. I'm sure I misheard him.

"What?"

He is quiet, staring at the counter. Confirmation that I did not mishear him.

"Wow. That was a low blow." I'm so shocked that I don't even register the hurt. I do register humiliation when my eyes fill with tears.

Matt is silent.

I stare at him, confused. "Why would you say something to purposely try to hurt me?"

"I don't know," he mumbles.

"Well, I suggest you figure it out. You saying things like that is not going to work for me," I spit out.

"I'm sorry," he says half-heartedly.

I get up and grab Murphy's leash. My apartment suddenly seems too small. I turn back toward Matt. "Don't say sorry when you don't even know what you're sorry for." I walk out the door with my dog.

I get back to my building after walking around for an hour and feel no better. Matt knows my failed marriage is my biggest sore spot. I cannot understand why he would so cruelly and impulsively throw it in my face. What does it say about him? About me? Is Nick something he'll hold over my head if we hit rough patches? Forever?

It's as if he has suddenly revealed a part of himself to me. And for the first time since I met him, it's something I don't like. And will not tolerate. The thought rattles me to my core, and I feel an overwhelming urge to pull the rip cord—to try to get out while I can, unscathed. An impossibility at this point, but the impulse remains strong.

When I walk in the front door, Matt has moved from the couch to the barstool. He's poured himself a drink, and the look he gives me is riddled with self-loathing. I refuse to feel bad for him.

"I am so sorry," he says.

I cross my arms.

"I am not used to navigating conflict. It is very uncomfortable for me. If I'm honest, I've probably been conflict-avoidant my entire life. I think I've managed by running away at the first sign of it, or sabotaging things so I don't have to deal with it. I think that's why I made that shitty comment. I am so sorry, Jules. Truly. I don't like arguing."

"You should probably work on that," I say, my guard up.

"I know."

"Maybe we should just take a breather. And figure out what we're doing and where we're going and how we're going to get there."

The words leave my mouth before I can stop them.

Matt jerks back like he's been hit. "A breather?"

"Yes."

"Like a break?"

I double down.

"I guess."

I feel the train coming off the tracks, careening toward something at breakneck speed, and I'm helpless to stop it.

"Because I made that shitty comment? I'm sorry, babe. I didn't mean it. A break? What does that even mean?"

"I don't know, Matt. I just think that when we're together it's hard to get any perspective. Maybe we need some."

"But we aren't together half the time anyway. We're three thousand–plus miles from each other for weeks on end, usually more."

"I didn't necessarily mean we needed a break from being physically together."

"Don't do this," he pleads.

"I'm not saying we're breaking up, Matt. I love you. I want us to work. I want us to last—forever. And I need a minute to figure out how to do that. I think you do, too. I know you've got a lot going on."

"But can't we figure it out and still be together? A break is the first step of a breakup. Come on, Jules."

The tiny fissures of doubt, insecurity, and fear I've felt throughout our relationship seem to have culminated in this moment. Despite the rising panic in my chest, I feel deep down that this is the right decision—for now, at least.

"Let's just see how it goes when you go back to LA, okay? I will call you."

"When?"

"When I get some clarity."

He puts his head in his hands, resigned. "Okay, I guess? Do I have a choice? What am I supposed to say to that?"

I walk over and wrap my arms around him. He looks up at me, his brown eyes miserable. I kiss him, and he resists, but only a for a minute. Then he leans in. I try to convey to him how much I love him, fearing I may have acted impulsively. He squeezes me tight, burying his face in my hair.

I want to grab him by the hand and tug him toward my bedroom so he can slowly undress me, and I him. So I can run my hands along his smooth chest, kissing each tattoo, saving the dahlia for last. So he can put his hands on my hips, my back, my breasts. So we can lie down skin to skin and he can get inside of me, fill me, stretch me, love me. So we can move together, our heartbeats thumping in sync. So I can make him feel so good, so loved. So he can make my body respond in ways that only he can. So I can remind myself that I am his, and he is mine. I want us to make love to each other and make everything better and fix it. Or, at the very least, distract us from it. The thought dangles in front of me, so close I can taste it.

I resist.

I tell myself that no matter how earth-tilting the sex is, it can't fix the schism that has developed overnight between us. Sex won't erase the uncertainty or answer the unknowns. Sex won't give us time to think about what we both need to make this go the distance. Sex isn't the solution. Instead, I settle for that one last kiss, then walk into my bedroom alone and close the door behind me. Only then do I let the tears fall. I'm so exhausted by the conversation I fall asleep.

I wake up later to the sound of the door quietly clicking shut. I walk out and see that Matt is gone with all of his stuff. Murphy stands in the middle of the living room, confusion in his eyes as he looks between me and the front door. I can almost hear his question: *Where'd he go?* I kneel to pet him, more tears streaming down my cheeks. I wonder out loud, "What have I done?"

Chapter Thirty-Eight

Being without him feels like an open wound. Everything makes the pain sear, even the air. I want to crawl out of my skin. The warmth of the sunny May days seems to be taunting me. It's all made infinitely worse because this entire situation was my doing. My brilliant idea. I have no one to blame but myself.

Despite the agony of the past few weeks, part of me still feels resolute in this decision. What I am experiencing now is exactly what I was trying to explain to Matt. Total consumption. I need to learn how to harness it. How to love him and be loved by him and still remember to come up for air. How not to lose sight of all the things and people in my life that make me *me*.

The past few nights I woke up in a blind panic that perhaps this sabbatical will not end the way I think it will. I worry that Matt will use this time apart to realize he does not want to be with me. That I'm not worth the fuss. Or he'll find someone else. Someone in LA. Someone who more accurately fits the idea he's had in his head for years, someone who predates me. I try not to let myself go there because it makes my heart feels like it's being squeezed in a vise.

I pull out my phone at least twenty times a day to call or text him, a habit I can't shake. He kicked off his spring tour two weeks after that last night in my apartment. I keep tabs on him and his shows. The reviews all agree the tour is a huge success. He hasn't called or texted me, but he is sending me emails. We didn't establish any ground rules for what this "breather" entails so Matt has taken it upon himself to send me emails, the first one explaining his stance.

May 2, 2025
To: julia.anderson11
From: mattyjohnson80
Subject: One.
Jules,
I'm emailing you because it's technically not talking to you. It's talking at you. You don't have to read them. You can have your breather. I still don't know what that means. I miss you. I love you.
Matt

The emails show up every morning. After several days of it, I realize they are satisfying my urge to connect with him and ultimately defeating the entire purpose of this. I make a folder so all his emails will automatically go there and I don't have to see them in my inbox.

I need to use this time wisely. I decide I'll give myself until my thirty-ninth birthday at the end of the month to figure out whatever it is I think I need to figure out.

I walk into the hospital and drop my stuff off in my office, noting my painting for the four hundredth time. The one that now constantly reminds me of Matt. And his insights. His intelligence that I love and admire. I think about taking it down, but that seems dramatic.

I walk to the other side of the building and grab a hard hat before entering the construction zone that is the pediatric behavioral health emergency department. It is a beautiful disaster of dust and drywall and saws, and a crew of twenty people is working to make it perfect. Coming here is a soothing little ritual that keeps me focused. I check in on the project every day. Something about seeing actual physical progress—a wall where there had been nothing—is immensely satisfying.

Outside of work, I try to balance keeping myself busy and deliberately not, so I can pay attention to how I'm feeling. My field hockey team wraps up the season with a winning record, and some of the girls talk about signing up for the Marine Corps Marathon in the fall to motivate them to stay in shape over the summer. On a whim, I decide to train with them. Now, on Tuesdays, Thursdays, and Sundays, the girls and I hit the concrete jungle to crank out miles. I am humbled every time by their youth, energy, and fully intact knees. Despite my aching muscles and blistered feet, I feel stronger mentally and physically. The running gives me room to think.

I make it a point to see a friend at least once a week, usually Meredith. The morning after Matt left, I sent her a text explaining what I had done, and an hour later she was at my front door.

"You are an idiot. But I love you. It'll be fine," she said, and pushed her way in with a bag of bagels, cream cheese, lox, and Veuve.

Lately Meredith has been heckling me about my upcoming birthday. "We are doing something. Whether you like it or not. It's the last year of your thirties."

I don't want to do anything, but I begrudgingly settle on going to dinner with her at one of our favorite spots. Pressure grows in my chest as I think about the fact that I won't be spending my birthday with Matt. I hadn't quite thought that part through. The idea bums me out more than I care to admit.

* * *

My birthday arrives with little fanfare—a few calls and texts from friends and family, and my work family orders in our favorite Thai and Crumbl cookies to celebrate. I show up to dinner with Meredith feeling more melancholy than anything. The sinking feeling that has been my constant companion intensifies as each hour in the day passes with nothing from Matt. No text, no call, no card, no flowers, nothing. There's a chance he sent me an email, but I haven't checked the folder, which takes every ounce of my willpower. I feel pathetic.

Meredith and I are two bottles of wine deep, and despite her good intentions and an incredibly generous gift—a cream Staud bucket bag—my mood is tanked.

"Jules. You've gotta perk up. You're a serious buzzkill."

"What is wrong with me? Am I a masochist?"

"Hmm ... Are you sure you want to ask me that?"

"I'm serious, Mere. Why am I pushing away someone I love so much? What am I doing? The whole argument that precipitated this break seems so dumb every time I think about it."

"I don't know if you'll be able to pinpoint an exact reason, but I'm pretty sure it has something to do with your past. It's not just you—Matt has a past, too. Maybe you're testing him, maybe you're scared, maybe you're trigger shy, maybe you don't want to get hurt again, but that's all bullshit, and you know it."

"I know."

"I don't think it was the wrong choice for you take a little break, to zoom out a little. You guys are intense, which is not criticism. But at some point, you're going to have make a choice. And to make that choice you're probably going to have to stop overthinking, stop worrying, stop trying to analyze every little detail. You've gotta jump in, hope for the best, and do what you can to make it last. And if it doesn't? So what? You start over again—that's not anything new for you."

She's right. And again, I think about what a gift girlfriends are.

"Enough moping. Let's get out of here. We're going *out* out—to a new place just around the corner. There will be music and dancing and bottle service. A bunch of my coworkers are there tonight, and I am not taking no for an answer."

"A club? Seriously?"

"Yes. It's your birthday, and even though you're trying your best to make it depressing as hell, I think we can turn it around. We are not dead. We are young and beautiful, and we are going out. Get up!"

"Okay, okay!" I smile for the first time all day, happy to hand the night's reins to Meredith.

* * *

We show up to the swanky club, a place I have not been in many years. I'd forgotten the allure of places like this—all low lighting, sexy furniture, loud music, and well-dressed, beautiful people sipping cocktails. Meredith's friends have taken over one of the lounge areas, and several bottles are splayed across the table. When I walk up, everyone cheers, "Happy birthday!" I thank them, and Meredith pours me a very strong drink. "Sit. Enjoy. It's your fucking birthday!" she demands.

I do. And I find myself able to get lost in the music, the conversation, and these very smart and funny New Yorkers I haven't been out with in a long time. I've missed this.

A man to my right strikes up a conversation.

"So what birthday are we celebrating? Twenty-five?"

"Ha. Good one."

"Yeah, not my best work."

"I'm Julia."

"Yes, I know, I've heard a lot about you from Meredith. I'm Andrew." He offers me his hand.

I take a good look at him—he's tall, at least six feet, and very muscular. I can see his shoulders rippling underneath his custom suit. His hair is dark, almost black, with salt and pepper on the sides, cut short and neat. But his eyes are the centerpiece—piercing blue and gorgeous, especially in contrast to his dark features.

It hits me that this is the corporate sexpot Meredith tried to set me up with months ago.

"I was supposed to take you out a long time ago." He gives me a warm smile.

"Ah, yes. It's all coming back to me now. Sorry it didn't work out."

"It's okay, I only wallowed for a night or two. But I was intrigued. Meredith is a fantastic saleswoman."

"That she is. And only a night or two of wallowing? Not weeks?"

"If I'd seen you, I would've wallowed longer. I guess I missed my chance. I do occasionally peruse the pop culture section of the news."

"Right." *He knows about Matt.*

"But your boyfriend isn't here?" He glances around the room.

"No, he couldn't make it."

"What a shame."

"Excuse me?"

"Leaving a beautiful woman by herself on her birthday."

It lands. And I'm startled at how intrigued I am by this man flirting with me. I can imagine life with a guy like Andrew so clearly. We'd be in New York forever. He'd work downtown, and I'd be at the hospital uptown, and we'd find a gorgeous penthouse somewhere in between and a house out East where we'd spend the summer. He might work late and travel on occasion, but he'd be home, and I'd be home, and we'd have dinner together with our kids almost every night and take Murphy for long walks in the park where no one would follow us or take pictures of us or weigh in on our relationship. It seems so easy, simple, to love someone like him. To make it work with someone like him. But as quickly as the fantasy enters my mind, it blows out like a birthday candle. And all I can think of is Matt. His messy hair, his worn jeans. His pensive face. His hands.

"We're celebrating in a few weeks when he wraps up touring," I lie.

I chat with him a while longer. Before I know it, I am two more cocktails deep and way more than buzzed, yet my thoughts remain clear. I excuse myself from Andrew and find Meredith in the crowd.

"You know he didn't do anything for my birthday. No call. No text. No nothing."

She stares at me dubiously, biting her lip. "Didn't you tell him to not talk to you?"

"Yes, but I guess I just thought he would. Maybe that means something."

I think her eyes might pop out of her head. "For the love of God, Jules! You are exasperating!" she screams at me over the music. "You can't tell him to leave you alone and then expect him to do something."

"I know. Whatever. He's probably fucking Ariana or Alessandra or some other LA chick right now," I mumble into my drink.

"He is not."

"How do you know?"

"Because, you idiot, he asked me about your birthday. He wanted to do something. Something big. And I told him not to. I told him it would be better for him to respect your wishes. Because I thought that is what you wanted!" She's incensed.

Shit.

I turn around and beeline to my purse sitting on the couch, fumbling for my phone. I open my email.

I open the folder.

I have more than thirty emails from him. But I only focus on the one from today. At the very top.

May 28, 2025
To: julia.anderson11
From: mattyjohnson80
Subject: happy birthday
Jules,

Happy birthday, babe. You're thirty-nine today. I had lots of things planned, lots of ideas on how I would celebrate you today and probably all weekend. Maybe all month. I'd been planning for weeks. I wanted to reciprocate how you made me feel on my birthday in Mexico. I wanted to make sure you had no doubts about how much I loved you. But a trusted advisor thought it best for me ditch my plans—to lay low and play it cool. To give you your goddamn breather.

In the past month I've ridden the entire roller coaster of emotions. First, I was stunned. Then I spent most of my time being sad, feeling sorry for myself, wondering what I did wrong, what I could've done differently, and mostly just missing you. Then I felt hopeful. Surely, you'd reach out to me soon, but today, it's been almost a month. I've emailed you every day and it's still radio silence. So now, I'm angry. I'm angry that you chose this and in the same breath told me how much you love me—it's a bit of a mindfuck, and something I never anticipated from you. Anyway, thinking about all of this over the past month has made me realize maybe you were onto something. And that this breather was the right call, despite my strong protest. I need the space to do some thinking, too. I'll honor your wishes and this will be my last email. I'll be back in New York on July first after tour ends. Let's meet then and see what we've figured out. Enjoy your birthday.

Matt

I read and reread it five times. *How much I loved you. Loved.* Past tense.

My heart is in my throat and tears prick my eyes. I run for the front door, in desperate need of fresh air. I walk two blocks before I catch my breath. I pull out my phone and order an Uber, then shoot a quick text to Meredith.

> Overserved, took an Uber home. Thanks for making me go out tonight. Love you.

On the short ride home, I frantically text my brother and book a flight to Denver for three days from now. I feel like I'm on the verge of a breakdown.

For the hundredth time, I wonder, *What have I done?*

Chapter Thirty-Nine

I land in Denver in the early afternoon. I spend the majority of the flight listening to the most depressing playlists I can find on Spotify. Many of them have Matt's songs on them, and the irony is not lost on me. I read through the emails he sent over the past month, over and over again. Also weighing on me is the fact that Matt is somewhere near Denver to headline a music festival at the Red Rocks Amphitheatre. I haven't received any more emails from him despite refreshing my inbox one hundred times a day, and I don't have the guts to reach out myself. The fact that we will be in the same city and not see each other seems absurd. I am holding out for our July meetup.

Ryan meets me at baggage claim with a homemade chauffeur sign that says, *Jenna Tills!*

It takes me a minute of saying it in my head before I laugh. We started this tradition years ago when we both moved to new cities. It's so dumb, and it cracks me up every time. I give him a giant hug.

"How ya doing?" he asks.

I burst into tears.

"That good, huh?"

"I think I'm fine. I just don't know what the hell I'm doing right now."

"Let's go find your bag and get some lunch. Let the mountain air clear your head," he offers.

I already feel better, being with my brother. Knowing he'll make decisions and usher me along as I sort through the mess I've made.

We stop by his condo to drop my luggage off before venturing out for lunch. Ryan lives in downtown Denver, right across the street from the capitol building. A classic forty-something, well-off, single guy place with very modern décor—all sharp edges, steel, and concrete minimalism.

"It still looks like a million-dollar elevated prison cell," I tell him when I walk in. "Would an area rug and some throw pillows kill you?"

"You sound like Mom." He shakes his head.

Ryan is an environmental scientist at a small firm headquartered in Denver. Much of his current work focuses conservation efforts and specifically, repopulating the native trout populations in the rivers here that have slowly been disappearing.

Growing up, my brother took environmental issues very seriously, almost too seriously for a kid. He went door to door in in our neighborhood to give a presentation on why each resident should opt into recycling, a new phenomenon at the time. He convinced my mom to install a rain barrel in our yard that she could use to water her garden rather than wasting water from the hose. Embarrassingly for him, he also went on a shower strike for about a week to conserve water, only to be told by the prettiest girl in his grade that he smelled like a jock strap. I was proud of him for turning his passion into a thriving career.

"How is the job? The new unit?" he asks as we walk to his favorite restaurant. The sun is shining, but the air is still cool. It's perfect weather—a perk of summertime in a mountain town.

"It's good. The construction is all done, now we're waiting to fill the staffing requirements and get everyone through training before we can open. It's so much waiting, it drives me nuts."

We order beers and a pizza and Greek salad to share. Never one for small talk, Ryan cuts to the chase.

"Tell me what happened. Why'd you break up with Matt?"

I start crying again as I fill him in on the entire story, trying to explain how I didn't break up with him, but it feels like I did, plus all my annoying thoughts and the series of events that led to this frantic trip to Colorado.

"I don't think it's as bad as you think it is," he says once I finish.

"What do you mean?"

"I mean it's nothing you can't rectify. You got scared and ran. So? That isn't that big of a deal. No one cheated. No one quit—though I can see how he might think you did."

"That doesn't make me feel better."

"I don't understand why you don't just call him."

I can't explain that part either.

"Can we talk about something else? I don't want to think about Matt."

After lunch, Ryan drags me out to the mountains. We hike a five-mile loop and stop for beers on the way home. When we get back to the condo, I barely have enough energy to shower before crawling into bed, where I sleep like the dead for eleven hours.

* * *

I wake up to my phone vibrating on the nightstand. I see an incoming call from Dave. He is a prolific texter, so the fact that he is calling makes me think something terrible happened. I answer.

"Is everything okay?"

"Have you been on Instagram in the last hour?" he asks.

"No."

"Well open it *right now*, Jules. Keep me on the line."

"What am I looking for?"

"Go to Matt's page. He is doing a Q&A."

I type in his profile and start tapping through his story. People have submitted questions, and he is answering them. An indirect interview, where Matt is completely in control. *What a good idea for him.* The first few slides are about his tour, new music, inspiration for songs, and a bunch of random questions about his favorite things.

The last question is, *Are you in a relationship?*

My adrenaline surges as I read his reply.

I have met someone who is very special to me. I think you all might have an idea of who she is, and I think you'll like her as much as I do. She makes me incredibly happy, and I feel very lucky to know her.

"Are you *reading it?*" shrieks Dave.

"Yes. I see it," I say, mind racing, palms sweating.

"It's already being picked up by TMZ, Us Weekly, Page Six. The pictures of the Grammys, the gala, and some other paparazzi pics of you guys."

I sag onto the bed.

"Okay? I don't know what this is supposed to mean. You know we're spending some time apart, Dave." My heart is hammering—I notice how Matt says everything using the present tense. Maybe I didn't ruin everything after all.

"Don't you get it? He has literally *never* spoken publicly about any relationship. In like, over a decade. And here he is, offering it up to the world, willingly, on a silver platter because he wants to. It's worth the risk. *You're* worth the risk. Don't you think he's trying to tell you something? Don't be an idiot!" he screams.

I take a second to digest this. Dave is right. I know Matt's press strategy has been rooted in self-preservation. That he is willing to throw that all by the wayside to send some kind of message to me is a huge deal.

I hang up with Dave and bust into Ryan's room. I show him the Instagram page. Ryan looks at me stone-faced.

"I told you."

"Told me what?"

"That you're making this a bigger deal than it needs to be."

"How would you know that?"

He's quiet.

I throw a pillow at him.

"I saw him. Yesterday morning. Right before I picked you up from the airport. You know he's here for a show at the Red Rocks."

"What?!"

"He reached out. We've stayed in touch since Christmas. I like him, he's a good guy. Funny, too."

"Ryan. Please elaborate."

Ryan smirks. "He asked if I could meet him for coffee. He wanted to pick my brain to get a different perspective on you. He wanted to understand more about where you were coming from. I told him stuff about Nick, stuff about Mom and Dad, some of the weird stuff you've been doing since you were a kid. I told him to hold steady and you'd come around—you just had to go around and around in your head like you always do. He laughed at that and said he knew what that was like. I also think he wanted to get me on board. Get me on his team for some backup. Which I already was. Like I said, I really like the guy."

Wow.

Matt hasn't used this time apart to quietly quit, to give up and move on. Rather, he's been working behind the scenes to figure me out, to fight for me, to connect with my people—it's unbelievable.

"What do I do?"

"I think you know exactly what to do."

He turns his phone around and shows me two e-tickets for Matt's show tonight at Red Rocks.

Chapter Forty

W e're late departing for Red Rocks because I spend the day trying on and dismissing every clothing item in my suitcase—and almost every clothing item in every store within a five-block radius of Ryan's condo. I settle on my favorite pair of jeans, a black tank top, and a new and insanely expensive green bomber jacket by Acne Studios that I found at a boutique around the corner. Money is no object at this point. I can barely keep my hands steady as I put on earrings and my watch, *the* watch, from Matt, spritzing myself with perfume as Ryan yells at me to hurry up.

On the drive over, I feel like I'm going to throw up. I'm sick over the fact that I let all the otherness of the world muddy what I feel for Matt and what I know he feels for me. I cannot believe I almost lost someone truly spectacular because of my own fears, my old wounds. I feel like I suddenly have complete clarity. As we speed along the highway, I reflect on how different my experience was with Nick.

Our marriage crumbled in isolation. It was only when we pared down every outside influence and were left with just each other that we realized how wrong we were together. We hadn't the wherewithal to take a second to think about what we wanted, where we were headed, how we'd navigate conflict, how we'd keep each other a priority—we blindly followed what we thought was 'right'. And then when things got tough, Nick shut down and couldn't muster up any fight for me. For us. That feels like an important thing for me to understand.

With Matt, our relationship turbulence is a result of the opposite. We are good together, just the two of us, *so* good. It was only when our love became something for public consumption that I let doubt and fear creep in. Matt has been fighting for me, for us, every step of the way. Even in our time apart, he has still found ways to tell me he's thinking of me, that I am worth it. We have a foundation, just the two of us, that is strong enough to weather the inevitable storms.

I hope I can tell him all this clearly.

I see the famous giant Ship Rock and Creation Rock formations looming in the distance as we pull up and find parking. As we make our way inside, the opening act performs on stage—Timmy Campbell, an up-and-coming bluegrass singer, local to Denver. Matt once told me how it important it was to him to help give musicians opportunities whenever he could.

"All it takes is one lucky night, one *Sliding Doors* moment, for a musician's career to take off. For their life to change. It's my little way of paying it forward. A lot of people gave me a chance, and I've never forgotten it."

I stand next to Ryan on the left side of the stage, several rows back. The lights dim and Matt walks out. His hair has grown longer since I last saw him—it curls over the tops of his ears. He has on his dark jeans, a T-shirt, and a pair of sneakers I don't recognize. His arms, the muscles, the tattoos, capped by a watch—his watch, the one I gave him for his birthday, the one that matches mine. Seeing him, even at a distance, after all these weeks is extraordinary. It's at once familiar and like I'm seeing him for the first time. I resist the urge to run to him.

I try to focus on him, which is no small feat because the crowd around me is going crazy screaming and cheering his name. The snare drum rumbles and the lights blast on as Matt's fingers drive down on the guitar playing the first notes. For the next hour as Matt performs, I grab for Ryan's hand—for emotional support and for something to hold on to so I don't float off into the thin night air.

As spectacular as the show is, I am eager for it to end. Only a few more songs and I can see him again. Touch him again. I watch closely as he walks up to the microphone. "This is something new I've been working on," he says softly.

I pour a glass of wine and see your smiling face
Why aren't you next to me? I see you in every place
Room four sixteen, my heart on the floor
I rocketed to outer space when you walked through the door
Your brown eyes, and the sunrise
I'm thinking about a house on a hill,
with a garden, and a room with a crib
The doors slid open
And brought me right to you
The doors slid open
What do I do
Are you feeling it too?
You're in bed, in my shirt, so damn beautiful, it hurts
The moonlight on your skin, makes me believe again
Could this be the love I've been looking for, finally coming to find me?
That mind of yours keeps me on my toes. I'll follow wherever it goes
The doors slid open
And brought me right to you
The doors slid open
What do I do
Are you feeling it too
Are you feeling it too
Are you feeling it too
I'm thinking about forever.

I turn to look at Ryan, who, once again, is smirking, looking at me like he knew all along that this is how it would end. The song isn't even over before something, a force, propels me toward the stage. I move not of my own volition, Ryan at my heels. I veer to the left side, where I see Marcus standing guard. His face breaks into a wide smile when he sees me. "Hey, baby girl! I was hoping I'd see you tonight. I know I'm not the only one." He wraps me into a giant bear hug.

"Can I come back?"

"You? Of course. Our boy is going to be ecstatic."

I turn to Ryan. "I'll meet you back at your place after the show." Ryan nods in understanding.

I move backstage and find my way to a dressing room full of familiar things. A to-go container with half-eaten grilled chicken, broccoli, and rice, a half-finished mug of Throat Coat tea, honey, candles, scratched-out set lists, and, of course, his collection of guitars. I know he has maybe one or two more songs left before the show ends. I try to sit on the worn leather couch, but my nerves are jumping. I pace the room, touching the familiar items—his coat, his extra soft T-shirts, his scuffed boots. I think back to the first day I met him, when he walked onto the critical care unit and into room 416. If I could go back to that moment and slow it down, maybe pay closer attention, I think I would know that this was it. That he is the person for me.

Forever.

The rest of our relationship plays through my mind in a series of short clips, the spectacular moments mixed in with all the ordinary ones. I try to steady my breathing.

The door flies open.

Matt walks in. His face is flushed, a sheen of sweat on his brow. When he registers me in the room, he stops and stills.

"Jules." He stares.

"Ryan brought me to your show. He told me you reached out."

He tucks his hands in the front pockets of his jeans, his eyes wide, body taut like he is focusing hard on staying still. Before he can say anything, I continue, hands sweaty, my body trembling, but my voice calm and strong.

"I saw the Q&A, what you said about me. That new song you just played. That was about us." Not a question.

"Yes."

"I need you to know, I love you. More than I ever thought possible. I thought I knew what love was, and I didn't. I thought I knew exactly what love should look like for me. I was wrong. When you walked into my life that day last July, I felt a calm, a peace, and at the same time it was like I'd never been more alive in my life. It's something I've never experienced before. I know I said our love was consuming, as if it was a bad thing. It's not...it's the *best* thing. And it dawned on me how incredibly lucky and rare and beautiful it is to love someone so much that you can fuse yourselves together in a way that can't be undone, in a way that vaporizes uncertainties, where there's no room for doubt because to question it would be as insane as questioning if the sky is blue." I take a step towards him.

"We can still be our own separate selves, but we get to walk through life with this added protection, this *security*. Loving you enhances my life, Matt. In every imaginable way. The last few months with you have been the best of my life. I have not a single regret, except for the fact that I almost let everything else—the noise—get in the way of what I know to be true.

"I am so sorry I suggested this break. I don't need a breather—not now, not ever. There have been a million things in the last few weeks that I have wanted to tell you, and to feel like I couldn't—for no reason other than I'm an idiot—was unbearable. I don't ever want you to wonder how I feel about you. You are the love of my life. I think I'm yours, too, and I don't want to spend another moment without you. I'm so sorry I put us through this." I exhale, tears streaming down my cheeks.

He crosses the room in three long strides and takes my face in his hands. "I love you so much, Julia. You are everything to me. I am equally responsible for letting the noise get to me, for my own shit, my own history, and my own stupid brain getting in the way of what I know to be true in here." He presses his hand to his heart. "Every word I sang in that song I wrote for you. I feel it in my bones. You have awakened and inspired me; you somehow manage to be the softest place for me to land while also making me want to be a better man. When I see your face, I feel like I am home. I cannot imagine my life without you. I've tried in the last few weeks, and it was impossible. I know it will not always be perfect or easy, but I have not a shadow of doubt that we will figure everything out, together."

I think my face might split in half, the way a smile bursts out of me. Relief courses through my veins.

He kisses me so deeply, so passionately that it feels like we somehow have cemented the words we've just spoken to each other. A promise. A vow. When I pull back, his eyes are shining with love and emotion that I know is reflected in mine. I rest my head on his chest, smelling his familiar scent and feeling calm wash over me.

Home. I am home.

Matt lets out a deep exhale as he leans down and softly whispers in my ear, "What's going on in that beautiful mind of yours?"

"Just thinking that maybe I'm the long-winded one now."

He laughs and kisses the top of my head. "Impossible."

"Hey, what's the name of that song?"

He pulls me tighter, smiling, his mouth pressed against my ear.

"Thinking About Forever."

Acknowledgments

This book was written almost entirely in secret.

Similar to the early days of Julia and Matt's relationship, I have considered disclosing my writing on a "need to know" basis. I've been surprised by how completely terrifying it feels to take something from inside your head and put it into writing, and then share it with the universe.

Writing a book has always been on my bucket list, but never in my wildest dreams did I think it would come in the form of *Thinking About Forever*. This book was written frantically, in a four month period, during what might be the busiest time of my life. Raising three very young kids, a husband with a demanding job, my own career separate from writing, and all the other trappings of modern life—it seemed like an impossibility.

And yet...

The idea of Julia and Matt hit me like a lightening bolt in a rare moment of solitude, and the story flowed from my fingertips like a woman possessed (though usually only in 15-minute increments).

So why *this* book?

The answer is simple: I wrote a book I wanted to read.

Somewhere in the murkiness of early motherhood and a global pandemic, I entered the world of romance novels, and they became a refuge for me in a way I hadn't experienced before. They were a respite from the monotony, exhaustion, and emotional roller coaster that accompanies the huge unconditional love and equally huge responsibility of raising children. Those books imprinted on me and inspired me. If my book can do that for just one person, I'll consider it a massive success.

And, while this book is a work of fiction, there are some truths in it, particularly about the children's mental health crisis. I, like Jules, am educated and trained as a social worker (there's a quote here about writing what you know...) and I would be remiss if I didn't use this opportunity to point out that the numbers and stats I included are very much based on reality. Right now, kids experiencing mental health crises are waiting in triage rooms across the United States, with nowhere to go, hoping and praying that a bed opens up some-where...for days, weeks, even months. It is an impossible situation for them, their caregivers, and the emergency department providers who, despite their best efforts, often have their hands tied by hospital poli-cies, insurance red tape, and other bureaucratic issues.

My fictitious vision for a wrap-around emergency department / short-term inpatient unit, like the one I wrote about at UCLA, is a dream. Maybe someone reading this—someone much smarter than me—might be inspired to make it a reality. If so, email me and count me in to help.

ANYWAY.

The fact that you are even reading this is a testament to some dumb luck, lots of Googling, and sheer stubborn will... because the self-publishing journey is intimidating and overwhelming. To say the least!!!

I owe the biggest thank you to Hilari - my editor. The stars aligned on the day we found each other. The single best decision I made in this whole process was to work with you. You gave me the confidence to move forward and answered every single question I asked (a lot!!!!). I refer to you as my literary fairy godmother. THANK YOU!

Thank you to Linda - my copy editor, for your attention to detail. You had the tall order of cleaning up my excessive use of commas, inappropriate m/n dashes, quotations placed incorrectly, verb tense issues, and many other grammatical blunders.

To Jennifer - who designed the cover for this book. I had an idea in my head, and somehow through a chaotic mood board and many rambling messages, you made it come to life. I am obsessed!!!

To E - who sat and laughed with me through one long night at the ER with one of my kids and helped jumpstart this entire process.

To my friends and family – who knowingly (many of you) and unknowingly (even more of you) helped me get here. Your encouragement and positive feedback about my writing over the years laid the foundation for this. You may even see parts of yourselves in all my favorite characters. Thank you!!!

To my dog – who is the inspiration behind Murphy but clearly can't read this. She sat next to me during many long nights while I typed and has been my constant companion for over 10 years. Dogs, especially mine, are simply the best.

To my children – who endured this season of life with a more-than-usual distracted mom that spent lots of time on a laptop. Thank you for hanging in there with me. I hope I make you proud and beyond that, I hope this book shows you that you can do anything you put your mind to. It is never too late to try something new, even if it feels very scary. I love you all to the moon. Also, you may never read this without my parental permission.

To my late grandmother – whose love of reading is now four generations strong. I wish you could see this and go to battle for my book to be your next pick at the Senior Citizen Center Book Club.

To my mom – who navigated life as a single parent with a very anxious child (me!). You loved me, pushed me, and always made me believe anything was possible, as long as I put my mind to it. This book is proof of that. If I'm half the mom you are, I'll call it a win.

To my husband – you were the first person to ever read this book, despite never having read a romance novel before. Thank you for saying, 'Wow, this is really good.' When I said I needed a weekend away to write...and then another, thank you for saying, 'Go, I got it covered here.' When I asked you to read other romance novels to see how mine stacked up, thank you for doing it, and for saying, 'Yours is better.' And when we sat down at dinner all those months ago, and I said, 'I'm thinking about self publishing,' thank you for saying, 'Let's do it.'

We did it.

And here we are.

I love you.

Lastly, to YOU, the reader. Thank you for giving me a shot. I hope you'll join me again in the Fall of 2025 for the next one!

A Sneak Peek of Chrissie's Next Book

The Yard
Coming Fall 2025

Chapter One

"No," I say for the fifth time. Its early afternoon on a Friday. The bitter end of the spring semester.

"Give me one good reason," Sarah shoots back.

"'No is a complete sentence," I cross my arms.

"Beatrice Marie Frisoli." She's patronizing me now.

"Yes, Sarah Beth Thompson?"

"A reason. Now."

I blow out my breath. "I have too much studying to do. If I don't ace this Torts exam next week, I am very, *very* screwed. Plus, I don't want to go. I can't think of a more boring recreational activity. I'd rather watch paint dry."

I stare down my best friend over the banker's lights in the library. She has been harassing me for the past ninety minutes. She is unrelenting. One of the many reasons she'll make a damn good lawyer someday.

"First of all, that's offensive. You're talking about America's greatest past time. Second of all, you do realize you'd never do anything remotely fun if it weren't for me, right?"

She slams my book shut and scoots closer to me. "Seriously Bee, you'd rot away your entire youth in this God forsaken library if I let you."

I roll my eyes. Since when did being goal oriented become a bad a thing? After years of being told to 'dream big' and 'stop at nothing' to get there, suddenly someone somewhere changed the tune, and *that* mentality was out and 'work-life balance' was in. I did not understand.

I also did not appreciate the added guilt from Sarah that I was missing out on something or that I might have regrets later. I put enough pressure on myself already.

"Two words. Crab. Pretzel."

"What?"

"I will buy you a crab pretzel. At the stadium. If you come."

My stomach growls almost immediately in response.

"Listen. I already have tickets. I will pay for all the concessions you could want. It's the last home game for the next two weeks, then they'll be on the road and then I won't bug you about it till next month," she says, exasperated.

Sarah is without a doubt, the Baltimore Orioles' number one fan. I've known this about her since we met over five years ago in under-grad. Pictures of her and her older sister, Meg, decked out in O's gear from birth to present are littered all over her parents' house in Roland Park.

I, on the other hand, could not care less about baseball.

Especially now.

I have another week of classes to get through, followed by final exams, and then approximately seventy-two hours to 'relax' before diving headfirst into my internship clerking for the Honorable Judge Adams in the U.S. District Court for the District of Maryland. It was a once and a lifetime opportunity—one that I had fought like hell against my peers to get. Once my internship was complete, I'd be back at for 2L year and the whole cycle would rinse and repeat again and again, until I graduated and had to take and pass the bar exam.

Tension seeps into my shoulders.

I look out the window of the library. The early May sun is shining bright, and it seems like all of Charm City is outside, laughing, biking, their faces turned up towards the warmth. I look back at my books, at the blaring blue light of my laptop, and feel my eyes burn. I can't remember the last time I've been outside for longer than the ten minutes it takes me to walk from my apartment to class to the library. A crab pretzel and a beer sound like the perfect antidote to the endless drone of lectures and readings.

"Fine. I'll come."

"YES!!!" she squeals and jumps out of her chair.

"Meet me at Pickles at 4pm. Don't be late. And please change out of this hideous outfit," she gestures to my sad stretched out gray high school soccer t-shirt and faded black leggings. It doesn't bother me... because she is right.

* * *

A few hours and a wardrobe change later, I stand in line outside at Pickles Pub, waiting to get in. My normally tight gray tank top feels loose against my body, same for my favorite pair of jeans, reminding me that I should probably put food a little higher on the priority list. As I wait, I watch the crowd from behind my sunglasses. The tiny pub right outside Camden Yards is bustling, filled to the brim with Orioles fans enjoying what feels like the true beginning of summer.

Once I get inside, I push my way through the crowd out front to the bar inside and order four Bud Lights. My drink of choice as of late because it's so cheap, only $2 a piece at most happy hours, and water-like enough to pretend I'm hydrating myself.

I get to the table where Sarah and two of our other law school friends, Kendall and Pete, are chatting about upcoming finals.

"There is no way Professor Griffin can expect us to know everything about civil procedure in twelve weeks. It's not possible," Kendall laments.

"He did say he'd grade on a curve," adds Pete.

"I don't even think a curve could help me at this point," Sarah groans.

"We'll all be fine," I pass out the beers.

"You mean *you'll* be fine, little Miss Top-of-the-Class," teases Kendall.

My cheeks flush. Though I work my ass off to achieve that exact status, I never want it acknowledged out loud.

"No more school talk. Tonight, we are on an important mission," Sarah says conspiratorially.

Pete raises an eyebrow at her. At this point in our friendship, we're all used to her outlandish ideas.

She pulls a folded-up piece of neon orange poster board out of her purse and then slowly unfurls it, building the suspense, a Cheshire grin spreading wide on her face.

"Guess who just got off the injured reserve?"

We stare blankly at her, conveying with our eyes for the hundredth time that not a single one of us watches or follows baseball like her. Or at all.

She turns the poster around, – a grand reveal. In thick black marker she's written:

Hey Christian, call me. 443-555-4567!!!
Go O's!

The three of us burst out laughing.

"This is next level. Even for you" Kendall cackles.

"I've gotta admit, its clever. Straight to the point," adds Pete.

"That is your *real* number, Sar," I shake my head.

"I know, it's brilliant right?"

"Brilliant would not be the word I'd use to describe it. But honestly, you're hot and even more determined so it might just work," Pete points out and takes a swig of his beer.

Sarah musses her perfectly blown out bright orange mane and

bats her thick black eyelashes at us. She is gorgeous, with more confidence than the three of us combined, and her obsession with the Orioles' left fielder knows no bounds. So, by default, the three of us know way more about the man than what is considered normal or perhaps even legal.

Christian Patriankos was a late round draft pick, right out of college but quickly rose through the ranks, leading the O's to three post-season appearances in his three seasons with the team. He is now Baltimore's very own demigod, and men, women, and children across the city worship him. The Baltimore Sun has dubbed him 'A Greek God of Charm City' and that's exactly what he is.

His Greek-American parents managed to produce an almost perfect specimen: 6'2' with olive skin, a full head of thick dark hair, and equally dark eyebrows. A permanent five o'clock shadow covers a square jaw, topped with a long straight nose, dark eyes and eyelashes. His body is chiseled in the way only a professional athlete's can be.

The owner of the Orioles publicly stated he could create an entire marketing campaign around the man. Christian is that incendiary. Which in turn has made Sarah that much more delusional. In addition to his baseball stats, I know (via Sarah) that he is intensely private with no social media presence at all – almost unheard of in today's day and age.

Perhaps because he also happens to be a notorious playboy, never seen with the same drop-dead gorgeous woman more than twice. And while I definitely do *not* count myself amongst his superfans, I am not so wrapped up in my own shit to miss the fact that the man is smoking hot.

"I traded my season tickets on the third baseline so we can all sit in left field. He can't miss us," Sarah says, beaming.

* * *

About the Author

Chrissie McCauley is a romance reader turned writer. She lives in Virginia with her family and functions in a constant state of chaos. She finds writing to be a singular refuge. *Thinking About Forever* is her first published work.

www.ingramcontent.com/pod-product-compliance
Lightning Source LLC
Chambersburg PA
CBHW020933260626
47169CB00006B/1701